P9-DWB-577

ALSO BY ELIZABETH MILES

FURY

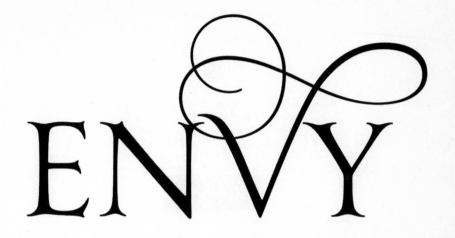

ENVY

BOOK TWO IN THE FURY TRILOGY

ELIZABETH MILES

SIMON PULSE

NEW YORK   LONDON   TORONTO   SYDNEY   NEW DELHI

SIMON PULSE
An imprint of Simon & Schuster Children's Publishing Division
1230 Avenue of the Americas, New York, NY 10020
First Simon Pulse hardcover edition September 2012
Copyright © 2012 by Paper Lantern Lit

For information about special discounts for bulk purchases, please contact
Simon & Schuster Special Sales at 1-866-506-1949 or business@simonandschuster.com.
The Simon & Schuster Speakers Bureau can bring authors to your live event.
For more information or to book an event contact the Simon & Schuster Speakers Bureau
at 1-866-248-3049 or visit our website at www.simonspeakers.com.
Designed by Hilary Zarycky
The text of this book was set in Bembo.
Manufactured in the United States of America
2 4 6 8 10 9 7 5 3 1
Library of Congress Cataloging-in-Publication Data
Miles, Elizabeth, 1982–
Envy / by Elizabeth Miles.
p. cm.
Sequel to: Fury.
Summary: High school junior Em researches Greek mythology in an effort to rid her Maine town of the returning, revenge-seeking Furies.
ISBN 978-1-4424-2221-6 (hc)
1. Erinyes (Greek mythology)—Juvenile fiction. [1. Erinyes (Greek mythology)—Fiction.
2. Supernatural—Fiction. 3. Revenge—Fiction. 4. High schools—Fiction. 5. Schools—Fiction.]
I. Title.
PZ7.M59432En 2012
[Fic]—dc22
2011044905
ISBN 978-1-4424-2223-0 (eBook)

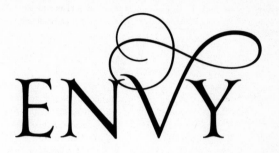

PROLOGUE

Henry Landon blew on his fingers to warm them. It was getting late, and he had to teach an early class tomorrow. As he stood to pack up his ice-fishing gear—a bucket, an ice saw, his bait, hook, and line—he thought he heard a rustle behind him. He spun around on the thick ice but saw nothing other than the muddy bank, the bare sweep of the hill, and the stripped trees beyond. The ice saw glinted in the moonlight.

"Hello?" he called. His voice echoed across the frozen pond. He shrugged, leaning over for the bucket, thinking about his empty house, how quiet it would be when he got home.

That's when he saw it—a face in the ice. There, just beneath his boots.

His heart thudded underneath his thick vest. It couldn't be.

He shook his head, blinked his eyes. He couldn't swallow.

As though encased in museum glass, a beautiful girl's face stared at him, her full lips the color of blood. Her blond hair was fanned beneath the surface like a mermaid's; it looked almost as though it was undulating in a current. She seemed to be clutching at the ice from below. In her palm was a scarlet flower.

He knew her face.

Landon gagged and coughed, struggling to catch his breath. When he closed his eyes, a memory surged: Several years ago, in California. At the beach. A blond girl in a white bikini had gone for a swim. The waves had been too much. She'd thrashed and called for help; then her body had gone under. He'd watched the whole thing happen—had *let* it happen. Not because he couldn't swim. Not because someone else was swimming out to save her. But because she was his student. An intelligent, Harvard-bound, sixteen-year-old student. Kaylie. And they were at the beach. Together.

She had been the one to start it, not him. Telling him he looked like George Clooney. Waiting after class. Flicking his silk tie with her slender fingers as she walked by. She'd worshipped him. And he couldn't help himself.

If the police had shown up that day, it would have been the end of his life as he knew it. He couldn't let her ruin everything. In that moment he chose to save his own life, not hers. He chose, and he ran.

He let her die.

And now she was here.

He opened his eyes. The girl below the ice came eerily into focus, as though she was glowing.

Suddenly her eyes snapped open, watery and white. Her mouth spread into a grin.

He couldn't move.

The crack was small at first. Sounded almost like a soft rip in fabric. But then it got louder, like a series of explosions, and before Henry Landon could step off the ice, it opened beneath his feet and he was falling. The icy water surrounded him, shot through his clothes, swallowed his legs and his torso while he flailed for something to hold on to. There was nothing. His bucket, with his pathetic catch of three fish, fell on its side; the fish flopped onto the ice, glassy-eyed.

He went under. The cold numbed him.

That day on the beach came back to him again. The sun. The waves. Kaylie's milky skin and trusting smile. Kaylie's body, disappearing beneath the waves.

His hands hit solid ice above his head. He gasped, choking on the freezing water, his lungs on fire. With the cold clarity of a razor's edge, Landon realized he would never take another breath. His body cramped and convulsed as it was overtaken by the first throes of a painful death. He heard the distant sound of girls' laughter.

Then: only whiteness.

ACT ONE

INNOCENCE, OR VANILLA ICE CREAM

CHAPTER ONE

"You say you wanna play around with other boys. You tell me that it's over, but all I hear is WHITE NOISE!" Crow grabbed the microphone and leaned forward, and for a second Em was sure he was looking right at her.

She leaned back into the beat-up armchair and wrapped her puffy down coat more tightly around her as she watched Crow practice his latest song, "White Noise." The sound of crappy, hand-me-down instruments and boys who love to play them reverberated through the garage. For the past several weeks Em had been spending more time with Drea Feiffer and her friends; as a result she was getting used to the buzzing electrical feed from the amps, the heart-pounding drum rhythms, and the screaming guitar solos. In addition to loving coffee and obscure movies,

Drea's alternative crowd loved music, especially the kind they created themselves.

Tonight they were at Colin Robertson's rehearsal space in Portland—if you could call a rug on a concrete floor, some ratty old couches, and a secondhand drum set a "rehearsal space." Colin's name had long ago been shortened to C-Ro, and that nickname had soon morphed into Crow. Em had never heard him called anything else. Well, except for when she and Gabby and some of their friends had referred to him as the Grim Creeper, back before he left Ascension. Not graduated, just . . . stopped coming. He was the only high school dropout Em had ever known.

Now Em knew he'd left to play music.

Crow strummed his guitar, licking his lips in concentration before opening his mouth to sing a verse. His longish black hair (it used to be bleached blond; this was better) often fell into his gold-green eyes, which always seemed just the slightest bit squinted—like he was still waking up, or like he had just gotten high.

Technically there were four guys in Crow's band, the Slump: Crow, who sang lead vocals and played rhythm guitar; Jake, the drummer; Patrick, the bassist; and Mike, who played lead guitar. They couldn't afford new instruments, but there was no question about their abilities. Other local musicians hung around the roomy old warehouse in South Portland, which Crow and the band rented for a cheap monthly rate. There was one guy who played the xylophone and another famous for his "found instruments"— a paintbrush on a metal tray, a wrench scraping against a birdcage.

Em couldn't believe this whole other world existed. And she *really* couldn't believe how cool it all was.

"Yo, Em, you want any of this?" From her perch on a ratty couch, Drea held up a Styrofoam cup of microwaved ramen noodles. Little-known fact that Em had learned recently: In Ascension, Maine, where Em and Drea lived, alternative types apparently subsisted on papery noodles in way-salty broth.

She made a face and waved her hand. "No thanks. Not hungry."

The room was starting to warm up—it was freezing when Em and Drea had first arrived—and Em started shedding layers. She unwound a thick burgundy pashmina from around her neck, shaking out the waves of her long, dark brown hair. As she stood up to take off her coat, she tugged at the belt loops on her jeans to hitch them up—they kept getting looser.

Her opinions of Crow and guitar solos weren't the only things that had shifted over the past few weeks. In fact, thanks to Drea, Em was seeing a whole new side of Ascension and its surroundings—and not just the green chai tea at the Dungeon, a hippie café downtown and a much preferable alternative to the watered-down Crappuccino next to the old mall. She was getting to know Ascension's "dyed-hair freaks." That's what she and

Gabby used to call them, anyway. She didn't like thinking about that side of herself. Especially not since Drea had recently dyed her hair purple.

These days she felt like she was straddling two worlds, often more comfortable amid Drea's friends and their loud music than at the Ascension parties.

Crow's gravelly voice hit the notes of a chorus—*"And my voice,"* he growled to the beat, *"it's white noise."*

Em pulled out her journal and wrote down some of Crow's lyrics. They really were good. Em had recently started bringing her journal with her everywhere. She'd kept one sporadically in the past, but these days it was like she couldn't keep her pen off the paper. Now that everything had changed—now that *she'd* changed—writing was the only way to keep her grip on reality . . . or what was left of it. It was the beginning of March; the showdown with the Furies had happened more than a month ago. She'd only recently begun to emerge from the practically comatose state she'd been in for weeks.

The royal-blue notebook was full of poems about love and regret. The snow. The cold. Her best friend, Gabby. And, of course, the Furies, who sought to punish wrongdoers for their sins. Em was a victim of their intractable wrath; the three beautiful-yet-hideous girls had exacted revenge on her because she'd spit in the face of love and trust by hooking up with Gabby's boyfriend. Now she was swallowing the bitter consequences. The worst part was that the guy, Zach, hadn't even been worth it. Nowhere close.

Well, no. The *worst* part was what had happened with JD Fount, her quirky neighbor, her childhood friend, and the boy she loved. The Furies had tried to kill him to teach her a lesson about lost love. She'd done what she had to in order to save him. But that included promising never to tell him, or anyone else, the truth about what had happened that night at the new mall, the Behemoth. And keeping those secrets put an impossible barrier between them. How could she apologize to JD without explaining what had really happened—and risk losing him all over again?

She wrote short entries in the journal every night, venting the uncontrollable feelings of sadness and hostility that seemed, sometimes, about to consume her. Writing eased her insomnia a bit, although it couldn't cure it. She cursed her pale skin, which made the dark circles under her eyes even more prominent.

Em blinked a few times, trying to snap back to attention. She wondered if Drea would want to go home soon—it was Sunday night, after all, and Em still had a chemistry lab to finish before third period tomorrow.

"We keeping you up?" Crow sauntered over, towering above the couch and raking his hand through his hair. "I know a pretty girl like you needs your beauty sleep."

"Sorry for blinking," Em said, sitting up straighter. While Crow had ignored her at first, he'd recently started to notice—and tease—her.

"Ah. The princess awakens!" Crow's eyes gleamed.

"I'm not a princess," Em blurted out. She'd been defensive lately, wary of people assuming that she thought she was better than everyone else. Like JD had. They'd only communicated once since that night at the Behemoth, the night she'd saved his life. One email, from him to her: *I'm not willing to be your Chauffeur anymore, Em. I won't be taken for granted ever again.*

Since then, nothing. No eye contact in the hallways, no waves from his driveway, where JD was apparently working on his dad's Mustang. Most days when Em came home, she glimpsed him lying halfway underneath the car, an open toolbox next to him on the freezing pavement. He never poked his head out to shout hello. Without saying a word, he was communicating clearly: JD wanted nothing to do with her anymore.

Telling him she loved him would be meaningless without an explanation about that night. Still, she thought about him constantly. His absence only made her realize how intense their connection had been, and how right he was—she *had* taken him for granted. One thing was for sure: Her feelings for him weren't like what she'd felt, or thought she'd felt, for Zach. Things with JD had never been tinged with betrayal. What they shared was warm and *right*. Or at least, it could be. It had been.

"Seems like you're slumming it, to me," Crow said stonily, raising an eyebrow. He was egging her on, and she took the bait.

"I didn't realize I needed your permission to be here," she

said. "We can go." She tried to keep her tone light—flirtatious, even—but she was surprised at the pricks of tears she felt at the backs of her eyes. She stood up and turned to find Drea.

"Whoa, no need to take off." Crow threw up his hands in mock surrender. "Never mind. My bad. You're a plebeian just like the rest of us."

Thank god Mike chose that moment to come over and discuss chord progressions with Crow. Em hoped Crow didn't see her face, which she could feel was burning bright red.

She leaned toward the couch where Drea sat with Cassie, an Ascension sophomore Em had never spoken to before last month. "Drea, are you ready to go soon? I've got chem homework." She crossed her arms and hoped her ears weren't turning red too.

"Sure, lemme just finish this up," Drea said, motioning to the tattoo drawing she'd started for Cassie on the back of an envelope. Em nodded and crouched down, pretending to dig in her bag for something.

"Hey, Em," Crow said, turning away from Mike.

She refused to look up at him, and instead kept her eyes on the toes of his ratty Converse sneakers. "Yeah?"

"Listen, I didn't mean anything by what I said. I was just thinking, you know, Sleeping Beauty and all." He tapped her knee with the tip of his Converse, and she finally looked up. "Are you one of those hot girls who can't take a compliment or something?"

"Oh, please." Now Em was really blushing.

"I'm serious. Look, I didn't mean to call you out for being here. I really hate that kind of shit—groups and types and all of that." He said it vaguely, but Em couldn't help but think of how many times she'd called him the Grim Creeper or stared at him and whispered as he walked down the hall.

"It's totally fine," Em said, embarrassed. Out of the corner of her eye, she saw Drea picking up her bag. She searched for something else to say to Crow, to convince him that things between them were cool.

"Awesome. So does your chem homework involve spewing blood?" He smiled at her.

Em stiffened. "What are you talking about?"

"Remember that badass volcano you made in sixth grade? I thought of it the other day. The lava just came pouring out, and you said it looked like spurting blood? That ruled." He laughed. "Emily Winters, mistress of gore. Put that on your prom queen résumé." He made a fake-scared face. "Just kidding. No princesses. No queens."

Em rolled her eyes. "Yeah, I'm thinking of submitting one volcano with each of my college applications," she said.

He snorted and shook his head. "Good stuff." And then Jake called out to him; break was over. "See you around." He touched her shoulder lightly with two fingers and she smiled shyly. Maybe she fit in with Drea's friends better than she thought.

Or maybe not. As she and Drea walked toward the door, she heard Crow call out her name. She turned.

"Hope you *grace* us with your presence again soon," Crow said over his shoulder, giving a slight bow. She glared at his back.

"We need to stop at the Dungeon when we get back to Ascension," Drea said as she merged onto the highway. "I am in des-per-ate need of some caffeine."

Em used to think she and Gabby were caffeine fiends, but Drea's coffee addiction knew no limits. It was like she needed a Red Bull just to have a conversation. "I thought you were trying to cut down," Em said lightly.

"I'll cut down tomorrow. Looks like you could use some too," Drea wryly pointed out.

Damn those dark circles. Em shook her head. "I'm having trouble enough sleeping. I definitely don't need a pick-me-up."

"That's not getting any better, huh?" Drea looked over at her. Their faces were illuminated every time an oncoming car drove by; it gave their conversation an erratic rhythm.

"Not really," Em said glumly. No need to tell Drea the lack of sleeping had actually gotten worse. She stared out the window. The winter had been a brutal one so far, but Gabby's mom, local weatherwoman Marty Dove, was predicting a milder end of winter. Em would be grateful for a break from the frigid temperatures, the hard creaking of icy branches outside her bedroom window.

"Well, think about it this way," Drea said, picking at her fingernails like she did whenever she was thinking hard. "All the creative geniuses in the world were haunted by something. I bet Hemingway, like, *never* experienced REM sleep."

Em looked down at the journal in her bag. Its contents were definitely not genius caliber. Nor were her grades, not since the Furies had come into her life. "I might be an insomniac, but I'm no genius," she said.

They were pulling into the Dungeon parking lot when Em spotted JD's car. Her stomach flipped. And there he was. She watched him push through the café's doors and stride toward his car. He had such a specific gait—like his feet had tiny springs in them.

She'd been silent for weeks, but tonight she was feeling feisty—which she could probably attribute to her exchange with Crow. Drea hadn't even pulled the car completely into the parking spot before Em hopped out.

"Where are you . . . ?" she heard Drea cry out as she hurried to intercept JD before he reached his driver's-side door.

"JD," she called, her voice ringing in the night air. He looked up and flinched. "Hold on for a second, okay?" It was better to corner him here, she figured, where there were few distractions.

For the first time in what felt like ages, she found herself face-to-face with him. She was standing between him and the Volvo; he'd have to move her if he wanted to leave. In regular jeans and a black jacket, he looked kind of subdued—only his tousled hair and a pair of thick-framed glasses betrayed his typically eccentric style.

As they looked at each other, trying to figure out who would speak first, Drea walked by, head down.

"Hey, Fount," she said to JD. "Em, I'll meet you inside."

"Hi, Drea," JD said, not taking his eyes off of Em.

Then, breaking the silence, JD asked coldly, "What do you want, Em?"

"Nice glasses," she said. Nothing. Stony silence. She sighed and continued. "Please," she said, pulling the ends of her scarf to make it tighter, "I need to know why you've been avoiding me. It's been weeks." She thought she was in fair territory—when they'd made their pact with her, the Furies hadn't forbidden asking questions, right?

"Clearly my strategy hasn't worked too well," JD said evenly. "I started coming here because I thought you preferred the Crappuccino."

"It's Drea . . ." Em said weakly. "She likes it here." She swallowed back the tightness in her throat. "JD, *please*. Please talk to me."

JD looked at her coldly. "I can't," he said. "Could *you* forgive *me* if I'd done what you did?"

Em stared back. What did he mean?

"And you want to know the worst part?" He barreled on.

"The worst is that you obviously don't even think it was a big deal. What happened that night . . . I thought things between us were going somewhere. The only place they were going, apparently, was the hospital."

She watched as his hand rose to touch his head where the pipe had hit him, the one that had landed him at the bottom of the mall's foundation and in danger of being buried by concrete. He would have been if she hadn't pulled him out. A reddish scar extended from his hairline diagonally across his forehead. She was desperate to know what he thought had happened that night at the Behemoth—the night she'd realized that she was in love with him.

The Furies had tried to kill JD in order to punish *her*, to teach her a lesson about lost love and betrayal, and she'd done whatever she could to stop them. And that included swallowing five glowing red seeds and promising to keep her mouth shut. Not to talk about it with anyone, in fact.

"JD—"

He cut her off. "Don't you mean *Chauffeur*?" She flinched. "Yeah, Gabby told me about your little nickname for me—she slipped up at the pep rally. I know that's all I am to you, Emily."

"JD, that was just a silly nickname. I don't feel like that. Things have changed. You have to believe me. You mean so much more to me than that." She put her hand on his arm. He shook her off.

"Things haven't changed one bit. You ditched me at the pep rally because something better came up." The disdain dripped from his voice. "You made up that story about Gabby being in trouble, and then you ditched me to go make out with some other guy at a construction site. That is low, Em. Especially for you."

Em was practically shaking. "I—I don't understand."

"No, you sure don't," JD spat out, grinding his boot into the slushy pavement. "I was worried about you, Em. Don't you get that? That's why I followed you. And when I saw that you'd just gone on some romantic rendezvous—" He broke off. "And, Christ, you *laughed* at me."

She'd laughed at him? No, she hadn't. But as he said it, the silver sound of the Furies' laughter, like a wind chime that wouldn't stop tinkling, resounded in the back of her mind.

"No—no. Gabby wasn't there. It was a trick. They tried to hurt you. I saved you," she said without thinking. JD's memories of that night . . . they were all wrong. And now she didn't know what was going on. She was letting things slip.

JD rolled his eyes. "You saved me? Oh, thank you, fearless warrior," he said with an exaggerated clasping of his hands. "Thank you *so* much for *saving* me by bringing me to the hospital after your new loser boyfriend—or whoever the hell that was—clobbered me with an industrial pipe. You really pick the good ones, don't you, Em?"

She took a step back, knowing that the insult was meant to remind her of Zach. How badly she'd misjudged. She wanted to defend herself, but she knew that she had to stay silent. She was on the verge of breaking her pact with the Furies.

"So no," JD continued, "I will not believe you, or trust you ever again."

"JD, please, you've got to listen to me. . . ." But then she trailed off, reminding herself that it was JD who would suffer if she screwed up. The Furies didn't play fair. And she refused to take that risk. She knew she'd already said too much.

"Nothing to say, huh?" JD took a quick step forward. "Then please get out of the way."

She moved away from his car mutely. There was nothing she could do. Her throat was so tight, it felt like it was clenching her windpipe.

JD paused, and then turned and looked over his shoulder. "You *laughed* at me," he repeated. "Why did you have to laugh?"

Then he threw open the car door, ducked inside, and was gone.

Watching him peel out of the parking lot, she choked back a sob as she wrapped her arms around her body. The cold seemed to reach inside her now. She wanted to go home.

Em managed to get Drea's attention through the window. *Urgent*, she motioned with her hands. And then they were driving home, Drea knowing better than to pry.

Drea didn't speak until they were nearing Em's house. "You want to get lunch tomorrow?" she asked. "Deli? I have this weird craving for a Reuben."

"Ummm, I don't know." Right now it was impossible to think about having to face school tomorrow. Her stomach hurt, and her heart hurt, thinking about how angry JD was. How she couldn't do anything to fix it. "I mean, maybe later in the week or—" Em cut herself off as she spotted a glint of white in the moon-silvered trees at the end of her street. She peered out the passenger-side window, trying to get a closer look. "Slow down," she said.

Sure enough, there was something white hanging from the oak tree by the small park at the end of her block. It was a sheet of sailcloth, just like what Em and JD had used as a signal flag when they were younger—he used to put it in his tree house as a sign that she should meet him there. She hadn't thought about that flag in years, but seeing it now made her heart speed up.

"Can you drop me here?" Em knew it was an odd request on this dark, cold night, but she was equally certain that Drea wouldn't care.

"A bit brisk for an evening stroll, isn't it?" But Drea stopped the car and didn't ask any other questions as Em gathered her things and said good-bye.

"See you tomorrow, D," Em said. Her words came slow, like she was in a trance—she couldn't take her eyes off the makeshift flag. It couldn't be a message from JD, she knew that. But the coincidence was too much. She had to investigate.

As Drea drove off, Em crunched across the frozen grass and made her way over to the sailcloth. Stretching onto tiptoes, she worked to untangle the flag, which the wind had wrapped several times around the oak branch. As she struggled with the canvas and her freezing fingers she thought of days spent chasing JD around the park's small circumference. The afternoon they decided to "trick" their parents by putting plastic ants on their cheese plate. The night they co-babysat JD's little sister, Melissa, and brought her here to play flashlight tag. Maybe Melissa had been playing with the flag and that's how it had ended up here? But no, even Melissa was too old for the flag now.

A gust of wind finally shook the flag loose. It flapped open, its edges whipping her face.

"Ow," Em said to no one, putting her hand to her cheek. But she dropped it and gasped as the flag came into full view. Through the center of it, there was an ugly gash, as though it had been knifed by an animal's claw. Years of play had never even frayed the material, but here it was, practically shredded.

And then, out of nowhere, the soft chimes of female laughter. Em whipped around, wriggling free as the flag wrapped around her wrist.

"Melissa?" she called out into the dark playground. "JD?"

No answer.

Em swallowed hard. Only a short while ago, in December, she'd been sitting on the swings when she'd found a note in her pocket. *Sometimes sorry isn't enough.* A note from the Furies. The thought made her palms tighten in fear.

There it was again. That eerie, beautiful laughter.

She knew that sound. She would know it anywhere.

The Furies. They were here.

Why were they back? She'd already been punished. Why show up here, why now? Would they reappear in her life whenever they felt like it? She thought of the fragments of the story she'd shared with JD in the parking lot. Did the Furies know? Had she brought them back?

She swung her head in all directions, but the laughter seemed to come from nowhere and everywhere at the same time. She started to retreat, moving backward slowly at first and then faster, faster. She turned, leaving the flag. Breathing hard in the night air. She moved toward the park gate, not daring to look behind her.

Suddenly, just before she reached the chain-link fence that bordered the park, a sharp icicle fell from above, soundlessly. Em yelped as it scratched her arm like the tip of a knife. And then icicles were raining down on her, piercing and deadly. Making no sound save the smallest *whoosh.*

She sprinted down the street but then tripped on a branch, landed on all fours, and skidded on the ice. She heard her jeans rip and felt tiny bits of dirt and salt cut into her knee. Her bag fell from her shoulder. And all the while there was that laughter, shimmering and bouncing like light on a lake. She couldn't *see* them, but they were here. She could *feel* them.

"Don't you dare come back here!" she shouted as she shakily got to her feet. "I stopped myself! I kept my promise!" She grabbed her bag from where it had fallen and frantically retrieved the stuff that had tumbled out of it. She could feel how panicked she looked, scrambling around on the dark street for her phone, her powder compact, her keys. It made her angrier. She yelled into the night air, "I've paid enough!"

She stumbled the last few yards to her driveway, then in through her front door, slamming it behind her, breathing hard. Only inside, away from the moon and the snow and the tree branches that seemed to grab for her, did the echoing laughter diminish.

Em pulled herself upstairs. *I didn't do anything wrong this time. I didn't say too much*, she told herself. *I'm safe.* But somehow she didn't feel reassured. This was a warning. She put her cold hands to her face in an effort to ease her burning cheeks. Either the flag or the wind had lashed her skin raw.

CHAPTER TWO

In the dusky tower of her aunt Nora's old Victorian on the corner of South Main and Maple streets, Skylar McVoy was unpack-
ing the last of her things from a purple duffel bag. She plugged
her iPod charger into the wall, arranged a small collection of nail
polishes on the rickety dresser in the corner, then draped a few
scarves over the edge of the mirror. She surveyed the room—its
hardwood floorboards, the bay window that looked out onto the
street below, the full-sized bed with its curved metal frame. Her
new home. It would take a while to get used to. The whole place
was so . . . New England—wooden, salty, and cold. Nothing like
her old home in Alabama, where the wall-to-wall carpeting and
cheap plastic furniture seemed to radiate with heat. She shivered, tucking her shoulder-length, dirty-blond hair behind her

ears before pulling the hood of her sweatshirt up over her head. Maybe she'd ask Nora for a space heater.

As if on cue, there was a knock on the bedroom door.

"Come in," she said, surprised at her aunt's respect for her privacy. With her mom and Lucy, there had been no knocking, no boundaries.

"How are you settling in?" Nora cast an eye at the scarves, the lineup of Skylar's shoes at the foot of the bed, the empty suitcases waiting to be shoved into the closet. Skylar was struck, as she always was, by how little Nora looked like her mom. Where her mom was skinny and hard and fake blond, Nora was soft and rounded, with wavy hair that showed just a few streaks of gray. And she smelled of plants. Dirt. In a good way. "Is there enough room in the dresser for your clothes? I put the flannel sheets on the bed—it can get pretty chilly up here."

"It's fine, Aunt Nora," Skylar said, smiling. "Thank you."

Nora had bought Skylar's plane ticket the very night her mom had landed in jail for driving drunk—for the third time. "You'll spend the rest of the school year here," Nora had said on the phone that evening, "and we'll see what happens after that."

But Skylar and Nora had both known the truth: Skylar was moving to Ascension for good. Life in Alabama was bad enough before Lucy's accident, but over the past year it had gotten unbearable. Her mom had been drinking more than ever, raging around the house when she wasn't smoking cigarettes listlessly in front of the television. She'd been bringing home random guys who didn't even pretend to want to learn Skylar's name. The emotional distance Skylar had felt for years became physical distance too. She would go days without even seeing her mother; sometimes she didn't even miss her. Her life had become a nightmare.

In effect, Nora had rescued Skylar. And so Skylar was determined to overlook and grow accustomed to all of her aunt's oddities, like her eerily encyclopedic knowledge of Ascension's history and her funny nervous giggle. Not to mention the fact that unlike Skylar's mom, Nora had a steady job—she was a dental hygienist at a local clinic—and therefore a steady income and a stable routine. Skylar was not used to any of these things.

Before she turned to go, Nora asked, "Would you like some tea? I'm just brewing some downstairs."

"No thank you," Skylar said. "I'm not really a tea person. But thank you for offering."

There she was again, eternally grateful. For so much. Because Nora hadn't just gotten her out of Alabama. She was giving Skylar a fresh start, a chance to be someone new.

"I'll drive you to the high school in the morning," Nora was saying, "in case there's any additional transfer paperwork we need to fill out. We should leave the house by seven o'clock, okay? Get some sleep, and let me know if you need anything else." She wrapped her burnt-orange shawl around her shoulders as she left the room. "Brrrr," Skylar heard her say as she padded back down the stairs. "What a brutal winter."

Skylar turned her attention back to her duffel bag, which was almost empty. There at the bottom was a large hardcover edition of *Aesop's Fables*, one she'd had since she was a kid. She'd always loved these stories, and had once suggested to her mother that she recite one for the talent portion of a beauty pageant. Her mom had scoffed. "You think anyone wants to hear you run your mouth?" Skylar had tap-danced instead.

She opened the book and flipped through, looking at the familiar pictures inside. "The Fox and the Grapes." "The Ant and the Grasshopper." She smiled and leafed through more pages. She'd always found comfort in stories.

And then, horrified, she dropped the book to the floor with a loud thud. A photograph that had been wedged between its pages skittered out onto the floor. It was a picture of her and Lucy before last year's statewide pageant, the terrible night when everything went wrong. Her: short and a little chubby, flat-chested, and looking off to the side. Lucy: tall, shapely, and gorgeous, beaming a smile at the camera with her painted red lips, her arm slung around Skylar's neck.

As always, Skylar marveled at Lucy's effortless beauty. "It's too bad Lucy got most of my features," her mom had slurred, more than once. Her mother had been a pageant queen too, before the smoking dulled her skin and the booze deadened her eyes. She'd pushed both her daughters to fulfill the dreams she'd killed for herself, entering them into beauty contests and talent competitions as soon as they could walk. For Skylar, they'd been repeated exercises in humiliation and rejection. But Lucy had excelled, wowing the judges with her easy grace, assertive strut, and killer dance moves. Lucy had everyone convinced she was perfect.

Almost everyone.

Skylar shuddered. How had this photo ended up with her things? She looked up and saw herself in the mirror. Nothing about her glowed. Her forehead was crinkled in concentration, her shoulders tight, hair limp. She could find none of Lucy's confidence in her own reflection.

No. The memory of that life was not going to follow her to Maine. Lucy couldn't cast a shadow on her now—not this far away.

Things would be different here.

Skylar walked to the trash can in the corner of her new room. Calmly and deliberately, she began to tear the photo apart. She ripped it into tiny pieces, and then she shredded even those, until there was nothing but a pile of glossy confetti in her hands.

It felt shockingly good to destroy the photo, in the same way that losing fifteen pounds, painstakingly, over the past year, had felt good; in the same way that the flight from Alabama to Maine had given her a guilty sense of relief. While she'd been flying through the air, her mother had sat behind bars.

Skylar gulped back a lump in her throat as she started laying out her outfit for the morning: a pretty white peasant blouse from Free People, a pink cardigan, her favorite dark-wash jeans, and gray ankle boots.

She had a chance to rebuild her life—no, to build a life, period. To be accepted. To be loved. Her eyes fell on a long silver necklace, and she smiled as she placed it next to the white blouse. Yes. At Ascension High, she would sparkle.

It wasn't like she'd never walked up stairs before. But the next morning Skylar's coordination was off, and at 9:18, between first and second periods, Skylar made her first big mistake: She tripped *up* a flight of stairs. *Boom.*

She launched forward, catching herself on her palms but practically face-planting. She looked behind her—nothing but a sea of nameless faces, moving together toward their next class. Somebody's boot struck her bag, and she scrambled to retrieve it before it tumbled down the steps. She got up and brushed herself off, trying not to make eye contact with anyone, her face burning with embarrassment.

Not that things had been going great before that. Her short meeting with Aunt Nora and the Ascension High principal had been less than reassuring. Principal Noyes had seemed doubtful that Skylar would be able to catch up in some of her classes; she'd suggested Skylar might have to take summer school. Then

Skylar had gotten lost trying to find math, first period. And now stairwell humiliation. She could have been wearing an invisible cloak and she still would have felt like she was being trailed by a spotlight.

After second period—French—Skylar found herself speed-walking through an otherwise empty hallway in what she thought must be the science wing, based on the fact that she'd just seen a portable skeleton dangling in one of the classrooms. The bell had sounded more than ten minutes ago, but she'd gotten lost making her way through the hallways. She was late for Honors Biology, if she could ever find it. She pulled out her crumpled class sched-ule, comparing the information there with the numbers on the doors. Finally she made her way to room 209. She opened the heavy wooden door with an apologetic expression, only to be greeted by twenty quizzical faces—and no indication that this was a biology classroom.

"Can I help you?" The teacher, a distracted-looking man with glasses and chalk on his wrist, turned away from the equa-tion on the board to face her.

"Um, yeah, I'm looking for . . . is this . . . I think I'm in the wrong place," she stuttered. The symbols scrawled on the board made it clear that this was a math class. She'd already had geom-etry first period.

The teacher didn't say anything—he seemed to be wait-ing for her to leave. The other kids—who, Skylar noticed to her embarrassment, looked older than her—kept staring at her blankly. Well, not just blankly. The girls looked her up and down. She was frozen with humiliation, and her cheeks were burning. She was sure they matched her pink sweater.

"Okay, thanks, sorry to interrupt." She knew that she should ask for directions. If this wasn't the science wing, then where was she? But she couldn't stand the idea of being on display even a second longer. She felt as exposed as the skeleton she'd seen just a minute ago, as though she'd been cut open straight through the gut. She turned to go.

And then a perky voice rang out across the classroom. "Where are you supposed to be, anyway? Maybe I can help. Right, Mr. Marshall? May I be excused for a few minutes? I really *get* this section anyway."

The voice came from a girl with a head of tousled blond curls. She looked just like an angel, Skylar thought, with a perfect, round face and sparkling blue eyes. The girl gave her a little wink, and Skylar breathed for the first time in what felt like minutes.

The teacher rolled his eyes. "I suppose so, Gabby. Just don't use this as an excuse to meet Ms. Winters for a hallway powwow. I expect you back here in five minutes."

"Obviously," Gabby said with a grin and a roll of her eyes. "Em's in English right now, anyway. She'd never bail." There were some appreciative snickers as Gabby sailed over to Skylar.

"Let's go," she said, grabbing Skylar's arm and tugging her out the door like they were on some kind of bonding mission, not complete strangers.

Out in the hallway Skylar fumbled for something to say. She was angry with herself for being nervous. Fortunately, the pretty blond girl saved her the effort of speaking first.

"Hi! I'm Gabby Dove." The name fit her perfectly.

"I'm Skylar. Skylar McVoy. I'm new," she answered, and then mentally kicked herself. Obviously she was new. She might as well have it tattooed on her forehead.

"Thanks for getting me out of there," Gabby said, as though Skylar had done her a favor on purpose. "I cannot stand math. Which is so stupid because I'm, like, actually okay at it. Not great, but I get it. I just wish it wasn't so painfully boring. Anyway, can I see your schedule?"

Skylar handed it to her mutely.

"Ah, you have bio now. Bummer. I do *not* get science. So, we're going to want to head back toward the cafeteria—you know where that is, right?—and then turn toward the back of the building." Gabby was walking now, tossing words over her shoulder, and Skylar scurried along to keep up. She checked out what Gabby was wearing—a deep-red tunic, black jeans, and black wedge boots that gave her at least three inches. Skylar could see that without them, Gabby would be short, like her. She tugged on her cardigan, which suddenly felt too small.

"So, how long have you been in town?" Gabby slowed down to let Skylar catch up.

"Just since Saturday," Skylar said.

"Where are you from?"

"I came from Alabama." She was about to offer a bit more information, but they passed a group of students standing by a row of lockers, and she clamped her mouth shut, suddenly shy.

"Hey, Gabs," several of them called out.

"Hi, guys," Gabby said, waving over her shoulder as she kept walking. Then she stopped, turned around, and kept talking to them as she walked backward down the hallway. "Can't wait to hear about the hot tub incident." They all cracked up as Gabby turned a corner. "It's right down here," she said to Skylar.

Skylar smiled too, as though she had any idea what the hot tub incident was and why it was funny. Maybe someday she'd make people laugh like that. Maybe someday she'd be in on the joke.

"Okay, here we go. Room 209. *That* was room 209 too," Gabby said, moving her head in the direction they'd just come from. "But it's 209A. Totally dumb system. Don't worry about it."

"Thank you so much," Skylar said, trying not to sound gushy. She'd already come off as enough of an idiot. It was important to try, but not seem like you were trying. That was the rule of the pageant circuit too. *Make it look easy.*

"No problem, happy to help. See you around, Skylar," Gabby

said as she turned back toward her math class. Skylar watched her go, then looked down to smooth her shirt before heading into bio. Ugh. All of a sudden she couldn't help but see herself as Gabby must have seen her—plain, lost, pathetic. With a knot in her throat, she opened the door to face the next humiliation.

Flat. Flat and stringy. Skylar hated hair spray, mousse, any type of hair product at all. The sticky-sweet smell made her think of being backstage at the pageants. But her hair, which she was currently fluffing in the bathroom mirror between third and fourth periods, fell limp against her head—nothing like Gabby's bouncy curls.

As she stared at herself she felt the slightest shimmer of a presence behind her. She whirled around, even though she knew that she was alone in the bathroom. She turned back to the mirror. And then, as though steam was clearing after a shower, the space behind her opened up and she could practically see Lucy smiling at her pityingly.

Oh, it looks fine, Dumpling.

Dumpling. The "affectionate" nickname Lucy and their mom had bestowed upon her in third grade. Skylar leaned against the sink and turned on the water, cupping some in her hand and gulping it down thirstily. She willed herself not to cry, ordering the Lucy in her mind to go away. *This is your chance to start over*, she told herself. She straightened up, rooted in her purse for a tube of lip gloss, and slammed out the bathroom door. She wouldn't be late for her last class before lunch.

When she finally made it to the cafeteria later, it was clear where she should try to sit—at the tables below the skylights, each bathed in white winter light, where students were gossiping, sharing plates of fries, and finishing last-minute homework. Everyone sitting at those sun-bathed seats seemed touched by a confident glow.

This was the popular crowd.

Clutching her brown bag—which held some carrots, a small container of hummus, and a yogurt, all packed this morning by Aunt Nora—Skylar headed in that direction. Was she being too bold, parading over to sit in the cool section? It wasn't like she was going to plop down in the middle of the action. She'd stay on the outskirts, try to smile at people, listen to the kinds of things people talked about here. Although, it might be difficult to hear anything, with that group of whooping boys wrestling and jostling each other just next to the cash registers. . . .

Just as she spotted the perfect chair, right at the edge of the light-drenched area, it hit her. Or rather, *he* hit her—a guy (one of the wrestling boys) came flying out of nowhere, slamming her shoulder and knocking his tray of spaghetti and marinara sauce all over her white top and pink sweater.

"You assholes! Now I have to get a new lunch!" The guy

who'd collided with Skylar was wearing an Ascension High football jacket and still hadn't noticed that his lost lunch was now covering the front of Skylar's shirt. She could feel its warmth on her stomach. A hundred eyes stared at her.

"Oh, jeez." The boy had just turned to look at Skylar. He had short brown hair, a square jawline, and broad shoulders. The name Travers was printed above his right pec on his football jacket. "Look at you."

She opened her mouth to speak, but nothing came out other than a squeaked "You—you ran into me." Great. Her second obvious comment of the day.

"Sorry about these idiots," he said just a little too loudly so his friends would hear him. "They don't know how to behave in public." He grinned at her. "Especially not around new girls. You are new here, right?"

Skylar actually had to concentrate to make sure her jaw didn't drop. This guy, this cute guy, had noticed her? "You—um—I— how did you know?"

"Hard to miss a pretty girl. I think you're in my geometry class, first period? I'm Pierce."

"I'm, uh, Skylar," she responded. She couldn't believe she was having a conversation—*with a boy*—in the middle of the cafeteria, while covered in spaghetti sauce. "Yeah—geometry. I'm the one who asked that dumb question about the sine and cosine stuff. . . ."

"Wanna know my secret?" Pierce asked, leaning in conspiratorially. He reached into his pocket and pulled out a graphing calculator. "Dorky, I know, but I carry it around with me just in case." He winked. "I also carry this around, for marinara emergencies." He took off his jacket and then pulled his sweatshirt over his head. It, too, was emblazoned with Ascension's football logo.

He put his jacket back on but held out the sweatshirt to her. She looked at it, and looked at him, not understanding.

"Take it for the afternoon—no one wants to smell like oregano through their last few periods."

"Are you sure?" Skylar took the sweatshirt tentatively.

"Yup. You can bring it to me tomorrow. See you in math, Skylar." And with that, he turned away and headed back to his table. As he approached his friends she saw him push one of them good-naturedly, and peg another one with a french fry. The guys started laughing and high-fiving.

Skylar felt a warm glow in the pit of her stomach. Pierce Travers. It was a perfect name, and immediately she coupled it with her own. Pierce Travers and Skylar McVoy. A football player who was also nice? She almost brought the sweatshirt to her nose to smell him, but remembered at the last second that she was still in the middle of the cafeteria.

In the bathroom she gingerly removed her stained top and replaced it with the sweatshirt. It was huge and hardly matched her boots, but who cared? She was wearing a boy's football sweat-shirt. If not for her nervous expression of a newbie, she might even be taken for the girlfriend of an Ascension High player—maybe even *Pierce's* girlfriend. With an unfamiliar confidence in her step, she emerged back into the hallway, ready to face the last few classes of the day.

The sweatshirt was a sign, she was sure of it—a sign that in Ascension, she would get the life she deserved.

CHAPTER THREE

"It's bad enough that I have to wait until practically dinnertime to eat lunch this semester," Gabby said, gesticulating with a fork held high above the Greek salad she'd brought from home. "But now I'm not even guaranteed the pleasure of my best friend's company? What is this? *Prison?*"

Em sighed. It was fifth-period lunch, and she and Gabby, along with Fiona and Lauren and the rest of the girls, were sitting at their typical table in the junior section of the cafeteria. Or rather, Gabby, Fiona, and Lauren were sitting, and Em was hovering next to the table, having just told the girls that she kind of had plans to meet Drea at the deli for lunch. Big mistake.

"I didn't know my presence provided such a ray of sunshine," Em said dryly, trying to smile. Her skin was still crawling from last night, and she couldn't shake the creeping feeling that the Furies were nearby. She'd agreed to lunch after all—she was going to meet Drea off campus (at the deli, so Drea could get her Reuben) in order to discuss the run-in at the park and the tattered flag; Em had been dying to share the details all day.

But just as she'd feared, and as harmless as it seemed, bailing on lunch was obviously going to hurt Gabby's feelings. It would destroy the daily routine—lunch under the skylights of the Gazebo, rehashing the morning's dramas—and forgoing it meant something was . . . off.

Of course, something *was* off. Obviously Em and Zach's hookup had caused a major rift, but over the past month or so, she and Gabby had been working hard to rebuild their friendship. Still, it was crystal clear from Em's distance and her new friends that things were different. Just as she couldn't tell JD what had happened that night at the mall, she had sworn to keep the truth from her best friend as well. Gabby had no idea what had happened—she didn't know about the Furies, and she didn't even know that Em had feelings for JD.

"The skylights provide the sunshine, sweetie. You can provide the skincare tips. What's up with your skin recently? It's, like, flawless." Gabby shook her head, wide-eyed. "I mean, I can't even see a pore. Sit down and spill. Do I need to change up my face cream?"

Em looked around at the familiar crowd of girls gathered

at their table. Lauren and Fiona were arguing over whether the new Bachelor was Hot or Not; Mindy and Caroline were sharing a plate of fries; Jenna was frantically penning her history homework last-minute. Em realized she needed this. She needed to sit down and talk about creams from Sephora and homemade avocado masks. She wanted to eat a slice of Ascension's thick Sicilian pizza and complain about how hard her French quiz had been this morning. To have Fiona lecture her on the dangers of white flour, and for Lauren to laugh so hard she shot Diet Coke out her nose. She wanted those things—normal things—not another hushed, clandestine conversation with Drea about the Furies.

"I'll stay," she said, tossing her bag under the table. Then, with a playful smile toward Fiona, she added, "But no lectures about my lunch."

"Like we could lecture her," she heard Lauren say as she walked toward the lunch line. "She's thin as a rail."

"It's not about *size*, Laur, it's about *health*," Fiona was saying. Em smiled as she walked over to the stack of trays.

As she waited in line for her pizza she pulled out her phone to text Drea: *Can't make it after all. I'll call you later.* She hoped Drea wouldn't be too pissed. As she made her way back to the table, it was like her ears had popped on the way down a mountain—her head suddenly felt lighter. She knew she needed to talk to someone about what had happened last night. But it could wait. Didn't she still deserve some semblance of a regular teenage life?

Back at the table, the girls were talking about Josie Swanson, another junior, whose parents were paying for her to have a private SAT tutor *and* a college admissions coach.

"May as well pay for her to have a personal academic assistant at college so she can keep scamming the system," Fiona said. "Doesn't she know that good grades and good schools are for, like, smart people?" Everyone knew that Fiona wanted to go to Harvard, and she wanted to get there all on her own. She'd balked even at buying an SAT review book.

"It really is kind of ridiculous," Gabby chimed in. "Do you know that she has a hot tub? I'm jealous. Apparently there was some impromptu senior party there on Saturday night."

Em took a bite of her lunch. Everything was the same—the thick dough, the too-sweet red sauce, the salty cheese. But for some reason, her guilty pleasure suddenly tasted gross.

"Speaking of hot tubs, Gabs, can you please ask your mom when it's going to get warm again?" This from Fiona, whose health craziness did not extend to sun damage—she started laying out in April and was usually brown by mid-June.

"Fee's dying to go back to that beach where we met those crazy USM boys last summer," Lauren said. "Gabby, do you *remember* how absurd that one guy was, the one who kept bringing you beach glass?"

"It was embarrassing," Gabby said with raised eyebrows. "I hope he found himself a nice girl his own age."

Em's eyes wandered over to the far left bench, where the junior footballers sat. She tried to look away quickly, before her gaze could linger on the empty spot at the end of the bench—the one where Chase used to sit, the one that had remained empty since his death, as if people feared it was haunted. And even though she wanted to think that was silly, she had to admit she was glad they were sitting several tables away.

". . . What do you think, Em?" Gabby nudged her.

"About what? Sorry, I was zoning for a second." Em pulled her hair into a low ponytail at the nape of her neck and tried to focus. All of a sudden sitting there in the cafeteria and gossiping didn't feel right. In fact, it felt distinctly jarring.

"That's a surprise." Gabby rolled her eyes. "I asked what we should do after the Spring Fling. Whether or not there'll be an after-party."

While Em tried to think of something to say—what would the *old* Em have said?—she watched Gabby's eyes drift over to the same table, the football table, and linger there for a second before snapping back to attention. Em knew she was probably thinking of Zach, who used to preside over that zone—over all the athletes in the school, in fact. Zach had gone off to boarding school last month, supposedly. But then last week Andy Barton had told them that he'd heard Zach had been involved in a nasty accident and was in some fancy physical therapy facility in Florida. Now there were rumors that he'd never be able to play sports again.

Em wondered whether Gabby felt bad for Zach . . . or if she felt the same sense of relief that he was *gone*, that his presence wasn't a constant reminder of how easy it was to make mistakes.

She watched as Pierce Travers, a sophomore and Zach's likely replacement as quarterback, caught Gabby's eye and smiled. He really was adorable. For a moment Em found herself back in social butterfly mode, hopeful that something might happen between Pierce and Gabby. At least that would prove that Gabby was really over that asshole. That Em hadn't broken up Ascension's best It Couple or something.

"I hadn't really thought about it," Em admitted. But she knew she had to do better than that. Post-dance parties were a big deal. "Will Ian's parents be out of town? They're always away, right?"

"I heard that they're going to be around," Lauren said.

"Plus we were just there last weekend," Gabby said. "I mean, I love Ian's house, but I'd also love a change of venue." She paused. "What about your new goth friends, Em? Do they ever have parties?"

She didn't say it meanly, but Gabby's message was clear: She'd noticed who Em had been spending more time with, and she didn't like it.

Em didn't have time to think of a response. Just then the whole table of girls was distracted by a french fry hitting their table, followed by some general hubbub. The boys had gotten into a shoving match and french fries were being used as weapons. For the second time in one lunch period Em was glad she and her friends sat on the other side of the cafeteria from the Sports Section.

They watched as the boys got rowdier.

"Can you believe we're the same age as those primitives?" Fiona asked.

They watched as a short, cute girl with dirty-blond hair—someone Em had never seen before—got blasted with a tray of spaghetti. They cringed, issuing a chorus of sympathy: "Ooooooh. Oh no!"

Em ducked her head. She hated watching other people get embarrassed. It was almost worse than being humiliated herself.

"Oh god, I know that girl," Gabby said, wincing. "She's new—I helped her find her bio class today. . . . I wonder—should I go, like, help her?"

Lauren pointed. "I think she's okay. Pierce gave her his sweatshirt!" They watched the new girl make a mad dash from the cafeteria.

"What a terrible way to start at a new school," Gabby said, turning back to the table.

"Hey, Laur, you want the rest of this?" Em shoved her tray toward Lauren, who could never turn down pizza—it was one of their shared vices. "I guess I'm not too hungry today."

"You should eat, Em. You're looking borderline rexy," Gabby said, grabbing Em's arm and holding it up as evidence. "Not to mention you're an icicle. Are you getting sick? Do you want to borrow my sweater?"

You're an icicle. The expression called to mind the dagger-sharp icicles that pitched down around her last night as though they'd been aimed by dark angels.

Just as she was about to make some snarky retort, she looked out the cafeteria window and saw JD and his friend Ned jogging across the parking lot, ducking their heads against the cold air. They were probably going to get a burrito from Chalupa's, where they went at least weekly to gorge on guacamole and talk computer programming. He told her once, *It's safer to talk about computer programming around people who don't speak English than around Ascension jocks.*

Her heart ached as last night's interaction with JD came rushing back. Like their shredded childhood flag, the past was slashed. Destroyed. And there was no way for Em to piece it back together. In fact, there was a chance that last night she'd made things even worse.

"Um, Em? Earth to Em?" Fiona was snapping her fingers lightly in front of Em's face. "Are you even listening to me? I'm asking what you think about Mr. Landon. Do you think he's coming back?"

"Yeah, I'd think you of all people would be interested in the disappearance of Ascension's hottest book-nerd teacher," Lauren said. "Didn't you have him this year?"

Em looked at them blankly for a second before nodding vaguely. "Yeah . . . the sub is meh. I'm bummed. I was looking forward to Mr. Landon's reading list this semester."

She couldn't think of much more to say. Honestly? She was thinking about those icicles and what it would feel like to have one stabbed into her heart.

CHAPTER FOUR

Skylar was still glowing when she arrived at school the next morning. Her hair was pinned back from her face, and she knew her green sweater made her hazel eyes shine. Pierce's sweatshirt was tucked in her messenger bag and still warm from the dryer—she'd slept in it, savoring his boyish scent—and gotten up early this morning to wash it. Right before shoving it in her bag, she'd spritzed it with a tiny bit of her perfume. Maybe when he wore it he'd think of her.

She saw him just before homeroom, standing near a bay of lockers with a group of his teammates. She had about four minutes before the bell rang. Should she go up to him and return the sweatshirt right there, in front of everyone? Should she call him aside? Should she wait until math class—which they had together next period—and put the sweatshirt on his desk then?

Why didn't she know how to do this stuff? And how come so many other people did? *Come on, Skylar. Be who you want to be.*

She took a deep breath and looked around to make sure no one was watching her, then she started to approach him. But just as she was about to say his name, she heard it come from someone else's mouth. She recognized the sweet, high voice from the day before. Gabby.

"Pierce!" Gabby called from down the hall. "Come here for a second!"

Skylar watched Pierce wheel around and jog right over to Gabby, who stood with a bunch of girls by the water fountain. Gabby casually slung her arm through Pierce's like it was nothing. Like she was in charge. They walked off together, Pierce towering over Gabby despite her wedge-heeled riding boots. Skylar wondered what they were talking about. She wondered if she'd ever be that comfortable around a guy.

By the time Pierce got to geometry (he must have walked Gabby to class, Skylar realized with dismay), there was no time for a flirtatious exchange. He slipped into the seat next to her just as Ms. Abrams was starting class.

"Here's your sweatshirt," she whispered, pulling it from her bag. "Thanks."

Pierce looked up with clear blue eyes and grinned. She felt that giddiness again. He was so cute—like army cute. Like southern cute, almost.

"Oh, hey, no problem," he said, taking the sweatshirt from her. "I'd almost forgotten about it."

"Well, here it is," she said, dumbly repeating herself.

He balled it up to put it in his bag, and as he did he took an exaggerated sniff. "This doesn't smell half as bad as it did when I gave it to you," he said. "Maybe I should lend you more of my clothes."

He noticed! Skylar smiled shyly and tried to think of something funny to say back. But then Ms. Abrams trumpeted, "Let's get started, people," and Pierce was digging in his bag for a pencil. So that was it. Opportunity officially missed.

She watched him jet out of the classroom as soon as the bell rang, and then realized, with a sinking feeling, that she had nothing else to look forward to that day. There was no one else she was interested in running into—in fact, she hoped to avoid anyone who might have seen her at lunch yesterday, pitiful and pathetic in her marinara-drenched shirt. When lunchtime rolled around, she took her PB&J and started walking up the hill off campus. She couldn't face more probing stares, or even the minor discomfort of sitting alone in the cafeteria. She thought she'd seen a little row of stores right around the corner from the school. Maybe she could hide out in one of them.

She trudged up the hill away from Ascension High, burying her face in her scarf to keep it from getting whipped by the wind and replaying her conversation with Pierce. He'd definitely been friendly, and there had been an undertone of flirtation. Right? She just didn't know how to follow through. Lucy would have known. Gabby probably knew. She sighed deeply, filling the scarf with hot, damp air.

As she rounded the corner she surveyed her hideout options: a Mexican place, a dry cleaner, a deli, and, right in front of her, an ice cream shop. She certainly didn't need the calories in a burrito—especially when she had already packed a sandwich— and she couldn't exactly ask to eat her lunch in the dry cleaner. Maybe she could just go into the deli and buy something to drink?

"Don't even think about it," a girl said. "If you're considering stepping foot in Chalupa's."

Skylar turned to see a beautiful girl, just taller than she was, standing in the doorway of Get the Scoop, the ice cream parlor. Her face was angular and pretty, in a pixie-ish way. Her wheat-colored hair was parted in the middle, long and choppy around the sides. Around her neck was a bright red ribbon, worn as a choker. She looked kind of like an elf. A beautiful elf. And she was smiling at Skylar.

"I'm—I'm sorry?" Skylar was startled; she hadn't seen the girl emerge from the shop.

"The Mexican place. I saw you eyeing it. The food at that place is like Styrofoam. Deep-fried Styrofoam, of course." The girl fake-shuddered. "Don't tell me you actually *like* it."

"I've never been," Skylar said. "I'm new here. I was just . . . I was just looking for somewhere to eat my lunch." Feeling beyond pathetic, she held up her brown bag.

"Oh. Totally excusable, then," the girl said brightly. Skylar was grateful she didn't ask why Skylar was eating alone, or whether she should be in school. "I was worried about you for a second there." She wiped her hands on the orange apron she was wearing and offered Skylar a beaming smile. "My name's Meg."

"I'm Skylar. Thanks for the warning about the Mexican food. I haven't really gotten much of a tour yet." Skylar thought she saw a flash of sympathy run through Meg's eyes.

"Listen." Meg leaned forward as though she was about to tell Skylar a secret. "My boss is out to lunch. Want to come in for a free ice cream? I can give you the lowdown on other establishments to avoid. Trust me—there are plenty."

It was a bit cold for ice cream, and she hadn't even eaten her sandwich, but Skylar couldn't turn down the chance to have a maybe-normal chat with a girl who seemed to be close to her own age. For a moment Skylar wondered why this girl wasn't in school. But then, who cared? If she wanted to make friends, she had to start actually *talking* to people. And maybe this girl was a freshman in college or something.

"I—I have to be back in twenty minutes, but I guess I could come in for a little," Skylar said, glancing at the silver face of her watch. It was delicate, but it always felt abnormally heavy on her wrist. She remembered receiving it for Christmas several years ago. Her mom had won two hundred dollars from a scratch ticket and used it to buy their presents. It was the one time her mom had ever purchased the same thing for both her daughters. She wondered where Lucy's was now.

"Nice watch," Meg said, and when Skylar noticed her staring at it intensely, she quickly tucked it under the cuff of her jacket.

"Thanks," she said. "It was a gift. From—from an ex." She blurted out the lie without intending to. But almost immediately she felt better. She relished the way the word "ex" hung in the air, propping her up, giving her confidence.

"Aw. That's nice that you still wear it," Meg said. "So, wanna come in? I know it's not really ice cream weather, but we've got good stuff."

Meg headed into the store, and Skylar followed her in. Maybe working in the freezer bins had desensitized Meg to the cold: Skylar noticed that Meg wore just a T-shirt, jeans, the orange apron, and the red ribbon tied around her neck. Skylar was shivering even in her coat and scarf.

"So," Meg said, surveying the bins of ice cream and adopting an exaggeratedly pensive expression. "Don't tell me, let me guess." She gave Skylar a once-over, then bent down and started scooping a flavor into a bowl, smiling mischievously over the counter at Skylar. Her eyes were blue-gray—like sparkling smoke.

"Here you go," Meg said, putting the bowl in front of

Skylar with a flourish of her hands. "Our best vanilla bean."

She was right. Vanilla, for all its lack of originality, actually *was* Skylar's favorite. She felt a surge of happiness. This mystery girl *got* her.

But as she was about to reach for it, she suddenly had the weird feeling that something—some*one*—was standing over her. And then she had a vision of Lucy, there next to her. Freezing breath on her cheek. *Are you sure that's what you want to be eating, Sky?* she heard her sister saying. *Baby fat is only cute when you're a baby.*

She squeezed her eyes shut for a second, trying to block out Lucy's voice.

"Was I wrong? It's not your favorite?" Meg's face fell. She sounded genuinely disappointed.

"No, no! It is. I just—I got distracted for a second." Skylar found herself strangely compelled to please Meg. "Do you think I could have some water?" As Meg turned to fill up a glass, Skylar looked behind her, over both shoulders. Of course no one was there.

She picked up a spoon and reminded herself that a few spoonfuls couldn't hurt. "How did you know? Do I just read vanilla?"

Meg giggled. "Just a guess. Go on, dig in. Have seconds if you want! You look like one of those sticks who could eat *anything* and never gain a pound."

Skylar blushed; she felt embarrassed and a little proud. She had tried so hard to lose weight after Lucy . . . well, since the accident. She clutched the spoon tighter and was about take a bite when Meg stuck out her hand.

"Wait! I almost forgot the most important topping!" Meg started rummaging around behind the counter.

"Oh, I don't need any toppings—I like it plain," Skylar said. But Meg was already tucking a flower into the side of the bowl. It was shockingly red against the white ice cream. For some reason Skylar found herself thinking of a nosebleed, the way a tissue looked when soaked with spots of blood.

"There. Perfect!" Meg stood back, admiring the bowl. Skylar smiled too, and finally took a bite.

"It's delicious," she said, letting a spoonful melt on her tongue. "Thank you." For the first time all day she felt her shoulders relax a little.

"I'm a Rocky Road girl myself," Meg said, running a hand through her hair.

"So, where do you go to school?" Skylar asked.

Meg's cornflower eyes met Skylar's. "I'm taking some time off," she said with a crooked smile, not offering anything else. Skylar anxiously wondered whether she'd overstepped some invisible line. Maybe Meg couldn't afford college and that's why she had the ice cream job.

"I like your hair," Skylar said to change the subject, and took another bite. The ice cream in her mouth, its texture and coolness, calmed her down.

"Oh, thanks! I kept it really short for a while, but I decided to grow it out last month." Meg waved a hand vaguely. "I change my look a lot. Luckily, my hair grows insanely fast."

Skylar pulled a handful of hair over her shoulder and examined it for split ends. "My hair is just so plain. Like my ice cream preferences, I guess. I'm thinking about changing mine too."

"Like how?" Meg asked.

"I don't know, like dye it even lighter, maybe? Or try bangs?" Skylar pulled her hair from the pins so that she and Meg could see it better. It felt nice to be chatting about hair with someone who wasn't just telling her to spray the back of an updo with extra-strength hair spray.

"Bangs could be cool," Meg said, pursing her lips like she was really thinking about it. "It's so weird how even the smallest change can really make a difference, isn't it?"

The prospect of changing her look made Skylar's heart thump in her chest. "Yeah. Like getting bangs could be a total makeover."

"Well, a *total* makeover would be a little more intense than a haircut," Meg said with a gently prodding smile. "What else would you do? What else would you change?"

Everything, Skylar thought. She thought about Gabby—how friendly she was, how popular she seemed to be, how effortlessly she'd beckoned to Pierce. Her tiny frame and her bouncy blond hair. It was impossible not to be reminded of Lucy: the unforced social ease, the cute laugh, and the smile that made people feel warm from the inside out, like hot chocolate or a good night's sleep. The way Pierce had simply jumped when Gabby called . . .

Skylar felt a familiar pang, one that spasmed just below her stomach.

"It's just . . . have you ever noticed how it's so easy for some people?" She pushed away the ice cream bowl and practically forgot that she was speaking out loud. "Sometimes I feel like I'd do *anything* to be one of them." She pulled the red flower from the bowl, wiped the dripping ice cream off it, and twirled the stem in her hands.

She was so lost in her own thoughts that it was a bit of a surprise when Meg responded warmly, "Anything, huh?" Then Meg grinned, her teeth glinting in the fluorescent lights. "I couldn't agree more."

ACT TWO

VANITY, OR THE FAIREST OF THEM ALL

CHAPTER FIVE

"We'll spend this class period in the library," said Mrs. Haynes, the substitute who was filling in for the mysteriously absent Mr. Landon, "but you'll need to do independent research on your own time as well."

The assignment of the research project was the single piece of good news Em had gotten that week. Maybe now she wouldn't fail out of school. Em had been unable to focus on schoolwork for the past few weeks, but now she perked up.

"You have until Friday to come up with a research proposal," Mrs. Haynes continued. But as soon as everyone dispersed into the stacks and to the bay of computers to search for topics, Em approached her with purpose.

"I know what I want to write about," Em said firmly.

"Already?" Mrs. Haynes pushed her glasses up her nose.

"Yes." Em nodded. "Greek drama. And myth."

"Oh, really?" Mrs. Haynes looked intrigued. "That sounds interesting. Although, that's a very expansive topic. Do you think you could narrow it down?"

Em picked at the cuff of her deep blue sweater, suddenly feeling nervous. "Well, I've heard of this . . . type of creature? They're called the Furies?" She left the word hanging as a question between them, hoping she wouldn't have to explain much more.

"Of course! The Furies. Female spirits who appear in most stories in a set of three, right?" Mrs. Haynes tapped her lip with her finger, trying to remember something. "Alecto, Megaera, and . . . oh, what was that third one's name?"

"Ty," Em said automatically, and she couldn't stop Chase's face from flashing before her eyes. Chase's sad, tortured face. So scared. So defiant.

"Tisiphone, yes!" Mrs. Haynes was thrilled.

Yeah, they're pretty great until they start tormenting you, Em thought.

"From what I recall—and forgive me, it's been years since I've really delved into the lesser Greek myths—the Furies were vengeful, correct? Inherently evil?"

"Yes." Em didn't even hesitate. "Evil."

"They exist to drive people mad," Mrs. Haynes said, nodding

briskly. "This sounds like an ideal topic, Emily. May I suggest investigating how and where they have been depicted by different authors? I can't wait to see what else you come up with."

Me neither, Em thought dryly. And as she walked toward the computers, Mrs. Haynes's words rang in her head: *They exist to drive people mad.* Was that what was happening to her? Her stomach turned as she remembered the five red seeds she'd swallowed at the mall that night. Could that be their effect? Craziness? Were the Furies going to make her insane?

Em took a deep breath and sat down heavily in front of a computer. She made a conscious effort to calm down. She had a chance here—some momentum. She could learn more about the Furies and maybe get a decent English grade. At this point she needed all the help she could get, on both fronts. Nothing good would come of hypothesizing worst-case scenarios. She'd been so paralyzed over the past few weeks that she hadn't had the energy to sit down and think logically about what was happening to her. This was her chance.

Furies, Greek myth. She typed the terms into the library's catalog search engine. Only four results came up, all of them located in the classics section toward the back of Ascension High's library. She marked down the call numbers, picked up her bag, and made her way over to the stacks. She felt a sense of relief as she did so—a sense of empowerment.

She found the books way in the back of the stacks, and she

allowed herself a moment to revel in their heavy bindings and musty smells. Old books were her favorite. She chose one at random and started leafing through it. The Furies were only mentioned as a footnote in the chapter about Greek sirens—beautiful creatures who lured sailors to untimely, watery deaths. Em replaced that book on the shelf and chose the next one and then the next one, running her finger down the indexes. She wasn't finding much. A small mention here, a note in the appendix there.

But she hit pay dirt in the fourth book. A full chapter was devoted to the Furies—their history, their appearances in mythology, their legends. She found herself sinking down right there in the aisle between the shelves, leaning her back against the bookshelves and devouring it. When the bell rang, signaling the end of the period, Em chose to ignore it—she could catch up on French later. At this rate she'd be happy to stay in the library all afternoon—at least through lunch, so that she wouldn't be forced to decide between Gabby and Drea. She pulled a granola bar from her bag and settled in.

According to stories in the book, entire towns and communities could be affected by the Furies' presence. The Furies had been blamed over the centuries for everything from droughts and epidemics to mass murders—and the problems always stemmed from the crime or conjuring of an individual or group of individuals. From there, the goddesses of vengeance spread their tentacles, often unjustly. It was like once the Furies had been summoned, they couldn't be stopped. They wanted more. More revenge. More misery. They wouldn't leave until they'd had enough. Some believed the Furies had to be specifically called up by an individual desperate for retribution; other myths claimed that the Furies would sometimes appear on their own. And Em read one story that suggested this: If the Furies thought they missed their mark, their wrath increased exponentially.

Em shivered. Again, Chase came to her mind. How guilty he'd felt over what he'd done to Sasha . . . then dead below the overpass, a red orchid in his mouth. And her own punishment for betraying Gabby's friendship and trust: losing JD, possibly forever.

Would the Furies spread their madness even farther?

Would they wreak havoc not just in Em's life, but through all of Ascension?

She tried to focus on the words, but they blurred together like a watercolor left out in the rain. Then a single phrase jumped out at her: *Atonement ritual.* She blinked and sat up straighter.

She read: *Although unsubstantiated, many ancient texts have indicated that the Furies may be appeased by a ritual atonement.*

Appeased. That meant they'd leave, right? Em turned the page, frustrated that the book didn't say what the ritual *was.* Still, she felt hopeful. Maybe there *was* a way to banish the Furies. She just had to figure out what it was.

With a burst of energy, she shoved the book back into its

place and scribbled *atonement* in her notebook. As she left the library the next bell rang. She picked up her pace.

"Drea!" Em leaned into the locker room, where girls were changing for gym class. This couldn't wait until after school.

Drea jumped, clearly startled. Her shirt was halfway over her head, revealing a delicate white bra that was completely uncharacteristic, Em noticed. "Jesus, Em! Stalk much?!"

"Sorry," Em said, ignoring the stares from other girls, who were likely wondering what the hell Emily Winters wanted with Drea Feiffer in the locker room in the middle of the school day. "Put your clothes back on. Come on. You're skipping gym."

"Hold on, hold on," Drea said, keeping her arms halfway out of their sleeves and pointedly refusing to move an inch. "Are you going to explain why you bailed on me yesterday?"

Em picked up Drea's hooded black sweatshirt and tried handing it to her. "Yes," she said. "In fact, I am presenting you with these low-caffeine teas"—she dug a paper box wrapped in pretty paper out of her bag—"to try to make up for it. You know, for your little caffeine addiction problem."

Drea took the teas with a begrudging smile, and Em continued, "Look, I'm really sorry about yesterday. Gabby was being a diva, and I've barely seen Fiona and Lauren recently, and—"

Drea held up her hand to cut her off. "I'm bored already. Just don't do it again, okay?" Then she started to put her Converse sneakers back on. "At least you made it up to me by pulling me out of gym. It's weight-training day," she said with a roll of her eyes. "So tell me what's going on."

"Okay," Em said, watching as Drea carelessly threw on the rest of her outfit. "So we have this English assignment. It's independent research. Whatever topic we want." She waited for Drea to understand the significance, but Drea just looked at her quizzically.

"You're making me skip class to tell me about a homework assignment?"

Em sighed. "So I proposed that I research mythology—specifically, the Furies." She stopped to take a breath, and Drea gathered the last of her things.

"Let's go." Drea motioned for them to leave through the back door of the locker room to avoid getting caught by any of Ascension's overly muscular gym teachers, a.k.a. People with Absolutely No Sympathy for Any Problem. "Okay. So go on."

"Well, I'm doing this research," Em continued, "and mostly it's just different versions of stuff we already know. Like, that the Furies characteristically appear in the guise of three women, or that they want to wreak vengeance for crimes. Snakes in their hair. That sort of thing."

Drea knew all this already, but Em could see that she was still hanging on every word. Em wondered for the millionth time why Drea was *so* invested in the Furies. It's not like they were chasing *her*. But she knew better than to ask. The first few times she'd brought it up, Drea had completely shut her down. Em didn't want to push it. Drea was the only one who understood, who didn't ask too many questions. Em had to return the favor.

"But then I saw something I've never seen, even in the articles you've given me," Em said, experiencing the same sense of fizzing excitement she'd felt when she first read the words "atonement ritual." They passed around the back of the gym toward the auditorium, where they'd be able to talk in both warmth and peace.

Drea paused and waited to hear.

"There's a way to end it." Em stopped walking too. They stared at each other.

"How?" Drea looked skeptical. She started walking again.

"I'm not sure exactly—yet. But apparently there's some type of ritual, some ceremony that you can do. It works. It said so in the book." She jogged a little to catch up with Drea. "Wait up, D. What do you think of that?"

"I *think* you look like you're going to freeze to death, Em. Let's go inside." Drea pulled open the door to the theater. Em was grateful to not see the gang of singing drama kids who usually called that zone home, and she was equally relieved that JD, who occasionally worked his techie magic lighting school plays, wasn't hanging around either.

"All right," Drea said, once they'd sat down on one of the

slatted benches that lined the lobby. "So what? We have to sacrifice a lamb or something? I don't know, Em. Sounds bogus
to me."

"It's not like that," Em said, although she didn't know that for
certain. "Come on, Drea, at least consider what this could mean."

"I'm sure that some people *think* there's a ritual that works,
Em." Drea was gentler now. "But I've read so much about the
Furies, and I've never seen *specific* instructions, like how you'd
actually *do* it."

It was true, the book Em had seen in the library didn't offer a
spell or a chant or information about what the rite might actually
entail. But Em wanted so badly to believe that there was some
way to get rid of the Furies. There had to be.

"Okay, I hear what you're saying," Em said, in the same über-
rational tone of voice she'd used when trying to convince her
parents to *at least* let her have the car on weekdays, when they
wanted to take away her access for good. "But aren't you the
tiniest bit curious? When's the last time you actually *tried* looking
for a way to get rid of them? It's like you want to know everything about them except the most important piece—how to get
them the hell out of our lives."

She'd hit a nerve, she could tell. Drea's face fell slightly. Em
watched as she fiddled with one of the safety pins in her ears, and
swallowed hard and fast like she'd bitten into something sour.
Then she gave in. "Okay. What do you want to do?"

Em exhaled. "Let's go to that library in Portland. The antiquities library you were telling me about?" She'd already written off the rest of the school day, and she hoped Drea would too. Tomorrow she'd start fresh, she told herself. Rededicate herself to her work and her normal life. But for today . . . today, she had to do this.

"Do you have your car?" Drea asked. It was the only answer Em needed; Drea was in. "I don't have mine, obviously."

"Well, yeah, but you know I can't drive it all the way to Portland," Em said with a sinking sense of disappointment. She'd forgotten that Drea only got the use of her dad's car on weekends. "My parents will kill me."

"Crow." Drea slapped Em's leg. "He'll drive us."

Em thought back to band practice and Crow's aggressive way of being "friendly." She felt a flicker of apprehension, but she shrugged. "If you call him, sure."

Crow's ride was a dark red pickup truck with silver stripes down either side. Em and Drea had taken Em's car home; now Crow, who had band practice later anyway, was going pick them up there and drop them at the library. Drea's dad, who worked on the docks of Portland hauling bait for local lobstermen, would drive them home later that evening. Em was happy her parents weren't home to raise their eyebrows at Drea's dyed hair or Crow's revved engine.

"You squeeze in back, Feiffer," Crow said out the passenger window as the girls approached his truck.

Drea looked at Em, then back at Crow, and then asked indignantly, "Why does she get shotgun?"

"Because I don't know where we're going, and you're a shitty navigator," Crow answered, leaning back in his seat and drumming mindlessly on the steering wheel. "Remember when you got us lost out near Sebago last summer? Not again, Fifes. I'm trying a new copilot."

Drea rolled her eyes and started climbing into the backseat.

"Plus this one's got longer legs," Crow added with a smirk as Em followed Drea into the car.

As they drove out of Ascension, Em leaned her head against the cold window and watched the trees blur by. With Crow's music—some drum-heavy loud stuff that didn't have any discernible melody—blaring on the car stereo, Em was grateful for a few minutes to tune out.

But once they were on the highway, Crow turned down the volume. "So, what's so special about this antiques place?" he asked.

"*An-tiq-ui-ties.*" Drea overenunciated the word, tapping Crow's shoulder with every syllable. "As in, related to Greece and Rome. Basically, it's a really quiet room in the USM library with a lot of really old books."

Em waited for him to ask why in the world they would want

to go there, but Crow just nodded, as if it was a totally normal place to visit. "Sounds cool," he said. He cast a sideways glance at Em. "Secret's out. I always knew deep down you were kind of a nerd. And not just about lava volcanoes."

"I guess I'm more than a spoiled princess," she tossed back.

Her self-satisfaction doubled when she was able to direct Crow to the library parking lot using only the map—no GPS, no smartphone. *You can still do* something *right*, she told herself.

The girls hopped out of the truck. "Take care of this one, Drea," Crow said, nodding his head toward Em. "She doesn't leave the compound much."

Then he cranked his music and peeled out of the lot.

Em felt Drea's eyes on her as they walked toward the entrance. She wondered whether Drea was as nervous as she was. It felt like there was a marching band in her stomach.

"I think he likes you," Drea announced.

This took Em completely by surprise. She wrinkled her nose. "Who likes me? What?"

"Crow. I think he has a crush on you."

Crow? Having a crush? On *her*? "Are you high?" Em scoffed. "Crow thinks that I'm Princess Popular. He's only nice to me because you and I are friends." And they *were* friends—Em realized it as she said the words.

"It just seems like he likes you, that's all. He was staring at you in the car. I kept thinking he was going to drive off the road."

Drea shrugged and looked at Em critically. "You are kind of having a good skin day."

Em shook her head, laughing a little. This was crazy. Since when did Drea talk shop about boys and skin? That was Gabby's job. "Let's go in, weirdo," she said.

The University of Southern Maine antiquities research room was a special section, wood-paneled and remote, near the top of the university library. A severe-looking woman with black hair and dark red lipstick sat at a desk by the door.

She sat up sharply when Em and Drea entered. "You have to sign in," she said, pointing to a sign that asked for photo ID.

"Can I help you girls?" she asked as she typed their information into the computer.

"We're just doing some research for a school project," Drea said, grabbing back her ID and sailing past the desk nonchalantly while whispering under her breath, "We're not gonna rob the place, lady." But then she did a double take. "I've seen that woman before," she said to Em as they moved out of earshot.

They searched *Furies* and made their way to a row of books about ancient Greece; the librarian watched them closely the whole time. She was in heaven, running her fingers over the books' leather bindings and gold-embossed lettering.

"Here's one," Drea said, heaving an oversized volume off one of the shelves. They brought it to a table and hunched over it;

meanwhile, the librarian had moved from her watchful perch and moseyed over to the search computers. Em saw, out of the corner of her eye, that the woman was trying to get a better look at what they had typed into the computer. They were definitely being watched.

"Okay, let's see," Drea was mumbling. "Erebus . . . Eurydice . . . Fates . . . Furies . . . Here we go. Page 282." Em could sense now that the librarian was hovering behind them.

They flipped to the page and Em pulled out her notebook, grabbing a pen cap with her teeth and tugging it off so that she was ready to take notes. She was ravenous for the information.

But page 282 offered nothing more than what they already knew.

"What's the next one called?" Drea asked as Em scanned the computer search printout.

"It's called . . . oh my god, Drea," Em gasped. "It's exactly what we're looking for. *Conjuring the Furies.*"

Drea craned her neck to read over Em's shoulder. "You're kidding. That's really what it's called?"

They eagerly scanned the call numbers; Em's pulse quickened with excitement. But when they got to the place where the book should have been, it wasn't there.

"Excuse me, ma'am?" Em approached the librarian politely, trying to contain her impatience. "We're looking for this book, here?" She pointed to the call number and the book title.

"It's gone," the woman said in a clipped tone.

"I thought you weren't allowed to check books out?" Em was *thisclose* to leaping over the desk and looking at the woman's computer herself.

"It's missing," the librarian told them. Em looked at her blankly. "It was stolen on November fifteenth. And frankly, ladies, I'm going to have to ask you to leave."

"What the hell?" Drea's voice got loud immediately.

"Drea . . . ," Em warned through clenched teeth. She turned to the librarian and spoke overly politely. "I'm sorry, Ms. . . . Markwell," she said, reading the woman's name tag, which showed that her first name was Hannah. "Are we doing something wrong? We're just trying to locate this book."

"I don't know what you girls are up to," she said, her eyes darting with distress between Em and Drea. Her lips were so strikingly defined that Em could not look away from her mouth. "But you can't do it here. You should leave."

The girls exchanged looks. There was something going on here, some undercurrent that neither of them understood.

"You can't just tell us to leave. We have a right to be here." Drea stood up straight and defiant.

Em rose slowly. This woman's nerves were clearly shot. She didn't want to startle her even more. She had a feeling—one she couldn't explain—that she knew what was rankling Ms. Markwell. But she wanted to hear her say it herself.

"Why do you want us to leave?" Em kept her voice steady. "Is there a problem with the . . . *subject* of our research?"

"Girls," she said again, her voice trembling. "I can't allow you to stay. I can't allow her . . ." She gestured with her free hand toward Em. Em drew back, feeling as though she'd been slapped. It was clear that this woman had a problem with *her*, not the book, and not even with Drea.

"Let's go, D," Em said quietly, tugging on Drea's sleeve. "Let's just go."

"This is bullshit," Drea said, picking up her bag. "This is total bullshit." But both of them could see the terror in the woman's eyes.

CHAPTER SIX

Visibility. That's what she was shooting for.

"You need to be *seen*," Meg told Skylar when they were in Skylar's bedroom a couple days later. With a flourish, Meg produced a black scarf covered in white skulls. It looked like something one of Ascension's goth kids would wear. Skylar had seen them in the halls, skulking around in their hoodies, skinny jeans, and crazy, heavy jewelry. She knew better than to smile at them.

"I don't know, Meg. . . . It's not really my style," Skylar said tentatively, not wanting to hurt Meg's feelings. "Why don't you wear it?"

"I have this," Meg said, touching the red ribbon she wore every day around her slender neck.

"Yeah, I've noticed," Skylar said. "Do you ever take it off?"

"No!" Meg responded as though the answer was obvious. "Then my head would fall off, silly!" She laughed then, louder than Skylar had ever heard her laugh.

"But really," Meg said, collecting herself, "Even if it's not your style now, it will be soon. I just saw it in *Lucky*. Plus it'll look hot with your new hair."

It was Wednesday evening, and the third time Skylar and Meg had hung out since they'd met in the ice cream shop two days ago. Skylar was getting used to Meg's strange sense of humor. Like the other day, she'd told Skylar that only "superclose friends" could visit her and her cousins at their house. "We pick them out special," she'd said. When Skylar had looked at her inquisitively, secretly wanting to know if she'd made the cut, Meg had giggled and said, "Don't worry, Sky. I chose you the moment I saw you."

This evening Meg had shown up brandishing a drugstore box with a blond model on it: "Let's highlight your hair!" And she'd massaged the dye into Skylar's hair—her fingers tracing wild patterns on her scalp—as Skylar sat there thinking, *At last. A friend.*

And not just any friend. A beautiful, cool, older friend. She felt a flutter in the back of her throat. What would Lucy have to say about *that*?

Now they were upstairs in Skylar's tower bedroom, Skylar's hair hanging damp around her shoulders.

"This is going to look *awesome*," Meg said, twirling a strand of it around one of her fingers. They both stared at Skylar's reflection in the mirror as Meg turned on the hair dryer. "You're going to love it once it's dry."

If only Meg went to Ascension. . . .

Because what Skylar wanted more than anything was someone to whisper with in the halls, to pass notes to in class, to giggle with in assemblies. *That* kind of friend. Someone like Gabby. She was embarrassed to admit it, but she'd become slightly fixated on her blond rescuer from day one. Gabby was everything that Skylar wanted to be. She represented the new life Skylar imagined for herself, far away from her old demons.

Meg pointed to a book on the dresser. "Is that the yearbook?" When they'd hung out yesterday, Meg had suggested that Skylar check out last year's Ascension yearbook from the school library. "Time for a crash course! Who do you know so far? Any cute boys at Ascension?"

Skylar felt warm, and not just because of the hot air being blasted at her head.

"I see that blush," Meg said gleefully, shutting off the dryer and plopping down on the bed. "You better tell me!"

And so they began poring over the book. Skylar turned the pages slowly, picking out Gabby and her friends among the candid shots at pep rallies and dances.

As she flipped through, trying to find the sports pages so she could show Meg a picture of Pierce, she passed the section that highlighted Ascension's artsy types. On the fine arts page she saw a charcoal drawing, heavy and dark, of an open eye surrounded by drooping flowers and bones. It was untitled, and done by someone named Sasha Bowlder. The picture startled her, and for a moment she couldn't look away.

"That's a beautiful piece," Meg said, touching it lightly with a slender finger. "Too bad someone defaced it."

Over the drawing someone had scrawled *Witch* in blue pen. The image, taken as a whole, made Skylar feel weird.

She was happy to find the sports section, and even more pleased to see a feature about Pierce: *Freshman Football Phenom*, it was called, and it described how last year Pierce was the first frosh to make it onto the varsity team in almost a decade.

"That's the guy I have a crush on," she said, feeling young and foolish. "He's a football player. He's really popular. Apparently he's going to be Ascension's starting quarterback next fall. He'd never notice me."

"Um, the football player who *lent you his sweatshirt*?" Meg cried, running the brush through Skylar's hair a few more times. "I'd say he's already ripe for the picking. And," she added as she finished, stood Skylar up, and spun her around, "if he didn't notice you before, he'll definitely notice you now."

With newfound confidence, Skylar strutted through the doors of Ascension High on Thursday morning, sporting her new scarf and freshly highlighted, blown-out blond hair. She'd paired the scarf with a black crewneck top and light-wash jeans.

She looked cool. Effortless. Not like the shy girl in the pretty pink cardigan she'd been on Monday.

Then she saw Gabby down the hall and stopped dead in her tracks. Blond, adorable, perfectly dressed Gabby—wearing the same scarf as Skylar. *Skulls and all.*

Oh god. Skylar knew she was violating one of the top ten Rules of High School: Don't wear the same thing as one of the most popular girls in school.

But when Gabby got closer, she smiled. "Hey—nice scarf," she said, and winked.

Skylar cleared her throat. "Yeah, it's—it's new." Was Gabby seriously giving her a break?

"I love how from far away the skulls look like tiny hearts," Gabby mused, examining it. "But then up close it's a little bit more hard-core."

Gabby was wearing the scarf with a button up white shirt and jeans; wrapped around her neck, the scarf looked casual and cozy—not goth at all.

"So, how are things going?" Gabby asked. "You finding your way around okay?"

"Oh, sure," Skylar said, as though she hadn't spent every day this week compulsively checking the school map to make sure she was going in the right direction. "Everyone's being really nice." Also a lie. But she was determined to appear confident right now.

The bell rang, and Skylar waited for Gabby to run back to her friends. But she didn't. Instead, she asked, "Where's your homeroom? Want to walk together?"

"It's in the humanities wing," Skylar said, her heart secretly exploding at the chance to walk through the halls with Gabby.

"Yay! Mine too." As they started walking, Gabby pointed to a colorful poster taped to the wall. "Are you coming to the dance?"

Skylar looked at the poster, which was adorned with bright flowers. The Spring Fling. A little over three weeks away. Terrific. Now on top of adjusting to a new school, she had a dance to worry about. As though she wasn't sufficiently aware of her loneliness. . . .

"I hadn't really thought about it," she said honestly.

"Neither has anyone else," Gabby said, suddenly sounding despondent. "I'm chair of the planning committee for all the school dances, but we've barely made any progress. My own best friend doesn't even remember the meetings."

This was her opportunity. Meg's voice sounded in her head: *Be seen. Be visible. Get involved.*

"I like planning dances," Skylar said, even though she'd never planned a dance in her life. "When's the next meeting?"

Gabby grabbed her arm and the thousand-watt smile returned. "Oh my god! You should totally join the committee!

Everyone is great—totally the cream of Ascension's crop—but we are desperate for some new blood. Come to the meeting tomorrow!"

Skylar McVoy. Planning dances. Friends with the most popular girl in school. She was liking the sound of this. And it was happening so fast!

"I just had the best idea," Gabby went on. "Are you free after school? Why don't we go to the mall and look around, brainstorm, see if we can come up with any great ideas for the dance—or for our outfits."

"I'm not booked yet," she said, dying to tell Meg about this fantastic turn of events. "That sounds great."

"Plus, I'm thinking of having a pajama party really soon. Maybe next weekend. Isn't that a great idea? So we can totally go to Victoria's Secret and look for some cute pj's."

Skylar could have broken into a happy dance. Had Gabby just invited her to go shopping *and* to a party? Skylar could only grin and nod.

In homeroom she pulled out her phone below the desk. *You were right about the scarf—and my hair,* she texted Meg. *I think I made my first friend (besides you)! Headed to the mall after school.*

On the way to the "old mall" that afternoon, the cold winter sunshine blazing through Gabby's windshield, Gabby went on about how excited she was for the day when all the best stores transferred over to the new mall, the Behemoth. "I just love shopping in brand-new stores. Everything's so clean and shiny," she chirped.

Skylar smiled.

When they got to the mall, Skylar trailed Gabby through several stores, fingering the same fabrics, smelling the same lotions, trying not to get too nervous.

Don't mess this up! she kept thinking.

"I want something girly and lacy," Gabby said as they walked into Victoria's Secret. "But also something that has coverage, you know? There will be boys there, after all."

A coed pajama party? Skylar bet Lucy had never attended one of those.

"How about this for you?" Skylar held up an orange-and-pink shorts set.

"That's the right idea," Gabby said, nodding encouragingly. "But I'm not a big fan of orange. Ooooooh, what about this one!" She was holding another set, this one with purple polka dots.

Skylar shivered involuntarily. "I'm not into polka dots," she said. "But I bet it would look cute on you."

As she made her way through the racks Skylar wondered whether Pierce would be at Gabby's pajama party. She imagined walking up to him, poised, smiling. It would be obvious that she was friends with Gabby and therefore one of the in crowd. She would giggle at the right moments and know what to say. And she'd be wearing . . . this. Her eyes fell on pink silk shorts lined in lime green. On the hanger they were paired with a lime-green silk tank top with a deep V-neck. Both pieces were edge with pink lace.

It was perfect—playful and sexy at the same time. Pierce would love it.

Gabby had already paid for a light blue nightie and blue capri leggings to match. She was standing at the doorway texting. So, with a deep breath and a promise to herself that she would look for a babysitting job this weekend, Skylar bought the pink-and-green pajamas, choosing to ignore the fact that they cost most of her weekly allowance from Aunt Nora.

Armed with their shopping bags, they made their way toward Macy's.

"I just want to take a quick spin through their dress department," Gabby said. "Not that I can even *plan* what to wear without knowing what the theme is going to be."

Skylar panicked slightly. The Spring Fling had to have a theme? Wasn't the theme, like, spring?

"Gabs!"

Gabby spun around. "Oh! It's Fiona and Lauren—have you met them?" Gabby tugged on Skylar's arm as she skipped over to her friends, who were standing by the indoor fountain. "They're the best. Other than Em. She's *actually* the best. But they're the other best."

Both girls were pretty brunettes. One wore black-framed, trendy glasses and the other had a bob with bangs. And then Skylar almost gasped out loud. Because standing right behind Glasses Girl were a few football players—including Pierce.

"Hi, sweetie." Gabby hugged one of the girls and pointed to Skylar. "Everyone, this is Skylar. Skylar, this is everyone. Fiona," she said, pointing to the girl in the glasses, "Lauren, Pierce, Sean, Adam, Andy." Skylar couldn't tell who was who, and none of the boys stepped forward to introduce himself. So she just kind of smiled and waved, hanging back, waiting for a cue about what to do next.

Gabby was pulling her blue pj set out of its bag and showing it to Fiona and Lauren while the guys whooped and hollered, trying to grab it out of her hands.

"You guys are pigs," Gabby said, laughing and shielding her purchase from them with her tiny body.

"That's hot, Gabs," one of them—Andy or Adam?—said. Skylar was relieved that Pierce hadn't said it. She watched Gabby blush just the right amount—enough to turn her cheeks pink. Not beet red, like Skylar used to get onstage.

Any confidence Skylar had felt during her one-on-one time with Gabby had dissipated, and now she didn't know what to say. Everyone ignored her; she obviously wasn't part of the group. Her breathing got shallower.

And then, just as in the ice cream shop, Lucy was there, next to her by the fountain. Only this time it wasn't a vision. It was a memory, vivid in Skylar's mind, like she was reliving it. Their mother was off looking for accessories for Lucy's summer pageant gown. Lucy, about to start her junior year, flirting with a bunch of gorgeous senior guys from their school. Skylar, a prefrosh, hoping one of them would notice her.

Lucy taking one glance over her shoulder, rolling her eyes, and saying, *Her? That's my sister. She's* special, *if you know what I mean.* Lucy laughing and Skylar's face getting hot. *She's supposed to start high school this fall . . . but my mom and I don't know if she's ready to go to school with* normal *kids.*

Skylar backing away, turning to go, to get away from this. Tripping on a shopping bag handle. Face-planting. And then Lucy helping her up, whispering in her ear, *I was just teasing, Sky. You have to learn how to take a joke. Those guys are jerks, and I didn't want them flirting with my baby sis.* Brushing her off. Skylar standing motionless, burning with embarrassment, the sound of the boys' laughter echoing in her ears.

"Want a sip?" All of a sudden Pierce was next to her, offering her a sip of his milk shake. "It's vanilla. Might put a smile on your face, Skylar."

Skylar's heart leaped and the corners of her mouth turned up into a smile—but not because he had shared the milk shake, or even because it was her favorite flavor. Pierce knew her name!

• • •

"Yeah, pageants are big in the South," Skylar told Gabby on the ride home. Gabby had asked about her old life in Alabama. "We grow up with them." She rubbed her temples. She didn't want to talk about her past, but Gabby had pressed her for details.

"That is so crazy," Gabby said, eyes wide. "I mean, I've only seen them on reality TV. Did you ever, like, win anything?"

"I won three crowns," Skylar heard herself say. And at that moment she knew she would keep lying. She would lie about the pageants and she would lie about her sister and she would lie about her whole damn life if it made her sound more like someone Gabby would be friends with.

"Really?" Gabby whipped her face toward Skylar, her curls bouncing as she did. "You'll have to teach me the walk. I've always wanted to walk like I'm on a runway."

Skylar knew Gabby was just being nice. She was clearly comfortable walking everywhere in three-inch heels—obviously the girl knew how to carry herself. But the idea of being able to teach Gabby anything—even a useless skill like pageant marching—was intoxicating. Skylar kept talking.

"My mom taught me the basics," she said, "before she got sick." In reality, her mom taught Lucy the basics before she got drunk and yelled at Skylar. But this version was so much nicer.

Gabby looked concerned. "So that's why you moved to Ascension? Your mom got sick?"

"Yeah . . . ," Skylar said, biting her lip. "She's off at some spa-rehabilitation place in Europe. It's recommended by all the best doctors." It's not like Gabby would ever check up on her story. She could say whatever she wanted. That her mom loved her. That she won pageants—even though the most memorable competition she ever attended was one in which she split her supertight pants during a performance of "Let Me Entertain You," revealing polka-dot underwear and earning her the nickname Dot-Crotch.

"Do you have any brothers or sisters?"

"No." Skylar said it firmly, looking out the window and fidgeting with the tassel at the end of the skull scarf.

"Wow," Gabby whispered. "I'm so sorry that you had to move. But you know what?" Keeping one hand on the steering wheel, Gabby used the other to pat Skylar's shoulder. "I'm really happy you're here."

Skylar's body tingled with pride . . . with the beginnings of transformation.

She hadn't been home from the mall for long before her phone dinged. As she walked to pick it up her skin prickled with anxiety. Back in Alabama she'd been used to getting "check-ins" from her mom right around this time of night, curt messages to the tune of: *Won't be home tonight.* For a moment Skylar's stomach ached with a familiar, sharp loneliness. Then she remembered that she wouldn't be getting any texts from her mom in jail.

The message turned out to be from Meg: *How did it go???* Wow. Meg really was an amazing friend to remember Skylar's "date" with Gabby—and to realize how important it was to her.

Skylar texted back: *It was great. I'm going to a dance committee mtg 2moro!*

Awesome, Meg replied. *Check yr email before bed. Hope to c u for lunch.*

When Skylar turned on her computer, she found an email from Meg, sent earlier that afternoon. *Hope you're having fun,* it read. *Here are a few songs from that Boston band I was telling you about—they're totally going to be the next big thing. See you soon!* There were a few MP3s attached to the email, and Skylar listened as she got ready for bed. The band—called the Dusters—was pretty good. A little rockabilly, a little indie. She downloaded the songs onto her iPod and went to bed humming them, her voice echoing in the old house. She prayed she would dream of her new life, not her old one.

Skylar's optimism extended into the next day, though it didn't help her come up with any brilliant dance themes (other than the theme of "make Pierce Travers fall madly in love with Skylar McVoy," which she didn't think the other girls would go for). Still, she practically skipped to the dance committee meeting after school.

"Hey, babe!" Gabby's greeting was chipper, but Skylar could

tell she was watching the door for someone else. "Now that you're here, I guess we're just waiting for Em." A whole cluster of other students—mostly girls, but a few guys, too—were in the room. Everyone seemed to be friends with everyone else.

One of the girls spoke up. "Could we just start without her, Gabby? She hasn't been here the last two times, and I'm missing part of practice for this."

Skylar could tell that Gabby wanted to stall. "She's probably just staying after class," Gabby offered vaguely. But after a few moments of shuffling papers, she took a deep breath and started talking, while keeping one eye trained on the door.

"So, we've got about three weeks to go, and not a lot figured out," Gabby said. Skylar made a mental note: The thing about really peppy people like Gabby? It was very easy to tell when they were off their game. "Um . . . what else? I'm glad the posters went up even without a theme, but we still need to have one for the actual event. We also don't have music figured out. . . ." She trailed off.

"What about the DJ we had at homecoming?" The suggestion came from one of the few guys on the committee. He looked artsy—he had a camera with a fancy lens on the desk next to him.

"No chance," piped up another girl, one Skylar had seen hanging around with Pierce and his friends. "He played the *worst* music."

"Um, I liked him," the boy replied.

"Me too," Sports Girl echoed. "Remember how he played all that dubstep? Perfect for dancing."

"That shit sucked, Sara," another guy, one of the ones from the mall yesterday, responded. "But when he played some of the harder stuff—"

"You mean the stuff that no one dances to," a young-looking girl with supershort hair cut in.

The conversation was getting weirdly heated. "Okay, guys, this isn't helpful," Gabby spoke up, but she sounded uncomfortable, and the debate about the music continued back and forth. Skylar knew that Gabby must be upset about the fact that this friend of hers—this Em she'd heard so much about—hadn't shown, leaving Gabby to corral the committee alone. *That's not how best friends should act,* Skylar thought. *That's not how I'm going to act.*

Notes of a Dusters song played in her head, and she got an idea. She sat forward excitedly, then checked herself and raised her hand timidly. "Hi," she said, smiling shyly, "I'm Skylar. And, so, I know I'm new? But I have an idea."

Gabby smiled at her. "Go ahead, Sky."

"Well, I just found out about this band, from Boston? They're called the Dusters. I think they'd be perfect—it's good dancey stuff but it could also just play in the background, you know? Maybe since they're kind of local, they'd consider it if we paid them?"

As soon as the word "Dusters" left her mouth, Gabby was squealing and banging her hand lightly against the desk. "Yes! Yes! That is such an awesome idea! Did you know that I'm going to *see* them in concert in April?"

"I've never even heard of them," someone said doubtfully.

But one of the other girls, the one who hadn't said much yet, nodded enthusiastically. "My brother *loves* them," she said. "I think that's a great idea."

"Sky, do you have them on your iPod?" Gabby asked.

Skylar silently thanked Meg for the music advice and the MP3s. "Of course," she said, digging her iPod and headphones out of her backpack.

"Here, listen to this, Jeff," Gabby said after pulling up her favorite song. She thrust the iPod in Photo Boy's face and turned to the rest of the group. "I am totally going to get in touch with them, like, today."

The girl who was friends with Pierce looked up from her phone, where she'd been texting. "I knew it," she said triumphantly. "I thought I'd heard of the Dusters from Angela McGowen—you know, she's a senior, she plays tennis?" Gabby nodded. "Well, she *knows* someone in the band! I just asked her, and she says her cousin is the drummer!"

Gabby squealed. "Are you serious?"

"Dead. Lemme ask her if she has their contact info."

Skylar couldn't believe her timing. Or, to be more accurate,

Meg's timing. It was like Meg was coordinating her life for her—perfectly.

"That's terrific, Gabs," Skylar said. She liked the sound of Gabby's nickname rolling off her tongue. The others nodded.

"If you think they'd play a high school, we should do it," Jeff relented, pulling the earbuds out of his ears. "This is actually pretty good."

So it was settled. Angela was going to call her cousin and set things in motion. Gabby would follow up the next day. If it fell through, they'd call an emergency meeting to come up with a backup plan. As the meeting broke up Gabby linked her arm through Skylar's. "This is, like, amazing luck. You should come with me to the concert," she said. "It's like fate brought us together or something—you're like my long-lost twin!"

Skylar squeezed Gabby's arm and grinned. Everything was falling into place. She allowed herself to relax ever so slightly.

Then they rounded the corner.

Skylar stopped and gasped. Right in front of them was Lucy, smiling, waving, and covered in blood.

"What's the matter, Sky?" Gabby squeezed Skylar's arm, breaking the spell. The girl in front of them was not Lucy. She was a blond girl about Lucy's height, draped in red streamers that she was removing from the ceiling. "You okay?"

"Yeah," Skylar said, still catching her breath. "I just thought I saw someone I knew."

CHAPTER SEVEN

The phone woke Em up at nine o'clock on Saturday morning. Gabby.

"Hey, Gabs," she said sleepily.

"You missed another meeting," Gabby said, without offering any greeting. "Another Spring Fling meeting. I called you and your phone was off."

"Oh no, Gabs, I'm so sorry." Em cursed herself for forgetting. She'd been at Drea's rereading a bunch of news reports about "accidents" that Drea believed had been caused by the Furies, trying to locate other copies of the overdue ("missing") book, and rehashing the strange run-in with the antiquities librarian. She'd been so stressed out recently that she hadn't charged her phone in days, and it had died. "I—I totally forgot." She felt like she should just start handing out preprinted apologies, the way she kept letting people down.

"You're supposed to be cochair of the committee, Em. Do you know how stupid I felt, waiting for you to show up?" Gabby's voice broke, and Em winced. She wanted so badly to be able to tell Gabby about what she was doing, why she was behaving so strangely. But she knew she'd sound crazy, and Gabby would never understand. Anyway, she couldn't tell Gabby—she'd made a promise to the Furies.

Instead, Em was left feeling awful—outside her own life, unable to talk to her closest friends about what was going on. She was getting doubly punished: first by the Furies, and now by Gabby and JD. She thought about what Mrs. Haynes had said about the Furies driving people mad. Maybe this kind of cycle of hurt and dishonesty was the core of insanity.

"I had—I needed to study for the SATs," Em said weakly. "My parents are really riding me about it. They made me turn off my phone."

"Em, you know how important this stuff is to me," Gabby said, lending each word a special amount of meaning. Em rolled onto her back and stared at the ceiling. It was true. For Gabby, much more than for Em, the dances and parties marked important milestones. They were symbols in her personal life. Just six months ago Gabby had announced her "V-Squared" Plan—her intention to lose her virginity on Valentine's Day, with Zach.

Then Em had hooked up with Zach. That asshole. Now he was gone. Off in some recovery facility somewhere—if the rumors were true. Em shuddered, thinking about the gossip that Zach had been in some kind of accident. Deep down, she knew the truth: the Furies must have gotten to him, too.

Without Zach around, Valentine's Day had come and gone with little fanfare, Em secretly agonizing over JD and Gabby acting more bubbly than ever to preserve her pride. Gabby was doing her best to keep up appearances, to still function as queen social bee of Ascension—even though Em knew that she must often still feel sad, betrayed, and embarrassed. Em dug her heels into the mattress, disgusted by the memories.

"I know, Gabby, and I'm sorry. I really am." She was. But seriously, a dance was the *last* thing she could think about right now. How could she get that across to Gabby without sounding like she didn't care?

"And when people flake, nothing gets done." The pitch of Gabby's voice raised. "This dance *has* to go well, Em, can't you understand that? I need it to."

"I get that," Em said. "And I'm sorry the committee sucks. But do you think, maybe, you shouldn't let it carry so much weight? I mean . . ." She spoke carefully, knowing she was treading on thin ice. "It's just a dance. In twenty years you won't remember any of it. The decorations or the music or any of the other stuff that's keeping you up at night. We'll just pick something out at the Party Shop this weekend."

"*The Party Shop?*" Gabby said each word as though it was a sexually transmitted disease. "Em, this isn't, like, our fifth-grade graduation. You know what?" Her voice quivered again. "Since this is obviously the last thing you care about, I'll find someone else to cochair. Someone who gets that the decorations can't come from the freaking *Party Shop*." And then she hung up.

Em tried calling back, but it rang twice and then went to voice mail. Fantastic. A fine start to her Saturday.

The fight with Gabby stuck with Em all day (which had at least one positive effect—for once, she wasn't thinking about the Furies) as she legitimately did try to study for the SATs. After botching yet another practice test, she threw her test prep book at the wall in frustration. Here she was, by herself on a Saturday evening, missing Gabby and wanting to make it up to her.

There was only one foolproof solution she could think of.

She called Chinese Dragon Palace and ordered delivery.

"We have food in the refrigerator," Em's mom said with raised eyebrows as Em pounded down the stairs to intercept the delivery man as soon as he rang the doorbell. "I'm glad you have your appetite back, but I'd prefer you feasted on something other than fried chicken and egg rolls."

"I know, Mom." Em pulled out a crumpled twenty and pressed it into the delivery guy's hands. "But Gabby and I are— Gabby and I kind of got into a little fight today. And I really want to do something nice for her. I want to bring her an olive branch," she said, motioning to the bags. "Or an egg roll branch, in this case."

"And how do you expect to do that? You know the new rule about weekend car use. It's for your own safety, honey."

After Em's car accident on Peaks Road, and then her secret drive out to the new mall construction site, which had ended in JD getting injured, her parents had laid down the law.

"Please, Mom. Gabby's is practically around the corner. I'll be home in a few hours."

With a sigh, her mom relented. "You better be back here by ten p.m., Emily."

Em was already halfway out the door.

As she was jogging to the car she heard the clanking of tools against JD's driveway. She looked over in time to see him sliding out from under Mr. Fount's Mustang, his mad-bomber hat framing his angular face like an astronaut's helmet. He'd taken his jacket off, presumably to use as a pillow between his body and the cold asphalt, and Em couldn't help but notice the way his bare biceps flexed when his arms pushed against the fender of the car.

Out of instinct, she shouted across the thin strip of lawn that separated their driveways. "Hey, you!" Almost as quickly, she remembered that they were barely speaking.

As he stood up, unfolding his tall and lanky frame, JD's eyes flickered over Em's face. For a moment he looked as though he was going to flat-out ignore her and go inside. But then his gaze settled on the bags in her hand.

"Let me guess," he said. "Fried pork dumplings."

"And sesame noodles—your favorite," she burst out eagerly. "Special delivery to Gabby."

He paused and toed the crusty snow with his boot. It was all Em could do to not charge over to him and wrap her arms around his waist. *Please, please, please forgive me,* she'd say. *I love you. I'll make you believe me.*

"You fixing your dad's car?" The answer was obvious, but she didn't want the conversation to be over yet.

"Yeah," JD said. There was a brief silence. "Well, I hope she doesn't hog the fortune cookies as bad as you do." His forehead wrinkled and he cracked a small smile, gone almost as soon as it came. Then he turned abruptly and went into the house.

As she unlocked her car, Em was elated. It was a short exchange, but it was progress.

The Chinese food may have been overkill, Em discovered when she showed up at Gabby's doorstep. And it probably hadn't been necessary for her to bring the stack of old DVDs that Gabby had asked to borrow ages ago.

Gabby answered the door giggling, clad in black yoga pants

and an oversized eighties sweatshirt that hung off one shoulder. She seemed both surprised and happy to see Em.

"Embear!" She threw her arms up for a hug. "Perfect night for a drop-by! I'm so glad you're here." And as Em leaned over to unlace her boots, Gabby whispered, "I'm sorry about before. I know I was a little harsh."

Gabby dragged Em by the hand into the living room, where a short, blond, eager-looking girl—the one who'd gotten doused in spaghetti sauce the other day—was sitting cross-legged on the floor. She was wearing running pants and a long-sleeved shirt that read ALABAMA BEAUTIES in small print above the breast.

"Meet my new cochair!" Gabby crowed. "Em, this is Skylar. She's new to Ascension—just started school on Monday. Sky, this is Em. The *best* of the best!"

Em wasn't really in the mood to hang out with someone she didn't know, but she was supposed to be making up with Gabby, and really, she should be thankful that this girl was taking over the dance committee. One less thing for Em to worry about. So she plopped down on the floor, where Skylar sat with an array of nail polishes in front of her.

"It's nice to meet you," she said with as much warmth as she could muster. Skylar's hair, she noticed, was in rollers, just like the ones Gabby used. Uh-oh—someone had a girl crush. Not surprising, really. Gabby had always had followers.

"Babe," Gabby said, reaching over as she scooched across

the couch. "Aren't you cold? Where is your coat? It's March!" She rubbed Em's arm, which was bare. As though she'd gotten dressed in a dream, Em looked down and saw for the first time that she was wearing just a T-shirt. No sweater, no jacket. Is this what she'd been wearing at home? Had her mom seen her leave the house that way?

"Oh . . . I must have left it in the car," Em said with a note of confusion in her voice. "I've been kind of absentminded recently," she added, as much to herself as to Gabby and Skylar.

"Yeah, I've noticed," Gabby said. But her tone wasn't mean this time. There was a combination of amusement and concern in it. "Want something to drink? An Irish coffee with some egg rolls? That'll warm you up." With that, she was bounding into the kitchen with the bag of Chinese food, leaving Em with this new girl, who had barely said a word.

"So . . ." Em leaned back onto her hands, stretching her toes out in front of her. "Pedicures?"

"Yeah," Skylar chirped. Her voice sounded strained. "I'm going to do this one," Skylar said, holding up a fuchsia color.

A classic Gabby color, Em noted. "Nice," she said, trying to seem enthusiastic. She picked up a bottle of dark red that appealed to her. It was so dark it was almost black. Em hadn't spent more than ten minutes on her personal appearance in the last month— and it showed. It couldn't hurt to at least pretend that she was a sixteen-year-old girl (who would be seventeen in just a few months).

Gabby came back into the room with a tray of Irish coffees.

"Here we go," she said, distributing them to Em and Skylar. "Chinese food is waiting in the kitchen for when we're done. I hope these pedis last until my pajama party."

The first sip of coffee burnt her throat, but Em didn't care. She gulped it down. It was weird, she really didn't feel that cold on the outside—she never would have noticed how underdressed she was if Gabby hadn't said anything. But there was this undeniable pit of coldness *inside* her. She didn't know if it was anxiety or sickness or those little seeds the Furies had told her to swallow, but she couldn't shake the strange feeling.

"So, soak, then scrub, then lotion?" she asked as the girls assembled their home-pedicure station.

"Precisely," Gabby said. Em began to relax. Gabby's favorite pop music Pandora station played in the background, the room smelled like flowery lotion, and warm whiskey was spreading in her belly. She felt almost normal.

"So, Skylar . . . I'm always curious how our guys hold up against non-Mainers," Gabby said with a giggle. "Who's hotter? Alabama boys or Maine guys? Who do you think is the hottest guy at Ascension so far?"

Em watched Skylar's face blanch and flush before transforming into an embarrassed smile. "Oh, I don't know," Skylar said, focusing intently on her big toe all of a sudden.

"There must be someone," Gabby pushed. "You can totally

tell us. I'm very good at keeping secrets, and Em is in outer space and will probably forget what you say in a few minutes anyway." She shot Em a grin.

Skylar looked back and forth between Em and Gabby, as though sizing up their trustworthiness. Then she spilled, all in one breath: "IguessIthinkPierceiskindofcute."

"Pierce Travers?" Gabby squealed. "Really? Okay, well, first of all, duh. He's definitely hot for a sophomore. And secondly, we could *totally* make that happen. Don't you think, Em?"

Em stalled, wiping her ankle with a washcloth. It was obvious to her that Pierce had a crush on *Gabby*.

"It's definitely a possibility," Em said slowly. "I don't really know him, but he seems like a sweet guy. You know him pretty well, right, Gabs?"

Gabby ignored Em's question. "Oh my god, cuteness! Well, okay, we'll get to work." She sounded like she was planning a tactical maneuver. Which, Em guessed, she was. "He's totally invited to my pj party, by the way. But none of the boys are allowed to sleep over."

"I can't believe he's a sophomore and he's set to be starting quarterback," Skylar said, suddenly seeming to loosen up a bit. She smeared lotion on her feet and ankles. "I heard a terrible story about the guy he replaced."

No, don't go there, Em thought, but before she could say it, Skylar was plowing on.

"That he killed himself? Is that true?"

Silence.

Gabby cleared her throat. Em ground a sandy scrub into the arch of her foot.

"Did you guys . . . were you guys, like—oh. I'm sorry," Skylar said, her brows coming together. "I should have known." She sounded genuinely apologetic.

"Well, he's replacing a guy named Zach, who left Ascension," Gabby said softly. "But you're talking about Chase, who's . . . really gone. And yes, we knew him. It's been difficult."

Difficult. Em chewed on the word. It was difficult to replay the night of Chase's death, wondering if she could have saved him from Ty's manipulations. It was difficult to hate him for how he'd tortured Sasha while his face continued to appear to Em in her nightmares. It was difficult that she wondered if Chase's actions had provoked the Furies' appearance in Ascension. If not his, whose?

"There were actually two deaths, very close together," Gabby continued gently, as Skylar stared at her openmouthed. "Another suicide that happened just a couple of weeks before . . . before Chase died. A girl named Sasha."

"Oh my god," Skylar whispered. "That sounds terrible."

"It was," Gabby said. "It is. Ascension is . . . Ascension is still healing." To Em that sounded simultaneously melodramatic and true.

"Sasha . . . her last name wasn't Bowlder, was it?" Skylar asked tentatively.

Em curled her knees into her chest.

"Yeah, that was her," Gabby responded.

"I saw one of her drawings in last year's yearbook," Skylar said. "I was looking at it . . . to get ideas for the dance. Anyway, the drawing was, well, interesting."

"I had forgotten about those drawings," Em said, nodding in recollection. "Wow. Remember them, Gabs?"

Gabby sighed. "Yes. They were a little bizarre. And they certainly didn't help her case."

Skylar looked at them quizzically.

"Sasha didn't exactly have the best reputation," Gabby explained. "She was a bit—what's the word?—eccentric. Right, Em? People made fun of her. Like, they said she was into witch stuff, spells . . ."

Em interjected with a derisive snort. "Among other things. Anyway, those were just rumors."

"I *know*, Emmy, I'm just catching Skylar up," Gabby said. "I once heard that she stole a frog from the bio lab just to sacrifice it in the woods!"

Skylar made a face. "Maybe she thought it would turn into a prince," she said.

"And there was another one about some special bag of herbs that she carried everywhere—"

"Can we go back to talking about parties?" Em interrupted again, and this time she made her meaning clear.

There were a few moments of silence, and then Gabby coughed again. When she spoke, it was quick and overly bright. "Parties, yes. Please," she said, shooting Em an apologetic look. "So, in addition to the pajama party—which is so soon, btw!—and the Spring Fling, I think we should have a special party for you, Skylar. Or rather, *you* should throw your own party."

Skylar looked doubtful, and Em raised her eyebrows. Gabby was really going all out on her little project.

"It could be like your coming-out party!" Gabby said, gaining steam as she always did when she was envisioning a social event. "Like a debutante ball, but Maine-style. I'll be pretty busy with dance committee stuff, but you could plan it, and I could help!"

Em watched Skylar's face break out into the most genuine smile she'd seen all night. It was clear that she worshipped Gabby, that her gratitude was miles deep. And whose wouldn't be? Ascension was a tough pool to dive into, full of social sharks swimming in established hierarchies. Gabby was giving Skylar an in.

Ping. Ping. Ping.

The freezing rain that Gabby's mom had predicted earlier this week began tapping against the window like tiny fingers rapping on the glass. The sound of the sleet lulled Em into a kind of trance until she heard Skylar's voice, as though from far away, saying, "What if we had it outside? Do people do that here? I mean, I know it's still cold, but we could have a bonfire . . . ?"

Now Gabby was the skeptical one. "A party outside? In March? March in Maine is still winter."

"You're right, it was a stupid idea." Em watched Skylar's face fall, and she couldn't stand it. She had to rescue her.

"Think about it, Gabs," Em said. "It could work. A big bonfire and a few of those heat lamps that your dad bought for his ice-bar party a few years ago? People would remember it, that's for sure."

Skylar smiled at her gratefully, and Gabby nodded slowly.

"It could work," she said. "We could tell people to bring thermoses, and flasks, and those little heat-pocket things that you put in your gloves." She was getting more and more excited. "It'll be like maple-sugaring parties! Except no adults! And no horse-drawn carriages!" She looked off into the distance, still scheming. And then a smile grew wide across her face. "We could have it at the Haunted Woods," she said. "Do you know about them? Out by the new mall?"

Every nerve on Em's body went on alert when she heard Gabby mention the mall. She hated even thinking about that place. For the thousandth time she found herself thinking about those red seeds, how gritty they'd tasted, how Ty had watched her swallow them. She began to tune out again, refocusing her attention on the sleet and the wind.

"There have been some pretty great parties out there," Gabby continued. "They call it the Haunted Woods, but it's really only haunted by awesomeness. Wouldn't you say, Em? Remember that one time—"

Skylar cut in. "My aunt said they really are haunted. By three women . . . three witches who burned in the woods, like, a thousand years ago. They're the ones doing the haunting. That's what my aunt says."

Em's attention suddenly became very focused. "What? What three women?" Her voice was thick, and she had to clear her throat.

"Earth to Em," Gabby said, shaking her head in mock disappointment. "You zone out, it's not our job to catch you up."

"I was just saying," Skylar explained after swallowing a mouthful of whipped cream, "that my aunt Nora—that's who I'm staying with—told me a crazy story about the Haunted Woods. I'm not sure I want to throw a party there."

"Don't be silly," Gabby interjected. "It'll be legendary! We'll invite literally everyone."

"What's the story?" Em asked again, laser-focused on Skylar.

"Oh, I don't really know much about it," Skylar answered nervously. "My aunt is just all into the supernatural, and she told me that there were three witches in those woods who were burned there a really long time ago. And supposedly they're the ones haunting the place." She rolled her eyes. "Crazy, huh?"

Em felt her heart rising into her throat. "I've, ah, I've never heard that one," she said. "Do you remember any more of it?"

"No, that's really all I can remember." Skylar laughed. "But hopefully they don't show up to my party!"

Three women in the woods—three wronged women haunting the woods? It hit too close to home, and Em started feeling itchy. She checked her watch and glanced again at the hail hitting the window. "I have to be home by ten, and I'm a little worried about the roads," she said, clicking the cap back onto the moisturizer she'd been using. "Thanks for letting me crash girls' night," she added as she got up to put on her socks and stretch her legs. "Gabs, save the Chinese for a study date tomorrow?"

"It was so nice to meet you," Skylar said with a little wave.

"Wait, wait, wait," Gabby said, running ahead of Em into the hall and pulling a Burberry coat from the front closet. "You are not leaving the house without a coat, young lady. I don't care how absentminded-professor you are these days." She thrust the tan coat at Em. "*And* I am going walk you to the car under the trusty protection of my dad's enormous golf umbrella," she said, brandishing the umbrella as she spoke. "I do not want you getting sick. Plus your hair looks fantastic right now, and you might be able to maintain it overnight if you don't get it wet. So. Let's go."

God. Gabby was like drill sergeant of kindness. It was worthless to even bother protesting. Em threw a hand to her forehead and mock-saluted. "If you say so, captain."

As they shoved their feet into their boots, Gabby twisted around to ask Skylar, "Want to come? There's room for all of us under that thing. It's like a tent."

"To the car?" Skylar looked confused, and Em had to let out a little snicker. Clearly, she hadn't been enrolled long enough in the School of Gabby's Whims.

"Yeah, just to the end of the driveway! It'll be a fun little adventure." The Doves had a very long driveway. Their big house sat on top of a small hill.

The three of them set out into the freezing rain, squished together underneath the umbrella, with Gabby and Skylar gig-gling about wearing flip-flops in the icy rain and Em feigning the same carefree joy. She shrieked when Gabby threatened to push her out from under their protective hood, and she told the girls she couldn't wait to pour herself a teensy glass of Bailey's from her mother's stash when she got home. But really, all she was thinking about was the story Skylar had told about the three women who'd died in the woods.

As they neared the end of Gabby's epic driveway and came within sight of the car, Gabby elbowed Em. "Hey, babe? Why is there writing on your car?" She pointed.

Em squinted into the darkness. Sure enough, all the windows of the Honda were completely fogged up, and on the rear wind-shield, in finger-scrawl, someone had written: *Who's the fairest of them all?*

She stopped short and stared. Her throat went dry.

The words had not been there when she'd driven over. She was sure of it.

But she couldn't let Gabby and Skylar see her freaking out.

"Oh, that? Probably Drea's idea of a joke," she said with a lame laugh.

"I didn't know Drea Feiffer was so into Cinderella," Gabby said dryly.

"That's actually Snow White," Skylar interjected. "That's what the evil stepmother asks her mirror every night because she's jealous of Snow White's beauty." Then Skylar broke off, clearly embarrassed by her knowledge of childhood fairy tales.

Who's the fairest of them all? . . . The words reminded Em of something, and she hated that she couldn't think of what.

"I gotta go," she said, grabbing Gabby for a quick hug. *"À bientôt, escargot,"* she whispered—their special way of saying good-bye—before slipping out of the jacket and handing it back to Gabby. "I'll call you in the morning."

"Em, keep it," Gabby pleaded. But Em was already in the car.

The rain dissipated on her ride home, leaving misty pockets where her headlights shone. She had wiped off the inside of her windshield, practically frantic, but still she thought she could make out the ghostly silhouettes of the letters there: *Who's the fairest of them all?*

She couldn't wait to be back at her house, out of this car, in her own bed. She didn't even want to turn on the radio; she was too jumpy. She tapped the steering wheel and bit her lip.

Her eyes flicked to her rearview mirror for a second. A face was smiling back at her.

Em screamed, nearly skidding off the road.

It was Ali's face. Ali with the white-blond hair, Ali with the bloodred lips. Ali who'd given her her first orchid.

Em hit the brakes, swinging her head around. Nothing. Her heart pounded heavily. Nothing but a few textbooks, an ice scraper, and a knit hat. No Ali.

She was shaking. She threw the car into park and swung open her door, getting out and into the backseat to wipe away, with ferocity, the words in the window. She banged her fist against the seat. Her cold fingers stung.

Back in the front seat, still not moving, the minutes on the car's digital clock getting ever closer to ten o'clock, she let her head fall back against the headrest. What did they want? What did it mean, to be bound to them? She knew it was worth it, to save JD's life. To save the life of the one she loved. But what had she actually agreed to? Had she agreed to be driven insane?

She couldn't stop the tears from coming. She swiped an arm across her face. "Quit it, Em. Shut up," she muttered. With eyes cloudy from crying, she looked into the rearview mirror and saw herself—paler than she'd ever been, with the circles under her eyes only adding to her ghostly appearance.

What the hell is happening to me?

She slammed her palm against the steering wheel and shoved her way out of the car. "I know you're out there somewhere!" she shouted. But there was no response, no movement. She spun around in the middle of the road, the wind blowing through her wild dark hair, her skin feeling like it was on fire. "If you have something to say to me, say it!" she screamed. Again, no response, just the sleet hammering against her face.

"Fine, then," she intoned, getting back into her car and slamming the door. She was starting to feel like this was war. She was up for the battle. The Furies were not going to fuck with her head anymore.

CHAPTER EIGHT

Skylar's second week at school flew by, filled with party prep and obsessing over her new crush. She was splitting her free time mostly between Meg and Gabby, and Aunt Nora was thrilled that Skylar was adjusting so seamlessly. "You'll have to bring your friends over so I can meet them," she said, bustling about in the kitchen one morning. Skylar nodded and looked down at her cereal. She'd been trying to avoid that, actually—she didn't want to risk bursting the lie bubble that she'd created about her former life. It would be just like Nora to overshare and somehow let the ugly facts slip.

Skylar wasn't lying only to her new friends; she was spreading her deceptions. She'd told her aunt that she was going to a party at Gabby's tonight (conveniently not mentioning the coed pajama part), but she hadn't divulged that *she* was throwing a party the following weekend in the Haunted Woods.

Skylar was excited for Gabby's party, but she was more psyched for her own. Everyone was coming. Skylar knew that people loved any excuse to drink, but she liked thinking that all those kids were coming to the party for *her*. According to Gabby's mom, it was even supposed to be unseasonably warm.

It was like the fates were smiling down on her. She'd been distributing invitations all week; they were printed on pink paper with an old-fashioned typeface that lent an antique edge to the lacy pastel.

In keeping with the old-fashioned theme, they were going to serve spiked cider and mulled wine out of kegs and oversized pots at the party—Skylar had already arranged for all of it to be delivered next Friday afternoon. (Meg was instrumental in this part of the process too—she had a fake ID.) Skylar felt a little bit guilty about the booze; it had been way expensive.

"Let's just get a few bottles of wine," she'd said to Meg early in the week, knowing she couldn't afford much more than that. "And maybe people will BYOB."

Meg had looked at her like she'd suggested serving cod-liver oil. "A few bottles of wine? For a party you want the whole school to know about? Sweetheart, you need to go all out."

"But . . . how am I going to pay for it?" Skylar fretted.

Meg had looked around Skylar's room, taking in the Victorian moldings and Aunt Nora's antique mirror that leaned against the wall. "You can find a way. You'll have to! Couldn't you ask your aunt for some extra cash?"

Skylar knew she couldn't ask Aunt Nora for money without telling her what it was for. So she'd come up with another plan. On Wednesday afternoon, her heart hammering with guilt, Skylar had crept into her aunt's bedroom and grabbed a few necklaces. Then she'd had Meg bring her to a dingy store on Route 1, where she'd pawned them for a couple hundred bucks. Skylar was betting on the hope that Nora wouldn't even notice. She had tons of jewelry! The earnings made up the difference in the alcohol bill, thank god. Still, as they drove away from the pawnshop, Skylar felt sick to her stomach. "Maybe we should go back . . . ," she'd started to say.

"Guilt is a pointless emotion," Meg had cut in with a soft smile. "Don't beat yourself up about it. You just did what you had to do." She'd looked at Skylar sideways. "Right?"

"Yeah, totally," Skylar had said, trying to believe the words. This party next week was so important for her. She *had* to give it her all.

More importantly, she would figure out some way to make it up to her aunt, or find a way to buy the necklaces back next month. Maybe Meg would get her a job at the ice cream shop after school. But she couldn't focus on that now. She had other things to worry about.

Like the pajama party. It was Saturday afternoon, and Gabby's Popcorn & PJ's party was starting in a few hours. Gabby claimed that it was going to be low-key and exclusive, just a chance for her and her friends to recharge after what had been a really hard winter in Ascension. *Two* suicides, not even a month apart.

Gabby's way of lifting people's spirits was to remind them that life was fun and worth living, and what better way to do that than with a cozy get-together? It was amazing, Skylar thought, the way people responded to Gabby's vibrancy.

Not only would tonight be a chance to observe the way Gabby played hostess, but Pierce would be there! Gabby had been so great about hounding him to make sure he was coming. And she'd been telling Skylar all about him, so that Skylar could dazzle him when they talked. Pierce was something of a football prodigy, with an arm that had astounded coaches since he was a kid. With Chase dead and Zach—Gabby's ex, about whom she'd said practically nothing—at boarding school, the Ascension football team was depending on Pierce to carry them through next season.

"I know nothing about football," Skylar had complained to Gabby earlier this week. "He's going to hate me."

"That's the whole point, silly," Gabby had replied. "Ask him about it! It's what he loves talking about! Besides, boys like when they get a chance to explain things." Gabby grinned, rolling her eyes.

Skylar had become slightly obsessed with the idea of Pierce asking her to the Spring Fling. He'd been talking to her a little bit more—asking her questions about the math homework, and dance committee, and Gabby (her pajama party, whether she was stressed out planning so many social events)—and Skylar was the tiniest bit hopeful that he was interested in her, too.

"Well, there's only one way to find out," Gabby was always saying. "Just be yourself, be open to it, and it'll happen if it's meant to be."

Skylar couldn't help but think, *That's easy for you to say.* And then she shook her head and reminded herself, *It'll be easy for me, too. Soon.*

Ascension had a tradition of naming a King and Queen of Spring at the dance. Unlike prom and homecoming courts, this honor was open to any student, no matter how young. Apparently, Pierce was a shoo-in for King of Spring this year, given how he'd already—gracefully, humbly—stepped up to fill the void in Ascension's athletic department. Skylar got butterflies in her stomach when she thought about the logical next steps: If Pierce was voted King, and she was his date (or better yet, his girlfriend!), she had a solid chance of getting the Queen of Spring crown. And that . . . that would be a dream come true.

Okay, Gabby kind of deserved the royal title. After all, she'd planned the dance practically single-handedly—"Until *you* came on board," Meg had helpfully reminded Skylar—and she was doing her best not to let Ascension turn into a permanent place of mourning. But still, Skylar wanted it. What a triumph it would be for a nobody like her to sweep into town and be voted queen after only a month! She already knew what dress she was going to wear. It was an old one of Lucy's—black, with a V-neck and a full skirt, belted. She would look great standing up there on the stage next to Pierce.

Maybe he'd even ask her tonight. For now, she had a lot to do: curl her hair, put on a fresh coat of nail polish, exfoliate her feet. She needed to look *perfect*. Skylar took a deep breath. Maybe she'd have some wine to loosen up before Fiona came to get her.

She found a bottle of something called "hydromel" in her aunt's pantry—a sweet honey wine that stuck to the side of the glass as she sipped it. She didn't usually like the taste of wine, but this drink was sweet on her tongue, like dessert. It reminded her of licking powdered sugar off fried Greek doughnuts with Lucy as a child. Then she took a long shower, using her mud scrub on every inch of her body. She shaved her legs. She applied vanilla-scented body lotion. She put her hair in rollers—Meg had gotten them for her as a gift—and listened to the Dusters as she waited for her hair to set. She went downstairs to pour herself some more. Then, back upstairs, a light coat of tinted moisturizer, a swipe of mascara, a smudge of blush. They were supposed to look like they were going to bed, after all. Rollers out, a flip of her head, on with the pj's. She spun in the mirror, happy with the way the lime-green and pink complemented her newly high-lighted hair. She looked like . . . she looked like summer. And the bit of lace that tickled her chest and hung from the hem of the shorts—it was just the right amount of sexy.

Fiona would be here soon. She had just enough time to paint her nails—a watermelon pink that matched the color of her pj's. She felt good. She belted out the chorus of her favorite Dusters song while texting Meg: *Hey girl, off to the pajama party—wish me luck!* And just before she turned off the light in her bedroom, Skylar caught a glimpse of herself in the mirror. She gave her head a toss, shaking out the curls, and smiled. She barely recog-nized herself.

"Who wants more cheddar popcorn?" Gabby came in from the kitchen holding a big red bowl. "And why is this the most popu-lar flavor?" She surveyed the still-half-full bowls of caramel and plain popcorn.

"Because it goes best with beer," Sean said from his perch on the living room couch, raising his bottle. "Cheers."

Skylar was in the living room, where a cozy fire was going. She was sitting cross-legged on the floor near the window with Lauren, Jenna, Nick, and a few other boys, trying to quell a feel-ing of frustration. The evening wasn't quite going the way she'd hoped.

Pierce was there, but he'd quickly settled in the kitchen to play poker with a bunch of boys wearing L.L. Bean flannel pants and white undershirts. Apparently, every boy in Ascension wore the same thing to bed. They were all whining, too. "If we don't get to sleep over, why did we have to wear our pj's?" Secretly, Skylar wondered the same thing.

Em was in the kitchen too; Skylar had seen her when she first came in. Em had been friendly enough, but Skylar couldn't help feeling that Em didn't like her very much. She just wasn't very warm. Nothing like Gabby. Skylar had a hard time understanding their friendship. One so bubbly, the other so . . . dark. It was like Em carried a heavy weight with her everywhere she went. Aunt Nora would say Em's aura was off.

Not that she wasn't absolutely beautiful. Tonight, with her flawless skin glowing against a dark-purple-and-black silk robe, which she'd worn over black leggings, Em looked sophisticated, urban, and lovely. Effortlessly cool.

"I'm going to go see if Gabby needs help in the kitchen," Skylar told group. She didn't want to hover, but she was dying for a chance to talk to Pierce, who hadn't even said hello when he walked in the door. "Do you guys want the rest of my cards?"

In the kitchen Skylar found Gabby laughing and picking up a popcorn explosion from the tiled floor. "Whoops! Men overboard!"

Skylar squatted down to help Gabby, tugging on the back of

her shorts to make sure she wasn't showing her crack to the rest of the room.

Just then Em came up behind them.

"Here's a dustpan," Em said, holding out a little pan and broom. "Might be a bit faster."

Of course *Em would come to the rescue,* Skylar thought, feeling unreasonably resentful. Like Gabby couldn't have found a dustpan herself.

"Thanks, Emmy!" Gabby swept the rest of the mess up quickly. "Much better. Now, should I try some cayenne on the next batch?"

"The spicier the better, Gabs," Em said. "But you'll have to tell me how it turns out. I'm heading home."

Em never stuck around, Skylar noticed. She was always leaving early—when she showed up at all.

"Already? But Em, it's only, like, nine p.m.!" Gabby pouted. "Guys, should Em leave yet?" she asked the whole kitchen.

"Thanks, sweetie, but I've really gotta go. I have a ton of studying to do tomorrow." Em started to wrap her scarf around her neck. *"À beintôt, escargot."* She gave Gabby a hug and a kiss on the cheek and smiled at Skylar. And then she was gone, to a chorus of "Bye, Winters!" before Gabby could protest any more.

"What's that *'bien escargot'* thing?" Skylar asked, feeling the need to fill the air left in Em's wake.

"Oh, it's Em's special way of saying bye to me," Gabby said with a smile. "We've been doing it forever."

How nice. Skylar made her way to the fridge. "Do you want me to make one more batch of the toffee-peanut kind?" she asked Gabby, desperate to be helpful. Gabby responded with a thumbs-up before running back into the living room, where someone had just called her name.

"Need help opening that?" Pierce suddenly appeared next to her, motioning to the jar of toffee sauce. She looked dizzily back and forth between him and the jar, so giddy at his approach that she didn't immediately grasp what he was talking about. Then she understood: He was being chivalrous.

"Sure," she said, heart leaping, even though she'd watched her mother crack open beer bottles on countertops more times than she'd care to admit. "Thanks."

"No problem," he said, towering over her and tensing his muscles as he twisted the lid. "Having fun?"

"Totally," she said, nodding eagerly. "And I'm excited for my party next week too."

"Oh yeah." Pierce looked like he was just remembering it. "That'll be fun." He handed her the bottle and her brain spun as she tried to think of what to say next.

"So . . . are you guys, like, practicing?"

He looked at her, puzzled. "Practicing?"

"I mean, I know it's not football season, but do you guys

practice during the off-season?" *Shit.* She sounded like a total tool.

"Oh. Um, a little. We do once-a-week gym sessions on Saturday mornings," Pierce said, before turning to go. "Be right back—bathroom break."

Great. Her sparkling conversational skills had done it again. She wondered if she should join the poker game so she could spend more time with him when he got back. But the table full of guys was intimidating. . . . And she barely knew how to play poker.

As Skylar went to get a mixing bowl from the cupboard, she saw herself in a small mirror that hung next to the kitchen doorway. She stopped short. She was a mess. Her forehead was shiny, her bouncy curls had fallen flat, her eyes had the dull glaze of someone who'd had beer for dinner. She saw herself in a whole different light. The skimpy spaghetti-strap top, the booty shorts. The garish green. The lace. She looked like she was trying too hard. No wonder Pierce had avoided her like the plague all night!

She changed her course immediately and left the kitchen, sneaking up to Gabby's bathroom on the second floor. She needed to clean herself up.

In the bathroom's harsh light she ran a comb through her hair and blotted away the oil with a piece of toilet paper. She took a deep breath and drank a Dixie cup full of water. When she got downstairs, she would put on her sweatshirt. It didn't match, but who cared? At least she'd maybe feel more comfortable.

She was on her way back to the staircase when she heard Gabby's voice, and another muffled one, coming from Gabby's room. Skylar listened more closely. There was no mistaking it. That was Pierce's voice. What were they doing up here? Her stomach flipped. Were they talking about *her*?

She tiptoed down the hall and tried to peer through the crack in the door, which wasn't fully closed.

Everything froze: her heart, her blood, her thoughts.

There was Pierce, leaning toward Gabby for a kiss. And Gabby reaching her arms toward his chest, as though she wanted to pull him closer. . . .

Skylar was about to burst into the room—she couldn't control herself—but then she saw that Gabby wasn't pulling Pierce in, she was pushing him away. She stopped herself just in time to watch Gabby say, "No, I'm sorry. Pierce, I just don't like you that way."

She scurried away before either of them could see her. Blinded by disappointment, she stumbled down the stairs. Of course Pierce liked Gabby. Could anything be more obvious? She had to get out of here, but she didn't know how she would get home. She couldn't walk—it was at least five miles from Gabby's house to hers, it was already after ten o'clock, and she was dressed in her ridiculous pajamas. Calling her aunt would be humiliating. She thought about calling Meg; she was certain that Meg wouldn't judge her, no matter how stupid she felt.

As if on cue, her phone beeped from the tiny pocket in her shorts. It was a text from Meg: *Hope ur having fun taking over Ascension's social scene! Just remember—if they can have it all, so can u!*

It reminded Skylar of what they'd talked about on that first day, in the ice cream shop.

I'd do anything to be one of them, Skylar had said.

Anything. And so she took a deep breath; planted a brave, giant, pageant-style smile on her face; and stayed.

CHAPTER NINE

As she left Gabby's pajama party Em wrapped her silk robe tighter around her. The heat must have been cranked in there; the cold air was a shock. She felt bad taking off, but she was feeling too restless to enjoy it.

As she pulled up to her house, she glanced next door out of habit. JD's Volvo was in his driveway, parked next to the Mustang, which had a tarp pulled over it. His metal toolbox was sitting out in the open. She shook her head. It wasn't like JD to leave things lying around.

Upstairs, she put her long hair into a braid and sat down at her desk, which she was finally using for its assigned purpose, and not just for clothing storage. She looked for the millionth time toward JD's window. The window where they'd once hung a string across to her window to transmit messages. The window where his blinds had been down for three weeks. Where his light was glowing warmly from behind the shade. She wanted to reach out and touch the glass.

The week had been quiet—no creepy messages left on her windshield, no deadly icicles launched by unseen demons. She'd spent much of the week driving around with Drea, listening to what Drea called "math rock"—long, intricate songs that switched gears frequently, never able to settle on one theme or rhythm—and waiting for the Furies to appear. But nothing happened. Em was starting to wonder if she could make the Furies disappear simply by the force of her will.

She surveyed the piles of books and photocopies and maps that she'd borrowed from Drea—their collection of disparate and confusing anecdotes. How was it possible to have so much information but so few answers?

She started flipping through the journal, rereading some old entries. A few days ago she'd made a list of everything she knew about the Furies. She was tracing the chain of events, to figure out when, and why, the Furies had suddenly appeared. This week Em had gone to the local library and tried to find evidence of the story Skylar had told—the one about three sisters burning in the Haunted Woods. On ancient microfiche, she'd found a mention of a fire in the early 1700s, set by townspeople, in which three "disreputable" local women died. She wondered if she should talk to Skylar's aunt and try to find out more about this piece of Ascension's history. But she was wary of digging deeper. The slightest slip could enrage the Furies even further. When she'd *almost* blurted out something to JD about what had happened that night at the Behemoth, the Furies had come back with a vengeance to torture her. She couldn't put anyone else at risk. She had to do this herself.

Of course, in their most recent incarnation, the Furies seemed to have been drawn to Ascension to punish Chase. But was he the first? And why had they been drawn to punish him? Surely there'd been other sinners in Ascension before him. Em knew that the gap in her knowledge about the Furies spanned centuries between the goddesses' origin and their current presence in town. Why had they come back now? On whose order? And what would it take to make them leave?

With a groan, she leaned forward in her chair, resting her head in her arms on the desk. She was tired, but she didn't feel like sleeping. So she sat up, grabbed her journal and a pen, and started writing.

The poem came quickly. Images and sensations—snow, skin, the light in JD's window, the words scrawled on her car, the feeling of being trapped in a cycle that was cruel and unfair—swirled together and landed on the page. She could tell this one was good.

She titled it "The Fairest."

It made her feel a little better. But still something was squirming inside of her. Some missing link was calling her, and she needed to find it.

As she started to close her journal, a phone number stood out among the scribblings—Crow's. With a burst of inspiration, she remembered JD telling her when they were freshmen about a brilliant slacker in his computer science class. It was Crow.

Em stared at the number for a few seconds, pondering his rebelliousness and hatching a plan even as she dialed his number.

"Hello?" He answered the phone like she was waking him up from a deep sleep.

"Hey, Crow, this is Em." Nothing. "Emily? Winters? Drea's friend?"

He made a sound of recognition. "Your Highness! How may I serve you?" He chuckled softly at his own hilarity.

She pursed her lips and pressed on, ignoring him. "I have a favor to ask you," she said. "It has to do with . . . information gathering."

"Will you pay me?" Crow asked.

The question took Em by surprise. "Um, I guess," she said, wondering how much she could borrow from her parents without raising suspicion.

"I take multiple forms of currency," he said, his voice dripping with innuendo.

"That's charming, really," Em snapped. "How about the

currency of my respect, which you are currently not earning?"

Crow whistled. "Hoo-ee. We've got a live one! Okay, okay. What do you need?"

Em took a breath. What did she have to lose? "I need you to hack the USM library computers and retrieve one single piece of information. I need to know who was in the antiquities library on November fifteenth. There's a book missing and I need to know who took it."

"School assignments sure have changed since I, ah, removed myself from the system," he said thoughtfully. "What book?"

"Does that mean you'll do it?" Em sat down with relief, realizing as she did so that she'd been pacing her bedroom for the whole conversation.

"What book?" Crow asked again, insistently.

Exasperated, Em told him.

He was silent again. And then, "All right, I'll do it." She could have embraced him, right then and there. "But I need one thing from you in return."

"What?" she asked warily.

"If I get caught, you don't tell anyone I was doing it for you. Your Highness."

She shook her head and hung up.

Thrilled to have put at least one plan in motion, she felt a sense of purpose that had been missing in her life for weeks. Her eyes went to the window again.

Knowing that JD was home made her ache with agitation. Was that a shadow in his window? Her legs shook, and she squeezed her hands together, trying to tamp down her energy.

In an attempt to create some order, she started organizing the papers on the desk. She shuffled them into piles: literary examples, local clippings, her personal run-ins with the Furies. As she did so a small scrap of paper floated to the floor. She bent down to pick it up. It was the note he'd left her in the wake of their fight a few months ago. *I just want to make you happy. Always. JD.* She remembered how she'd felt when she first read those words. Filled with desire and longing. She should have gone over and jumped into his arms right then and there.

Always. The word inspired a sudden flash of hope. If JD had felt so strongly, those feelings couldn't have just disappeared, right? She had to try again. She had to prove herself to him, make him realize that this was real, and that their connection wasn't going to fade. It *couldn't* fade. She could practically see him from her window. It would be pathetic not to try again, not to make him forgive her for the horrible things he seemed to think she had done. Somewhere, deep down, he must still know that they were meant to be together. She just had to uncover that buried feeling and bring it back to the surface.

His toolbox. He'd left it outside, and an icy mix of snow and rain was still falling from the sky. She knew he wouldn't want it to rust— maybe she would just bring it to his door. A gesture of goodwill.

She peeled off her leggings and the robe and threw on a pair of jeans and a sweatshirt. She ran downstairs and rummaged through the pantry, pulling out some Dr Pepper, and taking a pint of vanilla ice cream from the freezer—his favorite combo. Just in case JD wanted to talk. And in case the talk went well, she grabbed *Best in Show*, his preferred cringe-humor movie. She threw it all in a tote bag. Then she was out the door and running from her yard to his, stopping to pick up the toolbox.

Just as she was about to knock on the Founts' front door, she heard a big, hearty *girl's* laugh from inside. She froze.

Who was JD hanging out with on a Saturday night? The laugh sounded again, vaguely familiar. It wasn't JD's mom, and it wasn't Melissa, his little sister—but it was definitely a laugh that Em recognized. Guiltily, feeling a little like a criminal, she snuck around the side of the house to the window that looked into JD's TV room.

Through the frosted pane she saw JD sitting on the couch.

And Drea Feiffer practically sitting on top of him.

It took a moment for Em to register what she was seeing. Drea and JD, gabbing it up like best friends—like *more* than friends. They were bent over something on the coffee table, thighs touching, fingers practically interlaced. What she would have given to switch places with Drea right then. Seeing JD like that only fed Em's appetite—and her anger. She turned on her heel, ran back to JD's door, and blasted through it.

She wasn't thinking anymore. She was just moving, charging ahead, blind and furious. Through the entryway, through the foyer, ignoring a confused hello from Melissa, and into the den.

It wasn't until that moment that she realized, with sudden clarity, that she had no plausible reason to be there. Drea and JD looked up at her, both clearly startled by her sudden appearance.

"Um . . . hi?" JD finally said.

Drea just looked at her. Mute. And . . . guilty? Was that guilt Em saw in Drea's eyes? The moment was beyond awkward, and Em didn't know what to say. Thank god the Dr Pepper and the DVD were in the tote bag, where JD and Drea couldn't see them. She shifted on her feet, furious, confused, and unable to think straight. She and JD had barely spoken in weeks, and now she'd shown up like a madwoman, without being invited, and interrupted . . . something. Something between JD, her oldest friend and greatest love, and Drea—the only person she trusted with the biggest problem in her life. At least, she'd thought she trusted her.

"I—uh, I came over to borrow some coffee." The lame excuse flew out of her mouth before she could think of a better one.

JD raised his eyebrows. "Coffee? Now?"

"I have a lot of studying to do," she said sharply.

"Okay." JD shrugged. "Right this way." JD looked skeptical as he dragged himself off the couch and headed into the kitchen. Em didn't make eye contact with Drea as she followed him out.

She walked behind him down the hall, her heart breaking as she wondered how many times she and JD had hung out just like JD and Drea were doing. Probably hundreds. And she'd always taken it for granted.

"You want it, like, in a plastic baggie?" JD still looked confused as he pulled a tin of coffee out of the cupboard.

This was unbearable. She pointed to a small bag still on the shelf. "I'll take that one," she said. She had to get out of there as quickly as possible. Grabbing the coffee—which was the last thing she needed—she rushed out of the kitchen and toward the front door, calling over her shoulder, "Thank your mom for me. I'll pay her back."

She burst into the cold night, fighting back tears, and was at the bottom of JD's stoop when Drea appeared in the doorway, wearing socks and JD's flannel over her jeans. Em recognized the yellow lumberjack plaid. It made her want to scream; a cloud of black bitterness seemed to well up from her stomach, through her ribs, and into her mouth.

"Wait, Em!" The light from inside JD's house lit Drea from behind, making her look like a cutout silhouette. "What's up?"

Em exploded. "How could you?" She felt like she had no control over her words; they came flying out, surging on a tide of confusion and hurt. "What are you doing? You're into JD now?

That's odd, since you've *never* expressed interest in him before."
She felt like she was on a conveyer belt, being pulled farther and
farther away from Drea and JD. She was sliding backward, unable
to gain traction. "Or were you just keeping that a secret from
me? Were you using me to get to him? It must have ruined your
plans that we don't talk anymore, me and JD. Or did that make it
easier for you to move in?"

As Em spoke, Drea stepped outside and closed JD's front
door firmly behind her. Now she stood there, eyes flashing,
looking blindsided—and furious.

"Apparently, you don't keep very good tabs on JD—or his
friends," she practically growled. "We have American history
together this semester, and we've been hanging out. *Doing our
homework.*" Drea crossed her arms and glared at Emily. "I was
going to text you and see if I could come over after, but I figured
it was Saturday night, so you'd probably be out with Gabby and
your *real* friends."

Em flinched. Even though she knew that Drea had a point,
she still felt like her anger was justified.

"JD was just about to drive me home. Is that okay with you,
Em?" Drea's voice turned both defiant and syrupy sweet. "Do
you need to approve of my friendships now? You flake out on
me and then expect me to be there whenever you need me, and
now you show up random places and completely flip your shit.
What the hell is going on with you? What is this really about?"

"This is *about* you and JD," Em said, staring at Drea, willing her to deny it.

"Are you accusing me of something?" Drea's eyes narrowed. They stared at each other. Again Em felt a surge of emotion roiling through her body, making her nerves tingle. She tried to tamp it down.

"Just tell me," she said, willing her voice not to break. "Tell me what's going on." She'd thought she could trust Drea. Was she wrong?

"Look," Drea said, "we all know that you don't hang with JD and his friends, and he doesn't hang with yours—unless you ask him to. It's kind of like our friendship, isn't it? You spent most of your life ignoring me. Until you needed me."

Em opened her mouth to respond, but found she had nothing to say. Everything Drea was saying was true. And it killed her.

"Face it, Em. You *never* really knew what was going on with JD, or who he hung out with, or what he was doing when you weren't around. So now you're not around. And his life goes on. That's the way it is."

Em's fists clenched into balls and her cheeks went hot. A coil of fury burst through the tangle of her feelings, and Em shouted, "*Do not* try to educate me about JD! You don't know anything about him, or us. And you don't know anything about *me*, either," she added, kicking a planter for emphasis.

Drea jerked back an inch, but her face remained impassive.

"Listen to yourself," she said, infuriatingly calm. "Look what you're doing. You're acting crazy."

As Drea spoke, Em saw JD peering out the front door's window, trying to make sense of what was going on. It was too mortifying for words. She spun around without another word and stalked toward her house. Drea did not call her name; Em heard her go back inside and shut the door.

I am not crazy. I am not crazy. I am not crazy. She repeated the words like a mantra as she tried to will back the tears that threatened to blur her vision. That scene *had* been weird and suspicious, and she had every right to be furious that Drea claimed to know anything about her and JD. She was totally grounded. Not crazy.

Maybe if she said it enough times, she'd believe it.

She approached her front door and stopped short. All the breath slammed out of her.

There were marks all over her front door. Red marks.

No. Handprints. A dozen of them, smeared and sticky-looking, like a child's finger painting gone totally wrong. She snapped her head to look back over her shoulder. Nothing. A small whimper escaped from her throat.

She turned back to the door. The prints were rusty and red, unmistakably the color of blood. Bloody handprints, reaching up the door, like someone had been clawing to get in. Her legs felt weak beneath her, and for a second her vision flashed black. Again she twisted her head over her shoulder.

"Hel–hello?" she called out, even though she knew there was no one there.

Then she saw a flash of blond hair disappearing behind a copse of trees. She knew that hair. It was Ali. As in Alecto, the Fury who had stalked her, the one who avenged moral crimes according to the mythology Em had looked up. Ali, whose red-lipsticked smile was like the smell of flowers at a funeral—sweet but imbued with death. Was she here? Had her hands smeared their bloody mess all over her white door?

"Leave me alone!" Em shouted. But there was no one there, not even a shadow. For an instant she considered running back across the lawn to Drea. But she couldn't, not after their blowout just a few minutes ago.

She was totally alone.

Fear had blanketed her, making it hard to breathe. She stepped closer to the door. Closer. Her mind was full of hor-rible images: palms sliced open and fingernails ripped off. She thought back to the palm readings she'd done with Gabby in fourth grade—finding the Heart Line and the Life Line in the wrinkles on their palms. These prints were flat and unmarked by even the swirls and coils of fingerprints: just flat, shiny, bloody shapes.

She knew she had to get rid of the markings before her parents came home. She wrapped her sweatshirt cuff around her hand, careful not to touch any of the dripping red substance, and pushed open the door. She bolted inside, fumbling for cleaning supplies from under the kitchen sink.

Then, with her knees digging into the cold stone of her front stoop, she scrubbed and scrubbed until her hands were raw. The prints dissolved under the soapy water, staining the sponge a deep brownish red. It ran onto her sleeves, freezing her wrists. She gagged but kept on scrubbing until the stains grew faint. It wasn't until she'd dragged herself upstairs, exhausted and trembling, and turned on the shower as hard and as hot as it would go, that she realized—from the red eyes that stared back at her in the mirror and the tears streaking her cheeks—that she'd been crying.

CHAPTER TEN

It just before seven o'clock on Wednesday when Skylar's cell phone rang, and dread raced up her neck. She was sitting in the living room on one of Aunt Nora's cushy chairs, where she'd been trying to focus on her math homework. She closed the book instantly and sat up straight in her chair.

She knew who it was. Had to be.

It was her forty-second birthday, after all.

Her mom. Valerie.

She hadn't spoken to her mother in over a month now. When she picked up the phone from the coffee table, her hand was shaking.

"You would have forgotten, wouldn't you?" Her mom announced as soon as Skylar answered. Her voice was slushy, and it sounded like she was speaking with a cigarette in her mouth.

Skylar could picture her mom on the other end of the line, arranging her lips into a fake pout as she pulled her cigarette away to blow out the smoke.

Skylar tasted bile at the back of her throat. She cleared it.

"No, Mom, I was going to—" Skylar faltered. Had she really planned on calling her mother today?

Aunt Nora had encouraged Skylar to make a care package, or at least a card, to send to her mother in jail. She'd resisted. It wasn't that she didn't want to do it. She really was worried about how her mom was doing. She wanted to show that she cared. But she hated thinking about her mom's reaction. It would be overly effusive. "Look at what my daughter sent me," Skylar could picture her saying to her inmate pals. "We love each other so much." It would be a farce.

"Lucy would have remembered," her mom cut into Skylar's thoughts, making her stomach turn. "Poor Lucy."

Nora was hovering in the kitchen doorway, pretending not to eavesdrop. Skylar took a deep breath and willed herself not to cry.

"Yeah, Mom," she said. "I'm sorry. About everything. I was . . . thinking of you today, though."

"You better have been," Valerie said with a barking laugh. "After all I've done for you."

"I know, Mom," she said meekly. And then, with false cheer,

she tried to change the subject. "Well, things are going okay up here. I'm on a dance committee. And I'm catching up in my classes." Not that her mom had asked.

"Umm-hmmm," Valerie murmured. Then there was silence on the other end, probably while she took another drag of her Camel Light. Skylar snuck a glance at the clock.

Meg was due over any second. Skylar hadn't seen Meg in days—every single one of her teachers had decided to pile on the homework this week. She wanted to hear Meg's opinion about what had happened at Gabby's party. On the surface, everything was smoothed over. Skylar had stayed for the duration of the pajama party, but she'd gone to bed early feigning a stomachache. Then she'd ignored Gabby's calls on Sunday. On Monday she'd put on her game face. And it was a good thing, too, because Gabby came running up to her first thing.

"Hey, Skylar," Gabby said, her blue eyes shining and set off by a dusty-pink sweater. "Guess what?!"

"What?"

"The Dusters said yes!" Gabby squealed and slapped Skylar's shoulder. "And it's all thanks to you!"

Since then Skylar had done a great job of pretending everything was normal. The fact that Gabby was spreading the word that the Dusters had been Skylar's idea helped a lot. So yeah. Skylar had been distracted by things other than her mom's birthday.

"Skylar, we need to talk," Valerie said then, and Skylar's skin began to itch. Those were dreaded words.

"Mom, I don't really have time for . . . for a full conversation right now," she said, employing the so-called neutral tone that she'd read about in online forums about alcoholism. "I hope you're having a happy birthday, and—"

"Don't you patronize me, Dumpling," her mom said. "Remember who you're speaking to." She coughed, and suddenly her tone was sweet. "Anyway. I want to talk about what it's going to be like when I get out of here. What we're going to do."

What *they* were going to do? The words sat like curdled milk on Skylar's tongue. *They* weren't going to do anything. *Skylar* was alone. A team of one. And just as she was thinking of how to say that without hurting her mom's feelings more than she had to, the doorbell rang.

Shit.

"Mom, actually, I gotta go," she said into the phone.

As quickly as it had appeared, her mom's amiability melted away. The harsh tone returned. "Getting rid of me, huh?"

"It's not like that, Mom," Skylar said, feeling a familiar frenetic energy racing through her body. This call had to end. *I have to go. I have to go. I have to go.* The thought pulsed through her veins. "I just—I have a friend coming over. She's here now. I didn't . . . I didn't know you were going to call. . . ."

"I'll get it," Nora mouthed, stepping into the doorway.

Nora's face was etched with worry. Clearly, she'd gathered that this was not the smoothest mother-daughter reunion.

Skylar leaped out of her chair, hoping to simultaneously placate her mother and intercept Nora. Maybe she could get Meg upstairs before Nora started talking. Supposedly, her aunt was heading out for the evening, to a "breath workshop" in Portland. Skylar had been hoping she'd be gone by the time Meg arrived. "Okay, Mom?" she pleaded into the phone while she trailed Nora to the front door. "Please tell me it's okay. I don't want to get off the phone like this."

"Well, at least you had a few minutes for me," Valerie said in a wounded tone. And then, without giving Skylar a chance to respond, she hung up.

Skylar stood there for a moment, shell-shocked, listening to the dial tone.

It was then that Nora swung open her heavy front door and came face-to-face with Meg, whose eyes were glittering gray in the moonlight.

"I've been waiting *so long* to meet you, Mrs. McVoy," Meg said.

Nora began to respond in kind. "I finally get to meet the elusive Meg—" And then she stopped talking abruptly, her eyes falling over Meg's flowing hair, red choker, and silver shirt. The hand that was holding her mug of tea shook violently, splashing scalding water on Nora's wrist before she dropped the cup altogether. Nora let out a yelp.

"Aunt Nora!" Skylar rushed over. "Are you okay? Did you burn yourself?"

Nora didn't answer; she kept her eyes locked on Meg.

Meg took another step into the house, an expression of concern on her face. "Are you all right, Mrs. McVoy?"

"I'm—I'm fine," Nora said shakily, backing away from Meg. A nervous giggle emerged from her pinched mouth.

"Are you sure?" Meg dug in her purse. "I think I have some kind of salve in here. . . . I had a little bit of an accident myself a while back." She trailed off, dumping the contents of her bag onto the floor of the entryway.

Skylar approached her aunt and took her hand. There was a sharp red welt on her wrist. "Oh my gosh. It's all red!"

Nora pulled her hand away quickly and started gathering her things from the hooks on the wall. "I'll be fine," she said, hastily putting on her overcoat. "No worse than a cat scratch." And with that, she was out the front door and into the night. "I'll be back later this evening," she called over her shoulder.

As they watched her go, Skylar gave Meg an exaggerated shoulder shrug.

"I have no idea what that was about," she whispered. "She can be weird sometimes."

Then her gaze fell on the shards of china and the pool of cooling tea. It was unlike Nora to leave a mess. It was like she couldn't get away fast enough.

• • •

Upstairs, Meg sat in the high-backed chair in the corner of Skylar's sunny tower room, while Skylar sprawled on the quilted bedspread, trying to push her mom's injured voice out of her mind.

"I'm sorry my aunt is such a basket case," Skylar said, rolling her eyes. "Between her and my mom . . ." Meg was one of the only people who knew that Skylar's mom was, in fact, in jail—not sick.

"No, *I'm* sorry," Meg responded, all wide-eyed. "It's not because I came over, is it?" She tucked her legs beneath her on the chair. For the first time ever Meg looked slightly off her game.

"No, no," Skylar reassured her quickly, even though Aunt Nora had obviously been freaked out by Meg for some reason. "She's just bizarre. Don't worry about it. Trust me, it's the *least* of my problems."

She told Meg everything about the pajama party, right down to her total humiliation about Gabby and Pierce.

"Don't read too much into it," Meg said. Skylar knew this meant she was scheming up some idea.

"How can I not?" Skylar rolled onto her back and stared at the ceiling. "The message is obvious—Pierce likes Gabby. I have no chance. It's so unfair."

"But that's exactly it," Meg said calmly. "You have to even the playing field."

There was a silence between them; Skylar flopped back onto her stomach so she could look at Meg.

"Pierce doesn't like *Gabby*," Meg continued. "He likes what she *is*. What she *represents*. Think about it—he's a sophomore and about to be the new football star of Ascension. He probably feels like he's in over his head. He thinks he needs to follow a 'formula'"—Meg used finger quotes—"to live up to what people expect from him. It's almost like your mom and the care package." She pointed to the butterfly card and scented soap on the desk that Skylar had been planning to send to her mom. "She cares more about what people think of her than what she actually feels."

Skylar nodded, swallowing the lump that always appeared in her throat when she was reminded of her mother. What Meg was saying made perfect sense. She knew about the pressure of expectations. Skylar couldn't help but wonder, briefly, how Meg knew so much about people. It was like she'd lived hundreds of years and had seen it all.

"You are totally as pretty and smart and savvy as Gabby," Meg added. "It's just a question of getting Pierce to see that."

"At least I played it cool at school this week," Skylar admitted, hopping off the bed to gather up the things for her mother, and placing them in a bag under her desk for now. "Pierce smiled at me during geometry today. So I don't think he's, like, dwelling on it. Do you think I'm making progress?"

"Of course you are!" Meg rattled off a list, keeping track on her long, delicate fingers. "You're already friends with Gabby, so you're learning from the best. You're on the dance committee. You're one hang-out away from making Pierce like you. You're having your own party this weekend. You look great—your hair is so cute. You just have to keep going. Push it further."

As Meg spoke, Skylar's thoughts gained force, like a few flakes of snow whirling into a blizzard. Meg was right. Everything was going so well—she was on her way to living the life she wanted to lead. She wouldn't let one minor setback ruin her plans. Her party would be a social success. Her contributions to the dance committee would be brilliant.

It was simple: She would beat Gabby at her own game. And while she felt a pang of guilt, plotting against the person who had been so nice to her, she was sick of trailing behind. When she was around Gabby, she felt too much like the ugly, pudgy little sister again.

Anyway, wasn't it said that imitation is a form of flattery? It's not like people would stop paying attention to Gabby. It was harmless. Skylar would innocently spread the wealth. No one would get hurt.

Not like last time.

"Let's go shopping this week," Meg said with a wink. "You need something really special to wear to your party. Something killer."

• • •

As Marty Dove had predicted, the weather warmed up significantly in the days leading up to Skylar's party. Ascension teachers were unable to tamp down the burbling excitement that swept through the school, as it did whenever the brutal winter gave them a slight reprieve. The hardened crust of snow that had coated the ground for months had melted, leaving behind puddles of mud.

As soon as the final bell rang on Thursday afternoon, Skylar ran to the parking lot to find Meg. She was waiting in her maroon Lincoln with two other girls, whom she gleefully introduced as her cousins, Ty and Ali. All three of the girls were wearing sundresses and sunglasses, as though they were ready for a day at the beach.

Skylar raised her eyebrows and giggled as she waved to them. "Hey, ladies, I know it's sunny, but it's not officially summer quite yet."

"We run hot in our family," Ali said. "Come on!"

Skylar hopped into the backseat with Ali, the bottle-blonde, whose piercing blue eyes and full lips reminded Skylar of Scarlett Johansson.

"This is going to be superfun," Meg said, pulling out of the Ascension High lot with the windows down. "I love shopping trips! We're going to find you something amazing. I might get something new too."

"Where are we going?" Skylar asked meekly, pushing up her shirtsleeves. Ali was right. It was hot in this car. She hoped they would say Forever 21 or some bargain store. She didn't have much spending money, even after the pawning incident.

"There's really only one option at the mall," Ty said with authority. "If you want to really look special, I mean. We've got to go to Euphoria Boutique."

Skylar felt a flicker of anxiety. That place was *way* out of her price range. Didn't Meg know that? She'd never thought of Meg as having a lot of money. She worked at an ice cream shop, after all. But Meg just smiled at Ty's suggestion.

"Oh, well . . ." Skylar racked her brain for an excuse. "I was thinking more along the lines of, like, H&M? Because I kinda blew a lot of cash on the drinks and everything."

"Well, you'll just have to splurge a little more," Ty said, looking over her shoulder into the backseat, flipping a lock of flaming-red hair off her temple. Skylar was struck by how white her teeth were. Like Chiclets. "You deserve to have something nice for tomorrow night."

At the mall they dragged her immediately to Euphoria. It was an expensive store, full of beautiful, well-made staples and statement pieces. The stuff Gabby wore. The things Lucy would have liked.

Meg saw the doubt in Skylar's eyes. "Just pick out what you

like," she said, that familiar twinkle in her gray eyes. "There's no harm in trying things on."

"It's fun to play dress up!" Ali added, before scampering off to a rack of short leather skirts. "Do you think I should wear this tonight?" she called across the store, holding up a red suede miniskirt. Ty and Meg laughed and hooted.

Skylar tried to loosen up. She grabbed a bright green tunic, held it to her torso, and put a suede fedora on her head. The other girls were parading around in cropped blazers, a denim jumper, a pair of tight black pants with zippers at the ankles. They practiced their model pouts. And then, way in the back of the store, Skylar found a beautiful sweaterdress—navy blue, short, with detailing around the boatneck. The dress was cashmere and impossibly soft. There was a tiny pearl button at the nape of the neck. And it fit like a glove.

"Oooooooh, look at that!" Meg came running over. "It's perfect for you!"

Skylar blushed, but she walked over to the mirror anyway. Meg was right. It looked great—perfectly proportioned for her small frame, and making her boobs look a little bigger than usual. It was remarkably similar to something she'd seen Gabby wearing last week. Only this one was a teeny bit nicer.

Ty and Ali crowded around.

"It's made for you!" Ty said, motioning for Skylar to spin.

"Imagine that with tights and boots. Perfect for a bonfire

party," Ali chimed in. Yes. Skylar saw herself in the dress, flirting with Pierce by the fire. It was so warm that she probably wouldn't even need a jacket. Perfect.

But then, even as the fantasy danced in her mind, she snuck a peek at the price tag. As she'd expected: way too high. "No can do," she said with a sad smile. She started peeling off the dress.

"That doesn't seem *fair*," Meg said. "That dress should belong to you."

Skylar walked back through the store to return the dress to its rack—but her heart practically broke as she held it up one last time. Why should she put this back? Gabby wouldn't have to. Lucy wouldn't have had to; she would have found some way to get it. She would have found someone to buy it for her, or she simply would have taken it.

Skylar's mouth went dry.

She thought, suddenly, of the time Lucy had caught Skylar trying on one of Lucy's pageant dresses. "Is this mine?" Lucy had asked, fingering the strap. Skylar had pulled away quickly, and in the process, the strap had snapped. In a second Lucy's face had morphed from shock to outrage. "You ruin everything," she'd said, throwing her arms in the air. "*God*. How the hell did I end up with you as a sister?"

"I didn't ask to be part of this family!" Skylar had screamed back at her. When her mom had come running to see what the fuss was about, she'd grounded Skylar for touching something that wasn't hers, and Lucy had gotten a brand-new gown. The memory still made Skylar furious.

Meg's words echoed in her mind: *That doesn't seem fair. That dress should belong to you.*

Nothing was ever fair.

Taking a deep breath, she turned to head back over to the girls, who were standing near a rack of accessories. As she did a red box on the wall caught her eye. The store's fire alarm. She straightened her shoulders and walked like she was on a runway. And without another thought, she bashed her shoulder against the box as she passed it, then sailed quickly by.

BEEP-BEEP-BEEP. The sound was practically deafening, and it caused chaos in the store. Shoppers clamped their hands over their ears; employees scampered around from behind the registers, calling confusing instructions to one another.

After a few moments of looking bewildered, one store employee finally started shooing people out of the store. "Sorry for the inconvenience, folks," she said roughly, herding the customers toward the entryway and out of the store. "We'll have this all sorted out in a few moments."

Amid the hubbub, no one noticed that Skylar had stuffed the sweaterdress—and a headband, no less—into her bag.

"That was so amazing, what you pulled yesterday." Meg was still gushing the next day, when she, Ty, and Ali showed up to help

Skylar party-prep. (They'd snuck in through the back door, not wanting to elicit another weird reaction from Aunt Nora.)

"Totally badass," Ali agreed. Everything Ali said seemed somehow seductive, as though the words rolled over her curvy body as they left her mouth.

Skylar smiled sheepishly. "Anything is possible if you want it bad enough," she said, parroting back words that Lucy used to say to her. "Plus, Gabby's going to die when she sees this dress!"

Again that tiny twinge of guilt wriggled in her stomach. Gabby had been nothing but nice to her since she'd started at Ascension. But this was a special day, and Skylar felt like she finally had some guts. Not to mention . . . she'd never had a group of girlfriends before. Hanging out with Meg, Ty, and Ali was exhilarating, like being on a sugar high. Now, if only she could be this popular at school . . .

"So, hair?" Meg tapped Skylar's silver watch, sending shivers up her spine. "We're on a tight schedule, party girl."

While Meg wrapped Skylar's hair in curlers, Ali brushed foundation onto her face, blush onto her cheeks, and shadow onto her lids. Skylar felt like she was at a beauty salon, or on one of those before-and-after makeover shows. Ty hovered in the background—making Skylar a little nervous, to be honest. Ty seemed to have this balled-up dark energy inside her, even when she was smiling. It reminded Skylar, frankly, of Em.

"You've inspired me!" Ty exclaimed all of a sudden. "Watching you get this mini-makeover has given me an idea." She grabbed her purse and disappeared into the bathroom mysteriously as the other girls watched her go.

"Ty and her ideas . . . ," Ali said with a smile. "Can't wait to see what she's come up with this time."

Meanwhile, the girls pulled out patterned gray tights and heeled charcoal boots to go with Skylar's new dress.

"This scarf will look perfect too, especially with your watch," Ali said, holding a silvery one against Skylar's arm, where the glinting threads highlighted the delicate weave of the watch from her mom. Ali was right. It really was a perfect ensemble—and understated, for a change.

She was twirling around, trying to catch her butt in the mirror, when Ty reemerged from the bathroom. "Ta-da!" Ty struck a pose.

Skylar gasped. In twenty minutes Ty had completely transformed herself—she'd dyed her gorgeous, wavy red hair a deep chestnut brown, and she'd straightened it. Skylar hadn't even heard the blow-dryer. She couldn't believe how quickly Ty had reinvented herself.

"You like?" Ty asked, modeling for the others. "I figured since Meg changed her hair, I should change mine. Ali, you're next."

"I only grew mine out," Meg said. "You're like a whole new person."

Skylar stopped herself from confessing she preferred Ty before. "It's great," she said. The other cousins agreed, nodding vigorously.

But the truth was, with her newly darkened locks against her already pale skin, Ty looked almost like a corpse.

They were about to head out to the party when Meg got a phone call. She retreated into the hallway for a minute, and when she came back, she looked at Skylar apologetically.

"Family drama," she said with a grimace, and then, to Ali and Ty, "We have to bail pretty soon."

A small part of Skylar was relieved. Her new friends at Ascension didn't know Meg and her cousins, and Skylar didn't want to rock the boat. What if they all didn't get along and her party was ruined? It was better this way, really. Not to mention that she didn't need any *more* gorgeous friends to steal the attention away from her. But still—being around Meg and the girls made her feel almost powerful. How was she going to fake it without them?

"You're not going to come to the party at all?" Skylar pouted.

"Don't worry," Meg said, kissing Skylar on the forehead. "We'll go with you right now and help you set up. After that, we'll be there in spirit."

Ty winked at her. "You'll feel like we're right there with you. Oh! What's this?" She pointed to the red orchid Meg had given Skylar on the first day they'd met, which was still blooming as well as ever.

"Aw, you kept it," Meg said.

"I think it's the dream accessory," Ali piped up.

"You should wear it." Ty reached over and pinned the red orchid to Skylar's dress. "You know, for good luck!"

Impulsively, Skylar hugged her as the other girls squealed. It was time.

CHAPTER ELEVEN

"I really didn't know," Gabby told Em for the thousandth time, holding a gold dangly earring to her ear in front of Em's bedroom mirror. "I mean, he's a *sophomore*. He can't really think it would work out between us."

Em nodded. She was standing in her closet doorway, staring at her belt collection.

"I did think they'd be good together. I still do!" Gabby continued, fishing out a different dangly earring from Em's collection, this one full of bright red beads. She was wearing her hair up tonight and wanted to balance the look with some big jewelry.

"Do you think she has any idea?" Em asked, holding a black belt up to her jeans.

"I hope not," Gabby said. "I mean, she knows that I'm just

trying to be single for now, not date anyone, just focus on myself. You know? Which is exactly what I told Pierce, too. I'd go with the brown belt, by the way. The woven one."

"Thanks, Gabs." Em threaded it through her belt loops, noting distractedly that she had to buckle it into the tightest hole. She was thinking about how Skylar would feel if she knew her crush-object had fallen for Gabby. On one hand, the girl obviously worshipped Gabs. But Skylar was probably a bit jealous, too. Hell, Em knew *exactly* what it felt like to be overshadowed by Gabby. She recalled moments spent yearning for what Gabby had: the supposedly perfect life, the supposedly perfect boyfriend. Of course, memories of Zach made her think of Chase, and how for him, the desire for so-called perfection had been even more consuming. Bad enough for him to do terrible things. And then to have terrible things done to him. . . .

And while Gabby was stressing about stuff with Skylar, Em was equally remorseful about how things had gone down with Drea the other night. Now that she had some distance, Em was embarrassed and even a little scared by how she'd behaved on JD's stoop. That wasn't her. That was someone darker, someone worse.

She wanted to apologize, to explain herself. But so far, she hadn't found the words.

Gabby nudged her out of her thoughts with her elbow. "If you were Skylar, would you totally hate me right now?"

Em finished putting on her mascara. "I think you should just let it go," she said. "Skylar will get over it."

"But I want her to know," Gabby insisted, "that I would never do that to a friend. Especially not after . . ." She trailed off. Em's betrayal fell between them like a shade. "Anyway. Can I borrow these?" She held up a pair of long silver earrings.

"Of course," Em said.

"I wonder if the Dusters will be hot," Gabby mused as she put on the earrings. "Bass players are always hot, aren't they?"

"Sorry, who are the Dusters?" Em looked up distractedly from the pile of boots she was contemplating on her closet floor.

"Emmmmmmmm," Gabby whined. "They're *just* the semi-famous band I've been telling you about for a week. It was a total coup that we got them for the Fling. They, like, never do high school shows. But we had a connection through that senior, Angela something-or-other. Isn't it too perfect?"

"Too perfect," Em echoed. "Maybe I could interview them for the yearbook spread about the dance." She felt a glimmer of her old self.

Gabby flopped onto the bed and sighed. "I guess. The whole thing is going to be a mortifying disaster, of course." She looked at Em for a reaction.

"Um, why's that?" Em couldn't help but smirk at Gabby's flip-flopping between exhilaration and despair.

"Only because we don't have a theme and the dance is a week away!" Gabby groaned.

Em felt guilty that she didn't know. "We don't?"

"God, Em, no! Where have you been? Well, I know where you *haven't* been—at the planning committee meetings." All of a sudden, Gabby got quiet. "Seriously, Em, where have you been recently? Where has your head been? I can't shake the feeling that . . . Are you still hiding something from me?"

The question was so straightforward that it threw Em off. She tried to focus on lacing her boots, but her hands began to shake a little. She wished, desperately, that she could talk to Gabby—that she could tell her everything. Then she realized: There *was* something she could come clean about. She cleared her throat and stood up with one chocolate-brown boot in her hand.

"You're right, Gabs," she said slowly. "There is something I'm hiding from you."

Gabby stared at her, eyebrows raised, chewing on her lip. "I knew it."

"I haven't told you . . . the fact that . . . Well, this is going to sound weird, but . . ."

"Just say it!" Gabby made frantic whirring motions with her hands.

Em took a deep breath. "Okay. Well. I'm falling in love with—I'm *in* love with JD. Like, totally. Head over heels." She blushed, unable to believe that she'd said the words aloud. It actually felt . . . good.

Gabby was confused. "JD . . . Like, JD the chauffeur?"

"We really shouldn't call him that, Gabby," Em said. "He's more than that." But Gabby's reaction was no surprise. In public, Em had never treated JD as anything more than her personal driver. No wonder he thought she was a stuck-up bitch.

Gabby pressed for details. "So, when did you know? And doesn't he, like, totally love you back? He's always been pretty obsessed with you, hasn't he?"

Em threw her a small smile. "I think part of me has always known," she said. "Way down somewhere. But . . . I also think I lost my chance. I don't think he trusts me anymore. We kind of . . . we had a falling-out. And now he's more into fixing cars than hanging out with me."

"I can't believe you haven't told me about this," Gabby said. Em was relieved that Gabby sounded more exasperated than angry. Gabby swung her legs over the side of the bed, and in typical Gabby fashion, barked an order. "Come here, then. Is he going to be at the party tonight? If you want to make up with JD, you *have* to do something with your hair."

Em smiled sheepishly. "I was late for school this morning. I didn't have a chance . . ." She wondered if JD would be there tonight, and if so, whether the woods would be a good place to corner him and at least talk—about something, anything. Find some neutral territory. Some way to start things over between them. If she couldn't explain herself to him, explain what had happened that night at the Behemoth, well, at least she could apologize. Try to make him remember their chemistry. All the fun they used to have. Maybe she could at least get him to crack a small smile again like he had in the driveway the other day....

Gabby grabbed a comb from the dresser and motioned for Em to sit down on the bed. As she started working the knots out of Em's hair, it dawned on Em that JD really only went to parties with *her*—when she needed a ride. It was pretty doubtful that he'd make an appearance tonight.

Truth be told, as much as she was dying to talk to him, it was probably safer that things between them were so strained. She was having a hard enough time not telling him all the secrets the Furies had insisted she keep.

"There," Gabby said with satisfaction after a few moments. "Your hair is so dark these days, Em. It looks good with your coloring. I swear, you could be a Lancôme model or something."

Gabby grabbed some eye shadow from the dresser.

"I don't want—" Em started to protest.

Gabby cut her off. "Don't argue. I'm going to put some of this on your eyelids. That's it. You clearly don't need any other makeup."

Em felt a rush of gratitude. "Do you think I should wear my hair up or down?" she asked, smiling for what felt like the first time in months as she caught Gabby's eyes in the mirror.

• • •

The bonfire was blazing by the time they got to the Haunted Woods, and between the hot flames and the balmy night, spring fever had definitely struck early. People who had already arrived were running around in jeans and sweaters. Under the shimmering half-moon and against the flickering fire, the partygoers looked like they were moving in leaps and jumps—like characters in a flip book or dancers under a disco ball. The wood smoke was thick and smelled of pine needles. Em saw Skylar at the far side of the fire, struggling with a shiny metal keg. Had she set this up all by herself?

"Want help with that?" Andy Barton and a group of other jocks barreled past them, heading toward Skylar. Em noticed that Pierce was part of the group—he tried to say hi to Gabby, but she was distracted by Fiona and Jenna, who had just arrived with a portable iPod dock.

"Music!" Fiona shouted.

"Did you hear that Lauren is totally coming *with* Nick?" Jenna huddled into Gabby and Em. "I bet they're going to hook up again."

Gabby shrieked and Em smiled. The saga of Lauren and Nick was reaching legendary proportions.

"Let's go get something to drink," Gabby said. "There's spiked cider and beer. I think Skylar was planning on getting some mulled wine, too."

"Get me whatever, okay? I'll keep watch for Lauren," Em said, not quite ready to enter the group. There was raucous laughter coming from a group of sophomore and junior boys by the kegs.

"Remember freshman year? The Haunted Woods party? When Zach and Chase were doing keg stands?" Gabby laughed and Em realized, with a start, that she and Gabby had barely said Zach's name out loud since . . . the incident. She reached out and squeezed Gabby's hand.

"I remember. That was fun." She found herself, strangely, missing Chase—his party antics and his shameless flirting and his brusque chivalry. How many times had he refilled her drink?

"Okay, brb!"

As Gabby leaped off toward the drinks, Em stood back and observed the scene. She tried to imagine this as the setting for a fire that killed three presumed witches. Turning them into ghosts . . . or into Furies? These woods, with their darkly majestic pines and cacophony of foreboding creaks and hisses, made the supernatural seem closer than ever.

But so far tonight there were no signs of ghosts, just lots of drunk Ascension students. A bunch of seniors had commandeered some logs by the fire; they were sitting, roasting marshmallows and passing around a flask of whiskey. One of them, a band guy Em thought Crow might have been friends with before he dropped out, had a guitar with him. Several sophomore girls stood in a cluster nearby, singing a song they wanted him to play.

No sign yet of JD. Was he with Drea? She tried to dismiss the idea quickly. She was getting paranoid.

She watched Skylar handing out cups of the just-tapped hard cider. Skylar's dress was cute, and a silvery scarf was wrapped around her neck. She was taller than usual, thanks to a pair of heeled knee boots. Her hair was curled. *It's a mini-Gabby,* Em thought as Skylar approached Pierce and tried to get his attention, practically sticking her boobs in his face. If Skylar was going to be Gabby's project, Gabs needed to teach her the art of subtlety.

She was about to turn her head and do another sweep of the crowd for JD, when something caught her eye. A flash of red, there on Skylar's blue sweaterdress. She squinted and looked closer. Her breath caught in her throat, and she had a sudden, swinging sense of vertigo. There was a red orchid pinned to Skylar's dress. The party seemed to disappear; all she could see was the flower.

"Move. Excuse me. Sorry." Em shouldered her way over to where Skylar and Pierce were standing. She burst in between them.

"Where did you get that?" she demanded, looking down at Skylar's chest. She heard Pierce, behind her, mumble something about getting more beer.

Skylar seemed nervous. "At the mall. . . . It was pretty expensive, but I got a great deal. . . . Coupon—my aunt gave me a—"

Em cut her off and jabbed at the flower. "Where did you get *this*?" she said. "Where did you get this flower?" Her voice was high with panic; she could hear it.

"You don't like it?" Skylar whimpered, wobbling ever so slightly; Em wondered how much she'd had to drink while getting ready for the party. "I wasn't sure if it matched, but I decided to wear it anyway. But if you think it's too much . . ." Skylar unpinned the orchid.

Instinctively, acting on the hatred that the orchid sparked in her chest, Em grabbed it from Skylar's hand and threw it into the fire.

Skylar watched it fall, exclaiming, "Hey! That was a gift!"

"I'm going to ask you again: Where. Did. You. Get. It?" Em spoke with quiet determination.

"A friend gave it to me, actually," Skylar said, lifting her chin a bit. Em saw vulnerability in her face—desperation. This girl really just wanted to be liked. To be noticed. But still, that flower. It meant only one thing.

"Is your . . . friend—is she here?" Em's heart thumped. Images of Chase returned to her: His intense longing to be accepted. His feelings of being an outsider. How the Furies had preyed on that weakness. . . .

Skylar shook her head, distracted by a whooping cheer that came from the direction of the kegs. "She had some family thing," she said vaguely. "She might stop by later."

Em's mind clouded with visions of New Year's Eve: of meeting Ali on the train to Boston, of getting caught in the subway doors, of watching her orchid get chewed up on the subway tracks and then having Ali hand it to her, intact, just minutes later. What had Skylar done to deserve an orchid? Were the Furies now arbitrarily targeting Ascensionites?

Clearly, Skylar was in trouble. But she had no idea, and Em might be the only person who could help her.

Em coughed, feeling the scorching smoke scrape through her throat and nose.

"We should move," Skylar said, gulping down more of her drink. "The smoke's blowing right at us."

But Em barely registered her comment. She grabbed Skylar's wrist and squeezed it. "Listen to me," she said with the same quiet fervor. "You have to be careful. What do you know about this friend of yours? Does she . . . does she have two cousins? Two girls?"

This made Skylar light up. "You know them," she hiccupped. She moved in closer to Em, sloshing some cider out of the side of her cup. "Aren't they *so* pretty? Like you!" Skylar was talking nonsense, but it made Em's stomach flip.

"No, listen, Skylar," Em said, grabbing the girl's shoulders to steady her and stare into her eyes. Maybe it was worthless to have this conversation right now—Skylar was obviously already tipsy, and even without the booze, she was distracted by her hostess duties. But Em had to try. "I *do* know them. They . . . they hurt people, Skylar. You have to be careful. They think it's justice, but it's not. It's evil. It's revenge. Have you ever heard the expression 'An eye for an eye makes the whole world blind'?" She didn't wait for Skylar to respond. "Well, that's what they do. They make the world blind."

She heard herself speaking fast and furiously, and gripped Skylar's arms as though she was going to fall over. "They *know* things about us," Em pressed on. "Things that we're ashamed about. Things we did that maybe—that weren't right. And that flower," she said, pointing toward the fire, "it means you're in danger. It means they know something about you."

Terror replaced confusion in Skylar's eyes. Good. That meant she was listening. The flames lit Skylar's cheek, coloring it a rusty, glowing orange. The other side of her face was completely in shadow. She was shaking her head, starting to mumble.

"It's not my fault. . . . I didn't mean . . ." Then she jerked backward, out of Em's grip. "How did you find out? How do you know?" She stared at Em accusingly, as though *she* was the one to be afraid of.

"Look, I don't know anything," Em thought Skylar looked relieved. "I'm just trying to help. Start from the beginning. When did you meet the girls?" If she calmed down and got Skylar to open up, she could actually learn something. Maybe there was a pattern here, of who the Furies targeted.

But Skylar had shut down. She started backing away. "Look, Em, I don't know what you're talking about, but you're really freaking me out. I'm going to get a new drink."

Just as Em started to protest her phone buzzed in her pocket. As she fished it out Skylar used the distraction to escape.

"I—I'll see you later," she said over her shoulder while she walked quickly away.

It was Drea. Thank god. Em needed Drea more than ever right now. Their fight, her terrible words, rang in her head. She would find Skylar in a few minutes. First she would talk to Drea.

"Amazing timing," she said as she picked up, not letting Drea respond. "There's a new orchid. The Furies have marked someone else. We need to meet."

"Sweetheart, just tell me when and where." A male voice, full of confidence and swagger, came over the line.

Em took the phone away from her ear, made sure it really was Drea's name she'd seen on the caller ID, and then spoke again. "Who is this?"

Laughter, low and sleepy. "It's Crow," the voice said. "Drea left her phone in my car, and I wanted to get it to her. Is she with you?"

"Oh. Hi. Um. No, she's not with me. I don't know where she is. But I need to talk to her. As soon as possible."

"You sure do have a lot of demands, princess," Crow responded. Em rolled her eyes, glad that he couldn't see her blush. "If I see Drea, I'll tell her."

"Thanks," Em said, getting ready to hang up.

"Hey—what are you up to tonight?" Crow asked with renewed energy. "My band practice got canceled. Maybe we could all hang out? If we find Drea, of course."

Em hesitated. She liked Crow, and she wouldn't mind hanging out with him—there was something supremely relaxing about how little he expected from her, how easily she could defy his expectations—but there was no way that she could invite the Grim Creeper to an Ascension party. He'd ostracized *himself* from this group.

"I'm—I can't," she finally said. "Just tell her I called, okay? If you see her. Tell her I need to see her."

"Yes, Your Majesty," Crow said breezily. Em remembered Drea's words from the other day: *I think he has a crush on you.* There was no way. Absurd. She brushed the thought from her mind. "Oh, and by the way, I found that information you wanted."

Em's eyes widened. "You did? Oh my god, Crow, you're amazing!" she gushed.

"I know. I'm not sure if the information will help you much, though," he said. "The only person in the antiquities room that day was Sasha Bowlder."

The words nearly knocked her over; she had to put her hand against a nearby tree to steady herself. Sasha Bowlder. The rumors about witchcraft, about Sasha's weird activities in the woods . . . It was all too coincidental. Something was coming together, but Em wasn't sure what.

"You still there?" Crow asked, actually sounding earnest for once.

"Yeah, I—I just wasn't expecting that," she said.

"Neither was I," Crow said. "Hey, do me a favor. . . . Don't tell Drea that, at least not yet. She's too fucked up right now."

Em nodded vigorously, even though Crow couldn't see her. Of course. Drea and Sasha had been very close, and Drea was still grappling with her friend's death, going as far as to visit with the Bowlders occasionally to help them all get closure. "No, I won't," she said. "Thanks, Crow. Thank you so much."

She wished more than anything that she hadn't blown up at Drea the other night. What the hell had come over her? Sure, it had stung to see JD spending time with someone else—another girl, to be precise. But Drea was right. She had no right to be so upset, especially not with Drea, especially not to that degree. They were studying! Like normal people did when they were in high school! And even if she was justified in being pissed off, her reaction had been totally out of proportion.

She would reconcile with Drea before she did anything else. And then she'd tell her about Skylar, who was obviously in trouble too. Should they warn her? Was there anything they could do? She looked around, trying to locate Skylar among the half-shadowed partiers.

It was then that Em heard the screaming.

CHAPTER TWELVE

The scream sliced the thin winter air. Another shriek followed
the first, this one higher-pitched and more piercing. There was a
commotion over by the kegs.

Skylar headed in that direction, catching her foot on a branch
as she walked and kicking it aside with a jerking motion. She
called out when she was still several feet away.

"What's going on, you guys?" She hoped nothing was
wrong. More than that, she hoped nothing would happen to
ruin her party. She'd actually been having a good conversation
with Pierce. They'd been talking about geometry, and then the
Dusters, and then they'd somehow switched gears to talking
about reality shows. Cuteness!

Near the kegs a small group was clustered around two girls,

both of whom were now giggling nervously. Skylar recognized both of them—she thought they might be juniors—but she didn't know their names. The air was saturated with a high-strung energy.

"I swear I thought I saw something over there," one of the girls was saying.

"Me too," echoed the other. "Right behind those trees. Kind of . . . shimmering or something."

Surprised at the fear that fluttered in her stomach, Skylar scanned the woods in the direction they were pointing. She saw nothing but a curtain of pine-needled branches swallowed by swaths of black. Patches of moonlight penetrated the shadows. Nothing moving. Nothing shimmering. She turned back to the group. She didn't want to sound annoyed.

"All clear, I guess?" She poured herself another cup of cider as she spoke, hoping it made her seem cool and collected. She wanted to smooth things over as quickly as possible. What had she been thinking, agreeing to host a party in woods that were notoriously haunted?

Everyone was laughing now, making ghost sounds: *Woooooo, Woooooo.*

"Who you gonna call?" one of the boys shouted.

"I'm a Ghostbuster," another said. "Want me to go investigate?"

"Guys, shut *up*," the first girl whined. "I really thought I saw something!"

Relieved that this interlude would be a short one, Skylar tried to laugh along with the group, but it felt forced. Inside, she was still reeling from the exchange with Em. She rubbed her arms, trying to brush away the feeling of Em's nails digging into her shoulders, the feeling of Em's eyes boring into hers. And most forcefully, Em's words ringing in her ears. *It means they know something about you.*

It was as though *Em* knew Skylar's secrets. It was creepy. And it was official: Em and Skylar were never going to be friends, not really. Skylar barely understood why anyone was friends with Em in the first place. Sure, she was beautiful. And smart. But she was crazy! She wasn't at all suited for queen-bee status, or even to be co–queen bee. Em was nothing like Gabby. And, Skylar realized with a smile, nothing like herself.

Skylar pulled at the neck of her sweaterdress and hitched its skirt a little higher. She felt like she was running out of time— she had to get in at least one more good conversation with Pierce before the night was over. She cleared her throat, took one more sip of her beer, and prepared to find him just as a bunch of junior boys passed by. They were the cool, smart guys, the ones who weren't jocks but still fit in with Gabby and her group.

They seemed to be talking about underwear. *Her* underwear, she gathered from the direction of their gazes.

"Maybe it's polka-dot," she heard a guy named Matt say.

She whirled around, heart pounding.

"What did you say?" she demanded. But they'd already breezed off, chortling.

She held the cup of beer to her forehead, letting its cold condensation sweat onto her skin, then gulping down what was left. Her mouth was parched, and licking her lips did nothing to moisten them. Questions hurtled through her brain. Why had they said that? Of all things . . . But no. They *couldn't* know. There was no way that anyone could possibly know. It was a coincidence. Her Dot-Crotch days were dead and buried. That Skylar was gone. She touched her curled hair as if to convince herself.

Still, she couldn't shake the anxious, horrible feeling that people were watching her and snickering. That her secrets were unraveling, that old ghosts were emerging from shallow graves.

Suddenly the music cut off. Skylar whipped her head over toward the speakers, which were sitting on a pile of cinder blocks. Without the background music and its rhythmic beat, the staccato bursts of conversation sounded erratic and awkward. The night was suddenly filled with silent spaces, like black holes.

And then, into those holes, a tinny sound began to trickle and spread. Skylar froze, horror seeping through her whole body. It was a sound she'd recognize anywhere—an off-key warbling that she'd heard for years in her nightmares. Her own voice. Her own young, stupid, embarrassing self, singing "Let Me Entertain You." *And if you're real good, I'll make you feel good . . .*

She spotted a cluster of people hunched over a glowing iPhone screen. The air felt thick around her. She felt like she was moving through mud, drowning in the sticky darkness. The bonfire was no longer casting a glow—its flames had gone harsh, like a lashing strobe light cutting into the night. It made her feel dizzy.

She struggled toward the crowd around the phone, hating the way the machine's muffled sound made her terrible performance even worse.

"Found it on YouTube . . ." she heard one of the boys say.

There, over their shoulders, she saw it: her own mortifying routine, as a chubby eighth grader, singing loudly and—she recognized this now—desperately, attempting to keep a lipstick-coated smile on her face as she performed her ridiculous choreography. Some spins, some kicks, an attempt at a seductive shimmy that made the group roar with laughter. The song was about a *stripper*, for god's sake. Why had she ever let Lucy convince her that it was a good choice for the talent portion? Why hadn't her mother (who was visible on the sidelines in the video, watching her daughter with an expression of disappointed disgust) told her it was inappropriate?

And then the song's grand finale, with Skylar landing in an ungraceful split. You could hear the fabric tearing even over the music.

Skylar watched the train wreck as though she was seeing it for the first time. She watched her face—younger, pudgier, but unmistakably hers—crumble into confusion and fear as her pants, tight and spangled to match the bustier top that only highlighted her complete lack of a chest, split open, revealing her underwear. Purple and polka-dot. She watched her mother's face fall in embarrassment and then assume an expression of detached concern, almost as though Skylar was someone else's kid. The video zoomed in for a close-up as young Skylar scrambled to her feet, trying to minimize the exposure. It was impossible. The polka dots were practically all you could see, which is why her fellow contestants, mini-divas happy to see their competition go down in flames, had started shouting, "Dot-Crotch!" It followed her as she ran from the stage, and it continued until the host asked everyone (politely, barely concealing his own smirk) to stop.

Now Skylar was shaking. She remembered the event, of course, as if it was tattooed on her brain. But she hadn't known there was a video of it. Where did it even *come* from? She felt like everything she'd worked for was about to get sucked away.

It was Sean Wagner who was actually holding the phone in the middle of the giggling group. She grabbed his collar and dragged him to his feet.

"Whoa, whoa, whoa—Dot-Crotch is mad!" Sean's eyes were wide; he looked genuinely surprised at the strength of her reaction.

"*Wheredidyoufindthis?*" Her lips trembled as the words came pouring out. "Did you hear me? Where did you get this?"

"So it *was* you!" Sean started laughing harder. "Some chick showed it to me," he said between laughing gasps. "Some chick in the library. It's Dot-Crotch, right?" He held out his hand as though he was going to introduce himself.

Dot-Crotch. Dot-Crotch. Suddenly those words seemed to be everywhere, murmured and whispered and blurted out, spreading around the party. She heard Gabby asking what was so funny. She didn't see Pierce, but she knew it was only a matter of time until he found out. *Dot-Crotch. Dot-Crotch.* Lauren's and Fiona's faces blurred past. Even the trees seemed to be whispering it. The humiliation and devastation crashed over her as freshly as they had that night. She kept seeing her mother's face, harsh and humiliated. She had to get out of here.

"Skylar, wait!" Gabby called out to her as she ran away from the party. Tears were streaming down her face now, and she could barely see as she turned around.

"What do you want?" she sobbed, standing at the edge of the clearing, not caring whether all of Ascension could see her.

"Sky, I'm so sorry," Gabby said, approaching her with a pitying look in her eyes, coming around to cut off her escape route. "Are you okay?"

"No, I'm not okay," Skylar snarled, staggering a bit. She tugged at her dress, which now felt too short.

Gabby nodded. "Of course not. . . . But this'll blow over."

Only someone like Gabby would think that way: that it

would blow over. Skylar knew differently. She had built a structure of lies; this was just the beginning, the first wind that would blow everything to pieces.

"You know, I went out for social VP last year," Gabby offered gently. "And I was so sure I was going to get it. I was already planning things I would do and whatever. I even made this Facebook group for people to tell me their ideas for dances and stuff. It was mortifying. There was this group of older girls—"

Skylar cut her off. "Just stop." It was so condescending for Gabby to compare the Dot-Crotch humiliation to a minor social dilemma that obviously hadn't affected Gabby's popularity in any way.

She thought of Lucy's comforting arms when she'd run offstage that night—holding her, petting her, telling her that it would be okay and that everyone would forget about it sooner or later. But of course she thought that way. If *Lucy's* pants had ripped, if *Gabby's* underwear had been polka-dotted, it would be a whole different story. If you were unremarkable, it was the disasters that made you stand out. And even as Lucy told her not to worry about what people were calling her—because the nickname stuck, of course—she still encouraged Skylar to go on a diet, telling her about how her muffin top rolled over her jeans.

"But maybe if you just—" Gabby started to say. Here it came, the "friendly advice" with a clear message: *If you were more like me, these things wouldn't happen to you.*

"I said, *stop*." Skylar tried to push past Gabby. She couldn't take this anymore. She didn't care how loud she was, didn't care that everyone was probably staring at them. She didn't care that she was acting like her own mother—belligerent and irrational. Gabby reached out to stop her, catching Skylar's arm and throwing her off balance.

It all happened in slow motion. Skylar felt herself leaning sideways, losing her footing, realizing that there was no standing back up. As time dragged, she found herself wondering what her face looked like as she fell. Surprised? Scared? Angry? She landed half-draped over a log, her dress hitched up and her entire backside on display.

Her underwear was showing through her tights, she could tell. The air was cold against her butt. She was certain she heard mean laughter from behind her. She stood quickly and turned on her heel, yelling, "Show's over, assholes!"

"Skylar, stop, no one is—" Gabby tried to hush her.

Then Skylar heard someone shout out, "What happened to the polka dots?"

And then another jeered, "Is that a thong? Can we call you Thong-Crotch now?"

It was over. Her night was over. The party was over. The progress she'd been making—over.

"You did that deliberately," Skylar hissed at Gabby as she got up, scraping her hands on the rough bark of the fallen tree.

She didn't know if it was true, but it might as well have been.

"It was an accident! I didn't want you to fall!" Gabby protested.

But Skylar, her eyes blurred again with tears, didn't listen. She didn't stop running until she was out of the woods.

CHAPTER THIRTEEN

Everyone else had already forgotten about "the ghost," but Em stood at the edge of the clearing, looking into the forest, still on high alert. The screams, as short-lived as they'd been, had frozen her blood. She didn't see anything unusual. But she *sensed* that something was wrong.

She wished she could just forget about it—rejoin the party, have a good time, gossip with Gabby or maybe fend off a football player or two.

But no. The new Em was fixated on ghosts. Always looking for them. Thinking about them constantly. Obsessed.

She heard the music die behind her and then loud laughter. As she turned around to see what the big joke was, she heard Skylar screaming, "Show's over, assholes!" and tearing away from the party.

Damn it! They hadn't finished talking. Em had to get through to Skylar, had to let her know what was at stake. She tried to follow Skylar's path toward the darkness of the woods that would lead to the party's exit—maybe they could find a quiet place to talk. . . .

But in the time it had taken her to push her way through the party, across the clearing, she'd lost Skylar. She didn't know where she'd gone—it was just gnarled, bony trees and blackness as Em peered down the path to the Behemoth, where most of the kids had parked.

She turned and started trudging back over the muddy leaves toward the center of the party.

On the opposite side of the bonfire, she saw a glint of blond hair shimmering against the shadows. Em would know it anywhere, that shade of brassy blond. She squinted. The flames flashed before her eyes like curtains being rapidly opened and closed; she wished she could reach out and still them, just for a moment.

Then, as though she had wished it, the flames parted precisely and perfectly, framing for one moment the heart-shaped outline of a smiling face whose eyes appeared sunken in the quickly shifting light. There was no mistaking the face. It was Ali—laughing, maniacal Ali—the Fury who had stalked her. The Fury who had placed bloody handprints all over her door.

Em gasped; her knees buckled. Ali was here. She was laughing at Em—at Em's stupidity, at Em's delusion that the Furies were escapable. If Ali was here, the Furies, all three of them, were probably here.

She sucked in a deep breath and started toward the other side of the fire. She was going to find out what the Furies had in store—for her, for tonight, for Ascension. She might have heard Gabby saying her name, but she wasn't sure, and didn't care. She stumbled on a pile of rocks, nearly losing her balance, swaying dangerously close to the fire. She'd lost sight of Ali, but she could still see that sick smile. It seeped through her mind, turning her thoughts into tar.

She was at the other edge of the party now, where the crowd thinned out and the trees were closer together. A few steps away, in the woods, she heard something—a snapping branch, as from a footfall. She moved cautiously toward the noise and paused. Silence.

Em knew she should turn around. She was going to get lost out here if she kept going. But there was movement up ahead, she was sure of it. The flapping of a dress? The sinuous motion of a scarf? It was her. It was Ali.

She just knew it.

She pressed through the trees, branches springing back and stinging her face. A muddy trail, barely discernible, materialized below her feet, the underbrush parting just slightly; she followed it almost blindly, feeling roots and rocks through the soles of her boots. She went deeper and deeper, her path twisting and winding. As she walked she found herself thinking of a camping trip her family had taken with JD's years ago. Their parents had granted them permission to follow the river until it reached a small water-fall, but they'd strayed away from the water and gotten turned around in the woods. Em had gotten scared, but JD had reassured her. "Just be still for a moment," he'd said. "We'll hear the river."

With a flash of conviction, she realized she would follow this path to its conclusion, wherever that was. She had to. She held still for a second and listened.

How was it possible for a place to be so silent and yet so full of sound? Her breath was ragged in her ears, and the twigs, leaves, and icy slush whispered ominously. There was a low drone in the distance—a generator? The highway? She was completely disoriented now, not sure that she could find her way back to the party if she wanted to.

Then, at her feet, she saw something move. With an invol-untary shudder, she realized there was a snake writhing right in front of her, off to the side of the path. It was almost as though—and she knew how crazy it was to even *think* this—it was lead-ing her. Beckoning to her. So she followed it a few more steps before it disappeared under a bush. And as it did the trail opened slightly. Em found herself in a clearing. Looming and lit by the half-moon was an enormous house—Colonial, boxy, once beau-tiful, now ruined and dark.

The hairs on the back of Em's neck prickled.

Suddenly there was no doubt in her mind: The Furies were here. This was their home. She could feel them all around her.

I can do this. I must do this. Drea's face, and JD's, and Chase's—they crashed into her mind like waves, pulling her toward the door.

"Hello?" she called out. No response.

Creak. The front door swung open at her touch, and she stepped cautiously into a large, empty foyer. An acrid smell immediately seeped into her nose. It was the smell of burnt hair, like when Gabby left a tendril wrapped around the curler for too long. Em fought an impulse to gag, and instead brought her sleeve to her nose and breathed through it.

She looked for a light switch by the door reflexively, and then shook her head. Like there would be electricity in a place like this, which looked torn from the pages of her history textbook. She could practically feel the presence of mice in the walls, termites nesting in the wood: a house crumbling to decay.

The moonlight trickling in from outside was enough to illuminate rooms off to either side of the grand staircase. She took a tentative step into the one on her left, digging her cell phone out of her pocket and using it as a makeshift flashlight. This room was empty too, except for a wooden chair and a drop cloth laid below a wall that was covered in a garish shade of red paint. The paint reminded Em of something, but in her distraction, in her fear, she couldn't put her finger on what.

Beyond that: a kitchen with a swinging oil lamp hanging over a rickety table. Em circled around, taking in the layer of thick dust on every window, the black smudges that crept up every wall. The odor of ash and burnt wood was everywhere—but this wasn't like the bonfire she'd left at the party. No. This was different—sharper, fouler. She saw the remains of ivory curtains, just shreds, their edges curling and brown. There had definitely been a fire here, a bad one.

She forced herself to walk farther into the house.

The stairway banister was singed and crumbling. She could practically see the flames licking at the mahogany, the heat engulfing the staircase. Her toes curled in her boots. There were no dirty footprints on the stairs. No sign of Ali or Ty or Meg. But there was still the second floor—maybe there were clues up there.

Ever so lightly, she put her foot on the bottom step. Then, with deliberate motions, she climbed upward, taking only the shallowest breaths, trying to make as little sound as possible. She prayed the stairway wasn't rotten; she imagined it collapsing underneath her weight, sending her tumbling into a pile of splintered wood and fire-ravaged debris.

At the landing she paused, debating which way to go. She thought she saw a light turn quickly on and off in a room to her right. Her first instinct was to run. But she clenched her fists and stepped cautiously forward.

"Who's there?" Her voice was shaky. She cleared her throat.

She went into the room where she'd seen the light. Nothing. Had she imagined it? For a moment she saw herself as someone else would: alone, in a strange, dark, fire-damaged house in the middle of winter, looking for ghosts.

The Furies will drive you crazy.

Turn around, she told herself. *Turn around and go back to the party.* But she couldn't. She was still overwhelmed by the presence of evil nearby.

There was a scuffling noise behind her. Em whirled around, terrified, her breath catching in her throat and her arms going up as if she would defend herself.

An enormous rat, its long tail dragging through the dust on the wooden floor, scurried out of the room.

Em recoiled, then released her breath, letting her arms drop to her sides. She went back into the hall, which was dimly lit by a large, half-moon window set high in one wall. Turning to look behind her after every step, she walked farther into the house. Her footsteps echoed as her boots fell against the old floorboards. There, in front of her, was a closed door. She reached out, her fingers shaking as they neared the smooth metal doorknob.

"I wouldn't touch that if I were you."

Em spun around, her heart pounding.

Ty had materialized behind her, between Em and the stairs. She was watching Em with calm, wide eyes.

"You did something to your hair." Stupidly, it was the only thing that Em could think to say.

Ty smiled. "I wanted it to be like yours," she said. "You know, you really have a lot going for you, Em. You should be enjoying yourself instead of obsessing over me. I know *we're* having fun."

"I'm sure you are," Em shot back.

"It was wonderful of Sasha to invite us back to Ascension!" Ty said with sickly false innocence. "There are *so* many interesting people here. There always have been. . . ."

"Is that why you're here? Because of Sasha?" Em asked. She thought of the book about the Furies—the one Crow had said was in Sasha's possession when she died. Had she somehow *conjured* them?

"Right now I'm here to chat with you," Ty purred. "It doesn't seem like you have many people to talk to right now." The pout on her face made Em's fingers clench into fists.

"You've turned JD against me," she said, looking anxiously behind Ty, trying to gauge whether or not she could slip by her, down the stairs, out into the night.

"JD? Oh," Ty said, her voice fluttering with laughter. "Funny how people's memories are so malleable, isn't it? Because I remember that you ditched him on the night of the pep rally so you could meet up with someone *more your speed*. And I also remember that you told him he had no chance with you. I think he remembers that too." She gave Em a knowing smile. So these were the fictions the Furies had told JD.

For a moment Em saw through Ty's beautiful exterior. The . . . figure standing before her was hideous, old, withered, with eyes like coal. Em felt herself choking at the horror of it. "You took the only thing that mattered," Em croaked out. The room seemed to be pulsing, wavering in and out.

Ty shook her head and looked vaguely troubled. "We don't take," she said. *"You choose."*

"You punish people," Em said, growing increasingly angry. She felt like there was black smoke inside her, billowing, slowly settling in her veins. "You punish people even when they're sorry for what they did. Even when they want to take it back."

"Ah." A small, sad smile played on Ty's lips. "But you can't take it back, can you? Isn't that the lesson to learn?"

"It's not up to you to play teacher," Em shot back. There were only three feet between her and Ty. If she took one step forward, she could touch her. Em felt the urge to lunge for Ty's neck.

"The world is a very unfair place," Ty said, a calm coming over her face. "We just want justice."

"You don't care about justice. You just want revenge." Em's voice was a low growl.

Ty smiled again—this time, it was both beautiful and terrifying. "I guess we take what we can get," she said.

And then Ty was gone. As though she'd turned to ashes and scattered, dust blew around the room for a second and then settled.

Em was left alone, gasping as though suffocated by smoke and fire.

CHAPTER FOURTEEN

In the cold light of day—the air had literally cooled to a seasonal thirty-five degrees—Skylar knew that Gabby wasn't to blame for any of last night's disasters. It wasn't Gabby's fault that "Dot-Crotch" was still ringing in Skylar's ears; it wasn't Gabby's fault that when Skylar had looked up after tripping over the log, all she'd seen were faces distorted by laughter, like reflections in a fun-house mirror. But that didn't stop Skylar from obsessively recalling Gabby's face shining down through the shadows, full of pity. Every time Skylar pictured it, she wanted to puke.

Which was why she'd been screening Gabby's calls all day. She'd slept as late as possible, and then watched several hours of bad television while Aunt Nora was at the indoor farmers' market and running errands. Every time she finally started to relax, strains of "Let Me Entertain You" would seep back into her consciousness.

And out of her humiliated haze, she remembered Em talking to her. Her memories were fuzzy and Em had seemed to be babbling, but some of the words stuck with her—something about Meg and her cousins being dangerous? Something about them knowing her secrets?

She squirmed on the brown suede couch, finding it impossible to get comfortable. The question rang in her mind: Meg couldn't possibly know the full story of her Dot-Crotch past, right? No one could. It must have been a coincidence that those boys had somehow found that old video.... A terrible, humiliating coincidence ...

She just needed to lie low for a few days. Figure out how to do damage control. Maybe if she called Meg and asked her a few veiled questions, she could figure out how much people knew.... But when she dialed Meg's number, there was no answer.

She still hadn't heard from Meg by Sunday evening, nor had she picked up any of Gabby's calls. Or showered. Or changed out of her sweatpants. Or thought about her homework. Earlier Aunt Nora had tried to figure out why Skylar had been moping for a day and a half. "Anything you want to talk about, sweetheart?" Skylar had answered with a curt *"No."*

As her aunt continued to pry ("Did you go to a party last

night?"), Skylar's eyes fell on the turquoise pendant that hung around her neck. Guiltily, she found herself wondering whether Nora had noticed that some of her other necklaces were missing. If she had, she hadn't said anything about it.

"I hope you're hanging out with the right people, Skylar," Nora said. "I've been meaning to ask, have you run into a girl named Drea? Drea Feiffer? Her mother and I used to be friends—"

Skylar interrupted. She didn't need her aunt's social charity. "I have enough friends, Aunt Nora. I just need some space." Now her aunt was out cooking meals for an elderly neighbor, something she did every Sunday. Skylar was grateful for the silence. She was heating up a can of tomato-basil soup on the stove when the doorbell rang, interrupting her self-pitying reverie and causing her to drop the ladle with a clang.

She peered through the lace curtains that bordered the front door. Gabby was standing on the stoop, juggling her purse and a giant tote bag. "Let me in," Gabby mouthed. Skylar hesitated, but only for a second.

Then she opened the door a crack, finding it difficult to make eye contact and wondering vaguely what her hair must look like. "What do you want?"

"I was worried about you, Sky," Gabby said, pushing her way in the door and down the hall. "You haven't answered my calls."

"I've been . . . busy," Skylar mumbled.

Gabby raised her eyebrows, and Skylar could feel her eyes sweeping over the sweatpants, the ratty sweatshirt, the mussed-up hair. She knew she looked the opposite of busy.

But Gabby just chirped, "Are you cooking something? It smells good."

Skylar trailed Gabby into the kitchen, suddenly having lost her appetite. "Soup," she said sullenly, noting that Gabby, too, was wearing sweats—only hers looked fresh and stylish, like she'd just come from a clarifying yoga class.

"Skylar, babe, look at me," Gabby said as she unloaded her things onto the kitchen table, dropping her voice the way she did when she wanted to be taken seriously. She put her palms on the table and leaned forward. "I know why you haven't been picking up my calls. But listen. Do not give the party—or anything that happened that night—another thought."

"That's easy for you to say," Skylar choked out, turning off the stove as she smelled the soup starting to burn.

"I promise that everyone will forget about that video . . . and everything else . . . soon," Gabby said, coming up behind Skylar to peer into the pot. "Yum. Do you want me to dish some out?"

"I'm not that hungry anymore," Skylar said. Out of habit, she moved her hand down her arm to fidget with her silver watch. But she wasn't wearing it, so she was left awkwardly holding her wrist and staring at Gabby expectantly.

"Well, how about a bevvy instead?" Gabby said, walking

back to the table and digging in the tote, from which she pulled a half-full handle of Malibu rum and a carton of pineapple-orange juice. "Your aunt's not home, is she? Let's have a cocktail and relax. It's been a crazy weekend. Is that okay? I brought these just in case."

Skylar glanced at the clock. Nora wouldn't be home for at least two hours—she cooked at Mrs. Davis's house and usually took a long time dividing various casseroles into meal-size portions and labeling them for the elderly woman, who had lived right down the road for more than seventy years.

"No, but I have a lot of homework—"

Gabby cut her off. "So do I," she said with a grimace. "But we can do it later. I was thinking we could brainstorm about the dance a little bit. You know, get the creative juices flowing. I brought over this old scrapbook of other dances. So that you could see what we've done already?"

There was something so earnest, so undeniably sweet about Gabby's proposal, that Skylar couldn't say no. "Okay. But not for too long." She knew it was important to have Gabby in her corner. And if Gabby could overlook her embarrassing past, so could the rest of Ascension. She hoped.

"Yay! Good choice," Gabby said, opening up the cabinet next to the sink in a hunt for glasses. Skylar watched her pour, trying to figure out what was different about Gabby this evening. She seemed smaller than usual, and not just because she was wearing one of her few pairs of sneakers instead of platforms.

They brought the drinks—syrupy and sweet, "like summer," Gabby kept saying—into the living room and settled into the couch, placing the pint glasses on the coffee table in front of them and propping the scrapbook between them on their knees. Gabby took Skylar on a chronological tour of last year's homecoming, Spring Fling, and Valentine's Day dances, with a few nonschool holiday parties and summer beach bashes thrown in for good measure. Skylar noticed that she sipped from her glass after almost every page.

"Oh yeah, I remember when Fiona wore that dress—it had the coolest back." *Sip.* "See how the band was right in the middle of the gym at this one?" *Sip.* "Oh my god, I cannot believe I kept this picture in here, I look like a *whale!*" *Sip.* "I think last year's Spring Fling was the best one. My crowning achievement so far. . . ." *Sip.* Until her first drink was gone.

And then, out of the blue: "I have been so stressed out lately," Gabby said, just the slightest bit too loudly.

Skylar didn't know what to say. "Really?" *You could have fooled me. And everyone else.*

"I mean, looking at these pictures, it just reminds me of how much *work* goes into . . ." Gabby trailed off.

"Being you?" Skylar filled in, trying to keep the bite out of her voice.

"I guess so—even though I know that sounds dumb. I mean,

I know I am so lucky. You know? But I just find myself being, like, totally . . . I'm just tired." Gabby was staring down into her glass, watching the ice cubes melt. When she spoke again, her words had a staccato quality. "Part of me thinks it was easier when I was with Zach. One less thing to worry about, maybe? But now there's just so much. Too much. I mean, SATs and the dance and, you know, being single . . . It's like, what do I even focus on? I have to be perfect at all those things? Like my brothers. They're both at Duke. People expect me to be, like, a girl version of them." She ended her rant staring at an African mask that Aunt Nora had hanging on her wall.

Skylar still didn't know how to respond. It was shocking to hear Gabby talk like this. Gabby, who had everything and made it look so simple.

"I mean, and it's not even Zach that I miss the most," Gabby said, looking at Skylar again. "At least without him I always had Em . . . but she's never around anymore, and when she is, she's just being weird. I don't know what's up with her, and it's exhausting trying to figure it out."

Skylar listened, letting Gabby's words soak in. She tried to muster some sympathy, but it was hard. She wanted to say, *People expect you to be perfect because you act like you're* already *perfect.* And as far as Skylar could tell, Gabby was a lot like her older brothers—she had plenty of friends and admirers, with or without Em and Zach.

"I'm going to go make myself one more drink," Gabby said suddenly, standing up from the couch and heading back toward the kitchen. Skylar accompanied her, gulping down the remains of her own watered-down beverage.

Gabby poured equal parts of rum and juice into her glass. "It's not like I don't love being busy and helping plan things and, you know, being a girl—caring about clothes and my hair and stuff—but I guess I'm just . . . worn-down, or something," she said, holding her drink in one hand and absentmindedly fiddling with her key chain, which had been on the table, with the other. She was saying she was run-down, but her anxiety seemed to give her a frantic quality. "People don't understand that. They think it's all fun-fun-fun. But sometimes"—at this, her voice got quiet—"I just want a break."

There was a silence as her words sank in. "So why don't you take one?" Skylar finally asked. "It sounds like you're going to burn out." But Skylar knew that Gabby wouldn't take a break— why would she, when things were going so well?

Gabby nodded. "I know I should, but . . ."

But it's just too nice to bask in the glow of perfection, huh?

Gabby was staring down at her keys, still fidgeting. Dangling from the chain was a plastic frame about the size of a matchbook. Gabby thrust it toward Skylar. "Look at this," she said.

The photo was of Gabby and Em. They were both making funny faces, and their arms were draped around each other.

The photo was supersaturated; the colors were vivid.

"I know we look so immature, but I love that picture," Gabby said as she refreshed Skylar's cocktail. "We just took it this fall— my mom went to a broadcasting conference in New York City, and we went with her. That was in Times Square."

"This was just a few months ago?" For a second Skylar forgot she was sulking. She was genuinely surprised. "Em looks so different now." And it was true. The girl in the plastic frame was not the same girl Skylar knew. The Em that Skylar knew would never be so . . . silly. And the Em that Skylar knew had something heavy behind her eyes. The girl in the photo with Gabby—there was nothing in her eyes but joy.

"I know, she looks different these days," Gabby said, taking the key chain back and placing it carefully beside her purse. "She's skinnier. And paler. Not that she looks bad. I mean, she's always had great skin. . . . I totally envy it."

Skylar scoffed. "You have great skin too, Gabs."

"Well, thanks," Gabby said, blushing slightly—or was that the rum? "Thank god you've never seen me after I've eaten shellfish. I'm totally allergic. One bite and my skin gets all red and puffy. . . . I used to have nightmares about my skin being like that all the time." She shuddered.

As they went back into the living room Skylar had a vision of her and Gabby taking a photo that would replace the one of Gabby and Em. It gave her comfort. Despite the rum and juice,

Skylar felt like she was starting to see more clearly: Gabby liked her. Gabby was on her side.

Settled into the couch again, Gabby flipped to the page in her scrapbook dedicated to last year's Valentine's Day dance, which had an "eco-friendly" theme.

"Everyone was really on a going-green kick last year," she told Skylar, giggling a bit as she took another swig from her glass. "And you know, V-Day is all about *looooooove*. So the theme was We Heart the Earth. People liked it. All our stuff was recycled— you know, like the cups? And part of the proceeds went to Greenpeace."

Skylar ran a hand through her hair and felt how greasy it was; she wished she'd had time (or energy) for a shower over the last day and a half. Gabby may have been complaining about being tired, but she'd obviously still washed her hair. "Have you had any ideas about this year's theme?"

Gabby pouted and finished off her second drink. "No. I really want to come up with a killer idea—I've been waiting for the light bulb to go on over my head! But . . . nothing." And then, noticing her empty glass, she sprang up from the sofa. "I'm going to get one more," she said, scampering off before Skylar could say a word.

While Gabby was in the kitchen, Skylar checked the time on her phone: 8:15. Nora would probably be home within the hour. She'd have to get Gabby upstairs by then, considering how tipsy she was getting.

"I mean, if the dance has a good theme, I'm pretty much guaranteed to be the Queen of Spring," Gabby was saying as she walked back into the living room, her eyes locked on her almost-overflowing glass. "And that will prove to everyone that . . . I'm fine. I'm fine without Zach. I'm fine. Does that make sense?" She looked at Skylar with big doe eyes, one single curl falling over her left eyebrow. She sat, but her knee was bobbing up and down.

"It makes sense," Skylar said, nodding and putting a tentative hand on Gabby's shoulder. "I know you'll come up with something good. Even better than We Heart the Earth."

"Speaking of which"—Gabby perked up suddenly and brushed the errant tendril from her eye—"I was reading about all of these natural skin-care recipes—like, masks that you can make out of eggs, and oatmeal scrubs. We should do that! They're good for the planet *and* they make us prettier!"

Skylar looked at her skeptically. "What? Like, now?"

"No time like the present!" Gabby squealed. She was definitely tipsy. Skylar wondered how she would get home. She obviously couldn't drive.

Doing facials would at least get Gabby upstairs before Aunt Nora came home, so Skylar consented to Gabby's proposal and helped her rummage in the kitchen for ingredients: olive oil, oatmeal, and eggs from the fridge.

In the upstairs bathroom Gabby insisted they turn on the shower so that the steam could "open the pores"—another tip she'd read about in *Cosmo*. She was in a good mood again. The alcohol had obviously relaxed her. Skylar was glad that, for once, *she* wasn't the slurry one. And she decided not to point out the obvious—that running the water kind of negated the whole "save the planet" thing.

"It's lucky that you're into the whole natural thing right now," Skylar said as they cracked the eggs in small bowls that Skylar had set on the back of the toilet. "I don't really have a lot of fancy beauty products."

"Oh, neither do I," Gabby breezed, draining her glass. "The only thing I absolutely cannot live without is my La Mer face cream. My mom got it for me a couple of years ago, and it's absolutely crucial. Have you ever tried it? I can totally share mine with you. Next time we're at my house you have to put some on. It's like insta-glow."

Skylar knew what Gabby was talking about—she'd read about La Mer in *InStyle*. She knew it was extremely expensive—the kind of stuff celebrities used—and felt another flare of jealousy. But just then Gabby flicked her with a bit of olive oil, and Skylar couldn't help but giggle. They mixed the facials with their fingers, laughing at the gloppy mess that formed in the bowls.

"This is going to be fun," Skylar said, getting into it, loving the way the oil coated her fingertips, smelling sweet and earthy.

"The oil will be great for your skin," Gabby said, looking at Skylar intently. "It's supermoisturizing."

Was Gabby saying that her skin was too dry? Was there an insult cloaked in that "helpful advice"? She looked at Gabby through the mirror, searching for the Lucy look.

But Gabby was just staring kindly at her through the mirror. It gave Skylar a pang of sadness for some reason. She was so used to being tortured and humiliated by Lucy, or yelled at by her mom, that it was almost harder work to know how to act when someone was being *nice* instead of pitying or just plain mean. Skylar wanted so badly to just enjoy having a good friend. Someone who cared about her. But she couldn't relax. Couldn't stop worrying.

Maybe some girls just aren't meant to be happy.

That was what Skylar was thinking as she stared at Gabby's face in the mirror, where the steam from the shower was spreading slowly, forming white tendrils.

"That's pretty, isn't it? Kind of . . . smoky?" Skylar touched her finger to the steamy part of the mirror and made a streak.

And then Gabby's face changed completely. She slammed her hand to her forehead. "That's it!" She stood up, pointing at the mirror. "That's the theme!"

"What is?" Skylar said, snapping out of her sad mood.

"Smoke and Mirrors!" Gabby turned to Skylar with a wide, gleeful smile, then picked up her glass, gave a "Cheers," and tipped it back, slurping the last drops. "Smoke and Mirrors," she repeated, satisfied. And Skylar had to admit that it was a great theme.

After all, wasn't popularity pretty much just a big illusion?
Just like that, an idea started forming in Skylar's head.

"Ugh . . . I am *hung*over," Gabby said as a greeting when she and
Skylar met just before the dance committee meeting on Monday
afternoon. Last night, after her fourth rum and juice, Gabby had
ended up calling her parents, telling them that she and Skylar
were having a cram session (she'd enunciated *very* carefully to
avoid sounding as drunk as she was), and sleeping over. That
morning Skylar had reluctantly opened her closet to Gabby.
Skylar was embarrassed at her limited wardrobe choices, many of
which were too big even for Skylar these days.

"This is perfect." Gabby had grabbed one of Skylar's most
recent purchases—a silky lilac tunic—off a hanger. "I have leggings in my gym locker—did you know that I have a whole
emergency closet in there, practically?—plus a belt and my
crappy black boots. I'll be all set."

Skylar marveled over the fact that despite the lingering puffi-
ness under Gabby's eyes—and the fact that her hair was clipped
back, which it almost never was—Gabby still looked pretty, even
in the harsh fluorescent glare of the Ascension High hallway
lights.

"I'm sorry, sweetie," Skylar said, pulling a vial of ibuprofen
out of her purse. "Want some?"

"Savior!" Gabby shook two capsules into her palm and threw

them in her mouth, followed by a swig from her Poland Spring water bottle.

As she did so Skylar sighed dramatically. "Speaking of savior . . . I was hoping you might be mine, too."

"What's up?" Gabby asked, gulping back the pills.

"I spilled coffee all over my shirt last period. . . . Do you think you could lend me something to wear just for the meeting? From your emergency stash? I don't want to smell like coffee the whole time." Skylar made her eyes as wide as possible and pointed to her shirt, which did, in fact, have a bit of coffee on it.

"You can barely see it! You're being paranoid," Gabby said, linking arms with Skylar and turning in the direction of the committee meeting.

"Gabs, please? I just don't want to give people one more thing to laugh at, okay?" Her voice shook slightly, and for a split second Skylar didn't even know if the tremble was fake.

Instantly Gabby's expression softened. "I totally get it," she said, swiveling in the opposite direction. "But we have to run. I don't want to be late for the committee."

"Here's the thing," Skylar said as though she'd just thought of it. "I have to stop in and see Mr. Capron really quickly about my French homework. Why don't I do that, you run to the gym, and we'll reconvene at the meeting?"

As they went their separate ways, Skylar felt a rising sensation of both panic and exhilaration. Her plan was working. Sure, she'd had to lie (there was no homework in French today), and she'd stained one of her favorite shirts (on purpose), and yes, there was a chance the whole thing could blow up in her face, but it was worth it. It was all worth it. She kept channeling her conversations with Meg. *If you want something badly enough, you have to be willing to do anything to get it.* She felt a nagging thirst at the back of her throat, the same itch that used to overcome her backstage at pageants. She cleared her throat violently.

This was her chance.

She walked confidently into the classroom where the planning committee meeting would take place; everyone else had already arrived.

"Hi, guys," she chirped brightly, slinging her bag under a desk as she slid into her chair. It felt like her senses were on superalert—she could feel the smooth plastic chair through her boot-cut jeans, and the air seemed to slice through her shirt. "Jeez, is the AC on in here or something?" She made a show of wrapping her scarf—the skull scarf—tighter around her neck. Then she cleared her throat again before continuing. "Gabby asked me to start the meeting without her. She had to run down to the gym," Skylar said, doing her best to keep her expression neutral. "And I'm glad, because I am *too* excited to wait for her. You all know that the Dusters said yes, right?" There were nods indicating that they did. "Well, now I have even better news—I thought of a theme, you guys!"

"You did?" Photo Boy, a.k.a. Jeff, looked surprised.

You'd be surprised what I can do, buddy, Skylar thought with a small flicker of triumph. But instead, she adopted a shy, closed-lipped smile, and went on. "I think the theme of the dance should be . . ."—she added a dramatic pause before continuing—"Smoke and Mirrors! I thought of it the other night when Gabby and I were hanging out. I was thinking that we could get a fog machine and hang giant veils from the ceiling so everything's all hidden and dreamy? We'd set up a bunch of mirrors, of course. We could even hire a magician—"

A girl named Mara laughed. "A magician? This isn't my sixth birthday party."

Skylar started feeling warm, but she held her ground. "Well, the term 'smoke and mirrors'"—she put air quotes around the words—"comes from magic tricks, when magicians used to make things look like they were appearing or disappearing by using mirrors, or smoke."

"Thanks for the history lesson," Mara said dryly.

"And there are, like, cool magicians," Skylar added with a note of defensiveness.

"I actually think it's a great idea," said Sara.

"I agree," Jeff said. "Smoke and Mirrors is an awesome idea, Skylar."

Just then Gabby ran into the room, clutching a blue T-shirt in one hand. She looked confused. "Um, hi? Sorry I was late, I was just—"

"That's okay, Gabs," Skylar said, tapping the desk next to her, indicating that Gabby should sit down. "We *just* started."

"Skylar was just telling us about her awesome idea," Tim said. "This year's Spring Fling—Smoke and Mirrors." He shook his head. "It'll be great for visuals," he added as an aside to Skylar.

"Wait, what?" Gabby's eyebrows shot up. "Smoke and Mirrors was *my* idea." She turned to Skylar, confused. "Why didn't you guys . . . ?" She trailed off, rubbing her temple with one hand. She looked to Skylar, still holding the shirt she'd retrieved from her gym locker. "I thought . . ."

The others were talking over her now, and although Skylar felt a little guilty, she tried to bury the emotion. This little lie wouldn't hurt Gabby that much, but it *would* help Skylar get the kind of attention and respect she needed to make people forget about the party, and to win over Pierce. Really, what was the harm?

Gabby barreled over to Skylar. "Smoke and Mirrors was *my* idea," Gabby said quietly, trying to be subtle while the rest of the group was debating how to get fog machines.

Skylar spoke calmly. "The whole point was that we both blurted it out at the *same time*—don't you remember?" She smiled at Gabby like she was a child. Like Lucy used to smile at her.

"But I thought of it," Gabby said, insistent, louder now. The others fell silent, listening. It was rare for Gabby to lose her cool.

Skylar kept the same condescending smile on her face. "Oh

god, Gabs. I didn't realize you were *that* drunk," she said with a laugh. "Don't you remember? How we were waiting for the bathroom to steam up for our nature facials and we both said 'Smoke and Mirrors' at *the exact same time*? It was a total great-minds-think-alike moment!"

Her voice stayed level as she spoke, lending the lie—she hoped—credibility. She knew how this stuff worked. Gabby would only embarrass herself if she continued to claim it was her own idea.

Gabby must have realized the same thing. She stared at Skylar for one more second. "Totally," she said haltingly, mechanically. "I remember now. I love the idea. I can't wait to start planning."

People started buzzing again.

Mara asked, "So, Skylar, do you think I should go to the Party Shop and see if I can get a fog machine?" Skylar could feel Gabby actually flinch next to her.

"Sure," Skylar said with a toothy smile. "And I was think-ing, for tickets? Why don't we sell these 'invisible tattoos'—I saw them at Spencer Gifts at the mall. You put yours on your hand on the night of the dance, and then whoever's at the door flashes a black light on your hand, and the fake tattoo becomes visible, and that's your ticket in!"

"Whoa, that would be so cool," Tim said. The other girls squealed their approval as well. "Why don't you be in charge of ticket sales, Sky?"

Another girl, this one wearing her hair in low pigtails, jumped in. "I'll help, Skylar. Just tell me what to do. People are going to be so excited about this."

As the meeting continued everyone directed their questions about decor and details to both Gabby *and* Skylar. Hey, she was the new cochair, right? Plus, she reasoned, the tattoo idea legitimately *was* hers. And this turn of events might be exactly the teeny little advantage she needed—and really, she was barely evening out the playing field, as Meg had put it.

Despite her bewilderment, Gabby was still as adorable and perfect as ever, fielding questions and delegating tasks.

No. Looking at Gabby, Skylar definitely didn't feel *that* bad.

At home that evening, perched in front of her mirror, trying to squeeze a tiny zit on her forehead before it grew into a monster, Skylar finally got a text from Meg. *Sorry was out of touch. Family stuff. Let's catch up tomorrow. xo.*

She wondered what kind of family stuff had kept Meg out of touch for days. She pictured Meg's birdlike features, Ty's expressive eyes and mouth, and Ali's 1950s pinup body. *They must have, like, perfect genes or something.*

As she leaned in closer, trying to catch a glimpse of even one stray hair below her eyebrows, she knocked her eyeshadow onto the tile floor. It landed with a clatter, breaking the fine cake of powder into a silvery dust. Skylar sighed. *What a waste.*

Grabbing a tissue, she bent down, scooped it up, and threw it away. There was nothing in her little trash can but a leftover glob of the oatmeal–olive oil scrub.

Weird . . . Ty had dyed her hair in here just the other day when she and Meg and Ali were getting ready for the party. Skylar hadn't taken out the trash, not during her weekend of immobile moping. But there was no evidence of Ty's transformation . . . no used hair dye, no applicators. No wet towels, no errant dye stains on the sink or tub. She'd certainly never dyed her own hair so . . . neatly.

There was probably a simple explanation. Maybe Ty hadn't used all the dye. Maybe she'd taken the rest home with her. Maybe Ty had dyed her hair the same way she did everything else—flawlessly.

Which brought Skylar's thoughts back around to her mission: to get what she wanted and deserved. All the embarrassing stuff was going to be water under the bridge by tomorrow, when Skylar started selling dance tickets and leveraging her social prowess into social status.

A rush of adrenaline and power ran through her veins as she shut off the bathroom light. *It's working.*

CHAPTER FIFTEEN

Em had swallowed her pride and called Drea several times over the weekend; no answer. She'd even texted Crow: *Did Drea get her phone back?*

When Crow responded *Yes,* Em felt even worse. So Drea was deliberately avoiding her. It proved that Drea was still pissed. . . . Or could Drea be in trouble? Maybe there was another reason? Something to do with JD? Or the Furies? Em was getting anxious. Of course she wanted to apologize for freaking out at JD's, but she also wanted to tell Drea about the creepy house and how Skylar was wearing an orchid and probably knew the Furies. . . .

Despite the fact that their friendship was so new, Drea's absence gnawed at Em. It reminded her how much they didn't talk about. It was like there was something big that Drea wasn't spilling. A secret. Em was becoming increasingly curious about Drea's connection to the Furies. Why would she be so obsessed with them but not tortured by them in the same way Em was?

Em waited like a stalker outside all of Drea's afternoon classes, but there was no sign of Drea at school on Monday. On Tuesday, when Drea was still absent, Em ran around to each of her teachers, making up an excuse about Drea's "mystery illness" and collecting her homework assignments for her. It was the least she could do to prove that she cared.

It also provided an opportunity to spy on JD, who she spotted coming out of his and Drea's American history class, stuffing papers into his backpack as he walked. She looked at his back as he went down the hallway away from her. Working on his dad's car was bulking him up—he seemed more muscular than usual. She ached for him. And while she considered asking him if he knew where Drea was, she didn't want to know if he did.

Em's anxiety began to skyrocket. Had the Furies gone after *Drea*? There hadn't been any sign that Drea had been marked—the opposite, in fact. Drea had always seemed like the hunter, not the hunted. But still . . . people going MIA made Em extremely nervous these days.

At lunch Em sat down at the table intent on continuing her conversation with Skylar, who had become a fixture at their traditional table in the Gazebo—which was almost unheard of for a sophomore.

But Em couldn't get a word in edgewise. The whole vibe at the table was bizarre. Gabby seemed somewhat dazed and out of sorts, while Skylar was talking a mile a minute to an apparently rapt audience of Fiona, Lauren, Jenna, and the rest of their crew. Skylar barely glanced at Em when she sat down.

"So I'm trying to arrange a predance dinner with the Dusters—VIP only," Skylar was saying. "Isn't that the best idea?" The girls squealed.

Em had heard through this morning's grapevine that Skylar had been the one to come up with the Spring Fling theme. She knew that this turn of events must have stung Gabby's pride, given that Gabby had talked about struggling to find a theme just a few days ago, as they'd gotten ready for the party in the Haunted Woods. Em kicked herself for not having helped brainstorm. Not that she would have been much help. She could picture it now: *How about an insane supernatural witch-beast theme, Gabs?*

Gabby turned away from the other girls at the table, who were all babbling excitedly about the dance. "Bt-dubs, I wanted to ask you, were you at the old mall yesterday? I could have sworn I saw you." Gabby picked at her wrap. Em looked her over, taking in the drooping curl over Gabby's left ear, the frayed thread over the top button of her cardigan.

"Nope. Wasn't me," Em said. "Were you doing some retail therapy or something?"

"I went after the dance committee meeting, to return a

dress." Gabby leaned in and whispered, "It was so much like the dress that Skylar had on the other night. I wouldn't want her to see me wearing it and think I was copying her or something, you know? Or that I thought she was copying me."

That was so like Gabby—to be concerned for Skylar's feelings, and not realize that Skylar *was* blatantly copying her.

"I called out to you," Gabby continued. "I figured that since you skipped the committee meeting, maybe you didn't want me to see you, or something."

Em winced. Had she really been that bad of a friend recently, that her bff thought she'd blatantly ignore her in public? "I haven't set foot in any mall—old or new—in months," Em said, relieved to be speaking a truth for once.

"Too busy doing other stuff, huh?" The words breezed out of Gabby's mouth, but they bordered on bitter. She was studying her salad carefully. "I could have sworn it was you."

"I'd never ignore you, Gabs. And I'd love to look for sweaters," Em said, trying to steer the conversation back around to a normal zone. "Maybe we could go to that new vintage shop in Portland some weekend soon?"

"Yeah, for sure. Sometime soon," Gabby echoed.

But Em saw, with a pang, that Gabby didn't believe her.

Em struggled through her sixth- and seventh-period classes and was about to skip her last one to drive over to Drea's house. As everyone else scurried to eighth period, Em made for her locker; the skies were spewing an angry winter rain, and she needed her raincoat.

It was when she passed the library that she thought of it: the book. Crow had told her that Sasha Bowlder might have been the one to have stolen *Conjuring the Furies*. It was a long shot, but . . .

About a month ago Drea had pointed out Sasha's locker to Em. The administration had cleaned off the slurs (*WITCH* and *PSYCHO*), but Drea wasn't sure if anyone had ever opened up the locker and taken out what was *inside*.

"Maybe someday I'll have Fount help me break in," she'd said at the time, and Em had nodded, immediately distracted by thinking about JD's capable mind and hands.

Eighth period would be over in thirty-five minutes. She had just enough time.

Em speed-walked to the language arts wing and found the locker that looked scrubbed clean, with whitish patches where the words had been. She dug in her purse for her wallet and found her library card. What better use for it than jail-breaking a missing book?

Em shoved the card in where the lock was and started fussing with it, turning it this way and that. Nothing. Why did they make this look so easy on cop shows? She took a step back to reevaluate. Maybe if she used it to pry off the dial? About to give up, she gave the card another jiggle in the slot . . . and heard it click. She caught her breath.

The door swung open with a loud creaking sound, and Em peered around quickly to make sure no one else was in the hall to witness her break-in. Then she turned back to the locker and gasped. It was Sasha's stuff—strewn everywhere, just the way most kids' lockers look. Something about the haphazardness of all her things filled Em with a sudden sadness. *She was just like the rest of us.* And then, one day, she was gone.

Em tried to swallow the lump forming in her throat as she shakily bent down to pick up some of the old textbooks and an old crumpled black sweater she recalled seeing Sasha wear. And then there it was: a hardcover book, bound in leather with raised lettering on the cover. *Conjuring the Furies.*

Em's eyes got big. She looked to the left and the right; the hallway was still deserted. Her heart leaping, she took the book— the book Sasha had wanted badly enough to steal—from the locker and closed the door silently. She gripped the leather tightly and then walked deliberately, proudly, even, out of the building.

Drea wasn't at her house. Next stop: the Dungeon. By now school was over, and the parking lot was starting to fill up with cars. The Dungeon's windows were steamed up from the heat and the warm bodies inside. Walking through the double doors, Em scanned the low chairs and couches. No sign of Drea's purple locks, her half-shaved head, her raspy laugh. Em turned on her heel and headed back to her car, using a newspaper to cover her head (in her excitement over the book, she'd left her raincoat at school). She would have to go home and regroup, look at the library book, come up with a plan.

But when she reached her locked car and dug in her purse for her keys, she couldn't find them. *You have got to be kidding me,* she thought, peering into the driver's-side window. There they were, lying on the seat. Great. Now, thanks to her distraction, she was stranded at the Dungeon in the freezing rain.

Shaking her head in embarrassment, she dialed AAA. Then she ducked back into the shop to wait.

Once inside, she wished she'd denied the craving for caffeine. Because while she waited in line, someone tapped her on the shoulder.

She turned around. Crow was towering over her in a heavy green sweatshirt. He clearly hadn't shaved in a few days—his jawline was scruffy. He looked good. And kind of scary. Her stomach fluttered a little, and she had the urge to dodge him.

"I was just leaving," he said in that voice that sounded like honey on apples—sticky-sweet and smooth, with a bite underneath. "But if you're here, I could be convinced to stay. . . ."

"I'm actually waiting for someone," Em said.

"Ah, intriguing!" Crow said, grin never leaving his face. "Who's the lucky fella?"

Em allowed herself a self-deprecating smile. "The guy from Triple-A," she said. "Hot date."

"Bummer," he replied. "Want to come wait in my truck?"

"It would probably be more comfortable to wait in here," she replied haughtily.

"But there's something I want to show you in my car," he said, raising his eyebrows suggestively. "It's right there," he said, pointing to his truck just a few cars down from the Dungeon's front door.

She hesitated, watching the rain fall in sheets outside the coffee shop windows.

"I won't kidnap you. . . ." Then he added with a smile, "Even though I'd like to." Rolling her eyes, she nodded her consent.

The rain was coming down so hard that by the time they climbed into the cab of Crow's truck, she was soaked through.

The pickup smelled of wool and wood. Crow ran a hand through his wet black hair, then hooked his iPod up to the car speakers. The song that began to play was beautiful and mournful, one that seemed to perfectly match the gray day. She looked out the passenger-side window, watching the drops dance in the puddles and stream down the glass.

"Good thing I like purple," Crow said, and she turned to look at him quizzically. Then, the blush spreading from her ears to her cheeks to her neck, she realized what he was talking about— her bra. It was purple, and also completely visible through her wet shirt. The bra she'd purchased this Christmas, while obsessing over Zach. Em moved to cover herself, Drea's words rushing back: *He has a crush on you.*

"Relax," Crow said with a smirk. "I understand that members of the female species wear bras." He craned his neck to see what was stuffed behind the front seats and rifled through his messenger bag. He clearly couldn't find whatever it was he was looking for. Instead, with a sigh, he struggled out of his sweatshirt and started easing off his own shirt, a gray long-sleeved polo, which had stayed dry underneath.

Em watched with fascinated horror, unable to miss the fact that as he derobed the music seemed to swell. "Oh, no, you don't have to—I'm fine."

"While you do appear to be cold-blooded," he said, making her think of Gabby's recent observations, "I am not going to permit the Ice Princess of Ascension High to get pneumonia on my watch. I'll be stoned to death! Just take it." He thrust the shirt at her, and she caught a whiff of its boyness, like cloves and soap and fire.

"You really don't have to—" He put up his hand to cut her off, and she saw that underneath his right arm Crow had a snake tattoo along the side of his body. He was skinny, but his muscles were well defined. He threw his sweatshirt back on over his bare chest.

"Just put it on. This back-and-forth is boring," he said, and leaned forward to fiddle with his iPod.

Em realized that he was pretending to be busy so that she could change without feeling embarrassed. It was . . . gentlemanly. Still, she swiveled around and faced the rain-streaked window as she wriggled out of her wet shirt and into Crow's dry one, praying no one from school happened to pass by their corner of the lot.

"I came here in the first place looking for Drea," she decided to tell him. "She wasn't in school yesterday or today, and she won't pick up my calls. She's kind of MIA."

"Classic Feiffer," Crow said. "She's pretty hard to track. She'll come back, and she'll be fine. Then you can go back to watching Buffy marathons or whatever you girls do." For just a second Crow dropped the smile and looked serious. "Her mom died when she was young. I think that's why she has her dark days."

Em shivered, even in the warm, dry shirt.

"Em," he said, and his voice was different now, without the sarcastic lilt. "There's something I want to tell you."

Em's heart started beating faster.

He hesitated, but no words came.

"Yeah?"

"Oh, um, you look good in gray."

She was sure that wasn't what he'd wanted to say, but she didn't want to pry further. In the quiet, their breath began to fog up the car windows.

Then the music ended abruptly. He leaned forward and

began scrolling through the iPod again. The moment had passed. Em felt strangely disappointed. Crow turned on a new song, and the music changed, to something even more lovely—a lone guitar, picking a strange melody against droning background chords.

"This music is amazing," Em said, balling up her white shirt and putting it on the dashboard. "Who is it?" She pulled her damp hair into a low, wet bun.

Crow coughed. "It's . . . it's me. It's not finished yet. I'm still working on it. I can't quite see where it should go yet."

Em was momentarily speechless. "Wow. That's awesome, Crow. You're really talented."

"Don't sound so surprised, princess," he said shortly. "Just because I'm a high school dropout doesn't mean I'm an idiot."

"That's not . . ." But she didn't bother defending herself. She could see he was just playing with her. His eyes were smiling.

Em leaned back against the headrest and let out a big breath. It felt good to be in this truck, where nothing was expected of her.

Still, she couldn't help but continue to pry. "So, how long have you known Drea?"

Crow looked up, trying to remember. "Well, we started hanging out in middle school. You know, when things started to shake out. Cliques." He looked at her then, as though it was her fault that junior high school was a social nightmare. "We both hated that shit. And a crew kind of just . . . came together. A clique for people who hated cliques."

"I remember you then," Em said. "You used to skateboard at the edge of the teachers' parking lot."

Crow let out a laugh. "And got in trouble for it, like, once a week."

"I thought you were such rebels," Em said. "If I had gotten in trouble in middle school, it would have been the complete end of the world." She thought back to those days, when she and Gabby used to sit on the benches by the soccer field and make friendship bracelets and dream about dating boys in high school. She felt a quick spasm in her chest. Things were so simple then.

"We both were outcasts—she's practically an orphan," Crow continued. Em watched him, hearing the steady beat of the rain against the roof of the car. "And later, when I decided to drop out, she didn't harass me. Neither of us ever, like, pressured the other one. To talk, or to feel a certain way. We just both understood what it was like, I guess. To have things be . . . confusing."

Em thought about what Crow had said before—that Drea sometimes just needed to get away. "So you get it," she said. "When Drea wants to be alone." She wondered if Drea had ever talked to Crow about the Furies, but she didn't know how to ask.

"Not many people know how to be by themselves," Crow said. She thought about how alone she'd felt over the last few weeks. How she was getting used to dealing with stuff by herself.

All of a sudden she felt Crow's fingers against her jawline, tracing the curve from her neck to her chin. His fingers rested for a moment there, and then he turned her face toward his. He was leaning over the truck's bench seat, pulling her face gently to his. First he kissed her bottom lip, then her top, and then both together. She felt herself kissing him back, running her tongue along the soft skin of his lower lip, feeling him open his mouth slightly. They both shifted infinitesimally closer to one another, and an aching pressure filled Em's belly. She was taken aback and swept away at the same time; she could feel her hands trembling as they reached to circle Crow's neck. She couldn't help getting caught up in the urgency and rawness of it all: of being in his pickup truck, of their breath steaming up the glass while the rain continued to fall outside.

Then, without warning, he pulled away. Em looked at him, unconsciously bringing her hand to her mouth, not knowing what to say or do next.

"We shouldn't— We shouldn't be doing this," Crow stammered. "I'm not—you know I'm no good for you, Em."

"What?" Em took a deep breath, confused, attempting to quell the pulsing in her body as she tried to figure out what the hell was going on.

"It's just . . . I don't want you to get hurt." He looked at her imploringly as she cut him off.

"You don't have to say any more," Em said, grabbing for her things and noting, with great relief, that the AAA van was pulling into the lot. Even though her pride was wounded, she ached to kiss him again. *Jesus.* Now the Grim Creeper had rejected her. What was going on? "I have to go." She fumbled with the door handle and leaped from his truck, ignoring his single call after her and racing to her car, dizzy with mixed emotions. She barely felt the rain.

As the technician fiddled with her lock, she watched Crow's headlights swerve from the parking lot. What was she thinking? She was in love with JD, but here she was, letting another guy—Crow, of all people—kiss her in his pickup truck in public. JD's accusations, and his lack of trust, suddenly made a lot more sense. *Could you forgive me, if I'd done what you did? . . . You ditched me to go make out with some other guy.* That's what he'd said about following her to the Behemoth that night, about thinking that she was with another guy. It seemed now like less of a false memory and more of a prediction. Maybe JD was right—maybe she did, however unwittingly, toy with people's emotions.

She squeezed her hands against the steering wheel. *Get it together, Em.* The kiss with Crow was a fluke—a one-off. It had no bearing on her feelings for JD.

As she started to drive home she repeated it like a mantra: *It was a one-time thing. One-time thing.* But his words kept jutting into her consciousness. What had Crow meant when he'd said he didn't want her to get hurt? Was that his ego talking, or was he referring to something more?

Em turned onto Route 204, on the other side of the

Haunted Woods. A flash of purple caught her eye. Deep purple, reflected in her headlights against the falling dusk, bouncing ever so slightly. Like someone walking. As she got closer she saw that it *was* someone walking. And there was only one person in Ascension with purple hair.

"Drea?" Em pulled over and lowered her passenger-side window. "What the hell are you doing?"

"I thought I needed some exercise," Drea said dryly.

"Get in," Em ordered. "I've been looking for you for days."

Drea obeyed, getting into the front seat of the car along with a gust of cold air. The rain had caused her black eyeliner to smear into half-moons under her lower lashes, making her look both scared and tired. "I went to look at that house," she blurted out. "The one you mentioned in your voice mail."

"*Alone?* Why didn't you wait for me?" Em threw the car in park and turned her body to face Drea's. "Why didn't you call me back?"

"Nice shirt," Drea said, giving Em a once-over. Em knew that Drea recognized it as Crow's.

"Thanks." Em shrugged, avoiding the topic. "Now tell me what you did. Why didn't you call me first?" Em wanted to shake Drea for being so reckless.

"I needed to be alone," Drea said, avoiding Em's eyes.

Em exhaled slowly. Okay. If Drea needed to do things her way, Em would let her. It was better than losing her altogether.

"Listen, Drea, I'm sorry," Em tried to make her voice as level as possible. She tugged at the sleeves of Crow's long-sleeved shirt and was surprised to find that, like some of her own, this one had little thumbholes poked into the cuffs. "I'm sorry about the other night, at JD's. I'm just . . . I have some feelings for him—about him—that I'm not very used to. And I'm sorry if you think I'm a flake when I'm with my other friends. You're important to me. I've been really worried about you. . . ."

Drea waved her hand to cut Em off. "Okay, okay. Enough. I accept your apology. That's not important right now." She sucked in a deep breath. "The house, Em, the house you talked about?"

Em's heart sped up. "Did you find it?"

"Nowhere," Drea said quietly, and Em felt like she'd been punched in the stomach. "I made a huge loop. I've been out here for hours. No house."

Em felt like all the oxygen had been sucked out of the car. Her vision started to tunnel, the way it had at the bonfire. How could Drea not have seen the house? It was there. It was real.

"It was there, Drea. I saw it."

"I believe you," Drea said, turning to face her. "I know someone else who saw it once." Another pause.

"What? Who? Come on, Drea. Spit it out." Em thought she already knew the answer.

"Sasha," Drea said. "Sasha told me about a house in these woods. Before she died. That's when I gave her the snake pendant.

The one she was wearing when she . . . you know. Jumped." Drea cleared her throat and looked away.

Something deep within Em was spinning. Like a machine rumbling to life after a long dormancy. The book, the spells, the Furies. She was tantalizingly close to figuring out this awful riddle. But she bit her tongue. At this point, saying too much could get Drea in trouble too.

"And, Em? I found something else," Drea said, turning slowly back toward Em. She ran her hand nervously over the short-haired side of her head, which was starting to get messy and pixie-ish.

"What?" Em was breathless.

"You'll have to see for yourself. Go park at the turnaround," Drea said, pointing ahead. "I'll take you there now."

Despite the rain and her fear, Em parked without protesting and trudged with Drea into the woods, approaching, from behind, the clearing where the house would be. Em was certain she'd recognize the area when she stumbled on it, even as twilight continued to deepen around them. As they stomped through the rain, their shoes making sucking noises in the mud, Em looked for familiar signs. There had been a tall pine with a split trunk. She'd know it when she saw it.

"It's right around this bend," Drea said. "I can still see some of my footprints in the mud here."

Em looked up, squinting as hard rain fell into her eyes. There it was—the pine tree with two trunks, gnarled and stretching into the sky. The house should be right here. . . .

But it wasn't. There was the clearing, and Em could even smell the acrid scent of smoke, but there was no house here. Not even a foundation. Just a clearing, with something looming in its center. The trees moaned around them.

"This is where . . ." Em trailed off. She swallowed. "It was here. I swear it was."

"I believe you," Drea said again. But her eyes were hard. "Come look." She drew Em closer to whatever small structures were there in the middle of the circle.

Every nerve in Em's body was screaming for her to run away. Her skin was tingling; her breath was shaky.

"Come on, Em." Drea was insistent. They were both drenched.

With tentative steps, Em allowed Drea to lead her to what looked like small stone sculptures. No.

Not sculptures. Tombstones.

Three dark tablets, each marked with a carving of a flower. Em instinctively drew back. She knew those flowers. They were the same intricate orchids that the Furies carried. "What—what are these?" she whispered to Drea.

"Graves," Drea said grimly, as though that wasn't obvious.

Em's mind flashed back to Skylar's story—or rather, Skylar's aunt's story—about the three women who had died or been killed in Ascension's woods. Three women. Three stone graves. Three Furies.

"Something bad is going to happen soon," Em whispered. "I can feel it."

"Something bad is already happening," Drea said, her voice strained, as it had been in the car. "Let's get out of here."

Back in Em's car, they let an uneasy silence fall between them. Visions of crimson orchids ran through Em's mind—the one Ali had handed her in Boston, the one Skylar had had pinned to her dress the other night, the ones adorning those headstones back in the woods. The ones that meant you were . . . marked. In her mind, the flowers merged with images from Sasha's book, and with the stuff of pure imagination. Cauldrons. Bonfires. Sacrifice.

"Here," Drea said, breaking the quiet as she fished something out of her pocket. Em's breath caught in her ribs as Drea produced a gold-and-red snake pin from her jacket. "For protection. I noticed you lost yours."

Em reached out to take it, her hands still shaking. Here was Drea, trying to save another one of her friends from the Furies. Like two magnets with the same charge put together, something seemed to be pushing her hand away from the pin. As she made contact with the metal, she felt a sharp pain in her palm. She gasped, and the pin fell onto to the seat below.

"What's the matter?" Drea's tone was sharp.

"I—I must have pricked myself," Em said, examining her

hand. In the center of her palm was a deep-red mark and a bubble of blood forming where the pin had stabbed her. She wiped it away, leaving a bloody smear that led down to her wrist. She ignored the throbbing in her hand and stuffed the pin in her jeans pocket, Drea's eyes watching her closely. The rest of the ride home the pin stuck into her hip uncomfortably. Like a cramp, it was impossible to ignore.

So when she got home, she threw it hastily into the back of her T-shirt drawer. Obviously, this good luck charm wasn't going to work for her any better than it had worked for Sasha.

CHAPTER SIXTEEN

The idea had come to Skylar late last night: The dance ticket proceeds would go to the school activity budget, as usual, but the school could hold an additional raffle to raise money for the suicide prevention group Gabby had started in the wake of Sasha's and Chase's deaths.

The next morning she met with Mrs. Keough, a health teacher and Ascension's social activities adviser. "It's all well and good to talk about a suicide prevention club," Skylar said, furrowing her brow, "but what's the point if there's no money to fund it?" She'd arranged her face to look both innocent and concerned, and Keough had gone for it.

The announcement was made over the loudspeaker during homeroom: "Tickets are on sale today for the annual Spring Fling a week from Friday. We've got a great theme this year, courtesy of new student Skylar McVoy—so get your Smoke and Mirrors tattoo tickets while you can! And if you see Skylar in the halls today, thank her for organizing the first-ever Spring Fling raffle! Buy a raffle ticket for an extra five dollars and be entered to win a mystery prize! All raffle proceeds will go to the recently formed Ascension High Suicide Prevention Group. In other news, there's a swim meet today at . . ."

Skylar floated through the next few periods, feeling as though she was coasting on a cloud. Everyone—even juniors and seniors—smiled at her in the halls. In French, Jenna passed her a note: *Want to hang out after school?* The group of senior girls whom Skylar had noticed on her first day at Ascension— mostly field hockey players, with long, straight blond hair and equally good-looking lacrosse-playing boyfriends—approached her between third and fourth periods.

"Hey, you're Skylar, right?" said one of them. "I'm Jess. Awesome job with the dance and everything."

Skylar laughed like it was no big deal. "Oh, thanks," she said, letting her drawl drag out more than usual. She thought it made her sound more casual. "I'm just trying to bring some southern hospitality up north!"

The girls raised their eyebrows. Another one asked, "Oh, is that where you're from—down South? I heard that you just moved here, but I didn't know where from."

"Yeah, Alabama," Skylar said. Out of the corner of her eye she saw Sean and Andy walk by . . . which meant that Pierce was probably nearby too. She hoped he saw her chatting it up with these girls. "So, do you want to buy some tickets—I mean, tattoos?" She pulled a strip from the front pocket of her bag.

Jess nodded, digging in her jeans pocket. "We're thinking of pregaming with some of the football and lacrosse guys before the dance on Saturday. Want to come?"

"Like, with Sean and Andy?" She tried to sound as though she hung out with them all the time.

"Yeah, all those guys," another girl said, shelling out her money.

"Maybe," Skylar said. *You have to seem in demand.* That's what magazine articles always said about seeming popular and wanted. "I might have plans with Gabby and the girls. I'll let you know, okay?"

And then the cherry on top of everything: As she walked away from Jess and her friends Pierce appeared around the corner.

"Hey, Sky," he said with an easy smile. "I've been looking for you."

The feeling of elation made it difficult to breathe. "Really? Well, here I am!" She was going to be late for her next class, but she really didn't care.

"I wanted to talk to you about the dance," Pierce said, and

she could swear that he looked nervous. "But I've gotta run—I have an English quiz."

Pierce wanted to talk to *her* about the dance?! Skylar could have cartwheeled down the hall. Instead, she waved him off with a giggle. "Catch me at lunch," she said, as though she wouldn't have skipped the entire rest of the school day to hang out with him. "I don't want to get you in trouble." As soon as he was out of sight, Skylar did a tiny dance of joy.

Halfway into fifth-period lunch she did a mental tally. She'd already sold forty-five tickets today.

"Two tickets?" She smiled, syrupy-sweet, at the boy in front of her—cute, but a bit emo-looking, in a plaid blazer over a vintage T-shirt and jeans. He wore thick-framed glasses, like Fiona. She thought he might be a junior.

"Yeah, two please," the boy said, holding out ten dollars. Skylar ripped off two temporary tattoos and placed his cash in the metal box she'd been given by the front office.

Then, in a fake-stern voice, she issued a reminder: "Don't put them on until the night of. . . . We don't want their invisible powers to rub off!" She looked up at him. "Would you like to buy a raffle ticket for an additional five dollars? Proceeds go to the Ascension High Suicide Prevention Group."

"Shutting down the whole damn school would probably be more effective than starting a club, but sure, I'll buy one," he muttered, putting his books on the cafeteria table so he could get more money from his wallet.

"Great, thanks!" Skylar said, not really knowing if he was making fun of her or not. "What name should I put down?"

"I'm JD," the boy said, running a hand through his messy hair. "JD Fount."

As she racked her brain to think where she'd heard that name before, she caught a glimpse of Gabby's bouncing curls out the window that overlooked the parking lot, and a prick of anxiety pierced her bubble of confidence. She hadn't had the chance to run the raffle idea by her. Which she should have, of course, since Gabby was technically in charge of the dance. . . .

As Gabby and her companion came into clearer view, Skylar's heart sank even lower. Gabby was walking with Pierce. They both held waxy paper bags from Dunkin' Donuts, and their strides were in step. Now Skylar's bubble deflated entirely. A little off-campus coffee date. During the lunch period when Pierce was supposed to find *her*, to talk to *her* about the dance. She watched them circumvent the entrance to the cafeteria, presumably heading straight for their sixth-period classes. She swallowed hard; her mouth felt dry. She only sold two more tickets for the rest of lunch.

As soon as the last bell rang, Skylar headed for the ice cream shop. The hollow feeling in her stomach hadn't dissipated after lunch. With the image of Gabby and Pierce coming back from their lunchtime romp pounding in her mind, she'd skipped sixth period to find Meg, but when she'd arrived at Get the Scoop, she'd found the place bolted shut and dark inside. She'd pressed her face to the glass. All of the tables and chairs were stacked in a corner, almost as if it was closed for the season.

She texted Meg: *Why aren't you at work? I need to talk to you.*

I'll be there after school, Meg wrote back almost immediately. *See you soon.*

And she was. As soon as Skylar walked in the doors and saw Meg presiding cheerfully over the empty store, Skylar wanted to cry. Thankfully, she held it together.

"Hey, girl, what's the matter?" Meg leaped off her wobbly stool and glided over to where Skylar was standing, blinking fast.

"I came by earlier and you weren't here," Skylar said, pouting. "The whole place was locked up."

Meg waved her hand vaguely. "Oh, I just open it up when I need a shift," she said airily. "It is winter, after all. Not a big demand for ice cream. Now, tell me what's going on."

"Everything was going *so* well," Skylar choked out, trying to regain her composure.

"Yeah? They liked the raffle idea?" Meg put her skinny arm around Skylar's waist and maneuvered her toward one of the shop's uncomfortable wire chairs.

"Yes." Skylar sniffed. "But—it doesn't make any difference."

"Why not? What do you mean?" Meg motioned for her to keep talking as she leaned over to grab some napkins so Skylar could blow her nose.

"Gabby will always be cooler than me," Skylar burst out, "no matter what I do. And every guy will always pick her over me. Pierce will *never* like me back. Everyone in school was paying attention to me today. But he still chose her. He still went to Dunkin' Donuts with her." Skylar's voice rose to a whine as she finished her sentence.

"Hold on, hold on." Meg held up both hands. "That doesn't *necessarily* mean he likes her, Sky. You know that. Maybe it was just a friendly coffee date . . . ?"

Skylar frowned. "It wasn't friendly, just like it wasn't friendly when he tried to kiss her at the pj party. He said he had to talk to me about the dance, and then he completely flaked!" She let out a moan. "I hate her." She felt a twinge of guilt as soon as she pronounced the words. She didn't hate Gabby. She loved her. Gabby was her only friend. Besides Meg, of course.

Meg brushed one of Skylar's loose curls out of her face. "I can see how much you like Pierce," Meg said sympathetically. "And believe me, I know how it feels when someone else has what you want. But Pierce will notice you, I know it. He just needs to see that you have things to offer that Gabby doesn't." Meg tilted her head in the way she did sometimes, like a bird looking down at her from above. "Want some ice cream?"

Ice cream was the *last* thing she wanted right now. Even

thinking about it made her stomach turn. "No," she said. "I want to know what I could possibly have that Gabby doesn't. She's pretty and perfect, and that's why everyone loves her."

"I'm sure she has some weak spots," Meg said, her voice silky. "Everyone does. You just haven't found them yet. You've barely looked. And neither has Pierce. . . ."

Skylar sighed. She could feel the lump in her throat slowly melting. "I guess . . ." She was still doubtful.

"I'm telling you, nobody's perfect," Meg replied firmly, leaning forward so her hair framed her face like a curtain. "You just have to be willing to really *look* for your opportunity."

Skylar looked up. It almost sounded like Meg was talking about sabotage.

"Think about everything you've done to make this the best dance ever," Meg continued, smiling sweetly, still tilting her head ever so slightly. "You've worked so hard. Are you really going to give up now?"

The next day Skylar was just locking a stall door in the science wing bathroom when she heard two familiar voices swing through the door.

It was Gabby and Em.

"It's just that I feel bad for Skylar." That was Em's voice.

Skylar stepped up onto the toilet, praying they wouldn't try her stall. They didn't.

"I know, I know, me too," Gabby answered. "But, like, I just have so many people to worry about right now. I told you how I finally broke down and emailed Zach, right? Well, he never emailed me back, so last night I decided to just call him. Just to do it, you know? But his phone is off." There was a note of concern in her voice. "Like, off-off—like it's been shut off."

Both girls had exited their stalls by now and were washing their hands and primping in front of the mirror. Skylar could see them through the crack between her door and the wall.

"That's bizarre," Em answered, her voice sounding cagey.

"And I know I shouldn't have tried to contact him in the first place," Gabby went on, "but after everything I've been hearing, all this gruesome stuff about him not being able to play sports anymore . . . I just want to know what's going on, you know?"

"I totally get it," Em said. "I mean, he was a huge part of your life."

"And so that's why I think I've been reveling in the Pierce thing," Gabby continued. Skylar's breath caught in her lungs at the mention of Pierce. "It's not like I *want* to date him—I really do want to be alone right now. But it's nice to have some distraction."

Skylar stayed perfectly still—if they hadn't noticed they had company yet, maybe they wouldn't.

"I mean, I think that's fair. It's just . . . What about Skylar?" That came from Em.

"No, no, I still think they should be together!" Gabby's protest was high-pitched but earnest. "Like, if I can't take him right now, she should. She's totally adorable, and so is he."

Skylar tried to stop her legs from shaking. Here she was, Gabby Dove's pathetic charity case. Taking Gabby's leftovers, or the stuff she didn't want.

She listened to Gabby and Em leave and leaned against the inside of her stall door, letting the cool metal press against her forehead.

What about Skylar? The words echoed around in her mind; their pitying tone made her want to throw up.

She could barely contain herself during fourth and fifth periods. She called Meg immediately at lunch.

"Are you working today?"

"No, why?" Meg answered.

"Can you drive me somewhere?"

She skipped last period, met Meg in the parking lot, and directed her to Gabby's house.

"Wait down here," Skylar said as they pulled into the bottom of Gabby's long driveway. Skylar could see that there were no cars parked at the top of it; the Doves were still at work, and Skylar knew that Gabby had a spring cheerleading prep meeting after school. She was in the clear, at least for a little while.

"Are you sure you don't want to tell me what's going on?" Meg said, grinning. Skylar knew that Meg loved surprises.

"I'll tell you later. Just wait at the end of the driveway, on the street. I'll only be a few minutes." She pushed out of the maroon Lincoln and ran up the driveway toward Gabby's house. She was buzzing with anxiety; her fingers felt numb in her gloves. At the front door she rang the bell, just in case. No answer. Then she ran around to the back and knocked on the panes—again, she was just being cautious. But there was obviously no one home, and the Doves didn't lock their back door. Everyone who knew Gabby knew that. She and her mom were always forgetting their keys.

"Hello?" Skylar said as she stepped into the Doves' gleaming kitchen, where pictures of Gabby and her brothers covered the stainless steel refrigerator.

Skylar ran up the stairs, taking them two at a time, and into Gabby's bedroom. She took it all in. This was a reconnaissance mission. On the opposite side of the room, next to Gabby's neatly made bed, was a dresser, on top of which were all of Gabby's hair and face products. Her curling iron. Her face cream and scented moisturizers. Her makeup.

Next to the dresser was a chair where scarves and leggings and dresses were heaped haphazardly. Next to her small closet— "the absolute bane of my existence," Gabby was fond of saying— was a shoe rack, crammed with Gabby's trademark wedge heels in every color. Gold, red, teal, madras plaid. Straw heels, wooden heels, stacked heels.

Skylar allowed her fingers to brush against the downy, creamy comforter. It was hard not to think of Lucy as she made her way around Gabby's room, her feet sinking just barely into the plush wall-to-wall carpeting. Lucy, too, had had a room filled with pictures and trophies and stuffed animals—probably given to her by boyfriends. Lucy, too, had had clothes that fit her perfectly, and makeup that accentuated her perfect skin. Not like Skylar, whose closet was filled with clothes that would look good "once she lost a few pounds," whose makeup bag was packed with various tubes of cover-up to hide her seemingly constant rotation of breakouts.

Her determination started to wane. Her intent was to study Gabby and find her imperfections, but in this perfect room it was hard to imagine that Gabby had any weak points. Even as Gabby's own admission rang in Skylar's head—*I'm just tired. People expect me to be perfect*—it was becoming difficult to see anything but the pretty flawlessness of Gabby, her room, and her life.

Skylar felt the familiar sensation of jealousy beginning to boil, its hot fingers coiling around her veins, her throat, her tongue. It was impossible now to tamp down the burning shame that rose up every time she thought about what had happened at her Haunted Woods party, which was supposed to be her big "coming out"—instead, she had looked like a freak, and the only thing that actually "came out" was the color of her thong. No wonder Pierce would always choose Gabby over her.

Her sister had so fondly reminded her hundreds of times: *Some people are just late bloomers.* Of course, there was a tacit corollary to that statement: *Some people have it all, right from the get-go.* Her skin started to crawl with heat, as though she was in the spotlight of the unbearable pageant stage lights . . . as though she was covered in sticky, unflattering makeup . . . as though the laughing crowd was bringing a blush to her cheeks.

Skylar thought she heard a footfall behind her and spun around. Of course, she was alone. Lucy wasn't here anymore. Lucy would never hurt her again.

Still, blistering tears welled in her eyes. She let out a plaintive cry. She was *not* a loser anymore. She was a winner—and winners took what they wanted. It was the only way. She had seen that for herself.

She needed to tip the scales. If only Gabby could just be a little *less* cute—like if she got a bad breakout or something embarrassing—then she'd withdraw from the spotlight a bit. Just for a little while. Just long enough, maybe, to give Skylar a chance of being voted Queen of Spring at the dance?

Then she heard the sound of a car pulling into Gabby's driveway. She had to get the hell out of this house. Breathlessly, she ran downstairs and out the back door just as she heard the garage door start to grind open.

There was a woodshed off to the side of the house. She ducked inside it, peering through the slatted wood frame and watching as Marty Dove's car pulled into the garage. From somewhere above her she heard a faint buzzing sound. She tried to ignore it, but it only seemed to grow louder.

Skylar attempted to turn around without upsetting any of the rakes or grill instruments that leaned against the wall. Almost directly above her was a small, papery gray beehive attached to a beam. Shit. She whirled around too quickly, knocking against the wall and rocking the whole structure.

Bzzzz. Several bees came pouring out of the hive. Skylar swatted at one of them, driving it against the wall, where it thudded to the ground. Another one stung her on the arm. She winced and gasped.

She pushed out of the shed and fled down the driveway, hugging the treeline, praying that Mrs. Dove didn't choose that moment to look out her front windows.

"Hey, my little busy bee," Meg said with a smile as Skylar flung open the passenger-side door and leaped into the car, holding her cold hand against her neck as a makeshift ice pack. "Did you find any dirt on your queen?"

CHAPTER SEVENTEEN

The gravestone glowed in the moonlight, distractingly new next to the older, settled, moss-covered stones around it. Em sucked in her breath and tried not to focus on the dates below Sasha's name, the ones that showed her to be merely sixteen when she'd died. She tried not to think of Sasha in the hospital, her maniacal grin, the blood coming from her mouth. She tried not to think of anything but the task at hand.

The Furies spring from blood, the library book said. *Although they sometimes take the form of snakes, or appear with snakes as part of their visage, the Furies can assume many identities.*

She was taking a risk, she knew that, but she had a theory and she wanted to test it out. She'd made a deal with herself: She'd try this experiment tonight, and if it didn't work, she would tell Drea about the book, Sasha's involvement with the Furies, all of it. But if she could avoid dragging Drea in deeper, she would.

That's why she was here, alone in the graveyard on a moonlit night. She'd come on foot; the cemetery was less than a mile from her house. It had been a terrifying walk, and her imagination had run out of control. Figures behind every tree. Black birds circling overhead. An owl hooting in the distance. She didn't know what was real and what was her imagination. So she tried her best to filter out everything but her immediate plan.

Em was going to try to reverse-conjure the Furies. Just as they had been called up from their underground lair, she was going to send them back below. And she was going to do it here, near Sasha's burial place, because she was almost certain now that it was Sasha who had summoned them this time. Hadn't Ty said something to that effect? That Sasha had invited them back to Ascension? What else could she have meant by that?

Em kneeled before the grave, a knife in one hand and a paper bag in the other.

"I'm here, Sasha," she said out loud. "I'm going to finish what you started."

With a deep breath and a determined grimace, she dumped the contents of the pet shop bag onto the dirt. A snake slithered out. Em quickly threw her hand down on its middle before it could slither away, suppressing a whimper of disgust.

Holding the snake in place, feeling her stomach clench and

roll as the creature squirmed beneath her, Em pulled a knife from her pocket with her free hand. "I'm sorry," she whispered to the snake, which would likely have become a child's pet if she hadn't purchased it just a few hours ago.

Recalling what she'd read in the book, she raised the knife in the air. She hesitated and let the knife fall to the ground, turned away, gagged into the night air. She couldn't do this. This was insane.

Don't think about it. This is for JD. This is to make things right. This is to save Ascension.

She drew in a big breath, lifted the knife again, and brought it down, hard, between the snake's eyes.

The squirming stopped, and Em let out a tiny sob. She'd never killed a living thing before, other than an insect. She felt her whole body shuddering, but it was too late to stop now—she had to keep going with her plan.

She wiped her wet eyes with the back of her hand and talked aloud to herself. "You can do this, Em." She'd memorized what the book said to do next, and pounded on the icy dirt with her fist.

"Furies, return to where you came from," she intoned. She began digging a hole, doing the best she could in the frozen ground. When the hole was big enough for the snake, which she coiled into a neat circle, it was time for the next step.

"You spring from blood, then blood will bring you back,"

she said into the night air. She looked up, letting her hair whip around her face as she implored to the sky, "Please. Let this work."

Then she put the tip of the knife against her own palm. It felt smooth against her winter-chapped hand. The ritual called for drops of blood—five of them, to be precise. Just like she had swallowed five bloodred seeds. Once again she doubted she would be able to go through with it.

You have to. There's no choice.

She was about to press down and break the skin. She squeezed her eyes shut, not wanting to see the first spurt of blood. Scared of the pain. And then—

"Em! Stop!" The words came from behind her; she screamed and dropped the knife in front of her, leaping to her feet and ready to run.

There, standing behind a cluster of larger headstones, was JD. His brown hair was blowing in the slight breeze, and his hands were stuffed into the pockets of his bomber jacket.

Em couldn't believe her eyes. She fought to catch her breath.

"JD? What . . ." She barely knew what to ask him. How long had he been there? How much had he seen? Why was he there in the first place? But he didn't let her speak.

"What the hell are you doing, Em? Are you out of your mind?" He came closer. Even in the dark she could see the shocked look on his face. Gone was the normally goofy grin. He was speaking loudly, in a tone that Em barely recognized. "Thank god I followed you here. What were you—what were you *doing?*" He stormed up next to her, bent down, and picked up the knife.

She realized her hands were caked with frozen dirt—and they were still shaking.

"JD, I . . . don't know what to say," she said. Her mind was swirling; darkness clouded her vision, and she was suddenly worried she might faint. He'd followed her here? How long had he been watching? Had he seen her kill a snake? Call up to the heavens? Talk to Sasha Bowlder's ghost? It was too much. "I'm so . . . ," she sputtered. "Just please. Don't . . . don't tell anyone. This never happened. I was just—"

Anything she said would be too much. And so, in the same direction she'd come, she ran. Away from the graveyard, away from the dead snake and Sasha Bowlder's grave. Away from JD. "Em!" he called. But she ran faster, and lost him.

Wrapped in a thick robe after a long, hot shower, Em sat at the kitchen table and rubbed her temples, staring at her journal. The page in front of her was blank. She'd spent the last hour trying to warm her shaking body and calm down—while scrubbing the mud from under her fingernails. The scene at the graveyard kept replaying through her head, but she couldn't even get it down on paper. That poor snake. The blood. The dirt. JD suddenly appearing out of nowhere. She couldn't believe he'd followed her.

He still cares.

No. She wouldn't allow herself to entertain the idea. Still, she wondered if he would call, check up on her. Or—*god, no*—tell her parents? It was bad enough that her grades were running parallel to her social status, sinking as quickly as she was distancing herself from her old life. She had nothing to show for her distraction and disconnection, other than a handful of tests and papers bearing the dreaded inscription *See me*. If JD told anyone what he'd seen, she would pretty much be written off as totally insane.

The doorbell rang. A shot of anxiety ran through Em's whole body. She was home alone—her parents were both working their night shifts at the hospital—and while she had been happy for the solitude at first, she cursed it now.

Was it JD at the door, coming to harass her? Or (and she didn't know if this would be better or worse), was it someone else? Ever since the Ali incident, when the blond Fury had shown up on her doorstep like a bloodthirsty stalker, unexpected visitors left her with a thumping heart and clammy palms.

"Hello?" she called out from the kitchen. She started to move toward the front door. At the last moment she took a knife out of a drawer and curled her fingers around its wooden handle. Better safe than sorry. And if it was JD, well . . . he already thought she was out of her mind.

"Hello?" She said it again as she got closer to the door.

"Emily? Winters? It's Eileen Singer. Chase's mom." Em lost her grip on the knife, and it clattered to the floor.

"Mrs. Singer?" Em fumbled with the deadbolt.

"Are you—Emily Winters?" Mrs. Singer was wiry, small, and wrinkled: once beautiful, now raw. Em had only seen her a few times. She spoke with a tinge of the Maine accent that one rarely heard in the southern part of the state—drawing out certain sounds and narrowing her mouth around others.

"That's me." She motioned to her robe. "I, um, just got out of the shower," she added, as though she had to explain her ensemble to Chase's mom.

"I had to look you up," Mrs. Singer said, sounding relieved.

"It's, um, it's nice to see you, Mrs. Singer," Em said. What did Mrs. Singer want? What was Em supposed to say to her? "I hope . . . I hope you're doing okay. Would you like to come in?" She stepped away from the doorway, opening the view into the house, cringing at the sight of the steak knife lying in the middle of the floor in front of the stairs.

"No, thank you." Chase's mom jutted her chin toward a cardboard box at her feet. There was a spiral notebook sticking out of it. Em recognized it instantly. "I just came back to town for a few days, to clean out our house—the trailer."

Em nodded, remembering the night she'd met Chase there, after his fight at Galvin's Pond with Zach. She remembered the cramped kitchen, the stained countertop, the peeling linoleum. The way Chase's muscled body had seemed too big for the space.

"I'm leaving for good," Chase's mom continued, tucking her

graying hair behind her ears. "Heading for Pennsylvania. My sister lives there. Anyway, I was going through Chase's room—" Her voice caught here, and Em panicked. What should she do if Eileen Singer started sobbing on her stoop? But the meltdown didn't come. Mrs. Singer cleared her throat and went on, "These are some of . . . Chase's things. I kept the important stuff. But the notebook had your name in it. So I thought you might want it back. Or know what to do with the rest of it."

Em bent over to pick up the box, thinking about how awful it was that both Sasha's parents and Chase's mom had been left with nothing but some *stuff* to represent their children. "Are you sure you don't want to come in for a minute, Mrs. Singer?"

"I'm sure," Chase's mom said sharply. But she lingered still. They stood there for a moment. Then, "So, you two were friends? I didn't know many of the . . . other kids he spent time with."

There was another silence as Em weighed how to answer this question honestly. "We were always part of the same group," she said, placing the box down just inside the door. "Well, ever since eighth grade. My best friend was dating his best friend—Zach— for a long time. But it wasn't until recently that he and I . . . really started getting to know each other."

Chase's mom was watching Em talk with big, sorrowful eyes. They brightened a bit there.

"Not, like, in a romantic way," Em heard herself saying, unable now to stop the waterfall of words. "But I started to understand him more. We were working on some poetry together." That last part wasn't exactly true, but it was close enough.

"I worked all the time," Mrs. Singer said now, looking past Em at some unfocused point in the background. "I never got a chance to meet his friends."

"Well, he had lots of them," Em said with authority, tucking her fists into the cuffs of her sweatshirt. She flashed to the shirt Crow had lent her, how it had thumbholes in its sleeves, just as many of hers did. "He was an amazing athlete, and the boys loved him. And so did most girls," she said with a smile, trying to gauge Mrs. Singer's reaction. "He was very popular. We all ... I ... miss him. A lot."

Chase's mom exhaled forcefully, as though she'd been holding her breath. "Thank you, Emily," she said. "Thank you for saying that. I miss him too." Then she started back down the walkway, turning around just once more to say, "Good luck to you. And thank you again."

Em watched her go with a lump in her throat.

Once Mrs. Singer had gotten back into her car, Em closed the door and kneeled down right in the front hall to start picking through the belongings in the box. Most of it was crap: school papers, receipts, a small Best Sportsmanship trophy from Chase's sixth-grade rec camp, a cell phone charger. All of it seemed to be covered in a thin layer of dust, and Em kept having to wipe her hands on her pant legs to get off the grit. The lump kept swelling in her throat. It seemed inconceivable that this collection of random things could be her last connection to larger-than-life Chase.

At the bottom of the box were several printouts of the poems she'd "helped him write"—i.e., wrote herself—for Ty. And at the bottom of one of those was a small note, written in script.

Remember, you are bound to us, it read. Em squinted at it, read it again to make sure she was getting it right.

Had Chase written this? Was it a message? For her, for Ty?

No, it was obviously a girl's handwriting. With a shudder, she flashed back to those final moments at the Behemoth, before the Furies had disappeared into the night. The red beads shining against Ty's pale palm. Ty's words to her: *I'm warning you—they will bind you to us forever.*

Bound. Forever. What exactly had she promised the Furies? And why was the reminder here, with the rest of Chase's things?

Em ripped up the crinkled piece of paper, and then the other poems too. She brought the scraps into the living room and threw them into the fireplace. All of the memories those poems brought—of Chase, of Ty, of Zach, about whom several of them were written—made Em sick. Then there was the rest of the box too. . . . She was about to bring it down to the basement, when one last thing caught her eye. A small Mead flip-top notebook. It was full of brief jottings, written in Chase's messy chicken scratch.

Em flipped through the pages. The notebook seemed to be his "Ty cheat sheet"—short musings about their time together, things she'd told him, what she liked and didn't like.

They took me to Benson's last night, one entry read. *But not the biker bar. A different one, around back behind a Dumpster. I barely remember anything except red lights, amazingly hot women, and gold. Gold liquid, gold snakes, gold tongues. Weird. Route 23. Did we kiss?????*

Em read it over and over to make sure she had the right place. Benson's. She'd passed it a million times, and she, Gabby, Fiona, Lauren, and Jenna had a pact that they would go there this summer once they all got fake IDs to drink beer and do karaoke with the leather-clad motorcyclists.

But a secret swank club downstairs? Where the Furies hung out? It was hard to imagine.

Em knew she had to check it out as soon as possible. Any information was valuable information. And she knew she needed her partner in crime. She raced to the kitchen, grabbed her phone, and dialed.

"Hello?" Drea answered the phone like she always did—as though she was surprised, every time, that it would transmit her voice.

"Drea. It's me," Em said. Quickly, urgently, she told Drea about Mrs. Singer's visit, about the poems, the notebook, and the clandestine club. She left out the part about attempting a blood sacrifice at Drea's best friend's grave. "We need to go there. Like, tomorrow."

"All right," Drea agreed. "But how are we going to get in?"

"Well . . . Chase got in," Em said doubtfully, not wanting to admit that she hadn't considered the teensy problem of their age.

"He also happened to be with three gorgeous girls who happen to have supernatural powers," Drea sighed.

"So we'll get fake IDs," Em burst out, as though the matter was settled.

"In a day?" Drea scoffed.

"Drea! Do you have any better ideas?" Em felt the burning in her lungs, the painful determination to get as close as she could to the Furies as quickly as possible. The closer she was, the more chance she had of destroying them.

Drea said nothing for a few moments. Then she spoke with sly satisfaction. "Crow. We'll ask Crow. He can get them for us. I know he has one. I think one of those guys in the band makes them."

At the mention of Crow's name, Em got goose bumps. Involuntarily, she thought of his mouth on hers, her hand tangled in his hair. "Will he do it fast?" Em said, forcing herself to sound calm. She couldn't understand her own emotions. She didn't have romantic feelings for Crow, not ones she wanted to act on. So why did she still feel so attracted to him?

"Let's call him now," Drea said. Em didn't reply. "Okay, Em.

I'll call him. You stand by for more." While Em waited for Drea to call back, she threw her hair up into a bun. She was brushing her teeth when Drea's call came in.

"What'd he say?" she mumbled, her mouth still full of toothpaste.

"Well, he wanted to know what they were for," Drea said, and Em rolled her eyes. Like Crow cared that much about their well-being. "I told him we wanted to go to a twenty-one-and-over show in Portland. This band called the Low Anthem. Next time you see him, pretend you love them. I'll make you a CD."

"Drea, come on," Em said impatiently, spitting out the toothpaste. "Did he say yes or no?"

"He said a lot of things," Drea said teasingly. Em's heart stopped for a second. Had Crow told Drea about their kiss?

"What did he tell you?" she asked. She could feel her cheeks burning.

"Whoa, killer," Drea said with a laugh. "He said he worries about us and blah blah blah. I told him not to be a buzz kill. Anyway, he'll do it. He's going to pull our pictures from Facebook, and he says he'll get his guy to do it by tomorrow. That's rush delivery for us. But I think it's just for you."

"Shut up, D," Em said. But she was too excited to really be annoyed. Tomorrow they would be one step closer to the Furies.

• • •

They met Crow on Thursday evening in a 7-Eleven parking lot between Ascension and Benson's, just off Route 23. Both girls told their parents they were going to the USM library to study for chem and then do research for their independent projects. In reality, the chem test had been that afternoon, and Em was pretty sure she'd bombed it. As for her research paper, well . . . this was research. It was research about the only thing that mattered anymore.

In the parking lot Em could feel Crow's eyes on her. She felt as if he was absorbing her all at once, taking in everything about her: the skintight black jeans, her hair (she'd straightened it, and it reached to the bottom of her rib cage), and her heeled boots, which made her even taller than she already was. But he didn't say anything, didn't whistle, didn't raise his eyebrows. Nothing. There was no indication that they'd kissed, that he'd talked about not wanting to her, or that she'd run off into the rainy night afterward. He did, however, give Drea—who had forgone her typical safety-pinned layers in favor of a red miniskirt, patterned black tights, and a leather jacket—a long, low whistle.

"Shit, Feiffer, weren't you saving that outfit for prom?" Crow asked with a smirk. "I thought you were going to wear it just for me. . . ."

"Very funny, Crow," she shot back. "Are dropouts allowed at prom?"

"Probably just as waiters," he said, flicking the hair out of his eyes. With a flourish, he produced the fake IDs. "Here are your cards of false identification."

They paid, and as Em handed over her cash, Crow's fingers brushed her wrist. The goose bumps returned, but she ignored them. She resolutely refused to make eye contact with Crow. It was better to pretend that nothing had happened.

"We've gotta go, Drea," she said, as if they were thinking of hanging around in the 7-Eleven parking lot instead.

"She's a real taskmaster," Crow told Drea, cocking his thumb in Em's direction. "I'd watch out for her if I were you." Then, with a grin, he hopped back into his truck. "Seriously, though, ladies. I don't believe for a second that you're going to a concert in Portland. Whatever you're doing, be careful. I don't want liability, as the ID provider and all. . . ."

"How do you put up with him?" Em muttered as she got back into Drea's dad's car, which they had borrowed for the night.

"Sometimes I wonder how *he* puts up with *us*," Drea mused.

She'd been overheating for weeks, but as they pulled into the Benson's parking lot, Em felt freezing cold. Her nerves made her teeth chatter; her bones felt like they were going to quiver right out of her skin.

"You good?" Drea shot her a look of concern.

"I'm good," Em said, nodding emphatically. "I'm good. Let's

go." They walked around the building on the gravel lot, small rocks crunching beneath their feet.

Just as Chase had described in his notebook, there was a Dumpster flush against the wall back behind of the bar.

"This it, you think?" Drea asked.

"It has to be," Em responded. "Let's move it."

"Sure, let's move it," Drea said dryly. "Good thing I had gym today. I'm all warmed up." At the last second Drea pulled Em back. "Where's your snake pin?" she demanded. "You aren't wearing it." She had hers on, pinned just above her right boob.

"It's in my bag," Em lied. "Now come on."

They heaved and pushed against the metal container, and it glided aside as though it was on casters. Beyond it was a glowing door. Instantly it flew open; a burly bouncer stood framed in the doorway. Em wanted to back away from him. His eyes . . . There was something wrong with his eyes.

Then she realized: His pupils weren't black. They were red. Her whole body was shaking now.

The bouncer seemed almost to have been expecting them. He gave them both a once-over and didn't even ask for ID; instead, he waved them in toward a set of red-carpeted stairs. The space was so dimly lit that was impossible to tell what was at the bottom. Em could hear a faint rhythmic thumping. Drea did not let go of Em's hand as they started descending. Em looked at their linked hands gratefully. It appeared that unshakable Drea was scared too.

Just as the narrow stairwell began to widen—Em couldn't help but think of a mouth, stretching apart to swallow them whole—a prickling heat wafted over them. Em sensed fire, a tingling feeling of flames licking at her body. It was much like the sensation she'd felt in the old house in the woods. . . .

But this time it made her feel strangely alive, and alert. She was *sure* that the Furies were here.

"Whatever you do, don't lose me," Drea said right before they rounded the corner and entered the club. Em nodded.

Then they were inside, and Em had never seen anything like it. The cavernous room was low-ceilinged and shadowy, and full of people. Enormous golden birdcages hung from the ceiling, but inside there were no birds. Instead, lazy, watchful snakes hung from golden rods in the cages, their forked tongues darting from their mouths, twisting and writhing as though in time to the music.

All across the dance floor men and women were gyrating to pulsing music. Others were drinking from a fountain shaped like some crazy hybrid creature—a nude woman with enormous talons. Her mouth was open, and green liquid was dripping from her tongue; people were filling their cups with it.

Chase had been right. The people in this club were some of the most beautiful people Em had ever seen in her life. Her eyes were drawn to bare-chested men with tattoos, and women in skimpy dresses with heavy, smoky eyes. She suddenly felt very young, very angular, and very afraid.

She crossed her arms. She could feel Drea shaking a bit next to her. She, too, looked suddenly young. The music was too loud to try to communicate out loud. Em pointed toward a long bar, which was—like everywhere else in the club—packed with people. They started to make their way over to it.

The beat seemed to come up through the floor, causing Em's legs to vibrate, creating a slight sensation of vertigo. A hazy fog seemed to infiltrate every corner of the room—and every pore of Em's skin. As she squeezed through the crowd she felt increasingly out of control, like she was being possessed by something outside of herself. Men stroked her body with their eyes, smiling at her knowingly. Women, too. She tried to keep her eyes fixed ahead of her, but she was growing increasingly flustered. Should they leave? She turned around to gauge Drea's comfort level. Drea always knew what to do.

But Drea was no longer behind her.

Panicked, Em whirled around, searching for Drea's purple hair. They'd gotten separated. It was the one thing that wasn't supposed to happen.

She started pushing back toward the door. They were in over their heads. They had to get out of there.

And yet, despite her fear, the seductive mood in the room was seeping into Em's blood, beating its rhythm deeper and deeper into her body. Her mind began to feel cloudy with the sweet-smelling smoke, and as her thoughts softened, her limbs loosened up. A man, heavily tattooed, grabbed her hand to lure her into a dance. She resisted at first. Drea. She had to find Drea.

But she was unable to stop herself; the hypnotic music was like the pull of an insistent tide. She let the man put his hand on her waist. She let him keep it there.

The music . . . whispering . . . calling out to her . . .

She put her hand on his muscled arm, touching his smooth skin, feeling like she was in a dream. She inhaled his musky smell. It felt so good just to let herself go. . . . She closed her eyes for just a minute, moving her hips to the beat, allowing him to press against her. . . .

When she opened her eyes, they woozily focused. And the first thing they saw with clarity was none other than Crow. There. Across the room, by the fountain. She caught a quick glimpse of his dark hair, his searching eyes, and then the crowd closed in again and he was gone.

But she'd seen him, she knew it. Her mind snapped back to alertness.

What the hell was *he* doing here? Had he followed her and Drea?

Drea.

She wrenched away from her dance partner and began to elbow her way over to the fountain. But by the time she reached the spot where she'd seen Crow, he was gone.

Tap, tap, tap. She felt a finger on her shoulder. She jumped and let out a little cry. But when she turned around, she saw it was only Drea.

"Where did you go?" Em shouted over the music. Instead of feeling relieved, she felt a surge of unreasonable anger. She knew it had something to do with guilt; she wondered whether Drea had seen her dancing.

"I lost you!" Drea yelled back.

Em pulled her into one of the nooks carved into the stone walls; their voices echoed there, but at least they could hear each other.

"Crow is here," Em said, still speaking loudly. "I saw him, right over here."

Drea looked skeptical. "Crow? Here? Are you sure?" She cocked her head to one side and raised her eyebrows. "Are you sure that's not just wishful thinking?" Even in this atmosphere, Drea obviously had not lost her grip on her special brand of humor, which largely seemed to consist of giving Em a hard time. Clearly, the smoke hadn't gone to her head in the same way it had affected Em.

"Come on, Drea. Be serious," Em said, shutting her down quickly. The last thing she wanted was for Drea to get the wrong idea about her and Crow. What if JD found out somehow?

"Calm down. I was just joking," Drea said. She peered at Em. "Do you want a drink? Or some air? You look like you're freaking out."

Em shook her head. This was all wrong. The Furies weren't here—just a bunch of pleasure-fiending weirdos who were probably on drugs. The fake IDs, the money spent—all for nothing. "I think we should just get out of here," she said.

"Already?" Drea looked thoughtful. "We basically just got here. I haven't even had a chance to ask around—"

"Fine, then I'm going out for some air," Em said, realizing that she needed out. "I'll either find you down here or wait for you up there."

She fought her way back up the stairs, fidgeting as the bouncer moved the Dumpster to let her out, and gasping for clean air once she stumbled out into the parking lot. She paced, holding her arms and watching the way her breath fogged each time she exhaled. The feeling of dizziness started to dissipate.

And then, out of the shadows, a female voice: "Looking for someone?"

Em squinted. A girl was emerging from the darkness between two Harleys. Even before she stepped into the light, Em knew who it was. She recognized the lilting, taunting tone. Em was familiar, too, with the crawling sensation in her skin, as though a thousand snakes were writhing underneath it.

Ty.

Bitterness surged through Em. "I know everything about you," she spat out. "I know who you really are. You died in Ascension, and now you're back. For revenge."

Ty raised an eyebrow. "That's quite a theory," she said, her voice like a placid lake—no ripples, no waves.

"You're the reason that bad things are happening in Ascension. You're evil, and you're bringing evil to this town. You killed Chase," Em said. Then she added, "And I'm going to stop you."

"Em, evil feeds on itself, you know," Ty said, letting the words roll out of her mouth like she'd said them a hundred times before.

"What are you talking about?" Em felt the flames of anger blistering through her, and she decided to bluff. "I know your secret," she said. "I'm going to undo this—undo *you*."

Ty made a show of clamping her lips together and shaking her head coyly, as though vowing to keep a secret about a high school crush. Then she spoke in the merry-go-round singsong that made Em's blood curdle. "You can't just undo it, Em. And you shouldn't have tried. I almost felt sorry for you, back there at the cemetery with that poor snake. We made a deal. Don't you remember?"

Something in Em broke apart then, and she felt her muscles fill with adrenaline. She leaped at Ty blindly, more enraged than ever, attacking her with a fury that came from somewhere deep and hidden.

"Why don't you just leave? Leave me, and leave Ascension, alone!" she yelled as she struck Ty, knocking her backward.

When their bodies collided, Em felt a momentary surge, like a shock. Ty stumbled, but regained her footing. She came back at Em with her teeth bared, grabbing a handful of Em's dark, straightened hair, yanking it hard.

Em whipped her body back and forth to free herself from Ty's grasp. She kicked at Ty's shins, making contact, and in the process tumbling them both to the ground. Em felt the gravel stab through her jeans into her knees. Ty's hands felt like ice on her face, her neck, her wrists. All Em could think about was how badly she wanted the Furies out of her life. Now. The strength of that thought gave her conviction, and the conviction gave her power; she began to overcome Ty, who struggled and squirmed beneath her.

Then Em had her pinned to the ground. She dug one knee into Ty's bony chest and clamped both of Ty's wrists in one of her hands, pressing them into the frozen dirt.

She wrapped the other hand around Ty's long, slender neck—so like her own—and squeezed.

As she had at the Behemoth a few months ago, Ty started to waver in and out, like a picture on an old television. But she did not appear to be hurt, or gasping for breath, no matter how hard Em pushed on her windpipe. And then Em felt it—her grip on Ty's wrists getting weaker, their power reversing, then Ty's fingernails digging into her arm, breaking the skin, slicing into her.

"Shit," Em said, pulling away, gasping. Her arm was stinging, and tiny drops of blood began to bubble at the place where Ty had stabbed her.

"Don't look down, Em," Ty said tauntingly.

Of course Em did. The swinging sense of vertigo returned, along with a stomach-dropping sensation of airlessness. It took her a second to understand what was happening. She and Ty were both hovering about three feet off the ground.

Em jerked backward, breaking the spell and hurtling to the dirt below. Ty landed more gracefully, laughing as she taunted Em. "That was fun, wasn't it?"

Em couldn't respond. The air had been knocked out of her by the short fall to the ground.

Ty went on, "You see? We aren't so different, you and I. I see it, even if Ali and Meg don't. Even if you don't. We two, we'll do anything to get the things that we want. *We aren't so different . . .*" Ty repeated once more. And then, just like that, she vanished.

Em hauled herself to her feet and hunched over, cradling her left arm—the one that was bleeding. As Em heaved for breath, Drea emerged from downstairs.

"There you are," Drea said. And then, as she came closer and caught sight of Em, "Oh my god! What happened?"

"They . . . they were here," she croaked out. "Ty was here. I saw her."

Drea nodded grimly. "I saw one of them too. The one who wears that red ribbon around her neck." Drea scanned Em with concern. "Which one of them did this to you? I hope you at least got to throw a good punch. "

"I don't think I did much damage," Em said wearily. "It was Ty. What about you? Did you talk to her? Did she say anything?" Em followed behind Drea as they walked to the car. Every few steps she checked compulsively over her shoulder, as though Ty might materialize at any second.

They got into the car, both of them careful to close and lock their doors behind them. "She asked me if I was going to the Spring Fling," Drea said with a nervous laugh. "If I had a date. Then . . ." She broke off, picking at her fingernails and looking sidelong at Em.

"What? What did she say, Drea?" Em prodded.

"She said that they had special plans for you, Em. That I should watch out for you." Drea looked at Em now, searching her face as though trying to measure her reaction. They stared at each other.

"So what should we do about it?" she asked. They were losing time to come up with a plan.

Drea shook her head and started the car. "I don't know, Em. I think . . . I think this is bigger than we thought. I think the banishment ritual needs to happen as soon as possible. I think it's . . . I think you . . ." She didn't finish her thought, and worry fell between them like a boulder. Em contemplated telling Drea now about Sasha's connection to the Furies.

They drove home in tense silence.

In Em's driveway Drea fiddled with her snake pendant, still not speaking. Em reached down to gather her things. "That's weird," she blurted out. Her arm wasn't bleeding anymore. In fact, the marks Ty had left seemed to have practically healed.

"What?" Drea asked.

"I just . . . I could have sworn that Ty scratched me and broke the skin," Em said, putting her arm out so Drea could see. "I was bleeding. But now . . . it's, like, fine."

"Weird." Drea's voice sounded strangled. She put the car into reverse. "I'm sorry, Em. I gotta go. I have to get home." Em nodded and got out of the car. She had to step quickly to the side to avoid getting hit as Drea peeled out of the driveway.

CHAPTER EIGHTEEN

On Thursday afternoon after school Skylar took Aunt Nora's bicycle from the garage and rode it to the Haunted Woods, praying that no one would see her along the way. When she got there, the ground had refrozen where the mud had been, leaving craggy peaks and valleys on the forest floor. Everything was still, silent, and full of winter ache.

She'd realized during the week that she had no idea what had happened to her special watch, the silver one her mother had given to both her and Lucy. She hated the memories attached to it, but at the same time, she couldn't bear to lose it. Sometimes she wondered if she kept it out of familial loyalty or because she felt a sick desire to preserve the memories of the bad times. Wearing that watch was like a constant reminder not to feel guilty about what had happened.

That watch served a purpose.

She knew it was out here somewhere. The last time she'd seen it was right before she fell.

Skylar walked along a sun-dappled path that looked like the one they'd followed last Friday, keeping her eyes trained on the ground. She spotted mottled leaves, scarred sections of tree root, and brownish moss blanketing fallen logs. But no watch. The woods were brittle and motionless, drawn back into an early spring frost. Skylar pulled her knit gray hat farther over her ears and shoved her hands deep into the pockets of her pink flared peacoat, which had been Nora's in the 1970s.

She looked up to see the sun scooting behind a cloud, and the air turned gray as she looked around, trying to get her bearings. Through the trees she saw a large, boxy brown house, like something from the Colonial era, not more than fifty paces away. *That's weird,* she thought. *I thought this part of Ascension was uninhabited.* Seeing an unfamiliar landmark suggested to Skylar that she was lost, and she thought about turning around, retracing her steps, and trying to find a different path. But she quickly talked herself out of it. The woods weren't *that* big, and the party site had to be around here somewhere.

The trees were casting shadows now as the sun dipped lower in the sky. Their branches looked like fingers, poking their way down, grabbing at her. She tripped on a root but caught herself against some bark, rough and sandpapery.

She was less sure all of a sudden. This wasn't right; she'd been walking for too long. She was lost. What if the owner of that house back there came out and got her in trouble for trespassing? But there was light up ahead—another clearing. She would check it out. If that wasn't it, she would turn around.

Suddenly she found herself by a pond, where drooping, dead cattails ringed water that glistened with a paper-thin layer of ice. Larger pine trees stood around it, sentinels of this small woodland oasis. There were no benches here, no wooden signposts—this wasn't a popular watering hole, just a tiny, dark body of water.

Sitting on top of that thin sheet of ice was a red flower—just like the one Skylar had worn at her party. The one Meg had given her. A shiver went through her from head to toe, and she balled up her hands inside her pockets. Memories came flooding back—how Em's eyes had widened in fear when she'd seen the flower, how she'd grabbed it from Skylar and thrown it into the fire. And now here it was, or one that was almost identical, shimmering red among dead brown reeds and grasses.

As Skylar made her way over to it she felt as though she was walking through a dream. There was something not right about the flower, about the day, about the pond, but she felt unable to change course.

She stopped at the bank, her boots sinking into the slushy muck. The flower was just sitting there, as if it had grown out of the ice. And then, as she reached to grab it—it was *just* within her reach—her foot hit something solid in the reeds. Something that was not water, mud, or ice.

She kicked at it. It was dense and firm, kind of like a wet, decaying log. She bent down and swept aside the thick growth of tall, sun-bleached grasses.

It didn't quite register at first. She found herself stumbling backward, almost like her body understood what it was before her mind did. Her stomach heaved and bile came up her throat.

It was a leg. She'd tripped on a leg that was not a log and was lodged in the mud at the edge of the pond.

A leg.

A leg attached to a body.

Both of the corpse's legs were askew and washed up mostly on the bank; its torso and head were submerged, barely visible beneath the murky water and chunks of floating ice. But she could see enough to know that she was looking at a male face, which stared up at her from just below the surface.

She lurched again, still heaving. The sour taste of fear and nausea filled her mouth. Once she could stand, she backed up again, until she hit something—someone.

Skylar screamed, a high-pitched, frantic scream.

"It's okay, Sky. It's just me."

Meg was standing right behind her. She looked back and forth impassively between Skylar and the body.

"There's a—" Skylar blubbered. "I found a—"

Meg wrinkled her nose and cocked her head to one side. "Dead as a doorknob, huh?" she said, and Skylar realized she had already noticed the corpse. "Thank goodness we saw your bike out there. We wouldn't want you out here alone!"

"How did you know that was my . . ." She trailed off, noticing that Ty and Ali were there as well, the three of them arranged like the three points of a triangle.

The air went out of Skylar's chest. For the first time, she saw Meg—her lustrous hair and cupid's face, her red choker, her thin fingers—and was frightened. Who was this person, seeing a dead body and observing it calmly as if it was something you see every day?

Ty and Ali weren't any better. All three of the girls looked . . . blank. Skylar shivered as she was overcome by another wave of nausea. She leaned over and retched.

"Sad, isn't it?" Ty said placidly, shaking her head like she was watching a disappointing news report. "I think he worked at Ascension. I recognize him."

"Was he a . . . teacher?" Skylar said, wiping her mouth, still shaking. She found herself wondering what his face had looked like when he was alive. What his mouth had looked like when he talked. What his eyes had looked like when they weren't frozen in terror.

Ali tossed her blond hair over her shoulder and giggled, a jarring sound that made Skylar's toes curl in her boots. "Well, you could certainly learn a lot from him."

Skylar narrowed her eyes. "What are you talking about? Why are you laughing?"

Meg came up and put her hand on Skylar's back, rubbing it in small circles. "Come on. You've had a shock. We'll take you home."

Skylar's skin crawled where Meg touched, and she jerked away. "Shouldn't we . . . call the police?" Skylar choked out, trying to keep her eyes on Meg but finding them pulled toward the dead body.

"Why don't you do it when we get home?" Meg said, shepherding Skylar to a path on the other side of the pond. "There isn't any cell service around here. Come on," she repeated. "We'll drive you."

They walked a short distance in silence until they reached the Lincoln. Skylar's mind was spinning with questions, but each time she took a breath and opened her mouth—*Who was he? What happened to him? Why were you just . . . standing there, as though you'd been looking for me, or for him?*—she found herself too shocked and revolted to speak. Her nose was running; her eyes burned. More even than the sight of the body, she couldn't forget its feeling. How her boot had felt against human flesh and bone. She tried to stay focused. One foot in front of the other.

"I don't need a ride," she reminded them when they reached the car. "Like you guys saw, I already have my aunt's bike." Truth was, she really didn't want to get in the car with the girls. They were freaking her out.

"Don't be silly," Meg said, all sugary sweet. "You're in shock. We'll come back for your bike tomorrow."

Skylar didn't feel like she could argue back. She relented. Still, once all four of them were in the car, with Ali at the wheel, Ty in the front, and Meg and Skylar in the backseat, she tried again to speak. *How did you know I was in the woods?* she wanted to say. But just as she was about to voice a question, Ty turned around. Even with her dark hair and pale skin, she seemed to glow.

"Oh, here," she said, bringing her hand over the divider between the front and back seats. Clutched in her slender fingers was the orchid. The bloodred flower that had drawn Skylar to the edge of the pond.

Skylar drew back as though it was on fire. "Why—why are you giving me that?" She caught Ali's eyes in the rearview mirror; her mouth, as usual, was painted into a perfect bloodred grin.

She looked at Meg uncertainly, hoping to find some reassurance, and some answers. Instead, she saw only the tilted birdlike look that was becoming Meg's trademark.

Ty leaned over and used the flower petals to tap Skylar's knee. It was the lightest of touches, but it felt like a slice from a knife. "You dropped it in the woods!" Ty said, pouting. "I thought you wanted it!"

"I don't want it," Skylar insisted.

They were getting closer to Aunt Nora's house. Thank god. Skylar couldn't wait to get out of the car. How could the girls be acting so casual? They'd just found a *dead body*, for god's sake! And what was with that stupid orchid?

Skylar knew nothing about Meg or her cousins. But she still knew that something about them was decidedly off.

Skylar already had her hand on the door handle, ready to leap out of the car, when they pulled up in front of Nora's house. She thanked them hurriedly and moved toward the walkway. As she did Ty rolled down her window.

"*À bientôt, escargot,*" Ty said with a wave.

A sheet of cold blew through Skylar's body. In her whole life, she had heard only one person use that expression before: Em Winters.

CHAPTER NINETEEN

Ohmygod. JD wanted to talk. To her. To Em. To his lovelorn former best friend, who he had been shunning for months. On Thursday afternoon he texted: *We should meet.* Em's heart nearly exploded.

That's all it took, she thought wryly. *Boy sees girl attempting sacrifice in graveyard, boy falls back in love. Why didn't I think of that before?*

So around eight o'clock on Thursday night, after a strained dinner with her parents, Em threw her hair into a messy bun, put her Sorel boots over her sweatpants, and marched over to the Founts' front door.

One thing was clear: If she wanted to save her relationship with JD, it was time to talk. She might not be able to tell him the whole truth, but Em was determined to make him understand . . . something. Whether it took burying the past or explaining part of the present or fibbing around the truth, Em was going to make amends.

She knocked. As soon as she did, though, she lost some of her certainty. The last time she'd stood here, she'd been scream-ing at Drea. And the last time she'd seen JD, she'd been practicing witchcraft in a cemetery. But he hadn't said anything to anyone, at least as far as Em knew, and now he was reaching out to her. He was still on her side.

She heard JD yell, "I'll get it!" from inside, and his voice gave her a surge of renewed hopefulness, enough to make her crack a small smile.

She was still wearing the stupid grin when he opened the door; the sight of him in his slightly baggy jeans, white T-shirt, and favorite ratty cardigan—the one with the holes in both elbows and the coffee stain on the right cuff—was enough to make her smile even more broadly. His eyes were the color of autumn. She'd nearly forgotten how absolutely adorable he was.

But JD's tired, wary expression knocked the smile off her face. This wasn't going to be easy.

"So, our Reign of Silence is over?" she asked with false cheer as he swung open the door. He shrugged but didn't respond, just turned and let her follow him through the foyer and into the den.

They settled in the den, as usual, but the awkward silence

between them was unfamiliar. Em tried not to picture JD and Drea cozied up here on the couch. What if he'd told her about Em's crazy ritual? Then there was a girlish squeal from the doorway between the kitchen and the den.

"Emmmmmmmmmm!" It was Melissa standing there with her hair in a braid and a bag of tortilla chips in her hands.

"Hey, Melly," Em said, grateful for the distraction.

"Thank goodness," Mel said, crunching on a chip.

"Thank goodness what?" Em said.

"Thank goodness you're *here*," Mel said, as though it was the most obvious thing on Earth. "I was starting to think you didn't love us anymore!"

"We need some privacy, Melly," JD said. But his voice wasn't exasperated. It had softened.

"Whatever," his sister replied. "I have to go upstairs anyway. I'm in the middle of a chat."

Em laughed as Mel scampered out of the room and they heard her footsteps racing upstairs. "I swear, that girl is going to be in PR," she said. "She is constantly connected." Em and JD had always agreed that Mel could enter the *Guinness World Records* for fastest texter ever.

"I know. . . . She just about makes up for my being a social hermit," JD said.

"You're not a hermit, JD. More like . . . more like Mr. Darcy."

"Mr. Who?"

Em rolled her eyes. "You know, from *Pride and Prejudice*. At first everyone thinks he's aloof because he isn't into dancing and partying with the rest of them. But then, once you get to know him, you realize he has a heart of gold. And also a kick-ass mansion. And the only reason he didn't want to dance was because he sucks at dancing."

JD cracked a smile. "Sooooo, you're saying I'm not a hermit, I'm just a bad dancer?"

Em laughed. "Well, that wasn't really the point I was going for, but it's not exactly *untrue*, either." Without thinking, she reached out and poked him with a finger.

He swatted her finger away, and for a second it was like there was something warm in JD's eyes—that old familiar look. In its glow she saw that he, like her, was recalling all those shared root beer floats and epic thumb wars on the couch. Or maybe New Year's Eve in Boston, when he'd stood behind her during the fireworks, their bodies touching, his breath near her ear. Remembering it made a warmth spread through her lower belly, toward her heart.

But then his face went dark again. A lot had happened between then and now.

"So," she stumbled on, grasping for neutral ground, "what are you writing your English paper about?"

"Asimov, I think," he said. "Something about how humans tend to be their own downfall."

"I guess I should have known," Em said. JD had loved Isaac Asimov since middle school. She remembered a Fount-Winters family vacation in Cape Cod during the summer between seventh and eighth grades, when he'd summarized, in vivid detail, the plot of *I, Robot* to her on a walk from their cabin to the ice cream stand. It was the only time she'd ever cared about science fiction. JD, on the other hand, had been inspired. His love for all things technical—from computer graphics to stage lighting to car parts—made him fascinated by how humans interact with machines.

She looked at him, ready to share the memory, but found that he was staring at her intensely. He wasn't thinking about *I, Robot*.

He spoke suddenly and seriously. "Listen, Em, I texted you for a reason. We can't just avoid talking about what happened the other night. In the cemetery. What the hell is going on with you? People are worried. *I'm* worried."

Em offered a weak smile, one that she hoped conveyed something like sheepishness. "You were right, JD, about me being more affected by Chase's and Sasha's deaths than I admitted," she said, offering the answer she'd rehearsed at home. "I've been . . . a little off my rocker. I feel almost like I'm responsible."

"Jesus, Em," he said gently. "That's terrible. You know you're not, right? And you're hurting yourself because of it? You need to talk to someone."

"I know." She nodded seriously. "I'm taking the right steps. I'm figuring it out." That wasn't a lie, per se.

He seemed to accept what she was saying. But he wasn't finished.

"I have another question," he continued. "Why did you get in a fight with Drea that day . . . that night she was studying at my house?"

"I . . . We . . . Well, Drea and I have been spending a lot of time together. As you may know. Because, well . . ." Em blushed, knowing she was hedging the question. She didn't know how to tell him how jealous she was that night—ragingly, burningly jealous. She stared at the coffee stain on his shirt, trying to piece together a sentence that wouldn't make her sound idiotic. "It's kind of hard to explain," she finished helplessly.

When she glanced up, she saw that JD, too, appeared to be blushing. Her mind leaped to the best-case scenario. Maybe, somehow, he got it. Maybe if she just told him . . .

"I was just wondering," he said, with a shrug that was more like a jerk of his shoulders. "Seems like a lot of things are hard for you right now. So." He cleared his throat. "What have you been up to during our, ah, as you so eloquently put it, Reign of Silence?"

Once again Em felt trapped. She wanted to tell him everything. All of it. It was infuriating to feel so powerless. No wonder people called it madness.

She took a deep breath and shrugged. "Just spending a lot of time with Drea's crew," she said.

JD made a sound in the back of his throat, a cross between a "Hm" and an "Ah." Then, definitely red-faced now, he asked, "Anyone specific?"

Em raised her eyebrows. "No. I mean, Drea, obviously. . . . But no, definitely not anyone specific. . . ." Did he know about Crow? Her heart was beating fast now, pitter-pattering in her chest.

"I see." He didn't say anything more. Just sat there, looking at her intently, waiting for more. His hands were interlaced in front of him like a therapist's.

Em felt herself blushing all over. This was it. This was her chance. He was finally ready to talk, to forgive her, and move on.

"Listen, JD," she said. "I know things between us have been . . . weird over the last few weeks. But there are some things happening to me lately that don't make a lot of sense. I can't explain them. But I want you to be in my life. I need you there. I want to just bury the past and move forward."

Em couldn't stop the words from tumbling out of her mouth. She had the powerful urge to hold JD and never let him go—to make everything right between them. She felt their knees touching. Every nerve in her body was on alert.

But then JD jerked away from her. He looked confused— and not exactly on the verge of absolving her sins.

"I'm sorry that you're struggling, Em, I really am," JD said.

"And I'm glad we got to talk things over. But I'm not sure I can just 'bury the past.' Honestly? It doesn't sound like we want the same thing."

Em's joy morphed into mortification. Oh god—he didn't feel the same way. She was wrong. But how wrong? Had his feelings never existed in the first place, or had they dried up completely? A heavy smoke of anger started to billow inside her. This was all the Furies' fault. Had they planted false feelings in her, or erased them in him? Either way, they were doing their best to ruin her love story. And it was killing her.

"I'm sorry, JD. I thought . . . I guess I thought that things . . ." She was grasping at straws, and it was starting to seem like there was nothing here to rebuild—like what they'd had together had all been in her head in the first place. She looked at the cowlick over his left temple, the scruff on his cheeks, and she felt lost. She wanted him, but she could see that he was spinning further and further away from her. Or maybe she was spinning away from him.

"I guess I should take off," she said. "Thanks for listening."

"Good luck, Em," JD said, avoiding her eyes. "I'll see you around."

Back in her own room, she ran through the various ways in which the night had been a complete disaster. She'd basically confessed her love for JD, and he'd responded with repulsion.

He'd rebuffed her renewed attempt at reconciliation. He'd ended their conversation with "See you around," which basically meant "See you never, I hope."

She listlessly opened her laptop even though she knew she wouldn't get any homework done. Tears were welling in her eyes.

Almost instantly a chat message from Drea popped onto her screen.

Hey, Drea wrote, and barreled on without waiting for Em to write back. *Need to tell u something.*

It seemed, lately, that those words were always followed by horrifying news.

What? she wrote. Curt. Disengaged.

The police found Mr. Landon by the pond in the Haunted Woods, Drea told her. *I heard it on the news.*

The messages kept popping up, and Em couldn't look away.

They found something near him.

An orchid.

A red orchid. You know what I mean.

Em's breathing got shallow.

Em? Are you there? Are you reading this?

So the Furies had gotten him, too. An adult. Someone almost completely disconnected from Em, her life, and her circle. The weight of it hit Em like a wave, pummeling her with a horrible realization: The Furies wouldn't stop with Chase, or her, or even JD. They wanted to infect all of Ascension.

With frantic fingers, she typed out: *I need to tell you what I've learned over the past few days. Have you found out more about the banishment procedure? How to get rid of them?*

Drea's words came back almost immediately. *I'm on it,* she wrote. *Trust me.*

CHAPTER TWENTY

The garlicky smell of Aunt Nora's seafood risotto—steaming, salty, fresh—was wafting through the old Victorian, making it next to impossible for Skylar to keep her eyes on her textbook. She was starving. Her appetite had been insatiable over these last few weeks— it was like she was trying to eat away, or maybe bury, all of the stress and lies that were building up inside her. She'd barely slept last night after calling in the anonymous tip to the police station. . . . Instead, she'd crept downstairs and eaten pretzels dipped in sour cream. One of the few things she and Lucy had ever agreed on was that pretzels and sour cream were the perfect combination: salty, crunchy, creamy, tangy. Thank god her coping mechanism hadn't resulted in extra pounds—yet. Skylar reminded herself not to chow down too much risotto. She had to fit into Lucy's dress a week from Friday.

Aunt Nora was hollering up the stairs, "About half an hour more, Sky. Come down when you can and set the table." Just then the doorbell rang. "Could you get that? I'm in the middle of making supper," Nora yelled.

Skylar padded down the stairs in socks and her hideous holiday-themed pj's, which she'd put on the moment she got home from school. Those senior girls had invited her—along with Gabby, Fiona, and the rest of the crew—to some party, but she'd turned them down. She really did have to get some homework done, plus Gabby had been distant since the dance committee fiasco. Skylar wanted to give her a few more days to cool off.

She was shocked to see Em Winters on Nora's stoop. Were unannounced drop-bys, like, a thing in Ascension? She opened the door a crack, mortified to have been caught looking like this. It was like announcing that she had no plans on a Friday night.

"Um, hi?" She didn't open the door any wider.

"Skylar, hey, thank god you're home," Em said, smiling awkwardly and biting her lip. "I've been trying to talk to you ever since the night of the your party. It's so hard to catch you alone—you're like the Ascension cruise director or something!" Skylar could hear the false notes of enthusiasm in Em's voice. She'd never heard Em talk like this—like she was *trying* so hard. And still Skylar detected Em's usual darkness, her intensity, running underneath the words. She thought of the picture of the beaming, giggling girl in Gabby's key chain photo. *What had happened to that girl?* she wondered.

When Skylar didn't say anything, Em kept going. "There were . . . some things we talked about. That night. About some—friends we have in common?" Em looked at her pointedly then, trying to communicate something without saying it out loud. "I think we need to talk more about them."

Not only was it bizarre that Em, who had barely given her the time of day before this, had shown up on her porch . . . it was also uncomfortable that Skylar could barely remember anything about the conversation they'd had in front of the bonfire. All she remembered, foggily, was that Em had freaked out about the orchid and Skylar had said something about Lucy. Which was something she absolutely never did.

But Skylar couldn't exactly tell Em Winters to leave . . . not when she was Gabby's best friend (albeit a bit of a whack job) and still considered part of the A-list.

"Do you . . . want to come in for a minute? We're about to have dinner, but . . ."

Em was already halfway in the door. "Yes, thanks," she said, taking off her sweater as soon as she crossed the threshold. "It's warm in here . . . and it smells amazing."

"My aunt's making risotto," Skylar explained.

"Who is it?" Aunt Nora called from the kitchen.

"It's my friend Em," Skylar shouted back, glancing over at

Em to see how she reacted to the word *friend*. But Em was too busy looking around Nora's living room, which was cluttered with dusty antiques and nautical knickknacks.

"Well, bring her in here so I can meet her!" There was a clattering of pots as punctuation.

Shrugging, Skylar led Em into the kitchen. If Skylar was really lucky, maybe tonight would be the night Aunt Nora decided to really "get to know" her friends. But as soon as they walked in, Nora's eyes got wide and she dropped the lid she was holding, tripping over herself as she bent down to retrieve it, mumbling under her breath. She looked . . . terrified—much as she had when Meg had appeared on their doorstep. Was acting batty around her friends another one of Nora's charming quirks?

"Are you okay?" Em instinctively moved toward Aunt Nora.

"You'll have to excuse me," Nora whispered. "I'm . . . I'm not feeling very well. I'll have to ask you—Skylar—I'll have to ask you to wait a bit on dinner." She went to push past Em.

"Wait," Em said, her voice ringing out in the steamy kitchen. Nora stopped.

Em and Nora—one young, pale, vibrant; the other older, gray, shaking—stared at each other. Skylar didn't know what to do. She felt like she'd stepped into a bad dream.

Nora spoke with misgiving. "You're the one Hannah told me about."

"Hannah—you mean Ms. Markwell? The librarian?" Em asked.

Nora nodded slowly. "I have to . . . talk to Hannah," she whispered as she left the kitchen. A few moments later Skylar heard a door slam. It was obvious that Em was dying to go after her, but Skylar wasn't going to let this situation get even stranger than it already was.

"We're going upstairs," she said firmly, and practically hauled Em up to her bedroom. Em protested but didn't fight her.

Once they were in her room with the door closed behind them, Skylar turned to face Em, who was looking troubled. "Sorry about that," she said. "My aunt is just a little cuckoo—she's into, like, auras and spirits and stuff—and she acts like that around all my friends." Which, unfortunately, was kind of true.

"Like the friend you told me about at the bonfire party?" Em asked.

Skylar tensed—she wasn't sure if talking about Meg was a good idea. But Em kept going.

"The friend who gave you the orchid—Meg? How did you meet?"

Skylar sat down on the bed, picking at the quilted bedspread. "At the ice cream shop near school," she said. "I went in there one day and we started talking."

Em's eyes were boring into Skylar's, as though she was trying to memorize not just what she was saying, but everything about her. It made Skylar feel like she was under a microscope.

Em continued, "And you've met her cousins, right? Ty and Ali?" Skylar shrank back under Em's gaze; it was starting to look incendiary, angry.

"I've met them once or twice," Skylar said. "They're . . . nice." Even as she said it, though, she flashed to their curiously impassive faces as they stared at the dead body. And Ali had *smiled*. "I mean, I don't really know that much about them." Again, a truth.

"Has anything weird been happening to you?" Em persisted. "Do you feel okay? Have you done anything you feel . . . maybe . . . ashamed about?"

Skylar could feel the blood heating her face. She crossed her arms in front of her chest, digging her nails into her biceps. "Nothing's weird," she said stubbornly. "Everything's great."

"It's okay, Skylar," Em said gently. "You can tell me."

Her pulse pounded in her ears. She didn't like the way Em was looking at her. "Look, dinner's almost ready," Skylar said. "I have no idea what you're talking about, and I think you should leave." She stood up, opened her bedroom door, and waited expectantly for Em to walk through it.

But Em didn't move. "That girl and her cousins are dangerous," she said, and there was a pleading quality to her voice. "If you've done something, please tell me. You might not realize it yet, but something bad is going to happen."

Skylar stood there, thin-lipped, refusing to speak.

"Whatever they're trying to do to you, it isn't fair. I want to help you," Em pleaded. "Maybe we can work together. Mayb—"

With every bit of quiet force she could muster, Skylar interrupted. "Please leave, Em."

Em seemed to deflate like a punctured balloon. "Fine," she said, and Skylar could almost see her give up. They walked downstairs without saying a word. But right before she left, Em turned and spoke once more. "Please call me, Skylar, if you need anything. Or if you feel scared. I won't judge you." As she watched Em turn to go Skylar felt the strangest sense of déjà vu. She slammed the door after Em.

"I'll finish the risotto," she called upstairs to Aunt Nora, hoping it hadn't gotten sticky after being abandoned. Her stomach was actually growling now.

She poured some chicken broth into the pot and stirred the rice, which fortunately hadn't congealed into a gloppy mess. The clams glistened and the shrimp was pink and plump. She stirred absentmindedly, trying to distract herself from Em's prying questions by thinking about the dance, Gabby, and Pierce. She had barely seen Pierce in the past few days, and he still hadn't approached her about the dance as he had said he would. She had seen him with Gabby several times. For once, though, Pierce and Gabby weren't what plagued her. Em's words resounded in her ears. Was there truth to them? Em had said Skylar shouldn't trust

Meg, Ty, and Ali. But as far as Skylar was concerned, those three were the only ones on her side.

She thought about all the advice Meg had given her since they'd met. That she shouldn't allow herself to be so intimidated by everyone. That people might *seem* perfect, but it's just a matter of seeing people's weaknesses as well as their strengths. Em's weaknesses were clear enough: She was out of her frigging mind.

And what else had Meg said? That you had to want something badly in order to get it . . . because once you wanted it badly enough, you could do anything.

Skylar knew what she wanted.

But what were Gabby's weaknesses? Skylar was convinced she had none. And just then, as she poured more broth into the risotto, it hit her. The clams, the shrimp, the flaky bits of haddock—they reminded her of what Gabby had told her, right in this kitchen, last week. About her shellfish allergy, and how when she'd had a spot test for it, hives had popped up on her skin.

Bingo.

Skylar felt a surge of excitement. Meg had been right the whole time. Skylar was never going to get Pierce's attention if Gabby was always stealing her limelight—whether she was doing it purposefully or not. She needed to get Gabby out of the picture, just for a few days. Out of sight, out of mind, right?

If she just mixed a *tiny* bit of clam juice into Gabby's La Mer night cream—just a teensy bit—it would give her a rash, like

Gabby said. And what's a few hives? Just enough to make Gabby über-self-conscious, to put her in the background momentarily, which would allow Skylar to step in and show Pierce how awesome *she* was instead. It was just a practical joke. And a way to buy herself some time.

"Dinner's ready, Aunt Nora!"

Skylar spooned out the risotto as if she was dishing up liquid gold.

On Saturday afternoon Skylar asked her aunt to drop her off at Gabby's on her way to run some errands. "I just need to drop something off," she said. "Something for the dance."

Though Gabby had been acting aloof since the upset at the dance committee meeting, she seemed to relent a little bit when Skylar arrived at her house bearing a gift: a sparkly Vanessa Lorent headband that Gabby had been eyeing to go with her Spring Fling ensemble but was sold out at the VL store in the mall.

"I found it online," Skylar chirped, although the weird, coincidental truth was that Meg had given it to her in a bag of accessories. ("I was cleaning out my closet," Meg had said. "I figured you might look cute in some of this stuff.")

"Wow, thanks, Sky," Gabby said, pulling the towel she was wearing tighter around her torso. "It's freezing. Want to come in? I'm just in the middle of a home wax, but I'll be done soon. Maybe we could have a cup of tea. I feel like I've barely seen you all week."

"Sure," Skylar said. "I've never done a wax. Does it hurt?" She followed Gabby up the stairs.

"You get used to it," Gabby said over her shoulder. "The things we do for beauty . . ." Then she disappeared into her bathroom, leaving Skylar alone in her plush bedroom.

"Oh, and I have your sweater, from the other day?" Skylar called into the other room. "I washed it." She took out the carefully folded sweater from her bag.

"Cool," Gabby shouted back. "Just throw it in the hamper— I'll have to rewash it. Allergic to detergents."

Skylar looked at the carefully folded sweater—she'd even dabbed it with a tiny bit of perfume, just like she'd done for Pierce when she'd borrowed his sweatshirt—before sighing and dumping it into the hamper. Nothing she ever did was quite right.

She circled the room. Her eyes fell on a plaque she hadn't noticed the other day—an engraved certificate, commending Gabby for her charitable work at the regional food pantry. Then Skylar's eyes took in the framed photos. Gabby hugging each of her brothers on their graduation days. Gabby and Em, tan and smiling on the beach. Gabby, younger, sandwiched between her parents with her hair in pigtails and her face smeared with chocolate ice cream.

Butterflies began to flap at the bottom of Skylar's belly. Her purse, which she still had strung over her arm, was starting to feel heavy. She was having second thoughts. Gabby was nice. A good person. It's wasn't her fault everyone loved her. Maybe Skylar would just give her the headband and leave it at that.

Bing. A chat message popped up on Gabby's laptop, which was sitting open on her desk. Skylar sauntered over coolly, keeping one eye fixed on the door in case Gabby emerged from the bathroom. She skimmed the screen, and her heart stopped.

Pierce Travers had just chat-messaged Gabby. Her breath caught in her throat, Skylar leaned down to read the message.

Hey pretty lady. I have a present 2 give u b4 the dance.

Jealousy pounded through her like a flash flood. She felt desperate. Blinded. Disoriented. So Gabby *had* been leading Pierce on behind her back, just to feed her own damaged ego.

Without thinking, she sat down. Typed back: *when??*

Should be ready midweek, he responded with a smiley face.

At that moment Skylar resolved that no matter what, Gabby would not get Pierce's present—whatever it was. This had gone far enough. She had to make her move. She wrote, *meet me in the gazebo at 8 pm, Wednesday.* She added a wink for good measure.

You got it, he wrote.

And then, mind whirring, she added, *but let's keep it our little secret, okay? IM me at PinkLady13 from now on—my mom is a total control freak and she snoops in my account sometimes . . .*

Then, with several frantic clicks, she closed down the chat window and deleted it from the conversation history. She couldn't have Gabby find out about this. If all went according to plan, Gabby would be out of the picture for a day or two. Skylar would show up on Wednesday night instead of Gabby. She would make Pierce see that he and Skylar were perfect for one another. Gabby would never even have to know that Skylar had gone behind her back.

As the finishing touches of the plan came together in her head, Skylar heard motion from the bathroom. It was now or never. Tingling from head to toe, as though she'd been plunged into a vat of ice water, Skylar moved deliberately from the desk to Gabby's dresser, where her prized jar of La Mer cream sat next to a bottle of perfume and a shallow bowl of bobby pins.

The room felt almost windy as she unscrewed the cap on the bottle of clam juice. She whipped around. Was that a whisper? There was a prickle up the back of her neck, as though someone was watching her. But she found her hands still moving, as though they were not hers, as though they were possessed. She tipped a few splashes of the juice into the cream. Stirred it around a little with her finger so it blended. Quickly replaced the lid. Shoved the bottle back into her purse and wiped off her finger just as Gabby breezed back into the room, still wrapped in a towel, asking Skylar whether she wanted to join Gabby and Em at a movie.

"Em's supposed to be here in half an hour or so," Gabby said, meandering over to her closet. "I gotta get ready."

"Actually, I just came by to give you the headband," Skylar said, practically panting with nerves. "My aunt's probably already waiting outside."

She had to get out of the room before Gabby went near the cream.

"See you in school," she shouted as she ran downstairs. She slammed the front door so hard she could have sworn she heard something shatter.

CHAPTER
TWENTY-ONE

Persephone was down in the world beneath the earth. . . .

Em had shut herself up in the Dungeon all day, trying to do some work on her independent project for English before picking up Gabby for their movie date tonight. Despite two lattes and a regular coffee, she was—shocker!—finding it difficult to concentrate on school with thoughts of banishment rites weaving through her head. She'd been reading all about various sacrifice rituals, but it was only freaking her out. What could she and Drea do? It wasn't like they were going to kill a baby pig. Or another snake.

And now she'd stumbled on this stuff about Persephone, the beautiful goddess who was kidnapped by Hades. She was tricked into swallowing pomegranate seeds while in his dark netherworld, and as a result, belonged in part to that underworld, where she was forced to dwell for six months of each year for all of eternity.

Em heard Ty's silvery voice saying, *This will bind you to us forever.* The coffee between her palms was still piping hot, but suddenly she went cold—What had she done?

Impulsively, she pulled out her cell phone and called Drea. She wouldn't tell her the exact truth. But she could hint around it. She whirled one of her twin braids around her finger as she waited for Drea to pick up.

"We've got to talk," Em said as soon as she answered. "I'm freaking out."

"Hi to you, too," Drea said. Then her tone turned uncharacteristically earnest. "Why don't you come over to my place and let's talk this through, okay? I think I might have some good news that will help you."

Em agreed, hung up . . . and immediately realized that she had double-booked. She was due to meet Gabby in half an hour so they could get pizza before the movie. She typed out a text to Gabby—*Running late but be there soon. Promise!*—and was just about to press SEND when she heard a voice over her shoulder. "Tsk, tsk."

She looked up. Crow was standing above her, holding a coffee, wearing black jeans and a black leather jacket. "Persephone should've listened when Hades warned her," he said, pointing at her book.

She hadn't seen Crow since that night at the underground club, which wasn't to say that she was surprised to run into him here at the Dungeon—honestly, she wasn't sure whether she'd been hoping for the chance to confront him, or if she'd wanted to avoid him. It wasn't like she'd dressed to impress, in her ratty corduroys and green Gap shirt that she'd had since middle school. But there were tons of places she could have studied today, and she chose the coffee shop where Crow got his Red Eyes. That was an answer in itself.

Ugh. She didn't know *how* she felt. Everything in her life was messed up—that was the only truth she could cling to.

"What do you want?" Em asked, trying to keep her voice impassive and making a show of packing up her things.

"To give you this," Crow said, sliding a CD in a clear case across the small café table. Em stared at it blankly. "It's a song. I wrote it." He cleared his throat. "For you."

A single butterfly's wing fluttered in her stomach, but Em steeled herself to it. She tossed the CD in her bag as she stood up. "Thank you," she said, before switching gears. "Though perhaps I should be giving you a gift for acting as a bodyguard the other night?"

Now it was Crow's turn to stare at Em without expression. She noticed for the first time how symmetrical his features were—his straight nose, his thin lips, his square jaw. They were all set in firm lines.

"Come on, Crow—don't play dumb," she said. "You know what I'm talking about. The club below Benson's. I saw you there the other night. How did you even know about it—did you follow us?"

"You and Drea aren't the only ones who are hip to the local nightlife," Crow said, rolling his shoulders back in his leather jacket. "Some friends told me about that place."

Em pursed her lips and narrowed her eyes, looking up at him. "What friends?"

He laughed. "Why do you want to know? You jealous?"

God. He was infuriating. She didn't like his cocky attitude or the fact that he seemed to be hiding something from her. She wouldn't give him the satisfaction of continuing this conversation. She turned to leave and took a step away from the table.

He grabbed her wrist and pulled her toward him; when she turned around, his cockiness evaporated. "Yes," he said. "I—followed you there. But only because I was worried, and . . . I just want to make sure you're okay." He took a breath and seemed about to say more, but finished quietly, "There's a lot about me you wouldn't understand."

He was still holding her arm, and Em hadn't wrenched it away. She stood there staring into his eyes, just inches from him, unable to move. His yellow-green eyes were flickering hypnotically. And at that moment someone coughed behind them.

Em knew who it was before she turned around. She swiveled

and saw him watching them through eyes that were slits. "JD!" she said, her voice coming out high and squeaky.

From the look on JD's face, he obviously believed he had stumbled upon a major love scene. Em snatched her wrist out of Crow's grasp, but it was too late.

"If only there were more coffee shops in Ascension," JD said, his voice dripping with condescension, before giving her a knowing, angry smirk and slamming out of the Dungeon.

"Wait!" she called out.

Crow tried to grab her shoulders. "Em, hold on."

But Em could barely hear him—all she could feel was that the chasm between her and JD had cracked wider.

"Leave me alone!" she snapped, pushing past Crow and out into the parking lot, where she stalked to her car without a backward glance.

At Drea's, Em rang the doorbell and knocked a couple of times, to no avail. She knew that Drea was home—she could see the light on in Drea's basement "study" through a dingy cellar window— so she quietly let herself in, making sure to scurry quickly by the living room, where, as usual, Drea's dad was sitting practically comatose in front of the blue flickering television. She headed down basement steps, too lost in thought to announce her presence. When she parted the colorful curtains that cordoned off the space, Drea jumped from her seat and gasped.

"God! You scared the *hell* out of me, Em," she said, catching her breath. "You look like a ghost."

Em just stood there, trying not to cry. Seeing Drea made her think of Crow. Which made her think of JD. Which made her think of the Furies. Which made her head ache. It was like being strapped into the seat of a sickening roller coaster and not being able to get off.

"Fire," Drea said suddenly.

Em looked up, her trance momentarily interrupted. "What?"

Drea sat back down. Em looked at her, finally, and saw that Drea was full of nervous energy—her leg ticked up and down, and she kept rubbing her lips together. Drea pointed to a book in front of her. "I figured out the banishment ritual!"

The book was old and heavy, like the ones they'd seen in the antiquities library. *Hidden History: Tales of Small-Town Maine*, was called. "Where did this book come from?" Em asked.

"I managed to *borrow* it from that library after all," Drea said vaguely. Em knew what Drea meant: She'd stolen it. "It says in here that there were three sisters who were killed in Ascension—"

"Hold up, Drea," Em said. "Did anyone see you take this?"

Drea looked Em in the eye and said, "Let's stay focused on what's important here. So, like you told me the other day, these three sisters died in the woods, in a fire. But I found out more. As the story goes, the women were practically hermits—the townspeople thought they were witches, or evil seductresses, or some weird shit. Probably one of them had slept with someone's husband or something." Drea rolled her eyes. "Point is, they were practically prisoners in their home. They boarded up all the windows because kids would throw stones through them otherwise. But everyone in town still wanted them punished."

Drea stopped here, to make sure Em was paying attention. She was. She'd sunk down to her knees on the thin rug that lay on the basement concrete. The story made something deep inside of her ache. Vengeance that wouldn't be satisfied—she recognized the pattern. Surely, this was how the Furies had been born here, in Ascension, Maine. "Go on," she whispered.

Drea picked up the book and flipped the pages until she found what she was looking for. "Okay, so . . . the townspeople decided to smoke them out—using rags to light fires around the property. But one of the fires raged out of control, and the women were trapped inside. There was no way they could have escaped, no place they could have gone."

Em winced. There were flames licking at her chest, her cheeks, her hair. She put her icy fingers against her face, trying to cool off.

"You okay?" Drea looked up at her, concerned. "You want a Coke or something?"

"I'm fine," Em croaked. "So what happened after that?"

"Well, when the townspeople burst in to try and pull them out of the blaze . . . *they weren't there.* Only the body of a boy was found, no trace of the three women. It all fits together," Drea said, turning to look at Em. Her eyes blazed with intensity. Em felt weak.

"What do you mean?" she asked. "Who was the boy? What happened to him?"

"No one knows," Drea said. She stood up again and started pacing. "But don't you get it? The women didn't die. Instead, they became Furies. Or the Furies became them. Whichever. Remember how I said the Furies have existed forever, but in different forms?"

Em felt like she was at the top of a mountain looking down. She was at the edge of something powerful. She sensed it. "So, you're saying these three women . . . they *became* Furies. But how?"

Drea shrugged. "I don't know. Maybe their spirits were somehow trapped. Because the way they died—it wasn't right. They hung around, looking for revenge. They tapped into the eternal, shifting darkness that *is* the Furies. Anyway, that's not our problem right now. We need to get *rid* of them."

Suddenly she leaned forward and grabbed Em's wrist. "And I think I know how. It's just like the theme of the stupid Spring Fling—smoke and mirrors. It's all about mirroring. The Furies were somehow created by fire. Or during a fire. And by fire we'll get them *out*." With that, she pulled away and jabbed a finger toward a lighter on her desk. Next to the lighter was a pile of debris—bits of sticks and moss, a shredded piece of cloth, some crumpled pieces of paper. Did Drea want to burn that stuff?

"But—they're not human," Em said. "How can we burn them to death?"

Drea put on her *must I explain everything* face. "It's not like that," she said. "It's a ritual. We have to reverse the process. And we have to do it soon. Just trust me, okay? And I need you to be there. It won't work if you're not there." She stared at Em pleadingly, and Em began to see that Drea was dead serious.

"I'm just—I'm not sure," Em said. She was more than a little freaked out by Drea's plan. A fire ritual was even more intense than stabbing a snake. . . .

"Trust me," Drea repeated.

"Don't take this the wrong way," Em said, keeping her voice as friendly as she could. "But why should I trust you? Why are you so obsessed with the Furies, anyway? Don't you think I should have a say in how we deal with them? I'm the one who's being haunted by them. I'm the one who's being tortured."

"Em." Drea cut her off in a voice of infuriating calm, like she was talking to a child. "The entire world does not revolve around you. I have my reasons."

"Oh yeah?" Em took a step forward. "You have your reasons? Then please, spill. I'm all ears. Because so far, you haven't told me jack shit."

Drea looked away, and for a second Em feared she'd gone

too far. Drea would refuse to answer. But then Drea looked back at her, looking gentler and more vulnerable than Em had ever seen her.

"You want a reason?" Drea spoke in a quiet, measured voice, narrowing her eyes. "Fine. I'll give you a reason. Want to know why my dad hardly leaves the house? Why he can barely get out of bed? He blames himself, Em. He blames himself for my mom's death—he thinks she killed herself. They had gotten into an argument just before she died. He thinks he was the one making her unhappy."

A rock of sickness lodged in Em's stomach. Somehow, suddenly, she knew. It all sounded too familiar. "The Furies," she said softly. "They were after her?"

Drea nodded. "She was being haunted. I'm sure of it." She looked around the room, even though they were the only ones there. "After she died, I found an orchid. It was tucked underneath all her sweaters. There were notes, too. Taunting her." Drea's voice was barely audible now. "I buried the orchid and the notes in the backyard. And whatever it was they think she did, I'm sure she was innocent. I *know* it."

"What happened to her? How did she die?" Em asked gently.

Drea looked at her hands, still picking at her nails and her cuticles. Em could see that the skin around her right pointer finger was starting to bleed. "She worked at the Inland Diner—the one up on Route Four?—and it was a closing shift. The other waitresses and the cook said she insisted everyone go home, that she could handle locking up by herself. They said she seemed nervous, intense—but no one thought anything of it until . . ."

"They found her." Em murmured.

"The cook . . . the next morning. She was—" Drea swallowed hard. "She was inside the walk-in freezer." Drea yanked up the hood of her sweatshirt. "There were no wounds, no nothing. She—she just froze to death. She was trapped in the freezer for twelve hours. The inside doorknob had been broken off."

Em felt like she was about to be sick. "The Furies locked her in the freezer?"

Drea threw up her hands and spoke with a vengeance. "I don't know. Maybe. Or maybe she *was* trying kill herself. But it was their fault either way." Her eyes were shining with hatred. "They might as well have killed my dad, too. Sometimes I wonder how much he knew about the Furies—I have this vague memory of fire. . . . Maybe he tried to cast them out too?"

"Have you ever asked him?" Em said.

"No," Drea retorted firmly. "He's suffered enough."

There was no sound for a few moments, except for the rattling furnace and the faint noise of the television from upstairs. Em didn't know what to say. She could see Drea's shoulders rising and falling beneath her sweatshirt. She wanted to hug her. To comfort her. She tried to imagine what Drea had been through . . . and couldn't. Her mind wouldn't even let her go there. So instead, she went to touch Drea's back. But Drea flinched, pulling away.

"We'll figure this out together, okay?" Em said.

Drea offered a halfhearted smile. "The princess and the punk—whatta team."

Just then church bells sounded in the distance. Six o'clock.

"Shit!" Em cursed. She was almost an hour late to see Gabby. "I gotta go. I'm supposed to meet Gabby."

"Go," Drea said. "I need some time to be alone."

Emerging from Drea's basement, Em could see that she was irredeemably late. Gabby had sent several texts: *Where are u? . . .* and then, *We're gonna miss the movie . . .* and then, *Are you even gonna come over at all? . . .* and then, *Well, I guess I'll just get ready for bed, then. See you in school. . . .*

Em tried calling to tell Gabby that she was on her way, but there was no answer. Gabby was probably furious, and screening her calls. When she arrived at the house, Gabby's car was in the driveway and her light was still on. Good. She was still awake.

But there was no response when she rang the bell, or when she knocked on the door, or when she called Gabby's cell (again), or when she dialed the Doves' house line. She could hear it ringing inside, jangling. "Gabby?" Em yelled up at the house. Her heart started thumping, low and hard against her rib cage. This wasn't Gabby ignoring her. Something was wrong. She could sense it.

She made her way around to the back door, which she knew would be unlocked. She stepped into the Doves' huge kitchen. "Gabs?" No response, her voice echoing against the stainless steel.

She walked around to the front hall and started up the stairs. "Gabby?" She repeated Gabby's name over and over like a mantra.

Em pushed open Gabby's bedroom door slowly. It swished against the carpet. At first that was all Em saw—carpet, and Gabby's bed, and all the usual stuff. The smell of perfume in the air. And then, a foot. A bare foot with painted toenails. Gabby's.

Gabby was lying there, her breaths shallow, her face horribly puffy and swollen. Like bee-stung flesh. Like bread left in a bowl of water.

Em knew instantly what was going on: Gabby was having an allergic reaction. This was bad. Really bad.

"Gabby? Gabby! Wake up!" She barked at Gabby as she grabbed for her cell phone, hands shaking, and dialed 911. She knelt down and put her ear right up against Gabby's distended lips to make sure that she was still breathing. There was only the faintest breath, hot and thin against her skin.

"Yes, there's a girl here, 261 Allen Drive—I think she's having an allergic reaction," Em wept into the phone at the emergency dispatcher. "Please. Come. Come soon." Where was her Epi-pen? Em started rifling through Gabby's things, throwing stuff out of her nightstand drawer, dumping the contents of her bag on the floor. Nothing.

And as she ripped through Gabby's belongings, hot tears welling in her eyes, she began to hear girlish, catty laughter ringing through the air. Satisfied giggles that came from some unidentifiable place. Inside the house. Or maybe outside. Or maybe from within Em. It was impossible to tell.

As she gripped Gabby's hand, rocking back and forth on crouched legs and waiting for the ambulance to show up, only one thought raced through her mind: *Somehow, some way, the Furies had something to do with this, too.*

CHAPTER
TWENTY-TWO

Skylar smelled flowers long before she reached Gabby's room in the hospital. The scent was thick, overripe, like walking into a garden in mid-July, and it made her dizzy. She stopped for a moment to regain her composure.

She felt terrible, of course, for what had happened to Gabby. She'd almost *died*. Skylar put her hand against the wall to steady herself. *I didn't know.* She kept telling herself that, over and over. She'd had no idea that Gabby was *that* allergic to shellfish! She'd thought it was, like, a few hives. A little rash. Not this. She never would have . . . not in a million years . . .

I didn't know. It wasn't my fault.

Gabby had been in the hospital for more than sixteen hours. She'd gone into anaphylactic shock—been almost unable to breathe, puffed up like a balloon.

And it was all Skylar's fault.

Skylar had had to force herself to visit. It would seem weird if she didn't. Fiona, Jenna, Sean—they'd all called, asking if she wanted to ride with them, but she'd declined. Instead, she'd had Aunt Nora drive her over. She felt so ashamed. And terrified. She didn't want to be around anyone else, anyone who might discover her horrible secret. So there she was, alone in the busy hospital hallway, her stomach churning with nerves.

Skylar rounded the corner, and then stopped short. She had a clear view down the corridor to room 125. And honestly, it looked like a freaking florist, with bouquets and flower arrangements on every surface. Skylar could also see at least eight people from Ascension, all huddled around Gabby's bed. Her friends. Gabby's friends.

Skylar couldn't help but flash back to the time she broke her ankle in fifth grade during recess: how empty her hospital room had been (her mom outside flirting with the disinterested doctor, Lucy not bothering to visit at all), how bored she'd been as she healed at home. She didn't get one bouquet, and Lucy had made a game of placing things she wanted—soda, chocolate—just out of her reach. "It's physical therapy," Lucy had said.

She couldn't do this right now. She'd had too much of hospitals in her life. Her gut screamed that she should turn on her heel and hightail it away from room 125. She couldn't handle seeing all those people—not to mention Gabby herself—until she had things more under control. She froze, ready to make a run for it. But then her stomach sank as she remembered: the evidence. The cream. She was so stupid not to have thought of it before. Someone was going to find out—if they hadn't already—that Gabby's La Mer skin cream was dosed with clam juice. If she kept using it, she would continue to have these reactions. And once that came out, it would be an all-out hunt to find out how it had happened. Who had done it. She had to destroy the evidence. But first, she had to make an appearance at Gabby's bedside. Not to do so would only call attention to herself.

She pushed herself forward and hovered in the doorway of the hospital room until a nurse needed to get by. "Coming through," the woman said. As the crowd parted to let the nurse by, Gabby spotted Skylar at the back of the room, and her face broke into a brave, warm smile. It lacerated Skylar's resolve; she hoped her flushed cheeks would be interpreted as concern.

"Sky," Gabby said softly, motioning Skylar closer to the bed. "I'm so happy you came." Her parents were sitting on either side of her, looking haggard yet relieved. Their baby was safe.

Skylar thought that if guilt had a smell, it would be of cheap air fresheners or drugstore body oil—and she could swear that she was practically sweating the stuff.

"How are you doing, Gabs?" she asked as she approached the bed. "I'm so sorry that this happened. So sorry."

"Hey, I'll be fine," Gabby said. "I'm just grateful that Em found me."

Skylar nodded mutely. Then the nurse started shooing people out of the room: "That's enough excitement for now." Skylar was grateful for the excuse to leave. She didn't even wait for the elevator at the end of the hall; instead, she took the stairs down, two at a time. There wasn't much time to waste.

"Done so soon?" Aunt Nora looked up from her magazine as Skylar threw open the passenger-side door.

"Yeah," Skylar said breathlessly. "Um, we need to go by Gabby's house. She—she needs me to do something for her."

"Right now?" Aunt Nora searched Skylar's face, the wrinkles between her eyes furrowing with concern.

"Yeah . . . it's—it's something for school," Skylar said, zipping and unzipping her fleece nervously as she talked. "For the dance! I need to get this list from her desk and send out some emails later." Skylar tried to sound as chipper as she could. "It'll only take a second."

She knew no one would be home at the Doves'. She'd seen Gabby's mom and dad had been at the hospital, and Skylar was almost certain that they would stay with their daughter until she was ready to be released. Skylar made Nora drive all the way up the winding driveway, and then she went in the back door and ran upstairs. The cream was sitting uncapped on Gabby's dresser. It didn't look like it had been touched since "the incident." *Jesus.*

It must have happened so fast. With a shudder, she replaced the lid and pocketed the small jar, feeling a small sense of relief as soon as it was in her possession. Maybe she hadn't lost control after all. . . .

"I just . . . I feel really shitty," Skylar told Meg on the phone later that evening. "Gabby's never been anything but nice to me, and I'm the reason she's in the hospital!" She was lying on her creaky bed, staring up at the wooden slats on the ceiling. The cream was safely tucked beneath her rattiest T-shirts in a drawer. She wondered how long it would take Gabby to notice it was missing. The clam juice was in her bag, to be thrown away at school tomorrow.

"Skylar, don't beat yourself up," Meg said. Her voice sounded far away. "You had no idea the reaction would be as bad as it was."

"But I can't believe I did it at all," Skylar said. "This . . . this isn't me." *Anymore.* "What kind of person would do that?"

"Sky. Sweetie. You didn't mean for it to go this far, right? It was an accident, right? Just a practical joke that went a little too far. If anyone ever finds out—which they won't—your story is totally kosher."

Skylar sighed. She wanted to trust Meg, who seemed to have everything figured out, who always stayed so composed and collected. But her weird behavior the other day—the non-chalant way she'd reacted to finding a dead body in a pond—made Skylar see her in a new light. And there was something in her tone tonight that was only making Skylar feel worse.

A practical joke that went too far. Despite her breezy tone, Meg's words seemed carefully chosen, an echo of old words, old comforts. Once again Skylar wondered if there was some remote possibility that Meg knew about Lucy's accident. If so, why didn't she just come out and say so? Or was this just Skylar's guilty conscience acting up again?

"Babe, I gotta run," Meg was saying. Skylar had almost forgotten she was holding her phone. "Gotta go meet Ty and Ali. Call me if you need me!" She hung up.

Skylar curled up on top of her bed, laying her cheek against the worn fabric of Aunt Nora's patchwork quilt. Skylar's maternal grandmother had made it. Her mom's mom. Suddenly Skylar's whole body ached for her mother—someone to hold her and make her feel better. She rubbed the spot on her arm where she'd been stung by the bee; it was throbbing.

The pain reminded her of the night of Lucy's last pageant. They'd been in the dressing room together, getting ready.

Lucy leans in close to the long mirror, touching up her mascara, and Skylar is in the corner, pulling at the hem of her dress in an effort to make it fall evenly.

Lucy catches her eyes in the reflection. "Your arms look kind of flabby," she says, appraising Skylar's spaghetti-strap gown with a harsh eye. Skylar turns this way and that, trying to stand in such a way that her arms look slender—like Lucy's.

With a snort, Lucy caps her mascara, comes up behind Skylar, and pinches the back of her arm. Hard. So hard that Skylar lets out an involuntary yelp.

"I don't think you can camouflage this," Lucy says, gripping a fold of skin between her fingers. Then, releasing her fingers slightly: "Maybe you should borrow my shawl."

When Lucy lets go altogether, Skylar can still feel the pain. Pulsing.

Just like her arm was hurting right now. She got up to look at the bee sting in the mirror. Walking to the bathroom, she was aware of every step against the hardwood floor.

She flipped on the light in her bathroom and turned to face the mirror. What she saw there made her draw back swiftly. She gripped her hands around the door frame, swaying there for a moment. Squeezing her eyes shut. Maybe she was hallucinating. But no, it was still there when she opened her eyes.

A question was scrawled on her bathroom mirror in red lipstick:

Mirror, mirror, on the wall, who's the vainest of them all?

The writing was jagged and sharp. A shudder ran down Skylar's spine; her knees buckled. She turned to look down the hallway, half-expecting to see someone there. She didn't want to look back at the mirror, but she couldn't help but stare at the bloodred words. Was this a joke? For some reason, when Skylar heard the phrase in her mind, it sounded like it was coming out of Meg's mouth. Singsongy. Almost . . . deranged. She thought of

Em's warnings. Did Meg and her cousins have something to do with this?

And then she remembered that night a few weeks ago at Gabby's, when they'd walked out to Em's car. This very phrase—or one very similar—had been written on Em's windshield. The connection was too eerie. Terrified, Skylar forced herself to back away from the mirror.

She grabbed a wad of tissues and pressed them against the words, trying to ignore the way the lipstick smeared like blood. Her hand, shaking slightly, pressed down harder and harder. The letters weren't coming off; they merely bled into each other as Skylar scrubbed with increasing force. *Mirror, mirror. Mirror, mirror.* Even as they became illegible, the words still mocked her. She clenched her teeth and leaned in to the mirror even more.

With a loud splitting sound, the mirror cracked. Her hand swerved, but not quickly enough. The glass sliced into the side of her thumb, and blood immediately began to well up around the cut. The incision didn't hurt, exactly, but it sent a shock through her. She drew in a sharp breath through her teeth, trying not to look at how her blood matched the shade of lipstick almost perfectly.

Heart pounding, Skylar drew her thumb to her mouth and stared at her cracked reflection in the glass. The distortion made her grotesque. Like she'd been sliced, diced, and rearranged.

She looked like a monster.

CHAPTER TWENTY-THREE

As she shoved textbooks into her messenger bag before school on Tuesday morning, Em's hand fell on a square of flat plastic— the CD Crow had given her a few days ago, the same day Gabby had had her allergic reaction. She flipped the case over in her hands, but it was unlabeled, so she just popped it into her computer as she finished her morning routine.

Em recognized the first chords of the song as the ones Crow had played for her in his pickup truck. The day it rained. The day they'd kissed. She pushed those thoughts from her mind and tried to focus on the music. That day, he'd said the song was still in the works, but it was clearly finished now. It was good. The sea-shanty chords soared over a twinkling piano in the back- ground, and his words sounded clear and strong above it all. She paused from lacing up her boots and listened to the lyrics:

I don't know what tomorrow brings, or when the dark will come
Right now is all we've got—baby, let's be young

She could picture him singing it, his dark eyes narrowing as he reached for the higher notes, his hair falling in his eyes as he lowered his head to reach the gravelly tones. The vision was quickly eclipsed by thoughts of JD. The way he moved his hands when he got really excited about something; the way his forehead wrinkled when he was trying to figure something out; the way he always let her have the first piece of pie and control over the radio when they were driving. The way he looked at her like she was really there—no, like she was the only thing he could see.

Right now is all we've got. . . . The words leaped into her head and her heart, giving her a jolt of energy. She had the right to make mistakes, and the right to fix them.

Gabby returned to school that day. Her face was still red and raw, but she was in the clear, healthwise. She wore skinny jeans and wedge-heeled boots, a green scoop-neck top, and the sparkly scarf Em had gotten her for Christmas. It was an outfit that screamed, *I'm fine!* Still, their friends—and even near strangers—showered her with affection, care, offers to assist. She'd missed only one day of school, but it was as though she'd been away for weeks.

At lunch, sitting under the glaring winter light that came

through the skylights in the Gazebo, Em watched as Gabby carefully dressed her Greek salad, picked out a wilted piece of lettuce, and popped an olive into her mouth. It was like nothing had changed.

But Gabby had almost died. They were sitting alone; everyone else was still buying their lunches or trickling in from class.

Gabby cleared her throat. "I wanted to thank you. Again. We've barely had a moment alone since . . . this happened," Gabby said, brushing her fingers lightly against her ruddy cheek.

"I know. . . . We kept getting interrupted by your adoring fans," Em said with a gentle smile, referring to the steady stream of visitors and flower deliveries that had appeared at the hospital and then during Gabby's afternoon of home convalescence the day before.

"That was so nice of everybody, wasn't it?" Gabby shook her head in amazement. "But really, Em. Thank you. I know that you probably saved—you saved my life." Gabby's voice caught, and guilt swept over Em.

"Gabby, if I gotten there earlier—like I was supposed to—the reaction wouldn't have been so advanced." She hung her head, letting strands of her hair fall around her face. "I'm sorry that I was late, and that I didn't get your texts. . . ."

"It's okay, Em. We both know I'm lucky you got there at all." She threw back her shoulders and addressed the next question to the whole table, which had begun to fill up as they'd been talking. Lauren was feeding Nick french fries. Jenna produced a square of dark chocolate and presented it to Gabby as a get-well gift. "So, where are we going to pregame the dance?"

Just like that, Em knew the conversation was over. Gabby was back on. It was always a given that Gabs would coordinate both the pre- and post-dance partying. She always had.

Lauren and Fiona exchanged a quick glance.

"Skylar had said something about hanging out with Jess Marshall and those girls?" Lauren sounded tentative, and she was blinking a lot. "But, whatever. Like, whatever you want to do, Gabs."

Gabby gave her best newscaster smile and cocked her head. "Jess? Sure! I love Jess. She is such a sweetheart."

"I call no DD," Sean announced from his seat at the far end of the table. "I drove to homecoming."

"Me too," Lauren said. "You may remember that night, Fiona, as the one where you suggested going swimming even though it was mid-October?"

Suddenly Em had a burst of inspiration: the dance. That was where she would confess her feelings to JD. It was the perfect way to assuage any of JD's unfounded fears about her being embarrassed by him. Screw the Furies and their threats. They hadn't kept up their end of the bargain—to leave her alone—so she wasn't going to abide by the terms either. She wasn't going to let them manipulate her with the constant fear of retaliation.

She was going to tell JD everything. She would recapture the remnants of her former life, reestablish her best-friendships, and reveal the truth to JD—broadcast it, even, in front of everyone.

Not only was she going to the dance, she was going to go all out. Furies be damned. Instantly, she felt lighter than she had in weeks.

"I'll drive," Fiona was saying, pushing her glasses up her nose. "If I can borrow those blue suede Steve Madden heels, Em."

"Sure, Fi. I'm not wearing them," Em said.

"Which reminds me," Gabby said. "What *are* you wearing, Em? We've barely discussed it."

"Oh, I was thinking I would just wear my black wrap dress," Em answered. An old standby.

"Um, no," Gabby said emphatically. "You're too pale for black. You'll look vampy. How about that light purple one? The one with the sheer-ish skirt?"

Em smiled. "That's a great idea, Gabs. And I was thinking of getting my nails done after school," she added, spur of the moment.

"Boo, I can't." Gabby pouted. "I promised my mom I'd come straight home—it's like she thinks I'm going to break or something." Then Gabby beamed a smile at Em. "You should go, though. No offense, but you really need it."

"None taken," Em laughed. The lightness was still there. She *would* get her life back.

• • •

After school she drove to the strip mall—the one with Pete's Pizza and Princess Nails—to get a manicure. Back when Em's mom was working superlong hours (before she had seniority), she used to take Em here on her days off for a coat of nice, sensible pale pink polish. A special treat. "Taking care of yourself is the first step in taking care of others," her mom used to say. That's what Em was going to do today.

But just as she approached the salon door, Em froze.

There, in the window, was Ty. She was sitting with her nails under the dryer, her black-brown hair falling in waves over her shoulders. Em still couldn't believe that she'd dyed it, couldn't believe she'd gotten rid of that beautiful red mane.

They caught each other's eyes through the window. The afternoon sun burned orange in the winter sky, casting its reflection on the window, making it seem as though Ty was appearing beyond a thin sheet of flame. Ty raised her eyebrows and smiled, as if to say, *Imagine meeting* you *here!* Em curled her lip and watched Ty gathering her things.

"What the hell are you doing here?" she asked as soon as Ty walked out the door, trying to sound menacing. But she knew she sounded afraid.

As usual, Ty was underdressed for the frigid early spring air, wearing a loose T-shirt, jeans, and flats without socks.

Ty smiled. "Just getting my nails done. A good manicure

always brings me so much comfort, you know? It's like a fresh start!" Her voice was breezy, and it seemed to snake through the air, around her neck, tickling the hairs behind Em's ears.

"Did you know I was planning to come here?" Em's voice became small and shaky.

"I know one thing—you're a life saver," Ty said. "Thank god you were able to come to Gabby's aid." At the mention of Gabby's name, Em thought she heard those same high-pitched giggles drifting through the air. She couldn't tell if she was imagining them or really hearing them. "Things may not go so well for your other pals," Ty added in an offhand way.

"My other *pals*? What's that supposed to mean?" Em choked out.

Ty blew on her nails daintily and avoided answering Em's question directly. "Spring is my favorite season. Did you know that?"

The tone of Ty's voice confirmed Em's suspicions. The Furies were planning something. They were baiting Em, screwing with her. Well, she wouldn't bite. Not now.

"Get away from here," she spat, stepping closer so she and Ty were just a few inches apart. "Leave. Us. Alone."

Ty raised an eyebrow but didn't step back. "You know, maybe JD would like you better if you learned how to control your temper."

Immediately she figured out Ty's strategy: bring up JD in order to remind Em what was at stake—her love. Despite knowing it was a ploy to enrage her, Ty's words sent her spinning off the edge.

She lunged for Ty, the blackness inside her propelling her forward.

All of a sudden she found herself flattened, driven forcefully against the side of the brick building. It seemed as if Ty had barely moved. But she was very close now, practically whispering in Em's ear.

"You want to know about those seeds?" Ty breathed. "You feel it, right? Moving inside of you—that anger, that smoky rage. You know what I'm talking about, don't you?"

Em clamped her mouth shut, refusing to answer. But of course, yes, she knew.

Ty released her, examining her nails to make sure her polish hadn't smudged. "Careful, Em. Remember that we aren't so different, you and I."

"Get. The. Hell. Out. Of. My. Life." Em's words were packed like dynamite. "If you don't—I *swear* to you—I will extinguish you forever."

"I can't get out of your life, Em," Ty said. "We're bound together. Don't you get it?" Then she stepped past Em, toward the setting sun. For a second she seemed to shimmer in front of the orange-red glare. Then Em blinked, and when she opened her eyes, Ty was gone, as though she'd just burned away. The sound of laughter, however, lingered.

CHAPTER
TWENTY-FOUR

Tonight was the night: Skylar's surprise date with Pierce. He'd chat-messaged her—well, technically he had chat-messaged Gabby—a few times this week, and Skylar had played her part. She'd flirted with Pierce, planned their rendezvous, and reminded him that they should keep their feelings secret until the dance. She'd tried to play down "her" brush with death. The last thing Skylar needed was Pierce thinking that Gabby was some beautiful wounded bird or something.

There was enough of that going around at school. Skylar couldn't believe Gabby's luck—after missing *one* day of school, she'd come back as a survivor-celebrity! No one seemed to care about the rash on her face. On the contrary, Gabby's health scare only cemented how much everyone loved her, how much everyone missed her when she wasn't around, how crucial her bubbly personality was to daily life at Ascension.

But tonight was Skylar's chance to turn Pierce's eyes her way, to have him all to herself. And though he was expecting Gabby to show up, not her, Skylar hoped—knew!—he would be glad in the end that she was the one in his arms.

There were several reasons for her logic. First of all, he hadn't been *overly* effusive via chat. Maybe, now that he'd seen Gabby without her makeup on, he was more interested in being her friend than her boyfriend. Skylar hoped to provide some contrast—a perfectly put-together, perky prize.

Secondly, she was certain that once Pierce had a second to absorb, without any outside distractions, how much Skylar has grown and changed—like a butterfly, like a swan—he would change his mind. Tonight Pierce Travers would see that Skylar had it all. Everything Gabby had, and more.

And plus, as a last resort, Skylar resolved to tell him that Gabby had sent her, to convey that she wasn't interested, and that he should leave her alone. If he didn't naturally see Gabby as out of the picture, she would shatter the illusion for him.

Lip gloss. Hair pinned half up with sparkly bobby pins. Light purple eye shadow to bring out the green in her eyes. Black jeans, a magenta boatneck shirt, a bluish scarf, her gray ankle boots. Eyelashes curled, brown mascara applied—it looked less severe on blondes, Gabby had told her. Her legs were even freshly shaved, under her jeans. Not that she thought Pierce would touch them (tonight, at least), but because she'd been "getting ready" since three o'clock. Meg had helped, of course. And now every single tiny detail of her appearance was perfect. Or as close to perfect as Skylar would ever get.

"Lots of snow coming tonight," Meg mused as Skylar checked her makeup in the car mirror one more time. Skylar hadn't seen much of Meg over the last few days, not since the creepy incident at the pond. She didn't really miss her that much. In fact, it was amazing how much she'd learned in so little time. She could take care of herself now.

Tonight Marty Dove and the news reports were predicting at least a foot of accumulation. It wasn't rare for March in Maine, but it would be Skylar's first blizzard since she'd moved to Ascension. She hoped it wouldn't get too bad until after her tryst with Pierce. Although, walking outside together with snowflakes resting on their eyelashes and noses would be a romantic way to start their relationship. He'd told her once how much he loved being outside during nor'easters. Skylar couldn't help but sigh out loud, thinking about it.

Meg gave Skylar a pep talk as she drove her to school in her maroon Lincoln. More of the same. How she just needed to show Pierce how awesome she was, blah blah blah. Skylar didn't want to tell Meg she was only making things worse. Skylar was ready to stop talking about it and just put this plan into action. She focused on the beautiful flakes of snow, watching as they smashed into the windshield and became drops of slush.

"So, should I wait for you out here?" Meg cocked her head as Skylar did some last-minute primping in the high school parking lot.

"Um, no," Skylar said in an impulsive—and she hoped warranted—fit of confidence. "Pierce can give me a ride."

"That's the spirit," Meg said, nodding as if she'd expected that answer. "Good luck, babes—you earned it."

Skylar didn't feel half as self-assured as she was making out to be, but she tried to psych herself up as she let herself in through the auditorium doors and made her way through the back hallway of the theater and into the library wing, which led to the cafeteria. Her boot heels made clacking sounds that bounced off the walls and windows in the empty, dark halls. It was fun to be in school all alone. She hummed a little bit, and her voice reverberated against the lockers and classroom doors.

In the cafeteria she'd expected more moonlight to be shining through the Gazebo's skylight, but the glass overhead was already covered thickly with snow. It was dark and shadowy. Intimate. Pierce would have no choice but to fall for her. She grinned and spun in a circle, arms outstretched, on the freshly waxed linoleum. Her pink coat flared out around her. In the silence, despite the empty tables and benches, the curling posters, and the smell of school lunch still lingering in the air, it was easy to imagine herself as reigning queen bee.

And then she heard them—rubber-soled steps squeaking faintly in the hallway. Good. So Pierce had found the door she'd told him about. Her heart beat faster; she reached up with both hands to bring the hood of her coat carefully over her curls. She knew that from afar, she looked a lot like Gabby, and she was going to use that to her advantage, to draw him in close before making the big reveal.

"Gabby?" His voice resounded in the empty room. She motioned him closer; he grinned in the easy, flirtatious way he was known for. "Hey there," he said as he walked toward her. Even in the dark, she could see his strong frame, how his shoulders fit perfectly in his football jacket, the way his crew cut highlighted his strong jawline.

And then, when he was just an arm's length away, Skylar pulled the hood away from her face and stepped into a small patch of moonlight that shone through the skylight.

"Hi, Pierce," she said, offering her best pageant smile.

Pierce's shock crushed her almost instantly. It was more than surprise. It was discomfort. It was disappointment.

"Skylar?" He could barely speak. His mouth opened and closed like a cartoon guppy. "Hey. I wasn't . . . um . . . What are you . . . Where's . . ." He trailed off, looking mystified. And slightly angry.

"I know you weren't exactly—expecting me," she said, fluttering her eyelashes. "But . . . hi."

"I don't understand," Pierce said, staring at her and then at his snow-soaked boots. "I'm sorry, I'm confused. It wasn't supposed to be—"

"I know," she interjected. "But it *is* supposed to be me, Pierce." She gazed at him, waiting for him to understand her meaning.

"I—I don't get it, Skylar."

"It's been me all along," she said. "Online, at school, at parties—we have a connection, don't we? We're perfect for each other. Don't you see it? I've known since that first day in the cafeteria—when you lent me your sweatshirt? I'm just right for you. And you're just right for me. You know?"

He backed away ever so slightly. He ran a hand through his hair. "What the hell, Skylar?" He shook his head. "All this time—all this time, when I thought I was talking to Gabby, it was really . . ." He couldn't even finish.

Oh god. This wasn't working. Panic palpitated through Skylar's whole body.

"Pierce, *wait*. Can I explain? I mean, look—" Her words got all jumbled, and she was fidgeting with the tassels of her scarf. She looked and sounded like a scared little girl. This was nothing like the impression she'd hoped to make.

He cleared his throat and shifted his eyes toward her. God. He looked so uncomfortable. "Hey, Skylar," he said. "I know you have a thing for me. And look, I don't mean to say . . . You're great, okay? You're a nice girl. But I just—" He looked down again.

A nice girl. He might as well have reached out and slapped her. She knew what he was going to say next. "Gabby doesn't want you, Pierce," she said, suddenly regaining the ability to articulate. "So think about that." She crossed her arms and stood there.

For a moment it seemed like he was softening. Their eyes met. He smiled a little bit. Skylar's heart soared. To hell with Gabby—she had won Pierce after all. Her arms fell to her sides, fingers tingling, waiting for him to come closer.

Then Pierce just shook his head. "I'm sorry, Sky."

"But—but . . . I'm just as pretty as her," Skylar said, knowing she sounded desperate and jealous, but unable to stop the words from gushing out. "And I . . . the dance—I thought up all the stuff for the dance. Did you know that? And we're in the same class, you and I!" She swallowed a massive lump in her throat. "Why are you so obsessed with her? Why is everyone so *obsessed* with her?" She was near tears now.

Pierce gave her a sad smile. "There's just something about Gabby," he said. "She's a good person. She's always thinking about other people. She doesn't have anything to prove. She's just . . . fun."

Just fun. A good person. Nothing to prove. Nothing like Skylar, was more like it. In an instant it became clear: She wasn't anything like Gabby, no matter how much of Gabby's personality she'd tried to usurp.

Pierce started to walk away. "Wait!" she called after him weakly. He just kept going.

She stood there for a moment, motionless, trying to regain her breath. And then she heard something, a sound simultaneously far away and near. Like a shriek of laughter or a high-pitched creak. Or maybe . . . a footstep? Had Pierce changed his mind? But the sound was behind her. Skylar spun around; by now her eyes were well adjusted to the dark. Something was glinting on the table where Gabby, Em, and their crew usually sat. The popular table. The table directly below the Gazebo's glassed-in roof, the one where she'd sat for the past few glorious days.

She walked closer. It was a glossy photo with two figures on it. She leaned over to pick it up, but as she got close enough to see it, her heart started drilling in her chest. She staggered backward. *No. Impossible.*

It was the picture. The picture of her and Lucy that she'd destroyed weeks ago, when she'd first moved to Ascension. The photo she'd torn up. The memory she'd tried to get rid of. It sat in the middle of the table, taped together like an elementary school art project. The hair on the back of Skylar's neck stood on end. She didn't dare touch the image. She just stared at it as though it was alive. Like it was going to bite her, or slither up her side.

She was so focused on the picture that she barely heard the faint groaning from up above.

But then the sound got louder, and Skylar knew something was wrong. It was like the sky was moaning. She squinted out into the parking lot. Nothing. She looked out through the door Pierce had walked through. Equally still and silent. But something was coming at her—she could feel it, she could hear it, she could sense it.

The rumbling got louder still, something like a train coming from the distance, until it was whooshing into her ears. All this in a matter of seconds, but still she had time to wonder: *Is there going to be an earthquake?* And then: *It's like the sound of a bending ice cube tray, only a million times louder.*

That's when she felt the blast of cold air hit her scalp. She looked up with just enough time to see the ceiling collapse into a million deadly pieces under the weight of the snow.

It felt like slow motion; the way the snow mixed with the splintered glass was almost beautiful, like sharp white feathers. It took her breath away. Rooted to the spot, she marveled at their terrible beauty even as the giant shards rained down over her hands and face in a freezing blur. Through the almost deafening roar, she could swear she heard girlish shrieks again—maybe laughter—as her head hit the linoleum floor.

Then the roar, the laughter, became a searing fire of pain.

Then darkness.

ACT THREE

VENGEANCE, OR THE LAST DANCE

CHAPTER
TWENTY-FIVE

An accident? *Bullshit*. Em knew better.

They were saying there was something "structurally unsound" about the Gazebo roof, but the whole thing felt off to Em. Why had Skylar been at school so late in the first place? She'd been marked by the Furies—Em was sure of that—and now she'd paid the price. And hadn't Ty just said Em should watch out for her other friends? Not that Skylar was a *friend*, but her "accident" seemed all too coincidental.

While everyone else buzzed about what had happened and about the Spring Fling—which, it was decided, would still take place as planned ("The kids really need something positive," the administration had said)—Em was lost in darker thoughts, wondering how the Furies had lured Skylar to Ascension High in a snowstorm, how they'd tampered with the glass so that it would break right over Skylar's face. And what she could have done to prevent it, or at least better warn Skylar.

Still, as guilty as she felt, Em was also furious with Skylar for putting herself in this situation, for not listening.

She had to go see Skylar. She had no other choice, even though she was sick to death of hospitals. First Sasha. Thinking of that night still made Em's skin crawl. Sasha's dead eyes, her bloody smile . . .

Then Gabby. Surrounded by flowers—white, pink, yellow. No orchids, thank god. The hospital was not exactly a place you wanted to see your best friend.

And now Skylar, in a quiet hospital room, with her weird aunt Nora slumped and sleeping in a chair in the lobby. Em considered waking her up to find out what she knew. What she'd seen in Em that day at Skylar's house. Em harbored a strong suspicion that Nora was connected somehow to the Furies. But the poor woman looked so drained that Em decided to spare her further distress, at least for now. She still wanted to keep the Furies a secret from anyone who *didn't* know of them. The risk was far too great.

Skylar lay in the hospital bed; her face was totally bandaged, but her eyes were open, and they looked simultaneously wild and drowsy. She was probably delirious from the pain meds they'd pumped her with. All around her, machines beeped and buzzed in irregular rhythms.

"Skylar? It's Em," she said, standing about three feet from Skylar's metal hospital bed.

"Hiiii . . . ," Skylar mumbled. It sounded like she was speaking through a mouthful of tissues.

"How are you feeling?" Em asked, taking in the IV tube inserted into Skylar's arm and the part of Skylar's head that had been shaved so that the doctors could stitch up a gash on her scalp.

For a second Skylar just stared at Em blankly, and Em wondered if this whole thing was pointless. Was Skylar too out of it to even have a conversation? But then Skylar croaked out, "I—I did something. I did something bad."

You sure did, Em thought. *But what?*

"I made my sister Gabby hit her head," Skylar slurred.

"Your sister? What are you talking about?" Em leaned closer to make sure she didn't mishear.

"She's damaged," Skylar said. "I'm so ashamed. Is this why this happened to me? Is this why I can't be the queen?"

Em shook her head. She had no idea what Skylar was talking about. Gabby? Did Skylar somehow feel guilty about Gabby's allergic reaction, like she did? "If you think this is payback, you should consider yourself lucky," Em said. "Your *friend* Meg could have done a lot worse." She waited to see Skylar's reaction to Meg's name.

Through the bandages, Em could see Skylar's eyes narrow. "She told me . . . she told me I would be the queen of the dance. . . . They said it would all happen tonight," Skylar murmured, and Em's stomach dropped as she remembered Ty's words in the nail salon— *Spring is my favorite season.* An idea began niggling at the back of Em's mind.

Were the Furies planning on crashing the dance?

She thought of Gabby, who had put so much effort into planning the event, and her friends, who were excited to dress up and gossip about boys and stare at girls in too-short skirts. Normal high school people, doing normal high school things. And JD, and her plan to fix things between them tonight.

Em needed to know what Meg had told Skylar. She needed to know everything. "Skylar . . . ," she began.

But Skylar interrupted her. "Are you Ty or are you Em?" she asked in her dreamy, drug-induced haze.

"What?" Em froze.

"Sometimes I can't tell the difference . . . ," Skylar said, her eyes drifting over Em's face.

Em shuddered and stood up straight. "You—you think we look alike?"

"Ummmhmmm," Skylar said, starting to doze off, "both so pretty . . ."

Em remembered how she had thought the same thing when they were grappling in the gravel outside of Benson's Bar. Their long, wavy brown hair and their tall, lanky bodies. Now that she thought about it . . . she and Ty did look, if not identical, then at least . . . similar. Like they could be from the same family.

The very thought made Em feel like she'd swallowed something too big, or too hot. She watched as Skylar's head slumped to one side; Skylar was fully gripped now by a doped-up sleep. Em wouldn't get any more answers from her. Not now, anyway. She slipped out of the room as quietly as she could, hoping to avoid disturbing either Skylar *or* her aunt.

As she drove home she thought about what Skylar had said. *The queen. The dance. It would all happen tonight.* The more she turned the words over in her head, the more certain she was that the Furies were planning something that would go down this evening. Something that would affect not only her, not only Skylar, but Ascension as a whole. As Drea had said, the Furies could be plotting revenge against the whole town.

While she'd been determined to make an appearance for her own reasons, this new information made her less sure about whether to risk going to the dance or not. Would it be smart to show up and try to disrupt their plans? Or would it be safer for everyone if she stayed home? Were the Furies really after everyone—or just her?

Her brain spun with conflicting thoughts, plans, and desires. She was burning up; she checked to make sure the heat was off and then rolled down her window a bit to let in some cold air, gulping it in like it was water in a desert.

When she arrived at home, she ran upstairs and flung herself on her bed, burying her head in the pillows. She spoke to herself: *Calm down, Em. Okay. Relax. Take deep breaths.*

She tried to think rationally: What was her next step? The dance. She had to get to the dance and talk to JD.

She looked out her bedroom window and saw that JD's light was off. *Shit.* She grabbed for her phone. Dialed his cell; let it ring. No answer. She tried his land line.

"Hey, Mel?" she asked when JD's little sister picked up. "It's Em. Where's JD? I know his car isn't there"—she didn't care if she sounded like a stalker to a twelve-year-old—"and I need to talk to him. Like, now."

"Hiiiii, Emmy," Melissa drawled. "JD went to that Spring Fling thing. Weird, huh? He's so *weird* recently."

"Thanks," Em said hurriedly before she hung up. So he was going to the dance. She found herself wondering what he would wear: a crazy tuxedo like he did last year, or one of his top hats, like he did the year before? She spun a full circle around her room. She had to get ready quickly.

With every second that passed, Em felt increasingly sure that she was making the right choice. If the Furies wanted a fight, they were going to get one. She wouldn't let them stop her from attending the dance; she needed to find JD and Gabby and let them know how important they were to her.

She looked in the mirror.

It was time.

Somehow she'd make the Furies vanish, like smoke after a fire, or snow in the spring.

CHAPTER
TWENTY-SIX

Skylar drifted in and out of consciousness, riding a wave of awareness that pulled her slowly into her surroundings, allowing her to tune in to the sterile hospital room, the faint and constant beeping and buzzing, and her physical pain for just a moment before quickly tugging her back into a sea of memories. She floated helplessly, willing her thoughts back to shore but unable to escape the riptide that swirled in her brain.

Two years ago. Skylar and Lucy are getting ready for a pageant together. Skylar knows, the way you know in dreams—especially bad dreams—what's going to happen . . . that she's going to fumble during her talent portion, the pathetic cherry on top after a disappointing performance, and she will not even place at all in the pageant. Another dose of humiliation. Skylar wonders just how much of that she can take.

Meanwhile, Lucy will wow the judges with her pure singing voice, her graceful dancing, her pulled-together look, her radiant smile. But for now they are still backstage in a dressing room. Their mother is watching them, rather listlessly, from the corner. Offering the occasional "pointer." Lucy has already pinched Skylar's arm. Now she is helping do Skylar's hair. She's pulling too hard, probably on purpose, and it hurts. Skylar screams, it hurts so much. Lucy leans down close to Skylar's ear and whispers, "It's supposed to hurt. Don't you understand that, Sky-sky? Life is pain."

Pain. Skylar moaned out loud as the wave brought her back to full consciousness. She felt pulling at her scalp—as if Lucy was here with her, scraping a brush against her head. No. She was here in the hospital. The pain at her hairline was the stitching in her skin, holding together a gash in her scalp. The glass. The snow. The memories came crashing back, along with a searing sensation of pain.

But then the pain ebbed and she floated up into an eddy of warmth. Just as quickly she started to drift away, back toward the visions. . . .

When Lucy leaves the room, Skylar is furious. What does Lucy know about pain? The anger keeps cycling in Skylar's chest—and on every pass, it gets worse. Skylar looks around and spots Lucy's sparkly gold pumps—the ones she always wears for the talent portion of the pageant. The talent portion, in which Lucy would excel and Skylar would fail.

She grabs the shoes and snaps off both heels with a strength she didn't know she had. She throws them across the room. For a second her rage dissipates. But it's not enough. She wants more. Then, the idea: manically, speedily, she opens their "emergency kit" and digs out a bottle of glue usually reserved for last-minute rhinestone emergencies. She retrieves the shoes and glues the heels back on. They look almost normal, like nothing happened. Lucy won't be able to tell. It's perfect. They'll barely last until she gets onstage, and then the uneven pressure of her dance moves will break them. Skylar smiles with satisfaction, finally able to take a full breath.

But in the bed, now, she felt panicked, unable to fill her lungs with oxygen. She clutched the scratchy hospital sheet, trying to stay in this reality, to keep from rolling away in the next tidal surge. But there was no life jacket. She dunked under again.

Skylar is backstage as Lucy struts down the runway toward the judges. The lights are bright and hot, and Skylar can't see anything but Lucy's silhouette. Stumbling. Winding her arms almost like a cartoon character. Falling. Skylar can't see her eyes, but she knows what they look like: bright, wide, shocked. Then a sound like a crack as Lucy hits the ground.

No, not the ground. A footlight—a sharp, metal sheath around a glass spotlight affixed to the runway, shining up at the girls. The glass shatters as Lucy's head makes contact. Then nothing. The music stops. The audience is silent, even while the music keeps playing like a broken record. Skipping. Skipping on the image of Lucy's bruised face. Lucy is motionless. There is blood spreading in a butterfly pattern beneath her, as though she is sprouting wings. . . .

"I didn't mean it," Skylar mumbled. The skin at the sides of her mouth was dry and cracking. She brought her hands up to her face, felt the cloth wrapped around her cheeks and chin, the tape by her ears holding the bandages together.

The hospital. Doctors speaking in low voices; she watches her sister through a glass window. Frontal lobe damage. *Lucy cannot hold a pencil.* She may seem fine down the road, but things will have changed. *Lucy's hand shaking. Her head turning toward the window, looking at Skylar, taking a moment to register who she is.*

The machines next to her kept beeping. She imagined them like a lighthouse. If she could just keep swimming toward that sound, against the current, against these hideous recollections, she would be safe. *Beep-beep-beep—*

Lucy is staring at Skylar, crying. Then she is laughing. Pointing jerkily. "It's her fault, you know." Skylar sees the nasty set of stitches across Lucy's forehead. Like Frankenstein's monster. Men are taking Lucy away. Their mom is crying, saying her little baby is damaged forever. Skylar is crying too, and the doctors interpret it as heartbreak, not guilt. Lucy laughs the whole time.

That laugh. Where was it coming from? It filled Skylar's head, her whole body. Like a twittering bird . . . She knew that sound from somewhere. Meg. Meg with the red ribbon around her neck. She laughed like that. Did Meg laugh like Lucy, or did

Lucy laugh like Meg? It was impossible to tell. Skylar whimpered. She felt like a child, or a singing doll stuck on repeat. She closed her eyes and pressed her head against the thin pillow. *Stop. Shut up.* The dreamscape flooded back to her, even as tears began filling her eyes.

Skylar is on a stage with the lights shining too brightly into her eyes. Everyone is looking at her and pitying her and petting her and telling her not to worry, her sister will be okay. It is a lie. She is a liar. I'm sorry, I'm sorry, I'm sorry, *she says, and no one understands why.* You have nothing to be sorry about, sweetheart. Don't blame yourself.

"I'm *sorry!*" she cried. All of a sudden Skylar sat up straight in her hospital bed, sputtering and shaking, her bandages soaked with sweat. No longer onstage, but here at the Southern Maine Regional Hospital, in room 17. Alone.

She squinted. Her vision was still fuzzy. No. She was not completely alone. As she looked around, trying to catch her breath and her bearings, she saw a figure standing in the doorway—blond and beautiful, just like Lucy was. Like Lucy had been. She gasped.

Lucy was here. Lucy had come; she had come to make sure Skylar knew she was a terrible person, a horrible sister, a liar. Skylar hadn't visited her sister once after Lucy got shipped to the "rehab center" for people who had suffered severe brain damage. Skylar had made excuse after excuse until finally it was time to leave for Ascension.

"Lucy? Lucy? Is that you?" She sounded groggy. Maybe now she could explain and apologize. Maybe she could undo the wrongs.

"Hi, Sky-Sky." The girl stepped farther into the room. Smiling, all curves, with peaches-and-cream skin, the girl seemed almost to glow with an ethereal light. And her lips. Her lips were painted a deep, true red. Or was that blood dripping from her mouth? For a moment the girl looked like someone else. . . . She looked like Meg's cousin Ali. Skylar gasped and pulled back, feeling her head swaying a little.

The girl smiled again. "It's me," she said.

Skylar stared, trying to stay present, trying not to get sucked back into a dream state. The girl—it was Lucy, it had to be—fanned her face with her hand. "It's hot in here, huh? Come on. We're leaving. The nurses may not want you to leave, but we do!" She smiled conspiratorially. "I came to bring you to the dance."

Skylar let her eyes close while the girl began unhooking and unplugging various machines and IVs.

"How . . . how did you get out?" she murmured, listening as the machines stopped whirring one by one. The rehab facility was almost like an asylum—once admitted, patients were unlikely to leave. How had Lucy found her here? She grew tired trying to unscramble the mixed signals in her brain.

"They let me out," the girl responded brightly. "I wanted to come and see my baby sister."

If they'd let her out, she had to be fixed, right? "Then you're all better?" She looked at Lucy's face imploringly.

"All better, Sky-Sky," the girl singsonged in response, smiling a smile that was even more perfect than Skylar remembered. The words caused another wave of relief and euphoria to wash over her. "Now come on. I'll help you get ready once we get you out of here."

She was better. Lucy was better. She'd be forgiven after all. With hope in her heart, Skylar swung her legs over the side of the hospital bed and stood up shakily, still swinging between dream and wakefulness. Slipping quietly through the darkened halls, miraculously undetected by the few doctors and nurses they passed, Skylar followed her magically healed sister out of the hospital, still in her thin blue-green gown and bare feet, with bandages concealing her face.

They were going to the dance.

CHAPTER
TWENTY-SEVEN

Em got ready in a matter of minutes. She grabbed a short, flowy white dress from her closet—she'd worn it only once, to a party at Gabby's country club last summer—and a lavender shawl. On her feet, silvery flats. She was flushed with nerves and anxiety; it barely registered that this outfit might be more appropriate for a summer celebration than a winter dance. But with her hair pulled up into a tight dancer's bun, silver strands dangling from her ears, and a slick of berry-stain gloss across her lips—all this done on autopilot—she could see, with a quick look in the mirror on her way out the door, that she looked okay. Pretty, even. It didn't matter, anyway. She wasn't going to make a fashion statement. She was going to stop the Furies. She was going to make things right, to find Drea, to put an end to this cycle of hurt and revenge.

Hastily she transferred her things from her school bag to a simpler, smaller silver purse, noticing in the process that she had several missed calls on her cell phone from Crow. She hadn't spoken to him in a few days—not since their strained interaction at the Dungeon—and she felt a twinge of guilt. Sure, he could be an asshole, but he was also genuine. Weirdly, even though she hardly knew him, she felt like she could trust him. What was it he'd said? Something about just wanting to make sure she was okay . . . ? She was curious about the rest of his mysterious revelation.

But it wasn't Crow who she needed right now. It was JD. Her love.

She shoved the phone into her purse, vowing to call Crow tomorrow once all this was over. If she hurried, she could catch the last half of the dance.

Screeching into an illegal parking spot outside the gym, Em spotted Mr. Shields, a senior adviser and a government teacher, working the door. *Shit.* Em realized that in the chaos of the last few weeks, she hadn't bought a ticket. Ascension admin insisted that students buy tickets in advance in order to be admitted to school dances. Something to do with some drunken dance crashers from Trinity a few years back. She considered trying to sneak in; maybe she could go around the back? Sometimes smokers propped the door open. . . .

Shields was busy lecturing a freshman dance committee volunteer about keeping watch on the door, which was being held open by a garbage can.

Just as Em was about to make a run for it, Shields swung his face over in her direction. With his arms crossed over his barrel chest and a frown on his face, he looked like an actual bouncer. But as soon as she approached him, it was like he melted, or something. Like he was under a spell.

"Mr. Shields?" Em gave him her sweetest smile. "I think I forgot to bring my ticket, or lost it. . . ." She craned her neck, trying to see inside.

He looked at her distantly, as though seeing her through a fog. "Oh . . . that's fine, Emily. Go ahead."

She raised her eyebrows. *That* was easier than she'd expected.

A maze of mirrors had been set up throughout the dance floor, sheets of sheer fabric were suspended sporadically from the ceiling, and the gym was full of smoke from a fog machine. The air smelled overwhelmingly sweet, a combination of the chemicals in the fake fog and the Axe body spray used by most Ascension boys.

Em stood on her tiptoes, looking for Drea, for JD, for Gabby, for anyone. She needed an anchor, some way to tether herself and get her bearings.

It was easy enough to locate Gabby, at least. Em had arrived in the middle of the crowning ceremony. Pierce Travers was already standing awkwardly onstage, wearing a crown and a sheepish smile. In black dress pants, a white shirt, and a blue tie, this King of Spring was the picture of clean-cut cuteness, Em had to admit. She could see how he would be the next Zach McCord . . . only less skeezy. Hopefully.

Next up was queen, which was Gabby, no big surprise. As she made her way to the stage in the middle of a roar of whistles, cheers, and applause, Gabby literally sparkled. She was the perfect queen in a strapless pink dress, a white belt, white wedge heels, and a head of bouncy curls. Instead of demurely accepting her crown and going to stand near Pierce, Gabby grabbed the microphone and cleared her throat.

"Thank you so much for this honor," she said, her voice reverberating throughout the room, which went silent at once. "But I won't be wearing the Queen of Spring crown this year." Quiet gasps and whispers buzzed through the gym. "Instead, I'd like to give it posthumously to Sasha Bowlder, who left us too soon." She took a breath and continued. "Nights like these probably made Sasha miserable," Gabby said, and Em's heart swelled as she watched her best friend address the crowd. "We forget, as we go through our daily lives here at Ascension, that not everyone is as happy as we are," Gabby said. Em heard sniffling coming from some of the girls near the drink table. "I know I often forgot, while Sasha was alive. And so, I'd like to give her this crown tonight. It's a small gesture to show that we'll try to remember from now on."

Everyone, including Em, applauded wildly as Gabby walked off the stage on Pierce's arm, smiling and brushing off the crowd of people who instantly surrounded her. Gabby pushed her way to the corner where a bunch of shaggy-haired, vest-clad musicians were standing, probably urging them to get the music going again. Em started toward her.

Then she saw him: his hair, his shoulders, his neck. JD was standing just a few feet away, with his back to her. Her heart sped up and she could feel the heat rising up her neck and into her cheeks.

Then he turned, and she was even more flustered. He didn't look cute, like he usually did. He looked hot. His slim jeans, dark blazer, white shirt, and lime-green bow tie, the Converse sneakers peeking out from under his cuffs, his crooked grin—it came together just right.

"Um, hi," she said, hoping the dim lighting was enough to hide her raging blush. "I just got here."

"I know, I saw you come in," he said as the band started playing again. Em waited expectantly for him to say something more, but nothing came.

"Who . . . who are you here with?" Em didn't want to know the answer, of course, but she had to ask. She took one step forward to make sure she could hear his reply. He stayed put.

"No one," he said, holding up his spare ticket with a shrug. "I was going to ask Drea—just as friends," he added with a sarcastic roll of his eyes. As if he owed her an explanation. . . . "But she said she had some other stuff to take care of."

There was a brief moment of silence between them. His eyes went from her face to her dress, lingering for a moment at the draped neckline, which followed the lines of her clavicle.

Then he sighed, as though he didn't want to say the words that came out of his mouth. As if he just couldn't help himself. "You—you look beautiful," JD said. "You're, like, glowing."

Em's heart swelled. She had doubted she would ever hear such kind words from him again. She grinned and looked down at her shoes. "Oh. Thanks." She looked back up at him, right into his hazel eyes, the ones she'd looked at so many times before. She found something there, something she wanted to crawl into, like a goose down comforter in the middle of winter. "Can we talk? Someplace a bit . . . quieter?"

Just then the song changed. It was a slow one this time, and couples started pairing off on the dance floor. JD looked wary. "I don't know, Em. Things have been so screwed up. . . ."

"Can we dance, then?" She tried to keep her question light. She just couldn't let him get away, not this time.

He hesitated. Then: "Yeah, I guess. Sure." He spoke in a low, scruffy voice that Em had never heard before. She took his hand and led him to the edge of the dance floor; once they found a spot, neither of them knew how to proceed—how close to stand, or where to put their hands. Em thought about other dances, other guys—Steve Sawyer holding her hips at last year's homecoming dance, or Andy Barton putting her hands around his neck at the Spring Fling.

This was nothing like that. JD took one of her hands in his own and placed the other one on his shoulder. He put his free hand around her waist, and she could feel it there, burning through the white fabric covering her ribs and the small of her back.

She took one step closer. She could smell the clean scent of his peppermint soap. Being this close was overwhelming, exciting, and just as she'd imagined. It was like there was no one else in the whole room except the two of them. The music swept around them; Em imagined that both of their hearts were beating in time to its rhythm.

"Maybe I'm not so bad," he murmured into her ear.

"What?" she said, pulling back a little to look at his face.

"At dancing, I mean. Remember? You told me Mr. Darcy doesn't dance; he just has a heart of gold and all that crap."

Em laughed, and held him tighter. "No," she whispered. "You're not so bad at all. . . ." She felt her grin widening uncontrollably, and she pressed her face against his chest, breathing in his familiar smell.

"This is nice," he said, his voice quiet and gravelly.

"It *is* nice," she said, squeezing his hand in hers. Finally. It felt like they had begun to reclaim something. "It's always nice, with

us, JD. Or, at least, it used to be. We've had so much fun together."
Immediately, she scolded herself for being so inarticulate, for not
saying what she wanted to say: that she was happy with him,
always. Even when everything around them was falling apart.

"Fun. Right," he echoed hollowly. He took a step away from
her, running his hands through his hair, breaking the spell. "Good
old JD. Always good for a laugh and a ride, right?"

Em didn't know what to say. The song ended, replaced by
fast beats that made it hard for Em to hear herself think.

"JD, no. That's not what I was saying. You don't understand.
I came here . . . to tell you how I feel. About you. So I could see
you, and explain—"

He cut her off. "I don't think your boyfriend would be so
happy to hear this." He pointed to one of the fun house mirrors
in the gym—and in it, she was shocked to see Crow's reflection.
He looked as tall, dark, and disdainful as ever, scanning the room
full of his former classmates . . . looking for Em, she suddenly had
no doubt. Em could hear people around her begin whispering
and snickering, and all of a sudden Gabby was behind her, squealing, "What's the Grim Creeper doing here?"

Crow strode purposefully in her direction. When he reached
her, he pulled her aside without saying hello.

Em was aware that people were staring at her. Crow towered
over her, looking wild and paler than usual. She shook his hand
off her arm. "What the hell are you doing?" she whispered.

"Em, I just came from Drea's house," he said. "I rushed straight here to find you."

"How did you even get *in*?" Em knew that something must be very wrong, but her mind settled on this, the most mundane of problems: Crow was a dropout. No way he could have bought a ticket.

"Who cares?" he practically barked. "Listen to me. It's Drea. Something's up with her, Em. I think she's flipped a switch. I came to warn you—"

Just then, all at once, the music died, and all the lights in the gym went out. Someone screamed, and Ascension High was plunged into complete darkness.

CHAPTER TWENTY-EIGHT

Skylar had just arrived at the dance. She floated across the parking lot. A silk mask, made of delicate black lace that matched the somber black of her satin dress, brushed across her bandages. She touched her fingers to the mask, wondering where she'd gotten it, when she had put it on. The medication was starting to wear off, leaving a pounding sensation in her skull, making everything around her pulse in and out as though under a glaring strobe light. She couldn't remember exactly how she'd gotten here, to Ascension, to the dance. It was Lucy . . . ? Lucy had taken her . . . no. That didn't make sense. *Lucy can't go anywhere. . . .*

She was alone now. Alone at the dance. She drifted toward the freshman who was guarding the entrance to the dance. When he saw her, he stood up, knocking over his chair. He seemed . . . scared.

She smiled at him, not knowing if he could see her face through her mask. "One ticket for the dance, please," she said, barely recognizing her own voice.

"We—we don't sell tickets at the door," the boy said shakily, moving away from Skylar almost as though she was a wild animal. He wouldn't—or couldn't—look at her straight-on.

"One ticket for the dance, please," she repeated. Like one of those dolls again, who can only say one phrase over and over.

"Let me see if I can get Mr. Shields—to make an exception," the freshman said. As he scurried away, he shouted over his shoulder, "Stay here, all right? Just stay here." He disappeared through the double doors.

Skylar nodded dreamily, but she didn't listen. Pulled by unseen forces, she floated after him, pushing aside, then replacing, the metal trash can that blocked the door. It made a squealing noise against the linoleum floor, but no one noticed.

The scene inside was nothing like the romantic ballroom she had anticipated. It was dark and chaotic. The lights were out—and not, apparently, on purpose. There were sputtering wails of feedback coming from the front of the room, where the band and its amplifiers were set up on a makeshift stage. There was a deep, rhythmic thumping coming from the speakers—someone must have been testing the sound system.

Glinting with limited light from the Exit signs and a few flashlights, tall mirrors offered shadowy, distorted reflections that increased the sense of confusion in the room. Through her own fog and that of the swirling artificial mist that surrounded the students, it was like a subterranean maze. The pulsing in her head wouldn't stop. *Is Lucy here? I'm so sorry.*

Someone was speaking into the microphone on the stage— an adult—telling the kids to stay calm as the chaperones investigated the lights situation. Flashlight beams swept through the crowd and high-pitched squeals and giggles started to emerge from the corners of the room as boys used the darkness as an opportunity for a quick grope and girls pretended to be appalled. To them, this was a game. A fun twist to their night.

Maybe it *was* a game.

Skylar was all mixed up. *All this noise. I can't see. I can't hear.*

She took a step backward, back toward the double doors. But she was disoriented now. She couldn't tell which way she was going. There were mirrors everywhere, and they made it impossible to see straight. People spun by her, leering reflections with bug eyes and pointing fingers. Her breath started to come quicker, and fingers of panic licked at her arms and legs, encircling her, grabbing at her heart.

Where am I? Why am I here? The dance beat sounded increasingly like static. Was the rhythm real, or was that in her head? She took several impulsive steps forward, walking directly into one of the glass mirrors. The impact was enough to make her stumble backward, lose her footing, and fall onto the floor. As she did so her mask flew off, skittering across the waxed floor of the gym. She was uncovered now. No protection.

The drugs had mostly worn off by now, and when she glimpsed herself in the fun-house mirror, she felt like she had been shoved into a nightmare. Her starched pageant dress— *Lucy's dress*—was hideous and ill-fitting. Her skin was bloated and discolored—what you could see of it, anyway, beneath the crisscross of bandages and stitches. Her hair was only half there.

Skylar looked like a monster.

The beam of a flashlight swept over her and lingered there, like a spotlight. Then more flashlights, all circling around her, until she was surrounded in a pool of light. A scream, and then another. People calling her name and whispering. *Skylar. Skylar. Skylar.*

Through another mirror, Skylar saw Gabby, beautiful Gabby, a vision in pink and white with blond curls, comforting a freshman girl who appeared to be on the brink of a panic attack. Skylar watched Gabby soothe the girl and stroke her hair. Not even the distorted mirror could make Gabby appear ugly. No, she looked like a Disney princess, with disproportionately huge blue eyes.

Panic, humiliation, and confusion swept through Skylar. She tried to bring her hands to her face, to cover herself. She struggled to her feet and pushed through the crowd that had formed a ring around her. How could she get out of here? And then, through a different tall mirrored pane, she saw Em across the room. Bent over? Talking to someone? She seemed gigantic and leggy, with the body of a spider like the ones Skylar used to find in webby corners of her garage.

And her face, Em's face—it looked like someone else's. Ty's. Or maybe Ty had become Em? Either way, their features were nearly identical. Their beautiful, defined cheekbones. Their wide foreheads and deep-set brown eyes. Their dark hair. Their thin lips that widened into perfect, toothy smiles. It was like they were the same person.

Was Meg here too? Would Meg help her?

More screams then, and suddenly Skylar realized that people were screaming at *her*.

The freak. The beast. The monster.

Humiliation and fear boiled together in her belly, a rancid mix that burned and chafed at her insides.

She snatched the mask from the floor and ran, stumbling, for the doors, lost among the mirrors and smoke, searching for a red Exit sign that would be her beacon, a light at the end of this haunted tunnel. She pushed by the other students, who were becoming increasingly panicked. Was that a burning smell in the air? There was no order, no one in charge. Just screaming and shouting. People running out the doors. But Skylar didn't care about any of them anymore. She just cared about herself.

By the time she made it to the exit, Skylar was shivering

and sobbing. Her body was wrecked—by the cuts, by the drugs, by the bewilderment, by the mortification of being seen like this. *I'm sorry, Gabby. I'm sorry, Lucy. I'm so sorry.* She felt weak. A bunch of kids pushed past her, running out into the hallway and then out into the cold night. She wobbled and stumbled over the trash can in the doorway; when she didn't bother to set it right, it fell over and rolled down the hall. The door slammed shut.

But Skylar just kept running, and crying, and whispering her unheard apologies, so lost in her own misery that she could only barely hear the fists that almost immediately began to pound on the gym door from the inside.

CHAPTER
TWENTY-NINE

As soon as the lights went out, Em felt Crow try to grab her, but there was confusion, with people going in different directions, and Crow and Em were separated.

They were here, the Furies—she knew it. They'd plunged the Ascension gym into blackness, and whatever they were planning, it wouldn't be good. Panic filled Em's chest, along with rage. She had to find them, figure out what they were up to, and stop it. She had to stop *them*.

She became disoriented quickly in the dark; her senses were all screwed up. After an initial moment of silence, the sound had been restored to the gym. She heard the thumping bass of dance music and Mr. Shields's feedback-distorted voice on the microphone as he tried to make himself heard above the din. "The lights will be back on in a minute," he said. "Everyone, please stay calm." People were shouting—an adrenaline-fueled combination of confusion and excitement. The noise came as an assault, making it impossible to think. She felt like the room was spinning around her, and she really didn't know where she was going or what she was doing. She'd lost Gabby. JD. Even Crow. She was on her own, heading toward the shadows at the back of the gym, away from the crowd.

She ran smack into Drea. In jeans, a striped sweater, and her hooded peacoat, with a backpack on her back, Drea had obviously not dressed for the dance. Em felt a rush of relief; she wanted to throw her arms around her friend.

"They're here, Drea," Em said breathlessly, looking around for them as she spoke.

"I know," Drea said grimly. "That's why I came. The ritual has to happen now, Em. Before it's too late." She slung off the backpack and kneeled on the floor next to it, pulling out a pair of thick gardening shears. Em stared at them dumbly. "We need everyone out," Drea said, still digging in the backpack. Then she found what she needed: a flashlight.

"Hold this," she said, thrusting it toward Em.

Em didn't move. She felt rooted in one position.

"Fine," Drea sighed. "I'll do it myself." She turned it on and stuck it in her mouth so she could see and use her hands at the same time.

Em felt a new type of fear—a sharp, knowing dread—coil around her body. "What are you doing, Drea? What's this stuff for?" she asked. Mr. Shields still droned on in the background, imploring the kids to simmer down. There was a commotion on the middle of the dance floor, near where some mirrors were set up. The coil of fear grew tighter around Em's ribs.

Drea didn't answer. Instead, she took a deep breath, opened the shears until they were gaping, then sliced them quickly closed, through a bunch of cables that were attached to the giant speakers that lined the front walls. Then she did it again. And again. She hacked away as Em looked on, mystified.

"What are you *doing*?" Em asked, even though the answer was clear. *Why are you doing it?*—that was the more important question. Static started to hiss through the speakers, overpowering both Mr. Shields and the music.

"Trust me, this is the fastest way to get everybody out," Drea said, still sawing at the wires, the static growing louder and louder. And then the speakers went out entirely. Now the only sounds to be heard were those of increasing alarm. The fear in the room was becoming palpable.

"Drea, stop. This is crazy." Em reached out to grab her. They needed to talk this through, to get on the same page, to come up with a plan. But Drea whipped around, holding the shears between them. The flashlight was still in her mouth, shining out at Em, blinding her.

At the same time there was a cracking noise, and then the clattering sound of plastic against the parquet floor. "The punch!" Em heard someone yell right before she saw the red liquid start to stream around her silver flats. Someone must have collided with the beverage table. A river of red was now flowing across the gym floor. When it pooled around the freshly severed wires, sparks started to pop from the frayed copper strands.

Em experienced a few seconds as though they were in slow motion. The sparks burst into the air, their yellow-orange light casting flickering shadows. Then a spark caught on one of the paper streamers. Then another, and another. At first they just smoldered. But then small flames began to rise from the decorations. They leaped and swelled exponentially; Em had the bizarre sensation of watching a story unfold in a flip book. *Flip-flip-flip-flip*, and with every page the image moves faster, gets bigger, unstoppable.

Within seconds the fire was racing along the streamers, crisscrossing in a grotesque pattern. Soon the flames jumped onto the banners that hung from the gym's walls and ceiling: *2009 Field Hockey Regional Championships. Go Warriors! Congratulations to All-State Quarterback Chase Singer.*

The wooden bleachers would be next.

People were screaming. Smoke was starting to billow through the room. Em heard someone shout, "We're locked in!"

The door. It was locked, and all these people were inside, and

Drea had started a fire. Em scanned the room frantically, look-ing for a way out, or a solution, or—god, no, please—the Furies. Where were they? This was all their fault. . . . Were they just sit-ting back now, to watch and enjoy?

"Drea, come on!" Em yelled. "We have to get out of here. People are going to get hurt."

But Drea stared past her, gaze wide and terrified.

Em turned slowly, just in time to see Ty appear. She wore a short, ruffled skirt and a red top that made her skin look even milkier than usual. Still, it was impossible to look at Ty anymore without seeing the ghastly creature that Em knew was under-neath her facade.

"What are you doing here?" Em snarled. The smoke was get-ting thicker, and she began to cough.

"You're not the only one who can make new friends," Ty smirked. "Are you having fun at the dance?" She performed a small twirl. "What do you think of my outfit?"

"I told you to stay away from us!" There was the rage drilling through her again.

Ty just laughed, her lips curling into a wide, patronizing smile. "Don't be mad at *me*," she said. "Drea's the one you should be worried about. Are you sure she's on your side?"

Em shook her head, trying to keep her focus. "I won't listen to you." She moved toward Ty, who sidestepped her neatly.

Smoke continued to fill the already dark room, and the

shouting and banging intensified. Then Ty vanished behind one of the standing mirrors. Em darted after her, quickly becoming more disoriented. The mirrors were playing tricks with her eyes— was that Ty? She lurched forward, hands outstretched, and collided with a mirror; she'd made a lunge at her own reflection. The mirror toppled and shattered. Em screamed and jumped back.

"I'm over here," she thought she heard Ty whisper. But when she looked, there was nothing but vapor. Em bent down and picked up one of the shards of mirror. She held it in front of her, a weapon.

"Drea!" Em called out. "Help me!"

But Drea either didn't hear her or chose to ignore her. Instead, Em saw her crouched on the gym floor, oblivious to the fast-spreading fire, laying things out on the ground in a circular pattern. As Em leaned forward to see what they were, she felt a force at her back, pushing her from behind. She stumbled forward, landing facedown on the floor. The wind was knocked from her ribs through her throat.

She planted her hands on the ground and pushed up, then rolled over. There was no respite. Ty was there, with one high-heeled foot on top of Em's chest, pushing down. She leaned down and whispered in Em's ear, "It's starting. It's going to work."

"Drea . . . ," Em repeated in a strangled tone.

"I'm almost done, Em," Drea said urgently. "Hold on. This is going to save you. I promise."

Em swiped upward, using the shard of mirror as a knife, slicing a small gash into Ty's leg. They both gasped as a streak of blood oozed from the wound. Ty looked down, pale and suddenly shaken, and then into Em's eyes. It was the first time Em had ever seen Ty look anything less than completely in control. She took advantage of the moment, wriggling out from under Ty's weight and struggling to her feet.

And then—*whoosh*—Ty wavered like a candle flame and vanished in a wisp of smoke. She left a trail of cloudy white where her long legs had been. When her voice sounded through the blackness, it was angry and defiant: "Be careful, Em. Don't get burned. . . ." Then nothing.

"Come on," Em gasped at Drea. "We need to get out of here."

Drea shook her head. "Not until we finish the ritual." Over the past few weeks Em had seen Drea look fierce, angry, resolute. Sad. Sarcastic and disdainful, of course. But never like this. Never so singularly obsessed, never so fixated. Em got the feeling that even if Drea herself was on fire, she would still be crouching there, staring at Em with those wide, icy eyes.

Em struggled to a half-sitting position and spoke. Her voice came out ragged from the exertion and the smoke.

"The gym is on fire, Drea!" Em coughed. Several people brushed past her, nearly knocking her over again.

"No, Em. It's working, don't you see?" Drea gestured around

them. "The other ones—they've disappeared; the fire scared them off. Now it's just you."

"The *other* ones?" Em choked out. "You mean, the other students? Our *friends*?"

Drea was making a circle around Em now, and she had something in her hand. Between the smoke and the shadows, it was difficult to identify, but Em could tell it was a jar, and something was spilling out of it. "Pretty soon you'll be yourself again," Drea said. "You'll see. This is going to work."

Em took another gasping breath—the smoke was making her feel like her throat was closing up, like duct tape was being wrapped around her rib cage.

And then she smelled it. The sweet, oily smell of gasoline.

Drea was pouring gasoline around her.

The realization lit up in her brain like emergency flares. "Drea, stop! *Stop!*" She found herself screaming as she scuttled away from Drea, who continued to advance. She managed to get up on one knee, still shouting. "No! Drea, no! Stay away!"

She could see that Drea's mouth was moving. Saying something. But she couldn't hear—it was as though Drea was on mute. In fact, the whole world seemed to have gone silent. Em was inhaling smoke, she knew that, but it felt like there was smoke inside her too.

She was going to be burned alive.

And then, in one motion, with what felt like her last scrap of strength, she lunged at Drea, almost slipping on her knees on the wet floor. She'd have to force her to get out of here if either of them was going to live.

Other people were screaming, racing out of the building, knocking things over as they ran. It was total chaos.

"Get away from me," Drea growled as Em's hands made contact with her shoulders. As soon as she touched Drea, she could feel a huge power surge between them. Drea clawed at her arms, trying to push Em away. "Em! Don't fight me!" she shouted, turning her focus back on the gasoline she was pouring onto the gym floor.

But Em lunged again, determined to get in Drea's way and grab her. They needed to flee! As she and Drea struggled Drea tried to elbow Em—Em blocked her arm and shoved her to the side. The shove was far more powerful than Em had expected— it lifted Drea straight off the ground. Em fell forward, coughing, as Drea slammed to the ground and cracked her head against the side of one of the dance floor mirrors.

And then Drea stopped moving, except to blink, once. A trickle of blood emerged from her hairline and traced a shivering path along her angular cheekbone.

"Drea!" Em cried. "No!"

She crawled across broken glass, coughing as smoke got in her lungs and throat and eyes. She could barely see, but she made her way toward Drea, who opened her mouth slowly and began to speak with concentration, as if she was trying to translate commands between her brain and her body. "Em. You're . . . turning . . ." Her muttering trailed off.

Em looked down at herself—her stained dress, her ghostly skin, her quaking hands and legs. The dizziness and smoke overwhelmed her. What had happened? What had she become? The gym was emptying now—people must have found a way out, because the screams and shouting had become more distant.

The smoke kept swirling—around her, in her. There was nothing to do but dance with it, sway with it, succumb to it dizzily. She felt herself falling. Then all went black.

Em was riding a horse.

No. That wasn't right. It *felt* like she was riding a horse. Up and down, up and down, up and down. She turned her head groggily and was met by the peppermint smell of a clean white shirt.

She looked up. A scruffy chin, a pointy Adam's apple, sprouts of mussed hair. JD. She was in JD's arms. He was carrying her out of the gym while above them sparks rained down from the ceiling. She felt intense heat all around her.

The students must have gotten the gym doors open, or else they'd been busted down, because that's how JD got her out— through the double doors and out into the cold parking lot.

Her lungs felt as though they were coated in ash. She heard sirens wailing in the background and the sound of shattering glass. She took gulping breaths of air, trying to refocus.

Then it all rushed back to her—the power outage, the fire. *Drea*.

"No! Drea!" Em struggled in JD's arms. "We have to get her!" JD kept moving. He held her tighter.

"The whole building is on fire!" JD yelled. "They've evacuated the gym."

"But she's still inside!" Em was too weak to struggle.

"I'll go let them know. The firefighters are here, " he said, placing her down gently. "Everything's going to be okay." His face looked terrified, though.

In the parking lot the fire trucks were screeching to a halt, and firefighters were jogging toward the school, shouting orders to one another. The parking lot was bathed in flashing red lights.

Em watched the fire lick the sky. The walls must be on fire now. The bleachers. Everything. Firefighters entered the building. *Hurry. Hurry.*

The students had gathered in the parking lot, shivering and sickly fascinated by the scene in front of them, not knowing if everyone had gotten out safely. Friends found each other and cried with relief. Across the lot Em saw Gabby standing with Lauren, Sean, Andy, and the rest of them, looking around wildly. Looking for Em, no doubt.

"JD, we have to go over there—" She started to point to Gabby, but she was distracted by a sudden change in the air. She felt it.

And then: "It's gonna go!" She heard one of the firemen yell, and then they all started yelling it. *"It's gonna go."*

Em tugged on JD's sleeve. "What's gonna go? What's happening?"

He shook his head.

"There's still a girl inside!" Em screamed hysterically, a sob welling in her throat. But in all the commotion, no one heard her or paid attention except JD.

"Shh," he said. "Shh . . . They're doing what they can." She barely noticed that he took off his blazer and slung it around her bare shoulders. And then he kept his hands there, on her shoulder blades.

That's how they were standing when the gym collapsed.

The ceiling folded in on itself with a giant, heaving moan. The fire-weakened walls crumbled in and down, raining rubber and pebbles into the burning gymnasium. Screams ripped into the night, and it took Em a moment to realize that she was screaming louder than anyone else.

As the policeman led her to the ambulance, Em babbled uncontrollably. "I . . . I don't know what happened. Drea set the fire. I didn't know what was going on . . . and then I woke up and she was lying there, and . . ." She dissolved into sobs. She couldn't stop shivering.

Two EMTs helped her climb into the ambulance. They were

taking her to the hospital. Something about smoke inhalation and shock.

"She . . . she tried to *kill* me . . . ," Em stammered.

"Shh. It's going to be okay," JD said soothingly. "I'll be there at the hospital. I'll see you soon. I've got you."

All she could think was, *Drea tried to kill me. And now Drea is dead.*

The tears burned and her body ached. Her friend was dead, the only casualty of what newscasters would refer to as "another troubled youth's cry for help." Just a few hours later Em was at home in her bedroom, unable to sleep, unable to move, her face pinned to a pillow that was soaked with her tears.

She had been released from the hospital into her parents' care—miraculously, the doctors said, she had suffered almost no injuries. The smoke hadn't done any significant damage; she'd suffered no bruises or scrapes. Still, it had taken forever to get her parents to stop fussing over her, asking for extra tests, pain medication "just in case," the works.

Even if they showed up on no scans, Em knew her wounds were there. Drea, JD, Gabby, Skylar, the fire . . . Like bare feet pounding hot asphalt, these thoughts sent tremors of pain all through her body. She blamed herself. If she and Drea had been honest with each other about their motivations and plans, if they'd been more in sync, tonight would have gone much differently. Drea had only been trying to help. To save her. And Em had failed to save Drea.

So instead of trying to sleep, as her parents were doing right down the hall, Em was curled up in an oversized T-shirt with her journal. She'd frozen when she'd come to a page on which she'd marked Ty's words to her from a few days ago: *We aren't so different, you and I.*

Rap-tap-tap. A tapping at her bedroom window made Em spring to her feet. It was Ty. Or Ali. Or Meg. Tonight had come to no resolution; Em now knew her battle was far from over.

But no. It was only Crow. He must have hauled himself up onto the roof of the screened-in porch and made his way to her bedroom window. She felt a moment of fear, but it was followed quickly by relief. Crow might be insane, but Em trusted him, somehow.

He motioned urgently for her to let him in, and she did. There was a blast of cold air when she opened the window, and she could smell smoke—whether the wind carried it through the air or Crow carried it on his clothes, she didn't know. His eyes didn't have that faraway look, as they often did. They studied her deeply. He looked like crap, really—all pale and cold, with just a flannel shirt over his gray henley. His black boots were covered in ash, and his face was smudged, as though he'd been running sooty fingers around his eyes.

Em backed away from him, letting him climb in the window

but not making any move to help him. Having him in her room made her feel vulnerable, exposed. "Where did you go tonight?" she whispered, not bothering to ask what he wanted from her.

He didn't answer right away. Em watched him pace in front of the window for several seconds before he blurted out, "Remember when I told you to stay away from me?"

Em nodded, frightened by his wildness and his intensity. Maybe, she thought, she was wrong to let him in the house, in her bedroom. He cleared his throat. "I told you that because I care about you. I wanted you to be safe. And I'm dangerous. I'm—I'm bad luck."

She still hadn't sat down. She pulled at the bottom of her shirt, trying to cover herself more. She waited for him to say more.

"My whole life has been haunted by terrible luck—like I'm cursed, or something," Crow said. She could see that his knuckles were white as he clenched them around the edge of her desk. Part of her wanted to reach out, touch him, rub his shoulders. But she refrained. "I always seem to be around when bad things happen. And the worst part is, I *sense* it. Beforehand. I know that sounds crazy, but it's true. It's like I know when bad stuff is coming."

"So you knew something was going to happen tonight?" Em asked, her voice husky from the tears.

"I know it's *still* coming," Crow said, nodding gravely. "That was just the opening act."

"What do you mean?" Em demanded, fear tickling icy fingers down her neck. "What's next?"

"It doesn't work that way," he said. "I never get a clear vision. I just . . . I *feel* it. Something is going to happen to you. Something bad *is* happening to you right now."

She was silent. She knew Crow was right. She had known it for a long time.

"You have to let me help you," Crow continued. His voice rose and he stepped toward her. She could feel heat radiating from his body. "I tried to ask Drea, and she told me something . . . I didn't fully understand. I still don't. But I know it's why she was so obsessed with the idea of fire, with this exorcism she was planning for tonight."

"Exorcism? What do you mean?" Em's voice was a raspy whisper. For a second Crow didn't answer, and Em raised her voice. "What did she tell you, Crow?"

He sighed and sagged down onto her bed. "She said you had to be saved. She thought she was doing the right thing. But she didn't want to kill you. That was never her intention. . . ."

Tears pricked her eyes. "Crow, what are you talking about?" She sat down next to him, mostly because she felt she didn't have the strength to stand anymore.

He sighed, looking down at the carpet. "You two were looking for a banishment ritual, but it wasn't as simple as that. She didn't tell you the whole truth."

"So she wasn't trying to kill the Furies tonight?" Em asked skeptically. Crow shook his head, refusing to meet her eyes. Em felt a growing sense of frustration. "So if she wasn't exorcising the Furies from Ascension, what was the exorcism for?" But even as she asked, the idea was skirting the edges of her consciousness. She recalled lunging for Ty and hitting a mirror. . . .

"You." The word came from Crow's mouth softly. Like snow. Like deadly, burying, avalanche-inducing snow. "Drea said . . . she was trying to get it out of you."

"Get *what* out of me?" Em demanded, although the answer was there, unable to be denied, like boils on her perfect skin. She'd swallowed the seeds. She heard Ty's pronouncement: *They will bind you to us forever.* Most of all, she felt the blackness and the hatred inside of her. She knew what Crow meant. But she needed him to say it out loud.

And then he did.

"The Furies," Crow said quietly. "You're becoming one of them."

ACKNOWLEDGMENTS

To Lauren Oliver and Lexa Hillyer: I am full of respect and gratitude for both of you.

To Jen Klonsky: Thanks for your keen editorial guidance (and the kitten video).

To everyone at Simon & Schuster, especially Paul Crichton, Siena Konscol, Anna McKean, Dawn Ryan, and Carolyn Swerdloff; Michelle Blackwell, Maylene Loveland, and all at S&S Canada; Katheryn McKenna and the S&S UK team; Paper Lantern Lit–ers; Stephen Barbara and Foundry Literary + Media; and Stephen Moore at Paul Kohner, Inc.: You take great care of me and my books. I appreciate it.

To Jeff Inglis and Lorem Ipsums: Thanks for helping me exercise other parts of my brain.

To Mom and Dad, Aunt Madeline, the Brownings, the Reichers, the Cullens, the Finnertys, the Pintos, the Adamses, and Carolyn and Kasey McDonough: Hooray for a terrific family!

To Laura, Laura, Jackie, Dafna, Maggie, and Sonya: Let's go eat some pineapple pizza with baby animals on the Fourth of July and talk about how much we love each other. (Chris and Nick, you can come too.)

And to Keagan: I used to think a guy like JD was too good to be true. Then I met you.